THE TRADITIONAL WEST

An Anthology of Original Stories

by
The Western Fictioneers

TM

Table of Contents

Introduction

It's been said that the Western story and the detective story are the only two genuinely American literary art forms. The Western story is certainly the oldest, dating back two hundred years to James Fenimore Cooper's Leatherstocking Tales, which were set on what was then the American frontier.

Since then the Western story has gone through a considerable evolution, from the dime novels of the late 19th Century to the ground-breaking work of Owen Wister, Zane Grey, and Clarence E. Mulford in the early 20th Century, from the pulp magazines that flourished during the first half of the century to the hardback novels of well-respected authors such as Ernest Haycox and Elmer Kelton to today's line-up of Western authors who rank as the very best in their profession.

At one time the Western was the most popular type of fiction being published, just as it dominated the movie box-offices and the television ratings. While that's no longer the case, the traditional Western is still a vital genre, despite what some naysayers would have you believe.

New Western novels continue to be published at the rate of several hundred per year, both in paperback and hardback, and they still enjoy a healthy readership. More importantly, the Western is earning new fans among both readers and writers, and many up-and-coming authors are breaking new ground in the genre while veteran writers continue to expand its limits as well.

Western Fictioneers was formed in 2010 to celebrate and promote traditional Western novels and short stories. WF, as its members call it, is the only writers' organization devoted solely to Western fiction, and its roster includes many award-winning, best-selling authors. Its ranks are international, with members in England, Spain, and Japan as well as the United States. Every year it presents the Peacemaker Awards for the best in Western novels and short stories.

And now WF is proud to present what we hope is the first of many anthologies to feature brand-new stories by some of the top names in Western fiction. In THE TRADITIONAL WEST, you'll find as many variations on the genre as there are authors represented. There are epic adventure yarns, comical tall tales, noirish reckonings of Fate, slices of frontier life, and several stories that combine the Western and the detective story, those two distinctly American genres mentioned above.

Some of these stories will thrill you, some will make you think, and some will warm your heart. But above all, they will entertain you. If you're a veteran Western reader, you'll know the names of many of these authors and be aware that you're in for a great reading experience. If you're new to Westerns, you won't find a better place to start than THE TRADITIONAL WEST. This is the biggest all-original Western anthology ever published.

So don't wait any longer. Check out these stories, and you'll see why the Western is two hundred years old . . . and still going strong.

For more information about Western Fictioneers, visit the organization's website at www.westernfictioneers.com and the blog at http://westernfictioneers.blogspot.com

The Silver Noose

by Jackson Lowry

Jackson Lowry (a pen-name of Robert E. Vardeman) recently published his first novel, Sonora Noose. *The story included in the current Western Fictioneers' anthology uses the same character, Deputy Marshal Mason Barker, to explore a different portion of New Mexico Territory prior to the coming of the railroad. Another short story of Mason Barker's adventures, "Fifteen Dollars," is available for free at the website www.JacksonLowry.com. Under another pen-name (Karl Lassiter), his novel* Drifter *was nominated for a 2009 New Mexico Book Award.*

The loud screams from inside the way station caused Deputy Marshal Mason Barker to groan. He had ridden alongside the stage rattling over terrible roads from Benson because of Indians off the Tonto Reservation. But he had thought the duty would be easy enough, getting paid extra by the Butterfield Stage Company for riding home to Mesilla from delivering a prisoner. The entire trip through Arizona and into New Mexico they hadn't even spotted another rider, much less marauding Indians. Even getting past the notorious mining town of Shakespeare ten miles back west had been easy.

A new scream, shriller and more hysterical, echoed from the small adobe building out to where he sat astride his horse.

There had been two women and three men in the stagecoach. The women were homely and the men surly.

It suited him to ride rather than hitch his horse to the back of the stage and lounge in the compartment. His back was acting up and the hard coach seat would only make it ache worse, not that riding in the hot sun helped ease the agony. But the company was better.

He dismounted, reached down and took the leather thong off the hammer of his Colt, then went to the door. There was no telling what he would find inside.

A third scream cut through the air, but this one wasn't anywhere near as fierce. Deep laughter followed it. He pushed the door open with his foot, squinted and waited for his eyes to adapt to the dim light after being sun-blinded most of the day.

At first he couldn't make out what was causing the ruckus. Then he saw the body dangling from a viga, a noose around a scrawny neck. The hot wind whipping through the open door caused the body to turn slowly and gave him a better look. The hands weren't tied, and the man was dressed in his Sunday best.

"What the hell's going on?" he demanded.

"It . . . it's dead. They hung him!" The uglier of the two women pointed at the body.

This produced a new round of laughter. He stepped inside, pistol still out but without his finger on the trigger now. There wasn't any threat, at least not to him or the passengers. To one side of the room the driver and shotgun messenger clutched their sides, laughing. At the rear of the big room, a dilapidated man also laughed, wiping tears from his face and leaving dirty streaks on his cheeks. A man and woman stood to the other side of the room, both enjoying the spectacle of the passengers' shock.

"What's going on?" Barker asked. "Who's the gent with the hemp necktie?"

"He — " The man beside the woman caught himself before convulsing with laughter. As he settled down, he came over. "You must be the deputy marshal."

"U.S. Deputy Marshal Mason Barker." He slid his six-gun back into his holster and shook hands.

"I'm the station agent, Silas Lerman."

"And I'm Tillie," the woman said, coming over and putting her arm around the man's waist.

"Ma'am." Barker touched the brim of his hat, ignoring the tiny cloud of settling brown dust this act caused. "You care to explain?"

"Yes, Marshal, they, you, this is an outrage!" The less ugly woman passenger had found her voice. It matched her face and anger. "You don't hang men like this!"

"'Fraid she's got a point, Mr. Lerman."

"Call me Silas. Ever'body does."

"Don't think you're a lawman or a judge, and there sure ain't enough here for a jury. Why'd you go and hang him?" Barker walked closer and examined the man. From the dirt under his broken fingernails he was a miner. Might be silver specks, but there were too many minerals that produced a silver flash for Barker to be sure since he wasn't a miner and never had been. He had started working on a ranch as a cowboy, had been a scout for Colonel Carson during the Navajo War and had drifted south after getting hitched to the finest woman in Colorado to take this job as a lawman. That suited him mostly, except at times like this.

"We were just lookin' for a little fun, Marshal," Tillie said.

"He don't look like he's having much fun at your little party," he said, pointing at the dead man. The wind kept him spinning slowly. From the angle of the head, he might not have died of a broken neck. Barker shuddered. Strangling to death was a painful way to go, not that hanging was much better. Anyone who took the drop ought to deserve it. More than this, it should come after a fair trial.

"He was already dead when we strung him up," Lerman explained.

"We wanted to see what them passengers'd do." Tillie started chuckling again. "The look on their faces was priceless."

"How'd he come to be dead before you hung him up as a *piñata*?"

Tillie and her man looked at each and other, then shrugged eloquently.

"Don't rightly know. Henry back there found him alongside the road. Musta been throwed off his horse and died in the heat."

Barker motioned Henry over. The shabby man shuffled a little, a gimpy leg holding him back. He finally came over and looked up at Barker, and Barker wasn't that tall.

"As the boss said, found him out back."

"What's out back?" Barker asked. The road was behind him, out where the stagecoach stood with its team getting antsy at being neglected with the setting sun casting long shadows in front of them.

"He meant out on the road, didn't you, Henry?" Lerman fixed his hired hand with a gimlet stare.

"Why don't you show me where you found the body? And get him down. You're provoking the payin' customers for no good reason."

"It was worth it seein' their expressions," Tillie said. When Lerman made no move to take down the body, she poked him. "I ain't haulin' his sorry ass down. *You* get him down."

The two began arguing. Barker heaved a sigh, then shoved Henry in the direction of the body.

"Me and you'll take care of this."

The passengers huddled together and watched almost fearfully as Henry wrapped his hairy monkey arms around the body, and Barker used his knife to cut the rope. The sudden weight was almost too much for Henry. He staggered and swayed until Barker steadied him. Together they took the body outside.

"Where'd you find him?"

Henry frowned and looked around, as if trying to remember.

"Reckon I found him on the road since that's where Mr. Lerman said I did."

"Before that, where'd you find him?"

"Around back."

Barker leaned the body against the side wall and examined it for wounds. He scratched his head when he didn't find any. He had thought the man might have been shot. A road agent would have stolen his horse and gear. Going through the pockets in the fancy vest turned up a cheap watch and nothing else. The clothing was worn but decent, as if the man had come straight from church. It being Thursday, that might have been true, but Barker doubted there was a church within fifty miles. He certainly had never heard of one in Shakespeare.

If he had been to a Wednesday night prayer meeting fifty miles away wearing his celluloid collar and string tie, he had made mighty good time to die out on the road.

"He didn't fall off a horse," Barker said suddenly.

"How's that, Marshal?"

"Clothes aren't dirty, not like he tumbled from a horse." Barker flopped him over and looked. "Seat of his pants don't show he's ridden a horse lately. More like he drove a buggy."

He looked up and saw Henry shifting his weight nervously from foot to foot.

"You have a buggy here?"

"Got one out behind the barn."

"Lerman's? Or Miss Tillie's?" He saw the answer on Henry's confused face. Turning back to the corpse, he started a more thorough investigation. No blood on the clothing from a bullet or knife wound. The rope burn around the dirty neck showed Barker that Lerman had told the truth. The body had been strung up after he had died.

He shook his head and frowned.

"Might be he died of a heart attack?"

Barker never bothered to look at the handyman. As a lawman he had seen men and women die in about every possible way. Natural causes, a doctor might call it, could be anything from a heart attack to cholera. The body showed no sign of that. As Barker heaved the body back upright, the celluloid collar popped open. He pounced on it like a cat on a mouse.

"What'd you find, Marshal?"

Barker pressed his finger into a small hole at the back of the man's neck that had bled out a tiny spot on the collar.

"Looks like somebody drove an awl into his neck. Killed him outright. You got anything like that?"

"Toolshed." Henry pointed to a small building near the barn.

Barker silently walked to the barn and peered at the buggy parked behind it. He didn't know Silas and Tillie, but they didn't look like the sort to drive such a fancy rig. Not looking back, he went to the toolshed where Henry opened the door and pulled out a dynamite crate filled with tools.

"These are about all I got. Don't remember seein' others."

"You work here long?" Barker began poking through the tools until he found an awl. Holding it up in the last light of day showed only rust. He ran his finger over it, but there wasn't any trace of fresh blood. Tossing it back into the crate, he motioned for Henry to return it to the shed.

"Nope, just got here a week back. Needed a job real bad and Mr. Lerman he gave me one feedin' the teams and helpin' out."

"You sleep in the barn?"

"Surely do. Mr. Lerman and Tillie don't let me into the main house 'cept now and then."

"Like when you hung the dead man and for meals?"

"Don't let me eat inside. I make my own food."

Barker noticed that Henry didn't deny hoisting the body in the way station. He went over what he knew and couldn't figure out what was going on. There was evidence that the man had been murdered, but there wasn't any motive for the crime. He shrugged this off. Death came all too easy in New Mexico Territory.

"You want we should bury him, Marshal?"

"Not yet. It's getting cold, and the body won't rot too much over night," Barker said. He shivered a mite as he went back into the way station. The passengers huddled together near the fire, scooping food from tin plates into their mouths and looking furtively toward Lerman, the driver and guard. Barker didn't see Tillie right away, then saw her in the far corner in a rocking chair, slowly moving to and fro.

"You got a hankerin' fer some food, Marshal?"

"Yes, ma'am, that'd hit the spot."

"Ten cents a plate," Tillie said, using the motion of the rocking chair to propel her out. She laid aside her crochet work and went to the fire where a pot of beans hung. After wiping off a plate using her apron, she dished out a big wooden spoonful on the plate, added a smaller metal spoon and handed it to him.

"Obliged," he said. He fumbled in his pocket and found two nickels. They disappeared as if by magic into the folds of the woman's apron.

"You want more, ask," she said.

"I'm hungry enough that I just might," Barker said, but a mouthful of the partly cooked beans made that unlikely. Whatever spices Tillie had added couldn't cover the bitter taste. He worked on the food as he walked around the large room, studying the spot where the man had been swung by his neck and then moving closer to the rocking chair where Tillie had taken up her crochet work again.

"We ain't got nuthin' strong to drink. Company rules," she said, looking up at him.

"Most places have a little snort waiting since the company takes a cut." From her grunt he knew the answer. She probably had a bottle or two hidden away but was afraid, since he rode guard on the stagecoach, that he would turn her in to the company for keeping the money from the whiskey. She and Lerman had probably told Butterfield that they were Mormons and didn't cotton to hard liquor. If they sold one drink to him, it would have to show up on the records, in case he mentioned it to the company. The driver and guard no doubt got paid off in whiskey to stay silent.

"My missus knits. Never does needlework," he said,

peering at Tillie's work.

"I crochet pillow covers. Sometimes sell those to the passengers, along with a pillow to make the trip easier on their butts."

"Good idea. Take you long to put one of those fancy designs onto a piece of cloth?"

"Not long," she said.

"You know the dead man?"

"Never seen the cuss 'fore Henry drug him in. From the road."

"From the road," Barker said, nodding. He finished the beans and looked longingly at the empty plate. The food was terrible, and a bit more would go down good.

"Don't tell Silas, but I'll give you a second helping and not charge you."

"I don't want to do anything to cause trouble between you and your husband."

"Ain't my husband," she said. Tillie looked up, as if challenging him to complain. It didn't matter one whit to him if they were married or not. She grabbed the plate and slopped out more beans.

"Thank you kindly. And I won't say a word to Silas about it."

Barker wandered over to the table where Silas played cards with the driver and guard. From the look of the stack, Silas wasn't too good a player.

"Lookee here, Marshal," said the guard. "I 'bout cleaned him out! Did it bluffin' with a pair of deuces!"

The guard held up a small leather bag and shook it.

"Tobacco?" Barker asked.

"Silver. Silver dust, leastways."

"Last stage through had a prospector who paid for everything in silver," Silas said.

"Unusual seeing it in powder. Like it'd been scraped off a coin."

"Don't go lookin' fer a crime, Marshal," Silas said. "That's not too unusual men shavin' down a coin to make spendin' teeny bits easier."

"Milled coins," Barker said thoughtfully. "It's a federal crime to do that to a milled coin. The reason there's milling is to keep from shaving down a silver dollar and passing it off as a full ounce." He finished his meal and set the plate on a chair. He watched the card game a few more minutes, then said, "Lot of mining around here?"

"Shakespeare. And Silver City's not too far north o' here," the driver said. "Ain't misnamed, if you catch my meanin'."

"Don't get over there since it's in Marshal Armijo's jurisdiction," he said. He wandered off, found a place by himself in a dark corner and took out an old wanted poster for the outlaw he had escorted to Benson. He worked a spell using a stub of a pencil, smudged it up some, then tucked it into his pocket.

"Want to go tend my horse."

When he didn't get an acknowledgment from any quarter, he stepped out into the starlit night. The cold would have felt mighty good round about noon, but he would take the chill desert air now and try to remember when it got hot in the morning. He grabbed the reins of his horse and led it to the barn, stopping for a moment beside the body still propped against the adobe wall. Once more he looked at the tiny hole at the back of the neck and patted down the pockets before standing, feeling a twinge in his back and then going to the barn.

The smell of fragrant stew met him as he opened the barn door. At the back by the last stall, Henry stirred a small pot cooking over a fire made from dried horse dung.

"I finished curryin' 'and feedin' the teams, Marshal. I got hungry so I fixed dinner."

"You're not accountable to me. Silas is the one who hired you. I'm just passing through."

"Silas thinks you're a spy for the company."

"I got that feeling from Tillie, too."

"You ain't, are you?"

"Couldn't be farther from the truth." He put his mare into a stall, took off the saddle and began work brushing out the burrs. Folks complained about the desert being dead, but Barker had never found it that way. If anything, too much grew there. Cockleburs and cactus, devil's claws and ocotillo and more critters than he could name all prowled the barren land.

"Rabbit stew?"

"Yup." Henry looked at him, swallowed hard, then offered him a helping.

"As good as it smells, I already ate." Barker saw that the handyman had scant stew in the pot, barely enough for him. "How do you fix it to make it so good?"

That got Henry talking about his culinary skills. Barker slowly worked him around to Tillie's lack of cooking ability.

"She surely does good needlework, though."

"Couldn't say, but she goes around wavin' that crochet hook like it was a pointer." Henry looked a bit bashful. "That's why I quit school. The schoolmarm was always using that pointer to whack me when I fell asleep."

"There's a difference in size," Barker pointed out.

"Tillie can poke purty hard," Henry said, rubbing his arm in memory.

"Is there a cemetery around?" Barker asked.

"To bury Gus?"

"Can't leave him sitting upright. Having him hanging scares the passengers but sitting there where he is would scare off the animals." Barker finished his work on the horse, made sure the mare had fodder and settled down across the dung fire from Henry.

"How'd you know his name's Gus?"

"What? Who?"

"There's more going on here than you're telling me, Henry. That buggy? Gus rode up in it, didn't he?"

"Didn't see that." Henry turned sullen and looked away. "I was out workin' and don't know nuthin'."

"But Silas and Tillie do, don't they?"

Henry shook his head.

"They tell you they found Gus out on the road?"

"They tole me *I* found him there, if anybody asked. Gave me a glass of whiskey. So I reckon it was alright."

"And you helped string him up for the passengers?"

"Heard the stage comin'. Tillie and Mr. Lerman they argued, then told me to get a rope, so I did. They said it was gonna be a great joke. And it was. We danged near laughed our fool heads off when them women came in and saw Gus all strung up like that." Henry started chuckling.

"Quite a joke," Barker allowed. He settled back, studying Henry. "You want to play a joke on Silas and Tillie?"

"Well, I dunno. They been real good to me, not lettin' me die in the desert and all."

"It'll be a double-barreled joke," Barker said. "We'll fool them, and you might get something out of it, too."

"What?" Henry looked suspiciously at him.

"They might give you more whiskey."

That sealed the deal.

"What do I have to do? Don't think it'd scare them none if I hung Gus up again."

"This is a bit different, but just as much fun." Barker pulled the wanted poster from his pocket and handed it to the other man. "Give this to one of them — doesn't matter which — and tell them you found it in Gus' pocket when you moved him."

"But Mr. Lerman done searched his pockets."

"Bet he found a bag of silver shavings, too," he said, remembering the poker game. "Give this to him, and tell him you found it in Gus' shoe."

"Why'd I look there?"

Barker held down his impatience. The only thing worse than an honest man was an honest man who was a bit slow.

"Looked like his shoes might fit you. Your boots are getting holes in the soles."

"They are," Henry said, lifting one. "I put cardboard in, but that don't do much and a piece of wood hurt like the dickens as I went about my chores."

"Good shoes like that don't do a dead man any good."

"Never thought about it." Henry scowled. "But I can't take 'em. Not right stealin' from a dead man."

18

"You're right, Henry. But give Silas the paper."

The handyman took the wanted poster and nodded.

Barker spread his bedroll out on the straw in an empty stall and slept the best he had in a week or more. His back hardly twinged, and his dreams were all of home.

* * *

"We most certainly will *not* wait to bury that . . . that man!"

Barker didn't even take notice of which woman spoke. The other passengers chimed in, all agreeing as he had thought they would when he asked them to stay for the ceremony.

"You are right," Barker said slowly. "You folks got a right to be on your way. You've paid for tickets to get you to El Paso, after all." He motioned the driver over so he could talk privately. "You take 'em on ahead. I don't think there'll be any Indian trouble. I'll get the man buried and catch up with you when I can."

"I've gotta tell the agent you weren't along for the entire time, Marshal."

Whether this pleased the driver's ornery streak or he was simply being a loyal employee wasn't something Barker could discern easily. He put his arm around the driver's shoulders and moved him a bit farther from the way station and closer to where Silas and Henry stood over the body.

"It's my sworn duty to see this man in the ground and the matter of his death finished."

"Buryin' him'll do that, Marshal?" Silas asked.

"Some duty is more distasteful than others. This is one of those I'd rather not have to deal with, but I have to." To the driver he said, "I won't be too long. Maybe we can talk over how long I was, uh, out scouting for Indians, over a drink?"

"Now yer talkin', Marshal!"

He slapped the driver on the back and within a few minutes the stagecoach rattled away eastward, heading for Mesilla and then El Paso.

"I brung a shovel, but diggin' in this ground's real hard," Henry said.

"You hit caliche before you've dug a foot down," Barker said. "We got the same trouble over in Mesilla. You want to take the body on back to Shakespeare? They must have a town cemetery and undertaker."

"He'd end up in the potter's field," Silas said. "You don't want to go to that much trouble, do you? The town's a good ten miles back along the road in the direction you just came."

"Any sandy dunes around?" Barker asked.

"I know of one not too far," Silas said. "Bring the body, Henry." Silas set off into the desert. Barker followed with the shovel, letting the handyman wrestle the body up over his shoulder and stagger after them.

It took the better part of an hour to dig the grave in the shifting sand and lay the man to rest.

"Should have brung a marker," Henry said.

"We don't know his name," Silas said sharply.

"A cross, maybe. I seen graves with crosses and no names."

"All along the road," Barker cut in. "*Descansos*. Folks want to put up a monument but don't know who it is they are remembering."

"We kin do that later. It's gettin' mighty hot, and you have a ride ahead of you, Marshal, if you want to catch up with the stage."

"Right you are, Silas, right you are."

As they walked back to the way station, Silas spoke loudly to Henry about the day's chores and how he wanted the corral fenceposts reset.

"That'll take the better part of the day, Mr. Lerman."

"What am I payin' you for, Henry? Git to work." Silas Lerman turned and shoved out his hand to Barker, who solemnly shook it. "Have a safe trip, Marshal."

"Thanks. And a word of warning. Don't be doing pranks like you did with him." Barker jerked his thumb over his shoulder in the direction of the distant grave. "You might get a laugh out of it, but you saw how the

20

passengers acted?"

"No sense of humor. But if you say so, Marshal. Not likely to find a body layin' 'round like that again, anyway."

"Let's hope not."

Barker saddled his horse and rode into the sun, hat pulled down to shield his eyes. He glanced over his shoulder. Henry was already at work on the corral posts, and Silas and Tillie stood in front of the station arguing. Putting his head down a little more eased the back pain caused by his mare as she trotted along, but then when he had gone far enough, he drew rein and sat a little straighter, thinking hard on what to do. His back hurt but not too much. He ought to catch up with the stage and follow it into Mesilla.

There, he could beg off guarding the stagecoach the rest of the way into El Paso, get paid for the work he'd already done and be home for some of his wife Ruth's fine cooking. She might even do up an apple pie to celebrate him being home. He patted his bulging belly. If it weren't for her cooking, he might not have a gut like this hanging out over his gun belt.

But duty called. He rode off to his left a few miles, then turned westward and rode harder than he ought to in the heat. By the time he angled southward again to the booming little town of Shakespeare, the horse was tuckered out and so was he.

He went directly to the stable and dickered with the stableboy over tending his mare. It was worth fifty cents to see the dependable horse cared for.

Then he went to the saloon and glanced in. It was too early for the silver miners to have left their claims and come to town for liquid medicine to ease their aches and pains. He could use a shot or two of whiskey for his back, but he kept walking, toward the far edge of town and a small building where a buggy was parked outside.

He eased off the leather thong over the hammer of his Peacemaker, then went to the door of the land office and looked in. Barker stood a little straighter. This wasn't exactly what he had expected, but he wasn't too far wrong.

"I tell you, I am Gus Johansen's widow. He gave me this map to his claim. I want to — "

"Ma'am, I don't care if you're Queen Victoria, there's nuthin' I can do," the land clerk said.

"His claim is rightly mine! Here. Look at this map. It shows where his claim is." Tillie pushed across the wanted poster with the crude map Barker had scrawled on the back.

"This don't mean a thing. The landmarks are all wrong. There's no peak like that anywhere around here."

"Then his claim's *there*, wherever there is a peak like that."

"This isn't any kind of document I can use. And ma'am, Gus Johansen never filed a claim. He ran around town braggin' on how he had struck it rich, but he never filed a legal claim."

"Then you know he had a rich silver strike."

"Prospectors get all soused and say things they want, not necessarily what's real. I will say this. He was goin' to—"

"Ask the woman he loved to marry him," Barker finished. The land clerk looked over, and Tillie jumped as if she had been stuck with a needle.

"Isn't that right, Tillie? Gus got all dressed up in his best duds and rode out in his buggy to ask you to marry him because he'd struck it rich. What happened?" He saw her face flow like putty in the warm sun, then harden into a mask.

"Marshal! Silas killed him when Gus declared his love for me. Silas is a jealous son of a bitch and he killed him."

"That so?" Barker stepped into the small office.

"He done it. He killed Gus and said he'd kill me if I told you."

"I think you lied to Henry about the dead man."

"He's slow. What's it matter? He's no use to anybody."

"I told him to give Silas that map." He looked over at the land agent. "You're right. That's not a map to much of anywhere, except to prison."

"Prison?" Tillie pushed her handbag in front of her on the counter. "Whatever can you mean? You going to arrest Silas for killing Gus?"

"I suspect if I went back to the way station, I'd find Silas dead, just like Gus."

Tillie moved fast, and he had been boiling in the hot sun all day. That slowed his reflexes, but not by much since he had never taken his hand off his six-gun. As her crochet hook stabbed out at his face, Barker drew and fanned off a round. Tillie got a surprised look, turned a little and looked at the sharp-pointed crochet hook that had missed its target in his eye, then dropped it. Her boneless body followed the weapon that had killed Gus Johansen to the floor.

"You really a lawman?"

Barker pulled back his coat to show his badge pinned onto his vest.

"She killed Gus and just might have killed the station agent east of town."

"Why?" The clerk looked confused.

"Don't know if we'll ever find out, but I can guess. Gus hit it big and went to ask her to marry him. Either he wouldn't tell her where the strike was until she married him or maybe Silas killed him in a jealous rage. More likely Tillie killed him to keep the peace with Silas. But she had a second chance at getting a pot of silver."

Barker turned the map he had pencilled onto the back of the wanted poster around and shoved it toward the land office clerk.

"That look like anywhere around here?"

"Nope."

Barker shrugged. He couldn't expect to get lucky too many times. He had to be satisfied with bringing to justice a greedy killer ensnared in a noose of silver.

With any luck, he could be back home in Mesilla before sundown two days from now.

A Close Shave on Commerce Street

by Steven Clark

Steven Clark is the author of the novel The Guerrilla Man: Bloody Trail to Kansas, *available from Solstice Publishing. In addition to writing, he teaches economics and performs as a storyteller and musician. He lives with his wife in St. Charles, MO.*

As Conn Royal, town marshal of Jellico, leaned back in George Huxley's barber chair, he felt the beginnings of a complaint forming on his lips.

"How's that missus of yours treating you lately, marshal?" asked George as he whipped the shaving lather with a small wooden pestle.

Conn knew the question was coming. George always asked it early on, which was good because the marshal had come in today needing to vocalize a few things—perhaps even more than he needed the shave. Still, abiding by a long-standing convention between the two men, he started out reticent.

"Well, George, what can I say? Marriage is what it is."

The barber grinned, his friendly face glowing with good cheer. "Whatever in the world is that supposed to mean? You've only been married three months, so how can you say 'marriage is what it is?'And what exactly *is* marriage in your opinion, marshal? Hmmn?"

Conn shrugged. "You oughta know, George. You're married, ain'tcha?"

The barber nodded; the corners of his long, graying mustache twitched. "Twenty-nine years," he said. "But this isn't about me. It's *your* shave, marshal."

In the barber chair, Conn heaved a sigh as George began applying the lather. The marshal and the barber had known each other for some time. Ever since Conn had settled in Jellico, going on a dozen years ago now, he'd been stopping in George's place weekly for a shave or a trim. He always found the sessions calming and refreshing. The town of Jellico was no longer as wild as it once had been (nor was Conn, for that matter), but being town marshal still involved a degree of stress and strain. George always seemed to be able to help him untangle his thoughts, which had a tendency to get a bit knotted up at times. Conn figured that was at least half the reason folks visited the barber anyway.

After a fair stretch of silence had passed, the marshal (having carried the reticent act far enough) cleared his throat and began to unload his thoughts. "Don't get me wrong, George, Dagmar's a real good woman. *Real* good. Great cook and companion at mealtime. She listens well when I have something to say. Laughs when I mention anything funny. She washes and mends my clothes, cleans my boots, and just takes real good care of me all around."

"Real good care, you say?"

"Mmm-hmmn. She's even oiled and polished my gun a time or two," Conn said. "Just this morning, in fact."

The barber raised his eyebrows and glanced over at the holstered Peacemaker that sat just a few feet away on the shelf. The pistol and holster were wrapped loosely in the marshal's worn old gun belt. "Impressive," George said. "Thought I noticed something different about your gun when you walked in."

"And listen to this," Conn went on. "Last month I told her that I wished the buttons on my favorite shirt was a different color. You know what she gone and did?"

"Sewed new buttons on, did she?"

"She sure did. Sewed new buttons on and there

wasn't even anything wrong with the old ones."

"They were the wrong color.You said so yourself."

"There wasn't nothing wrong with the color of those buttons, George. It was just an idle thought I happened to utter out loud one day. Wasn't even sure if I'd meant it when I said it."

"Well, then it appears you bes' watch closer what you say around your house, marshal."

George set aside the mortar that held the shaving lather, then drew up the razor strop that hung from the side of the barber chair. He began running the blade of the razor back and forth along the leather strop. "Got a woman who'll polish your gun for you," he said, shaking his head slowly from side to side. "Idn't that something?"

"It's something all right," said the marshal. "She must've spent all morning working on it. I told her that pistol's so shiny now the bullets look like lumps of clay in comparison."

George glanced over at the Peacemaker a second time. "I'll have to say, it's the prettiest I've ever seen it."

All became quiet in the barbershop for a few moments as George pulled a hair from the side of his own balding head and used it to test the razor blade. Satisfied that he'd sharpened it adequately, he lowered the blade to the marshal's throat.

"So what's your problem then, marshal? Sounds like you've got a real good woman. One in a thousand."

"Dagmar's one in a million," Conn said, correcting the other man.

"Pardon me," George said, "one in a million. So I'll ask it again, marshal. What *is* your problem?"

Conn waited for the barber's blade to pass over his Adam's apple before he launched in. "I guess what you might say is that Dagmar, sweet and loving as she is, is almost *too* good a companion."

"*Too* good?" George's voice rose in surprise.

"That's right. That woman takes *too* good a care of me. So good I've almost forgotten how to do certain things for myself."

"Really now? That surprises me a little, marshal. What sorts of things you mean?"

Conn thought for a moment. "Well," he said, "take frying an egg for example."

"Frying an egg?" George's hand paused, the blade hovering beside the marshal's right cheek. "You've really forgotten how to fry an egg?"

"I haven't forgotten how to do it, George. I'm just out of practice. I tried frying one up the other day and I ruin't it. Dagmar was mad that I hadn't allowed her to cook the egg for me. And mad at me for making a mess of her frying pan."

"Can't blame her for that. Frying an egg's not all that hard to do."

"I know it's not hard to do. That's my point, George – it's almost like she's spoilt me and now I've forgotten how to take care of myself. I'm afraid one day I'll get too soft to be town marshal anymore."

George glanced down at the marshal's midriff, at the paunch jutting out from under the barber towel. "I've noticed you've gotten a little softer around the middle since you married, marshal," he said. "But that happens to the best of us."

"I wasn't talking about my middle, George!" Conn snorted. "I was meaning my mind!"

"Oh? You mean to tell me your it's your *mind* that's going soft?'

"In a manner of speaking. She's always making such a fuss over me, I get to the point I can't think straight no more. Let me give you a for instance."

"Hold on just a second," George said, and he leaned in closer to the chair, biting down on his lower lip as he eased the razor up under the marshal's right ear. A few seconds later, he wiped a big dollop of lather on the barber towel and said, "All righty, marshal. Go on ahead with your for instance."

Conn cleared his throat. "Now don't laugh when you hear this . . . A couple weeks ago I walked out of the house with my shirt all buttoned up wrong and my hat on cockeyed. Didn't even notice till I stopped off at Bo Luckenbill's store. The folks in the store that morning got a good chuckle out of it, and I chuckled along just to be congenial. But really I didn't think it was none too funny. I'm marshal of this town, George, not some circus clown."

"You've got a good point there. How're folks supposed take you seriously as marshal looking all out of sorts like that?"

"And that ain't the worst of it, George. Three days ago I walked out of the house wearing my gun belt, but I'd forgot to put my pistol in my holster!"

George's hand paused again, the razor stopping just under Conn's nose. "My goodness, Marshall Royal. Your wife's going to get you killed one day."

Conn sighed. "It wouldn't be out of meanness, though. Best way to say it is that sooner or later, if she keeps doing like she's doing, that woman's gonna love me to death."

The barber glanced over once more at the Peacemaker. "You've got your gun now, though," he said.

"Yes, I do."

"And you came in with your hat on straight, and your shirt seemed buttoned up right. So it can't be an everyday occurrence, this 'softening' of your mind," said George.

"I needed to be ready today," Conn said, lowering his voice slightly. "Can't risk having nothing out of sorts today."

The barber narrowed his eyes. "You expecting some kind of trouble today, marshal?" he asked.

The marshal, sitting up a little straighter in the chair, looked George directly in the eye. "Possibly," he told him. He sighed again, then said, "More than likely. Can I trust you not to tell anyone? Don't want folks getting worried needlessly."

"Of course, marshal. I never repeat anything you say when you're in my chair."

Conn nodded. He already knew that his secrets would never leave the walls of the barbershop, but he still appreciated hearing the other man say so. "The express box on the afternoon stage will be carrying a bigger load than usual," he explained to George. "An informant from over in Hemlock told me the Cryer boys may be planning to hit it. Shotgun man on that particular stage line is good, though. Has a tough-as-nails reputation. If the Cryers are planning on making a move, they'll most likely wait till the box is in the express office and the stage has gone on."

"That sounds like a serious piece of business, marshal." The barber had stopped working; had lowered the razor to his side. "Where's that greenhorn deputy of yours?" he asked.

"Homer had to take care of something down in Sadieville today," Conn said. "Probably won't get back till evening time."

"Can you handle this all by yourself, marshal? Sounds like some serious business."

"I've handled worse than the Cryer boys on my own, George. There are only three of them, word has it none of the three are very good marksmen, and they don't know I'm on to their plan. I'd say the odds favor me."

"If you say so, marshal." George sighed as he lifted the razor and moved it toward the marshal's upper lip. "You're the professional lawman here."

"I am still that," Conn said, easing back slightly in the chair. "No matter how soft my middle has gotten."

* * *

Later that afternoon, Conn was finishing a second cup of coffee at Mattie Akin's restaurant when, across the way, on the other side of Commerce Street, the stage from Kansas City pulled in from the east. Ordinarily he would have gone out to greet the driver and the shotgun rider, but he didn't wish to make his presence widely known just yet. Earlier in the day, the marshal had planted a rumor among the patrons of the Keystone Saloon that he and Homer Bodkin would be out of town most of the day on business. The saloon regulars were struck by the news, as it was rare for both the marshal and his deputy to be absent from town on the same day. Conn knew the rumor would spread quickly.

He continued to watch through the window as two passengers stepped down from the stage and the stage workers unloaded their luggage. Shortly thereafter, the clerk from the express office—a young man named Jaffey who'd only been in the job a short time—came out to claim the express box, which the driver removed from the stage's front boot. The shotgun rider stood off to the side watching the transaction closely, the barrel of his scattergun laid across his chest. After the express box was moved safely into the office, the driver and the shotgun rider each took a turn at the privy behind the express office building, and then, within fifteen minutes of its arrival, the stage pulled out, headed due west.

"More coffee, Conn?"

The marshal turned his head and saw Mattie Akin, the restaurant's proprietor, standing beside his table, her eyes beaming as she looked him up and down.

"No thanks, Mattie. You mind if I just sit here a while, gather my thoughts some?"

"You can sit in my place any day of the week, Conn Royal," she said, her smile broadening. "Way I see it, having you here only serves to beautify the place."

Conn quickly drew his gaze away from the woman. Mattie Akin often spoke to him that way; it was no secret around town that she still harbored strong feelings for him. The marshal had courted Mattie for a spell several years back, and at one point had even considered asking for her hand in marriage. Their union hadn't worked out, but she would never let him forget the time they'd spent together.

How would that have turned out? Conn wondered as he swung his gaze back toward the window and the scenery along Commerce Street. *Would Mattie Akin have made me soft, too?*

"Dang it," he muttered under his breath. "I ain't soft."

"What's that, Conn?"

Looking up, he saw that Mattie was still standing close by. "Nothing," he said. "I was just thinking about something George Huxley said earlier."

"Don't listen to nothing George says," she advised him. "He thinks he knows everything. Alls he is is just a nosy little barber."

"Well, Mattie, strikes me that that nosy little barber knows more than most people in this town 'bout most things."

One of Mattie's other customers summoned her from the other side of the big dining room. Relieved the conversation had ended, Conn returned his attention to the scenery outside.

Focusing through the restaurant window, the marshal shifted his gaze from side to side, taking in a wide view of the storefronts along Commerce Street. It was nearing the end of the business day, and so traffic on the street and the boardwalks was relatively light. There were a few pedestrians ambling along the boardwalks, one lone rider on the street moving at a lope from the eastern edge of town, and a buckboard rolling in from the west. Nothing in downtown Jellico seemed out of the ordinary for the time of day.

After a minute, the buckboard stopped almost directly in front of the express office. At almost the same moment, the lone rider swung his horse in close to the wagon. The two men who'd been riding on the buckboard's seat jumped down to the ground.

Conn had never seen any of the Cryer boys in person, but, as he studied them carefully through the window, he concluded that these three men fit the general descriptions he'd heard from his Hemlock informant.

Conn got to his feet and started toward the door, calling to Mattie, "Sorry to run out without paying. Start me a tab?"

"A tab?" She smiled at him across the room. "That means you'll be coming back soon?"

"Soon enough," he answered, then he opened the door and stepped out into the afternoon light.

Across the street the three men had already entered the express office. *Smarter bandits would have posted a lookout,* Conn thought. Throughout his career he'd faced some smart outlaws and some very foolish ones; he could usually tell the difference between the two types right away. "Definitely a one-man job," he mumbled to himself as he moved briskly across the street.

Well before he reached the boardwalk in front of the express office, Conn had drawn his weapon. The Peacemaker felt good in his hand, it occurred to him; like wearing a favorite shirt.

He could see that the bandits had left the door of the express office slightly ajar. *Another mistake on their part,* he thought. Rather than turning the door knob and giving them a moment's warning, Conn could kick the door open and take them by surprise.

Fool's mistake!

When he kicked the door open, as he'd been hoping, he caught the three bandits wholly off guard. Only one of them had his gun drawn, and that one had the barrel of his pistol aimed at Jaffey, the clerk, who stood at his post behind the counter with his hands held high.

"Drop it now," Conn said in a voice that was calm and clear.

The bandit with the gun dropped his pistol immediately and it *ker-thunked* loudly against the wooden floor of the express office.

"You two." Conn nodded toward the other two bandits. "Take your pistols out nice and slow and drop 'em on the floor. Two fingers only."

The bandits did exactly as they'd been ordered. Conn then glanced across the counter at Jaffey, who appeared to be in a state of semi-shock at the moment. "Come on 'round here and pick up these pistols," the marshal instructed Jaffey.

Before the clerk could get around to the front side of the counter, footsteps sounded on the boardwalk just outside the express office door, which Conn had left standing wide open behind him. His heart began to sink as it occurred to him that perhaps the three bandits had another accomplice – a fourth man – who was now coming in on the marshal's back side.

Before he could contemplate turning and looking behind him, he heard a voice.

But it was not the harsh, gruff voice he expected. Instead the voice was soft . . . feminine.

Not a fourth bandit, he quickly realized. *Not another man. A woman*!

"Conn, darling," said the voice, and the sound of it caused the marshal's back to stiffen. The tone, the cadence, the accent . . .

The voice of his wife, Dagmar.

"Darling, I tought I heard you talking in here," she said as she breezed forward into the express office. "You vent off today and left someting important."

"Not now, dear," Conn said without turning to look at her. "Can't you see I'm working here?"

He felt her move closer, and within seconds she was standing directly behind him.

"But I tought you would want to have deese, darling," his wife said.

Her hand came up beside him. When Conn glanced over and saw her palm open up, his breath hitched in his chest and his knees gave slightly.

In the palm of her delicate gloved hand the marshal's wife held a half-dozen .45-caliber bullets. The casings of the bullets were gleaming like pieces of polished jewelry.

As Conn stared in disbelief at the bullets, he could sense the confusion of the other men in the office. The three bandits and the clerk spent several seconds glancing around the room, first looking at the bullets, then the woman, then the marshal, and then one another.

Finally, one of the bandits spoke up. "Uh, she's holding six rounds there, fellas."

Another member of the trio said, "So that must mean . . ."

The bandit's voice trailed off, and all at once, as if reacting to a silent signal, all three Cryers dove toward the floor for their guns. Jaffey's face went a shade paler than it had been previously, and he quickly ducked down behind the counter.

Conn shifted his body and fanned his arms out wide, attempting to throw up a shield in front of his wife before any of the bandits could get off a shot. As soon as he'd finished assuming his defensive posture, Conn heard another voice from just outside the express office door. The shouting voice was full of anger.

"Everyone in there freeze, goldarnit!"

It was another voice familiar to Conn, though he'd never before heard it raised to a shout.

Two of the bandits, following the command, instantly froze in place. But the third continued to reach for his pistol on the floor.

"I said freeze!" George Huxley hollered as he came forward, crossing the threshold into the express office. Out in front of him the barber held a Winchester rifle, which he pointed at the third bandit.

The bandit paused with his hand just inches away from the grips of his pistol. For several seconds he seemed to waver, his bloodshot eyes narrowing on the barber's face. Conn turned his gaze on George's face as well, and was surprised by what he saw there. Nothing remained of the barber's usual friendly countenance; the balding little man was all steel and grit. Conn knew the look of a man who meant business, and his old friend had come in ready to handle some business.

The third bandit swallowed a lump in his throat, then drew his hand away from the pistol. Slowly he uprighted himself.

"Now get your hands over your heads!" George growled. "All three of you."

Without the least bit of backtalk, the bandits did as they were told. A moment later, Jaffey poked his head up from behind the counter and scanned the room before rising to his full height.

"Sure am glad to see you here," Conn said to George.

The marshal blew out a sigh and then, turning toward his wife, reached over and scooped the bullets out of her open palm.

"I thought maybe you could use a little backup," George said. He still had his Winchester aimed in the general direction of the Cryers; he was still eyeing them hard.

"How'd you figure out it was more than a one-man job?" Conn asked as he loaded the bullets into his pistol. After he closed the cylinder, he raised the Peacemaker and trained the barrel on the largest and surliest-looking of the Cryer boys.

George shrugged. "Kind of a hunch, I s'pose. After your shave, when I picked up your gun rig from the shelf to hand it to you, I was thinking that it felt a little lighter than normal."

Conn looked over at the barber, who was still staring intently at the three men in front of him. With his squinty-eyed gaze and his tight-clenched jaw, the barber had the look of a hard-case gunfighter staring down a hated enemy. Conn took in the sight for a long moment, and then, without intending to, he started snickering.

"What's so funny?" George said, creasing his brow.

Conn, still snickering, said, "I was just thinking that maybe you missed your calling, George. Maybe I should hire you as my deputy."

"Oh, dat is a very good idea," Dagmar said, nodding enthusiastically. "He can help you bring in outlaws, and den at de week's end he can give you a shave."

Conn reached over and patted his old friend on the shoulder. "Or maybe we'll just stick with the weekly shave," he said. "Like we've been doing . . . for how long now, George?"

"Twelve years," George said.

"That's what I thought," Conn said. "Long time."

The marshal was still grinning as he proceeded to march the captured bandits out to the street and toward the jailhouse. George came along, walking beside him with his Winchester clutched tightly in his hands. All around them, people began pouring out from the saloons and cafés to watch the jail-bound procession.

Midway down Commerce Street, the marshal turned to George and said, "I expect that for a long time to come folks in Walden County are gonna be talking about the day the mild-mannered little barber helped deliver three desperadoes to the Jellico jail."

George, paying no mind to the gawkers who now lined both sides of the street, glanced over at Conn and replied, "Or the day the marshal of Jellico tried to stop a crime in progress with an unloaded Colt Peacemaker."

Conn Royal nodded. "That too," he said.

As they stepped up onto the boardwalk in front of the jailhouse, the marshal was trying hard to keep his laughter in check.

He knew that in just a week his old friend, the town barber, would hold another freshly sharpened razor to his throat.

Lost Mountain Pass

by Larry D. Sweazy

*Larry D. Sweazy (www.larrydsweazy.com) won the
WWA Spur Award for Best Short Fiction in 2005, and
was nominated for a SFMS Derringer award in 2007. He
has published over 50 articles and short stories, which
have appeared in* Ellery Queen's Mystery Magazine; The
Adventure of the Missing Detective; Boys' Life;
Hardboiled, *and other publications and anthologies.
Larry is the author of the Josiah Wolfe, Texas Ranger
series (Berkley), and his first standalone mystery,* The
Devil's Bones *(Five Star), will be released 02/12. He is a
member of MWA (Mystery Writers of America), WWA
(Western Writers of America), and WF (Western
Fictioneers). Larry lives in the Midwest, with his wife,
Rose, two dogs, and a cat.*

Three pairs of boots pointed straight down. A long
second of silence followed, the crowd waiting, uncertain,
until the ropes quit swinging. Murmurs grew then,
almost in unison, like an amen at the end of a long
prayer. The entire town stood still, nervous to leave,
eyes shaded toward the three dead men, making sure
the twitching and breathing was finally done and over
with.

It had been a picture perfect day for a hanging in
Kosoma. Part celebration, part melodrama that had
come to a quick, neck-breaking end. More than
anything, the hanging was a cause for the boomtown to
grind to a stop, and witness the execution of Cleatus
Darby, and his two younger brothers.

The Darbys were legendary in Kosoma now—or not—

potentially lost names in a long line of lawless men whose bones would crumble back into dust, and become nothing more than the dirt from where they came. Memory or records of their deeds might never be spoken of again, unless absolutely necessary. The only ounce of fame the Darbys owned while they walked the earth was for their meanness, for their unrelenting efforts to bring suffering to all of those that got in their way, and some that didn't. Someone new would surely fill their place. Meanness in and around Kosoma was as plentiful as rain in the early spring.

"Looks like my job here is done," Oklahoma Circuit Court Judge Gordon Hadesworth said. He was as tall and thin as a cornstalk, stately with a well-trimmed white goatee, and a suit that, like all of his suits, was shipped to him directly from New York from a company called Brooks Brothers.

"I suppose you'll be wantin' a bite of dinner before we start toward Enid?" The questioner was Hadesworth's protection and escort, Deputy U.S. Marshal Hank Snowden—most often referred to as "Trusty," by judges and outlaws alike.

Hank Snowden had never lost a judge, and more than a few lawless idiots had thought they could outwit him, finding themselves at the smoking end of his Henry rifle, or dangling from the gallows, like the three fellas before him—though he had nothing to do with their capture, sentencing, or the quick send off to meet their maker.

"Between you and me, Trusty, I'd just as soon get out of this stinking town as soon as possible," the judge said, lowering his voice so no one could hear or take offense to his comment.

Kosoma actually meant "place of stinking water" in the Choctaw language. There were a myriad of bubbling, steaming springs fingering off the Kiamichi River, and they were all thick with stinky sulfur. A slight breeze pushed the pungent smell of rotten eggs straight down Main Street of the new town, and then into every nook, cranny, and alleyway, soiling any pleasant aroma it could find. There was nothing to overcome the putrid smell, and no way to escape it. You just got used to it...or you didn't.

Not even the smell of opportunity found in fresh cut lumber, that was so prevalent now that the St. Louis-San Francisco Railroad, more commonly referred to as the Frisco, could vanquish the residue of the springs from the senses or threads of your clothes.

The Frisco had built a new rail line running from the north to the south, straight through the Choctaw Nation, connecting Fort Smith with Paris, Texas, and Kosoma was perfectly located to capitalize on the new line, smell or no smell.

The railroad followed the Kiamichi River, exploiting the water for steam and power. Living with the stink was a small price to pay when there was more than a pile of money to be made. Kosoma was a classic territory town; a field of nothingness one minute, a bustling center of commerce the next, and there wasn't much of anything, smells or otherwise, that could keep the hopeful, the schemers, and the dreamers away. Especially now that order of law had been enforced judiciously, fairly, and without prejudice. The Darbys were longtimers, some of the first whites to settle the area. They were immune to the smell but not to the new ways of accountability and laws that stifled their unseemly behavior. Murder had been frowned upon long before there was ever a town, but the Darbys didn't understand that.

Hank Snowden figured he hadn't been in town long enough to reach the point of immunity of any of his senses, and had no intention of staying any longer than necessary. He was greatly relieved to hear the judge wanted to leave immediately.

"Not one of the nicer smelling places I've ever been," Hank replied to the judge. He didn't take to the nickname much. He thought referring to himself as Trusty was boastful and dangerous to believe in. Truth be told, he knew he'd just been lucky more than once, regardless of how prepared, or how good a shot he actually was.

The judge smiled, and nodded. "Not from the stories I hear tell. There's a line of whorehouses from San Antonio to Abilene that still tell of your exploits."

"You'd think a judge would be immune to hearsay."

"We get bored, Trusty. We like a little rumor and gossip as much as any other man. Besides, you've a reputation to uphold, I'm just contributing to your resume."

"Some of those spots smelled right nice." Hank's face flushed red. There was no question he liked the company of women. One in particular, but she was a hundred miles away, married to another man, his heart still hers, though, any time she came asking, silver braided ring or not. "Ain't nothin' but tales about me anyways, Judge. The past is the past. I'm a reformed man."

"You mean you've found Jesus?"

"Not lately, anyways, not in the places I've been. Course I haven't been lookin' much for Him, neither. I was just an energetic youngun', that's all. Women tend to complicate a man's life, at least this man's life."

"You just keep thinking that, Trusty, and we'll all have plenty to talk about for a long time to come."

Hank laughed uncomfortably. "Let's get your belongin's from the hotel and dust our way out of here before the sun starts to dive west too fast. I'd like to get through Lost Mountain Pass before night settles in."

"Expecting trouble, Trusty?" the judge asked with a raised eyebrow.

"Always, Judge. I'm always expectin' trouble. 'Specially after a hangin' as well-deserved as this one."

* * *

Hank cinched the saddle on his horse, a paint gelding that he'd never got around to naming. He called the horse Horse, and it didn't seem to mind. The two of them had traveled a lot of miles together, knew each other pretty well, but Hank wasn't one to hold a high affection for any animal on a long term basis. There was a job to do, and that was that. Attachments were a danger to the job as far as he was concerned. The escapade with the married woman had taught him that, along with a long string of hard lessons learned before then that he didn't care to revisit any time soon.

"I was hoping I would find you here."

The voice was a female's. It startled Hank. He hadn't heard anyone come up behind him, which at once concerned and scared him, but he didn't show it. Letting your guard down for one second on a day like today could get you killed, and he knew it. Another stroke of luck as far as he was concerned, as he took in the woman standing before him.

"I'm sorry, ma'am, do I know you?"

She shook her head no. "No sir, you do not." She was more a girl than a woman. Lucky to be twenty years old, at that, probably younger. Dressed in a plain white blouse, and a long skirt, deep blue, almost black, parts of it matte, other parts, shiny, sewed in a tight horizontal pattern, along with traveling boots, and a straw bonnet with dangling chin straps. Her face was hard set with a bird-like nose, eyes the color of granite, and dark brunette hair pulled back and swept up under the bonnet—all of which was stacked up on a skinny, flat body. There was nothing about the girl that Hank found attractive. She instantly annoyed him, considering her stealthy skills.

The livery was quiet, not much going on. It was just the two of them as far as Hank knew. A few stalls over, a horse snorted, then took a healthy piss.

"I understand you are on your way to Enid?" the girl said.

"Yes, ma'am, that would be correct."

"I would like to secure passage in your company."

Hank wiped his hands. "I'm sorry, ma'am, I'm a Deputy U.S. Marshal, not an escort. You'll need to make other arrangements. I don't hire out."

"Are you not Trusty Snowden?"

He flinched at the nickname. "I am. Sure as it's daylight, I am. But most folks call me Hank."

"Most folks call you Trusty, and that is the only

41

reason why I have sought you out. Your reputation as a drinker and a womanizer is overridden by the fact that your gun skills are rumored to be superb, the best in the Territory from what I understand. I need protection, deputy, or I will surely not make it out of Kosoma alive."

"Your life's in danger? How's that?"

The woman stared at Hank like he had just asked the stupidest question in the world. "Fine. This was a waste of my time, just as I suspected it would be," she said, spinning in perfect balance on the heels of her boots, pushing off with the intention of stalking off. "My blood is on your hands, deputy. Remember I said that," she added, snarling over her shoulder.

By the time Hank caught up with the girl, she had gone about twenty feet away from him, nearly to the barn's double doors that stood wide open. A slight breeze pushed stinky air through the barn, mixing with the horseshit and piss. He really wanted to get the hell out of Kosoma.

"Wait," Hank said, grabbing the girl's arm, bringing her to a stop. "There's no need to go gettin' all haughty, just tell me what's going on. If you're in trouble, that's another thing entirely."

With a glare that cut through her tear-filled eyes, she said. "It's too late. I might as well succumb to my fate. You are my last chance. I will approach this journey on my own, and take my chances, thank you very much."

Maybe it was the tears in her once rock hard eyes, the vulnerability now apparent, but her features had softened. There was a beauty to her, a sweet smell, that Hank had failed to see, somehow had overlooked at first glance. She was not the kind of woman he'd consider pursuing, but she wasn't an ugly bird at all.

"Let's start over," Hank said. "What's your name, ma'am?" he asked in his softest, most seductive voice he could muster at the moment.

"Matilda. Matilda Darby." She watched Hank's reaction closely, surely accustomed to a negative response. When his face showed no change, she continued. "Cleatus was my brother. Horace and Rascal, too. And just because I'm of the same blood, people think I'm a killer, thief, and a liar, too. Folks around town think we're all just meaner than snakes, and not fit to walk on this earth. That I'm just like them. I guess I can't blame them. The three boys robbed anyone with a nickel, and when they finally took to killing, they did it like it was fun. Old man Robinson, the one they hanged for, was target practice. They emptied their guns on him long after he was dead. Why should I be surprised then, that everyone, and probably you, think I'm no better than them?"

Hank let his hand slide away from Matilda's arm. "I'm sorry, I had no idea."

"How could you, you're not from these parts."

"I'll talk to the marshal, see about gettin' you some protection. Maybe it'd be best to just let things settle down a bit before you go makin' a rash decision like leavin' town."

"I have had pig's blood thrown on my porch. Service refused me at the mercantile. No one will extend me credit, or hire out my skills as a milliner. I am nearly broke, sir, left with no kin to fall back on, or any prospects for the future in this town at all, other than the certainty of my death. Just this morning, someone fired a gunshot through my front window. It is only a matter of luck that I was not walking through the front room, or I would be lying in a coffin along with my brothers up on Poor Man's Hill. I fear for my life, deputy, surely you must understand that."

Hank shifted uncomfortably. "How do I know that this isn't some kind of ploy to exact revenge on the judge for renderin' a well-deserved death sentence on your brothers, ma'am? How do I know you don't have a plot to kill him? I'm sorry to ask, ma'am, but I have to, the judge is my charge. I have taken an oath to die for him, if it comes to that. You sure don't look like a killer to me, but I've seen some sweet ones, let me tell you."

Matilda stared at Hank with her deep gray eyes unflinching. She had wiped away her tears, and it was like they had never existed in the first place. "I would expect that you would think of such a thing. Three things should be reason enough to believe me, deputy. One. I have never hurt a fly. Never. You can ask anyone in this town. Two. I am the last of the Darbys in this town. When I am gone, there will be no legacy for anyone to shoulder, and all of my family's debts will be paid in full. The Darbys will be a bad memory, quickly forgotten, and unknown to the greedy hordes that are filling the town in search of their fortunes. Three. I hated my brothers and what they stood for. They deserved to hang. They were cold-blooded killers, and earned their punishments, what they got in the end. I have no mind for revenge, no need to set the record straight by bringing any harm to Judge Hadesworth. My only desire is to start a new life as far away from Kosoma as possible. It is that simple, deputy. That is my story, and there is nothing I can add, other than the guarantee of my word that I mean no one any harm, especially the judge."

Hank took a deep breath, and stared up at the rafters. "I'll have to clear it with the judge, you understand."

"No need," Matilda said, "I already have."

* * *

They rode toward the end of town, three horses abreast. A few people stopped on the boardwalks and glared. Some even turned their backs, shunning Matilda Darby purposefully, leaving no question to what their intention was. The sighting of such disregard fortified Matilda's story, made it seem true. Hank was relieved, more than he was appalled, by the sight.

Matilda stared straight ahead, her eyes set on the horizon, not allowing one gaze that fell upon her to dent her attitude or touch her heart. At least that she showed on the outside from what Hank could see.

Hank had his trusted Henry rifle lying across his lap, and one hand dangling inches from his six-shooter, a Colt Double Action Army .45. The .45 had an enlarged trigger, making it comfortable for Hank's fat finger. He was a big man, over six foot tall, and fit, but not skinny.

His father had been a smithy in St. Louis, outfitting trappers and explorers in the early days, and Hank had inherited his father's stout body, and ability to build and keep muscle on as needed.

Horse had his ears erect, alert, sensing the tension in the air. One ear was white, the other, red, or strawberry roan, depending on who was doing the describing. Hank liked to think Horse's ear was red. Like a sunset falling behind a snow covered mountain. Strawberry sounded sissified, and there was nothing about Horse that suggested he *was* sissified.

Just as they were about to cross the last street before leaving Kosoma, a wagon passed in front of them, causing all three horses to come to a stop, and wait.

The wagon was loaded with the Darby brothers' coffins, and was heading toward a cemetery on the opposite end of town, the place Matilda had called Poor Man's Hill. There was no parade of mourners following along. The preacher sat shotgun, next to a glum teamster, both of them stiff, and on tenterhooks, as if they expected something to happen at any second.

Judge Hadesworth shifted uncomfortably in his saddle. "You sure you don't want to attend the funeral of your brothers, Miss Darby?"

"No, sir. I have no more tears left to shed for those three. Rascal held the greatest amount of promise, and I will miss him the most. But in the end, his deeds were influenced by the other two, competing to be noticed and accepted, so they wouldn't treat him as a dunce or a punching bag. It never happened. Rascal died still trying to impress Cleatus. Whatever awaits them on the other side of this life will be no different, I imagine. If there is such a thing."

"You are not a believer, then?" the judge asked.

Matilda turned her attention away from the coffins, and stared Judge Hadesworth directly in the eye. "Let's just say I have questions. And you, Judge?"

Hank stayed out of the conversation, his eyes darting to the rooftops, and to the shadows of the alleyway that cut alongside a mercantile and an empty storefront with a "For Rent" sign in the front window.

"My father was a Methodist minister," the judge said. "I was raised in the ways of the Lord. But I am not one to proselytize, so you have no need to worry of my pestering you for a conversion or deep conversation based on verses put to memory as a child."

"That is the least of my worries on this journey, Judge," Matilda said.

The wagon moved on, and the way forward cleared. Dust settled to the ground, and a thin, wavering cloud of flies chased after the coffins, drawn by the smell of death, and the opportunity that a human body provided. Three dead men were a jackpot of food and a virgin breeding ground. Flies obviously knew a boomtown when they saw it, too.

"Your decision is final then, ma'am?" Hank asked.

"Yes, Trusty, it is. The sooner I'm out of this town, the sooner my new life begins."

* * *

Hank trailed behind, keeping a short distance behind Matilda and the blond sorrel she rode. The sorrel looked a little old, and a little lazy. Hank wondered if it could make the trip all the way to Enid, but kept those concerns to himself. And Matilda was not an expert rider. The sorrel had a habit of snatching fresh grass that had sprung up alongside the well-trammeled path, eating at every chance it could find, slowing them down. If the act lasted much longer, Hank knew he would have to say something about it. Safe time on the trail was running out.

Judge Hadesworth was in the lead, pushing them up the trail as it eased away from a fertile valley. There was a clearing about halfway up that Hank had camped in before. He hoped they made it before dark, disappointed that time had run out on them.

They had taken longer to leave than Hank had planned on, helping Matilda finish up packing. She traveled light for a woman. Especially a woman planning on setting up a milliner shop in Enid, but she had explained that most of her materials had been sold or given away with the knowledge that she would be leaving town—or be dead, one or the other. Fleeing was more like it, so Hank supposed her easy load made sense. Still, it troubled him some.

The sun was falling west rapidly, and pink fingers stretched out in front of the three riders, fading sunlight reflecting on the underside of long bits of clouds, like arrows pointing them in the right direction.

A breeze had followed them out of Kosoma, but thankfully, the stink of the springs had been left behind. The higher they rode up the trail, the cooler it got, and long before night set in, Hank was sure he'd need his duster. Spring was a trickster, fickle with its weather. Hot days, shivering cold nights. Lucky for all of them that there were no storms on the horizon. At least, not that Hank could see at the moment.

Without Matilda along, as had been originally planned, Hank and the judge would have more than likely rode side by side, when possible, participating in a slow, but interesting conversation about the law, politics, and most assuredly, women. And they would have been much farther along, through the Lost Mountain Pass, and safe on the other side in an open stretch of land, skirting Spirit Lake.

The sorrel grabbed another mouthful of grass, forcing Hank to slow for the last time. "You're gonna have to get that horse of yours under control," he said, after kneeing Horse, and whipping the reins to the right, urging the paint into a slight run up next to Matilda.

"He has a mind of his own, deputy." Matilda's face was tense with frustration. Her eyes were hard, and cut through Hank like he was a schoolboy about to get his knuckles rapped. "Do we have much farther?" It was more of a demand than a question.

"No, ma'am." Hank let off the reins, slowing Horse, letting him fall back to his position. He was in no mood to offer horse riding lessons to a testy little woman who was short on manners, and long on attitude, no matter how fine she talked.

The pink fingers quickly turned gray, and though they were still heading upward on the trail, Hank could see the blackness of night eating into the grayness of twilight. The first star was visible, and the ghost of a crescent moon began to take form, its tips stabbing into a cloudless sky that would bring glory and thrills to coyote and nighttime hunters.

* * *

The fire crackled comfortably, and the smell of boiling beans, with a hint of bacon tossed in for flavor, permeated the air throughout the camp.

There hadn't been enough time to hunt a rabbit, or any other eatable varmint before the sun crashed below the horizon, leaving the threesome in the dark, and with only a minimum of supplies.

Hank had counted on getting farther, on being able to use his rifle skills to feed them for the remainder of the trip, but that had not happened. He was almost certain that Matilda was slowing them down on purpose, and it was that thought, that inkling of discomfort that kept him in camp, close to the judge. Acquiring trust was more dangerous than naming a horse as far as Hank was concerned.

The ground was flat, and a collection of boulders, some as big as sheds and houses, shielded them on three sides, while the thick torso of the mountain stretched upward, towering over them, dotted with a collection of pine trees that provided shelter and food for a variety of birds, deer, and an occasional mountain lion.

From where they sat, the view looked east, out over the valley, out over the Kiamichi River, as it snaked from behind the mountain, back out to Kosoma. The town wasn't visible, but there was no question it was there, still within a good hard ride.

"Quite a spot you picked here, Trusty," the judge said. He had not abandoned his jacket and hat. Like Hank thought, the night had grown chilly. But Hadesworth sat comfortably, sucking on the end of his pipe as he arched a safety match to the bowl, offering the smell of tobacco to the pleasantness of the camp as the bowl came alive, glowing like an ember from the fire.

Hank sat next to the judge, square in the middle, between him and Matilda. "Been forced to use it now and again. It's good if the weather kicks up like it's apt to do. Fire reflects off the walls, gives us plenty of light, some warmth which we'll appreciate come the middle of the night. Critters usually stay away."

"We can probably be seen from a mile away," Matilda offered with a scowl.

The Henry rifle was inches from Hank's hand. He tapped the stock. "If anything should be called Trusty, it's this old rifle. Don't you worry none, ma'am. I'll keep watch. This is the best spot we could be in. There's an escape passage between them rocks over there. Takes us right down to the valley floor in a hard minute if it comes to that."

"You seem pretty sure of yourself, deputy."

Before Hank could say another word, the judge interjected. "You've no idea of this man's skills, Miss Darby. Of all the U.S. Deputies that I know, and have ridden with, Trusty, here is the best."

"I'm aware of his reputation, Judge Hadesworth," Matilda said.

Hank stiffened. "Don't believe everything you hear."

A coyote yipped in the distance, not that far from them, off the trail. The call echoed upward, dashing into the night like a warning, a conversation about to begin. But nothing followed.

Hank eyed the judge, and Hadesworth, a veteran of trips under the dark of night, slid his coat to the side, exposing a holstered Peacemaker. A nod from both men followed, and Hank stood, edging into the shadows, stopping at the rim of the open arc of boulders.

The horses were tethered together behind the judge and Matilda, as far back away from the fire as possible, hard to see, but close to the passage Hank spoke of. They were suddenly tense, slightly pulling at the ropes, not yet in a full fledged panic, but working up to it. Even the sorrel showed some spunk, some concern.

Hank looked over his shoulder, and the judge had pulled Matilda back along the rock, huddling together like they were seeking protection from a hard rain, the Peacemaker in full view, cocked and ready to go.

Plans had been previously laid between the judge and Hank if any concern showed itself. Matilda was not part of the plan, but an active participant now.

At the rim, the whole valley laid before him, along with the trail that led up to the camp. It was one of the reasons he had chosen the spot so long ago. It wasn't perfect, but it was the only offering of comfortable and safe shelter until you were on the other side of the mountain.

The crescent moon offered a little light, but not the brilliance a full moon would have happily provided. Still, Hank was able to see pretty well once his eyes adjusted from the fire. He saw nothing, no movement on the trail, or below. The coyote remained quiet; one yip, that's all. Now Hank was not even so sure it *was* a coyote he'd heard.

He stood still for several minutes, giving whatever it was a chance to show itself, before he relaxed, and sat the Henry rifle back down. Finally, it became obvious to him that he'd overreacted, that it was his tension the horses were reacting to, that he was just being too darned cautious.

The beans smelled good, and his stomach rumbled with a request to be tended to. Hank drew a deep breath, and turned around, ready to call off the alarm.

He found himself facing Matilda with a gun pointed at him, a derringer, she'd obviously hidden under her skirt.

Matilda was a step away from the judge, who looked just as surprised as Hank. Before either man could say a word, in the matter of a split second, thunder boomed from above, crackling like a familiar song in Hank's ear, and flashing instantly, an odd poof of orange lightning catching his eye. It wasn't thunder; it was a gunshot.

Hank's fear had come true. Bringing Matilda along

had been a huge mistake. His mouth went dry, and as the bullet hit its target, shock and dismay were pushed aside as all of his training and instinct kicked in. He whirled around, firing the Henry rifle up onto the first exposed ledge, into the shadows, at the first sign of movement.

He hit the man with the second shot. The shooter tumbled forward, bouncing down on the rock, his skull crashing hard, breaking in an audible crash. If the bullet didn't kill him, then the fall did. The shooter landed flat on the ground with a thud, and a quick glance told Hank that he had no idea who the man was—but that wasn't his concern, at the moment.

Matilda lay on the ground, face up, staring at the stars, blood oozing out of her shoulder. She hadn't pointed the gun at Hank, she was protecting herself, them.

"She's been hit, Hank," Judge Hadesworth yelled. "She's been hit bad." He was already at the girl's side, putting pressure on the wound, his fingers bloody.

Matilda coughed, and drew in a breath, as Hank reached her. "I knew they'd come after me," she said, her voice weak.

"Who?" Hank asked. The derringer lay a few feet from Matilda, lost when she took the hit. She had been prepared for the attack, but it hadn't done any good. Another second and Hank would have taken her for the shooter, the threat, like he had supposed she was, and just might of shot her instead. He shuddered at the thought.

"Old man Robinson's son. He said his family wouldn't rest until there were no more Darbys walking on this earth. I believed him then, and I believe him now. I told you that I had to leave that town, and I meant it."

"He's dead," Hank said. "He can't hurt you now."

Matilda nodded, tried to force a smile, and coughed again.

"You need to get her back to town, Hank," the judge said, his voice booming with authority.

"We do."

"No. I'll only slow you down. I can look out for myself."

"I can't do that, Judge. It's my job to look after you. He might not be the only one. More might be waitin', aimin' to take revenge on you for shelterin' her."

"There's only one son," Matilda struggled to say.

"You can't let her die, Trusty. I'll be fine. Take her into Kosoma, and find a doctor."

Matilda grew pale, and as she attempted to say something else, to put her own two cents into the conversation like they had come to expect of her, the shock and pain of the injury became too much, and she lost consciousness.

"Now, Trusty, before it's too late! Get her to a doctor now!" the judge ordered.

* * *

The sun came up in Kosoma, barreling up into the sky like it had been shot from a cannon. Along with daylight coming on strong, the stink seemed stronger, more potent, thicker than Hank recalled from just the day before. But then again, he'd been sitting motionless on a bench outside the doctor's office for more than five hours.

There was no wind, nothing to move along the stink or his worry. Just because Matilda said there was only one Robinson left, set on revenge, didn't make it true. He was as concerned about the judge's welfare as he was Matilda's.

The door finally opened, and the doc walked out, a young man with spectacles, fresh from one of the schools back East. "Looks like she's going to make it, Deputy. But she'll need some care, and a good dose of peace and quiet for a while."

"She hasn't got any family," Hank said. "Can she stay here?"

"I've only got two beds, and it's just me. Maybe for a day, but not for as long as she needs tending to."

Hank sighed. "You're sure?"

The doc nodded. "I'm sorry, but she'll need to be

moved out of here."

"All right, I'll see what I can do."

* * *

A week later, a knock came at the door. "Telegram!"

Hank stood up from the chair, and looked out to the balcony. The French doors were open and a breeze was blowing in, ruffling the thin curtains, offering a peaceful wave into the hotel room. Matilda sat outside, sunning herself in the late afternoon light, her right arm bound tight to her side, a calm, rested look on her face.

Hank pulled his Colt out of the holster, hugged it to the side of his leg, then opened the door cautiously. Kosoma still posed a threat to Matilda as far as he was concerned, and as soon as she was able to travel, they were going to complete their journey to Enid.

The runner from the telegraph office smiled broadly at Hank; he was just a boy, maybe twelve, wearing knickers and an expectant look on his face. "You Trusty Snowden?"

"I guess I am," Hank said with resignation.

"Telegram for you, then." The boy handed the paper to Hank, who took the paper, and dug into his pocket for a nickel.

The boy groaned as he took the coin, then spun around and disappeared quickly down the stairs.

Hank closed the door, locked it, and opened the telegram. It was from Judge Hadesworth.

ARRIVED IN ENID. STOP. RECEIVED NEWS OF MATILDA'S CONDITION. STOP. SPOKE TO MARSHAL LANDON. STOP. TAKE LEAVE UNTIL YOU ARRIVE BACK IN ENID. STOP. BEST WISHES. STOP. JUDGE GORDON P. HADESWORTH, ESQ.

Hank walked out to the balcony. "Telegram just came from the judge. He arrived safely, and arranged for me to take as much time as I need to get us back to Enid."

Matilda looked up at Hank and smiled. "That's good news."

Hank returned the smile, put a hand comfortably on

her opposite shoulder, the one that wasn't bound. "I'm going to my room to get cleaned up for dinner, do you need anything?"

His room was right next door.

"No," Matilda said. "I think I have everything I need." Her face was soft, just like her features now that she'd relaxed, and come to peace with the lack of threats—or it may have been Hank's constant presence. He was never far, looking out for her like a mother hen, or a judge put in his charge. It was difficult for him to walk away from her, to leave her room.

In a short time he'd come to learn that there was little question that Matilda Darby was more woman than girl. He was a little older than her, but it felt good to have someone need him.

Only time would tell whether or not she'd be the one he'd settle down with. She had potential. But until that time, Hank planned on taking it slow and easy—and getting out of Kosoma as soon as possible.

The Poker Payout:

A Calvin Carter Adventure

by Scott D. Parker

Scott D. Parker's first western, "You Don't Get Three Mistakes," was published in the anthology Beat to a Pulp: Round One. *He writes on his own blog http://scottdparker.blogspot.com and is a contributor to the group blog, Do Some Damage http://dosomedamage.blogspot.com. He lives in Houston, Texas, with his wife and son.*

Sitting at a poker table, Calvin Carter smiled. It took him awhile, studying the movements of the dealer and the other men around the table, but he finally figured out how they all were cheating. The deck was marked. That much was clear. He, however, didn't have time to figure out what the markings were. Percy Johns was too busy winning another pile of chips.

"What are you smiling at, Carter?" the man across the table asked.

Carter fingered his tie and made his smile bigger. "I just can't get over how lucky Johns here is."

"It ain't luck," Johns growled, throwing a menacing look Carter's way. Johns's suit was rumpled and his tie askew, owing to his constant fiddling with it on his winning streak. "It's all skill."

"Oh, it's skill alright." Carter cocked eyebrows. "But I'm not sure it's yours."

The man across the table paused in the act of raising his highball glass to his lips. The light of the oil lamps overhead glistened on his shiny cufflinks. Slowly, he lowered the glass, the whiskey still swilling in the glass. "What are you implying, Mr. Carter?"

Carter held up his hands, palms out. "Absolutely nothing, Mr. Tobias. I was merely noting that every man here at this table has a certain degree of skill at this game. Sometimes, a man's skill at poker can win him more hands than the cards indicate. Other times, a man can falter, no matter how good he is." He patted his chest. "My skill just seems to be lacking here tonight and Mr. Johns is the benefactor."

A small crowd had gathered around the table as Johns racked up his winnings. A game of chance had sprouted among the onlookers, seeing as there wasn't going to be a vacancy at the table for the time being. With each successive hand, money and coin exchanged hands, to the choruses of cheers and grunts. A few of the working ladies hung on the arms of some of the men. Despite their earnest entreaties, none of the men would leave.

Jeffery Tobias drained his glass and held it up over his shoulder. One of the dark-suited men directly behind him took the glass and waded the crowd to the bar. With a last, long look at Carter, he said, "Well, Mr. Johns, I don't care what Mr. Carter thinks about his own lack of skill, you're playing a mighty fine round of poker. If I count your chips correctly, your winnings are rapidly advancing on a little bonus."

"Bonus?" Johns said, lacing his voice with extra curiosity.

As a trained actor, Carter felt the massive urge to give Johns acting lessons. Nonetheless, Carter smiled to himself. Things he had suspected were coming to pass.

Tobias sucked in his cheeks as he took a lungful of smoke from his cigar. He let the smoke waft upward as he spoke. "Yes, Mr. Johns. A bonus. Any man who earns four hundred dollars at the table is entitled to a room with one of my ladies." He paused and smirked. "Free of charge."

Johns actually blushed and Carter fought the urge to

roll his eyes.

"Let's get on with the next hand," Peter McKay said. He sat to Carter's left. He was a bearded man and had sweated through his clothes, clogging the smoky air with his stink. Absently, McKay wiped his forehead with the back of his hand. It made a wet sound.

Carter sniggered, "You must like losing more than I do, McKay."

"Shut up," McKay said. To the dealer, he said, "Deal."

Anderson, the dealer, looked at Tobias who nodded. The cards began flying across the table. Carter kept his cards face down, pulling up the corners to determine what he had. As usual, it was junk. He examined his small pile of chips in front of him. He might be able to stretch his presence at the table for a round or two more but, after that, he would have to leave.

Time to force the issue. But first, he was going to have some fun.

Of the six men — five players and one dealer — Carter was confident that four knew about the con and were in on it: Tobias, Anderson (as splendid a card sharp as Carter had ever seen), Robert Townsend (the man sitting next to Tobias and in his employ) and, of course, Johns. Poor McKay was most likely the only one not in on the con. Granted, the four conspirators didn't realize Carter was on to them.

He kept the raisings going around the table, throwing away three cards and being dealt an equally poor replacement set. The only difference was that Carter acted as if he had just been dealt a royal flush. The tells he had invented for this assignment became more exaggerated, even making attempts of trying to stop showing them. His performance was so well done that Tobias's countenance grew more worried as the round wore on.

"Call," McKay said through clenched teeth. His pile of chips was smaller than Carter's and he clearly knew this round wasn't his.

The rest of the players echoed the call and all showed their hands. Johns won again. Half the throng surrounding the table let out a cheer and more than one howled in anger. Carter, for his part, let out a huge groan.

Johns elbowed him. "Thought you had a winner, eh?"

"Yeah," Carter said, shaking his head, "I did." He slid the cards, face down, towards the dealer.

"Unless I'm off count, Mr. Johns," Tobias said, "you have just won the bonus. I see you have at least four hundred and twenty dollars in your hands." He grinned slovenly.

Johns all but started to pant.

Tobias raised his hand and made a signal. From behind him, Carter saw movement and then the crowd parted. What Carter saw next floored him.

The woman was tall and elegant. Her raven hair was pinned up so that both of her ears peeked from behind flowing locks. She was dressed in a blowsy, white shirt, tight, crimson velvet corset, and a flowing red and gold skirt.

It was her eyes that caught Carter's attention. He knew those eyes. And they didn't belong here. Those eyes peered back at him, twinkling, but there was something else. Fear? Doubt? Resolve? Whatever the emotion, Carter knew that Evelyn Paige was in over her head.

They had first met a few weeks ago. She had taken it upon herself to find evidence to acquit her brother's imprisonment for theft. Coincidentally, it was Carter's assignment to discover how the recent train robberies had occurred and who was responsible. He had interviewed Simon Paige in jail and had come away with a hunch that the man was innocent. Carter had told her his thoughts over a scrumptious dinner in Austin, but the lady refused to stop.

Now, he wanted to stand and escort her out of the saloon, tell her that he'd found the men responsible for her brother's false imprisonment. He was just looking for solid evidence. These thoughts flashed through his mind, but her beauty had startled him. Truth be told, she looked prettier now than she had two weeks ago when their paths first crossed and they realized they were after the same thing. But he could do nothing without compromising the both of them.

Tobias must have noticed Carter's reaction to Evelyn. He frowned and turned. His startled look warned Carter that Tobias suspected something.

"Where's Helen?" Tobias said. "I specifically told her to wait for my signal."

Evelyn smiled demurely. "She was waiting for you, Mr. Tobias, sir, but another gentleman, um, insisted his time with her was more important. Madam Ruth told me all about the bonus." She winked at Tobias and turned her attention to Johns. "And I know just what I'm going to do to him."

Tobias's frown deepened. He snapped at a man standing behind him. "Find Ruth."

Evelyn put a hand on Tobias's arm. "Please don't trouble yourself, Mr. Tobias, sir. Madam Ruth told me *everything.*" She lowered her voice so that only the men around the table could hear her voice. She patted his arm.

He threw off her hand. "No one tells me what to do in my own saloon." Tobias caught himself in an instant, realizing his voice had carried to the crowd surrounding the table. Visibly, he corrected himself and pursed his lips. He picked up his glass and threw back the whiskey. He grimaced and set the empty glass down. "Very well, Miss..."

"Evelyn."

Tobias stretched out his arm as if presenting Johns for her. "Very well, Miss Evelyn, show our big winner just how much he has won."

Trailing a finger across the shoulders of the men around the table, Evelyn slunk towards Johns, never breaking eye contact with her target. A couple of the onlookers stopped drinking their beers, their mouths hanging open. When she touched Carter's back, she jabbed him just above his collar with her nail. Johns quickly gathered his chips and plunged them into the pockets of his coat. He stood pushing back his chair. In his haste, the chair toppled. He didn't notice. The leer on his face showed his excitement.

He took Evelyn's hand when she offered it. The crowd parted again with hoots and hollers and cheers from many of the men in the saloon. As the two began to ascend the stairs, Evelyn risked a peek at Carter.

He wished she hadn't. Everyone in the hall saw it.

Carter picked up his cigarette case from the table, withdrew a pre-rolled cigarette, and lit it. He reached for his beer mug. Just as he was about to take a swallow, a loud cry erupted from behind him. He turned and a body smashed itself into his arm.

The mug left his hand and the liquid cascaded across the table, hitting Anderson. The beer soaked the dealer's shirt and hair, flattening the fabric on his chest. Dark hair showed in relief. The deck of cards he had been using got soaked.

Carter spun around, stood, and grabbed the man who had bumped into him. "What the hell do you think you're doing?"

"I'm sorry, sir," the man squeaked. Carter smelled the beer on the other man's breath and it nauseated him. "Can't straight walk, er, walk straight."

Carter put his face within a hair's breadth of the man's nose. "A man who can't hold his liquor shouldn't drink." He shoved the man backward. The drunkard couldn't put his legs under him and he spilled out onto the floor. Laughter exploded from everywhere as men — some more drunk than the poor boozer in the black duster — pointed and laughed.

"Mr. Carter," Tobias said, his voice rising, "I think I can handle things from here." He pointed, and two burly men broke free from the crowd. They reached down, in unison, and dragged the man toward the front door. Scattered applause was heard in the saloon. The piano player resumed his song.

Carter adjusted his suit, making sure his cuffs and sleeves were properly arranged. He looked at Anderson, who was trying, in vain, to mop up the beer from his shirt. The deck of cards was already curling.

"You can't use those cards," Carter said, indicating the warped deck.

At Carter's words, Tobias turned and noticed the cards. McKay noticed, too. He let out a cry about his lost money and how he wanted to get some back.

McKay said, "You got any more decks."

Tobias fixed Carter with a stare. Carter returned it equally. After a moment, Tobias said, "Get Hamilton."

Disgusted, Anderson left the table. Carter, with something of a swagger, rubbed his hands together.

Tobias narrowed his eyes. "You that good a card player, Mr. Carter? You've shown no signs of it yet."

Carter spread his arms. "I feel a second wind coming on." He indicated McKay with a thumb. "Who knows? Even Mr. McKay might have some luck."

Tobias sat and glowered at Carter, the cigar burning away in his mouth. Despite the piano playing and general hubbub of the saloon, the area around the table was strangely quiet. Hamilton arrived with the new deck and took his seat. Another man picked up Johns's chair and sat next to Carter. He was dressed in a dark blue suit slightly too small for his frame. The arms of the coat were stretched thin, trying vainly to keep the man's large, powerful forearms contained. He had a scar on his left ear, a small "V" carved out of it by some former misadventure.

Carter extended his hand to the newcomer. "Calvin Carter."

* * *

The other man didn't accept the proffered hand. "Rance."

Carter looked slighted as he lowered his hand and turned back to the table. He called for another beer as Hamilton dealt the cards. Carter paid special attention to how Hamilton dealt the cards. He was not as good as the first dealer, his movements a fraction slower. It didn't matter, really. These cards appeared older, more worn around the edges. They were still serviceable but Carter noticed that the markings were the same. He guessed it was too much trouble for a saloon keeper to maintain more than one set of marked cards.

The game played out as Carter suspected it would. Townsend took the first hand, Tobias, the second. Then, Hamilton made a mistake. Carter's hand was still a jumble of random cards but McKay brightened noticeably. Tobias's outlook grew grim.

McKay called for only one card and, with Carter having called, McKay won the hand. Tobias threw his cards at Hamilton and called for more whiskey.

"Looks like someone's luck is changing," Carter sing-songed, patting McKay on the shoulder. He turned and looked at Hamilton. "Maybe I'll be next."

Hamilton pursed his lips and shuffled the deck. The sweat on his brow glistened under the oil lamps. He reached up to wipe away the moisture but Carter intervened.

"Ah-ah, Mr. Hamilton. Let's not mark the cards for your boss." He pulled his own handkerchief from his coat pocket and extended his arm towards Hamilton, in front of Rance.

Rance smacked Carter's arm back. Carter looked offended and massaged his arm.

"I think you're too flippant with all this talk of marked cards, Carter," Tobias said, dropping his cigar in the ashtray and grounding out the fire. "I run a clean establishment here and the folks in this town love me. If there were anything illegal going on here, the law would shut me down."

When he was an actor, Carter obsessed about his cues. Now that he was a railroad detective, he didn't often get a cue as obvious as the one Tobias just provided. Carter smiled, putting his handkerchief back in his suit coat pocket. This was his favorite part of the job, the part where he told the offender exactly what he did wrong. He nodded and placed both hands flat on the table. "Not if you buy the law."

Tobias leaned on the table with both elbows. He glowered at Carter and fixed him with eyes of steel. "What are you implying, Mr. Carter?"

"I'm implying nothing. I'm merely here to tell you that you made three mistakes when you decided to rob the West Texas Railroad Company."

McKay stopped counting his chips. Hamilton stopped shuffling the deck. The din of the men surrounding the table died. Rance shifted his body so that he faced Carter. Townsend, across the table, unbuttoned his coat.

Tobias laughed. It was wild, the kind of laugh that came after a particularly funny joke.

"I wouldn't laugh too much, Tobias," Carter said, dropping all traces of formality. He reached over to his cigarette case and lit his final cigarette. "You're little scheme was actually very well thought out." He clapped his hands. "I applaud the effort."

If at all possible, the room grew even more quiet.

Tobias cocked his head, the smile still living on his face. "I think you've had too much to drink, Mr. Carter." The smile died. "Rance, throw him out."

The big man made to stand but Carter held up a finger. "Your first mistake was not broadening your scheme to other railroad companies. Once the thefts started with the West Texas Railroad Company and no other rail line had similar robberies, that vastly narrowed down the focus."

Townsend pushed his chair back from the table but remained seated. Hamilton's hands remained on the still deck of cards. Rance cleared his sidearm from his coat.

Carter continued. "I have to hand it to you, Tobias. Your method of bribing the security guards for the railroad was very ingenious." He spread his hands around the poker table. "Poker was a brilliant, and quite public, way to pay them off. Bravo!"

Tobias snarled at Carter and was about to speak when a large woman, dressed in the French fashion, broke through the ring of men. "You wanted to see me, Mr. Tobias?"

Extending his hand, as if presenting her, Carter said, "Ah, yes, Madam Ruth Rose." He clucked with his tongue. "That would be your second mistake."

Ruth frowned down her nose at Carter. "Who's this, Mr. Tobias, who insults me like that?"

"Someone who hasn't got long to live," Tobias said.

Carter leaned back in his chair. "About that second mistake, Tobias. You knew about the various shipments my railroad carried. That information is easily bought. You knew that in each major shipment, the goods were protected by two guards. One guard, the more senior man, kept the key on his person at all times. When it's time for him to sleep, he gives it to his partner who remains awake throughout the night or some other designated time."

"Your problem was simple: how to get the key. Sure you could break into the boxcar and steal whatever you liked but what's the fun in that when you could just have the key and go in and out at will. I suspect you could have expanded your little operation, had you more time."

Carter motioned toward Madam Ruth. "Thus, you came up with the idea of the bonus for all the men you bribed. Any man who earned more than four hundred at the table was entitled to an appointment with one of Madam Ruth's ladies. While the man was being *entertained*, another of the ladies made a wax impression of the key. Viola! Extra key!"

Tobias's face was rapidly becoming crimson. Madam Ruth looked around, trying to find a way out. Carter kept going.

"Your third mistake was the biggest: murder. The first two times my company discovered the stolen merchandise, they reassigned the security guards on whose watch the robbery occurred, usually the junior ones. They did it quietly as they wanted to avoid any embarrassing publicity. The third guard's employment was terminated. Something tells me you paid for his silence." He paused and put a finger to his lips. "What was the problem with Melvin Cameron?"

Tobias remained silent. His face had regained its

normal color and a look of resolve had taken hold.

"Not saying?" Carter said. "Well, my guess is that Cameron wouldn't stay quiet. He had won cash here at your saloon. He was one of the guards acquitted of any wrong doing. The problem was that his partner, Simon Paige, was accused of the crime and now sits in prison. But Cameron was going to talk so you had to quiet him. Murder is usually an utterly complete way to silence anyone. The problem is what is left behind."

Townsend stood. Rance did, too. Hamilton left the cards on the table, rose, and backed away. McKay pocketed his chips and sat very still.

Still smiling, Carter never broke eye contact with Tobias. "If you decide to remind someone that they owe you their silence, it's best if you don't write it down. And if you do," he cocked a thumb at Rance, "be sure to remind your oxen to search the body after they kill a man." He paused and blew out a smoke ring. "Granted, I'm here to make sure that never happens again."

Tobias nodded once. Rance reached down and grabbed Carter's right arm and hauled him to his feet, cigarette ash fluttering on the table. Townsend started to move around the table to Carter's left.

Tobias remained seated with an air of nonchalance. "I don't know who you think you are, Mr. Carter, but you've concocted a story so wild that no one will believe you. Besides, you'll be six feet under in a few hours and no one will – "

From the balcony, a huge crash emerged as one of the doors smashed open. Johns emerged, his shirt off and his pants half falling with only one suspender over his shoulder. He was shoeless. Three gashes lined his cheek.

In one hand, Johns held a revolver. In the other, he gripped Evelyn around the neck. A thin stream of blood trickled from the corner of her mouth down her chin, and onto her skirt. He looked down and locked eyes with Carter. "I know you're in cahoots with this here lady, you goddamned detective. I'm gonna kill you both, but your lady friend gets a bullet in her head first."

Carter looked up and saw Evelyn. He gritted his teeth and decided that if he got out of this predicament alive, he'd kill her himself.

Carter took the lit cigarette from his lips and mashed it onto Rance's hand. The other man screeched with instant pain, let go of Carter's arm, and shook his injured hand. In his peripheral vision, Carter saw Townsend in the process of throwing back his coat to draw.

Carter punched Rance in the stomach with his left hand. The man doubled over. Carter grabbed him at the collar and belt and, with a great heave, hurled him at the table.

Rance's weight carried him forward, taking the table along with him. Poker chips rained into the air. Ashtrays and whiskey glasses shattered on the floor. The table rammed into the still-seated Tobias and knocked down Townsend, who had cleared his gun.

Townsend discharged a shot. The bullet hit a brass lamp overhead and ricocheted back to the floor. The women in the saloon screamed and began running. The men around the table instinctively ducked. Rance, not on the floor but a second, started to rise.

When Carter planned this confrontation, he knew Tobias would not come quietly when presented with the facts and the truth. Carter even predicted that he'd have to fight his way out of the saloon. Now, however, he had an added burden. He needed to escape and rescue Evelyn as well.

He pondered the situation a second too long. From his blind side, a fist smashed into his face. Seeing stars, he staggered, trying to get his bearings, knowing one thing: a second fist was on its way.

Carter dropped unceremoniously to the floor, landing on his haunches. Amid the uproar, he heard the grunt of surprise from Rance as his fist met air. Carter shook his head, cleared it, and saw Rance's boots. With a mighty shove as if he were pushing a loaded wheelbarrow, Carter grabbed the man's legs and moved forward and up. Rance tumbled over Carter's back and landed, face first, onto the wooden floor.

With that one action, Carter had cleared the ring of onlookers surrounding the poker table. He spun around to take stock of his situation. Tobias now stood, his chair on the floor behind him. Townsend stood next to him, bringing his gun to bear. McKay was on hands and knees, scooting under the table, picking up more poker chips.

"Kill him," Tobias roared. The men, as a group, moved forward, blocking Townsend's aim. Carter took a step backward, his legs hitting a chair. He reached behind him, grabbed it, and held it in front of him.

Another shot rang out, exploding the wooden chair leg into splinters. Frowning, Carter wondered where the shot had come from. The men in front of him hadn't drawn their guns. Another shot shattered the seat of the chair, breaking it in two.

That's when Carter realized the origin of the shots. Johns, up on the balcony, had a clear view of all that was happening on the ground floor, and he was taking aim at the defenseless detective. For the moment, Evelyn was forgotten.

In a split second, Carter hurled half of the chair in the general direction of Johns. He threw the other half at the men in front of him. He plunged his left hand into his coat withdrawing his gun from the shoulder holster. Carter raised the revolver and fired at the oil lamp chandelier. One shot and liquid fire cascaded on the men. They grunted, howled, and slapped at their clothes, trying to put out the blue flames raining on them.

Carter turned and ran toward the foot of the stairs. A look back told him that Townsend was aiming for him. Carter got off a second shot at the same time Townsend loosed one of his bullets. Carter's shot sailed high over Townsend's head, cracking the large mirror behind the bar. Townsend's shot landed in the wood not six inches above Carter's head. He widened his eyes in surprise and launched himself up the stairs, taking two at a time.

For a moment, he couldn't see Evelyn or Johns. He heard a high-pitched squeal and feared the worst. Ducking Townsend's bullets, Carter crested the top of the stairs. He got off a shot, trying to give himself an extra second. He gave a start when he saw what lay in front of him: Johns, clutching at his leg, with a thin blade protruding from his thigh, howled in agony. As Evelyn bent down to pick up the abandoned gun, Johns withdrew the dagger from his leg and turned to her. She didn't see him.

Carter did and he got off two quick shots. The first shot embedded itself in the floor of the balcony. The second found a home in Johns's ass. Immediately, he dropped the dagger and grabbed his backside.

A moment later, Carter slammed into Johns. With a sweep of his arm, he threw Evelyn down beside him as three shots blasted away at the door frame.

"What the hell do you think you're doing here?" Carter shouted at Evelyn.

She gripped Johns's revolver and, using Carter's body as a make-shift cover, rose just enough to take aim at the men on the ground floor, rapidly making their way to the foot of the stairs. "Saving your butt," she said and emptied the Colt in the direction of the men.

One bullet blasted the railing but the other five bullets made their way to the charging men. One fell, clutching his shoulder. The others ducked.

Evelyn clicked on the empty chamber. She dropped it and, catlike, jumped to a crouching position. She grabbed her dress in her hands. "Time to go. Follow me." She scurried back into the bedroom.

Carter fired once more at the area around the top of the stairs and scrabbled, on hands and knees, into the room. He rose and slammed the door. The spare room had only two wooden chairs, a bed, a bedside table, and a mirror. He grabbed one of the chairs and wedged it against the doorknob.

"That won't hold them long," Carter said. From outside the door, shouts could be heard, the loudest being Tobias who was ordering his men to exit the saloon and cut off their escape.

"Forget the window. Tobias has his men . . ." He spun around, looking for Evelyn. Instead of being at the window, she put her hands on a large, metal-looking grate from a far corner of the wall. Next to it was the other chair with Johns's clothes draped over the back.

"Where are you going?" Carter hissed.

"Out," Evelyn said. She lifted the grate with ease and flung it across the room. At Carter's look of surprise, she said, "Wood, painted to look like metal. It's how the ladies managed to sneak into the room and make a copy of the keys."

Carter stood straighter for a moment. "Now, look here, Evelyn. I told you I'd find evidence to clear your brother. I told you not to – "

A crash at the doorway cut his words short. The men were trying to break down the door.

Evelyn pointed at the opening. "You have the only gun. You go first."

Carter moved swiftly across the room and eyed the opening. It was about three feet square. He could see a knotted rope trailing away down the wooden shaft into dimness. "Where does it lead?"

"The laundry basket at the back of the saloon," Evelyn said, cocking an eyebrow. "Didn't you scout the grounds before you made your plan?"

He frowned. "My plan isn't working quite the way I thought it would since I had to include saving you."

She wiped at the blood on her cheek. "I didn't need saving. I only needed the evidence to clear Simon." She patted her dress. Carter heard something hard clunk underneath the garment. "And I have it."

Another crash at the door and one of the slats of the door burst. A face appeared, looking in.

In one, fluid motion, Carter spun and fired. The man didn't utter a sound as a small, black hole opened in his forehead.

Evelyn gave him a wry grin. "You *are* accurate."

Carter opened the cylinder of his Colt and emptied the spent cartridges. He reached in his pockets and started loading his gun. From outside the door, they could hear an argument amongst the men as to who should go next. That gave Carter just enough time to finish reloading. He spun the cylinder and handed the gun to Evelyn.

"Ladies first." He indicated the shaft.

She didn't hesitate. She sat on the lip of the shaft and, keeping to the left side, vanished into the darkness.

Three bullets burst into the room from the stairs. Carter didn't wait. He threw himself head first into the shaft and started sliding.

He landed on Evelyn and a bunch of soiled linens in a giant barrel in the alley between the saloon and the general store. The dirty clothes tangled him. His spurs got caught and he had trouble gaining his feet. When he did, he realized Evelyn wasn't moving. She had her hands raised, Carter's revolver hanging limp from one of her fingers. Looking around, he saw why.

Surrounding the barrel were five men with Tobias in the center. All had their guns drawn and aimed at Carter and Evelyn.

"Game's up," Tobias said, sneering the words through a gritted grin.

"Not quite," Carter said, raising his hands, and grinning. "You still made one, last mistake."

"What?" Tobias said, cocking the hammer on his gun.

"You forgot to watch your back."

Carter nodded.

A loud volley of gunfire erupted. Evelyn screamed. Carter remained still.

The four gunmen surrounding Tobias crumbled. A look of shock crossed Tobias's face. He scanned the area in frustration. Then, he looked up and his mouth dropped open.

On top of the saloon and the general store, six men appeared over the edges of the buildings. Their rifles aimed directly at Tobias.

Growling with rage, Tobias turned to run. From the side of the laundry barrel emerged a man. He was dressed in a long, black duster. The smell of alcohol and whiskey wafted in the breeze. In two long strides, he had the barrel of his gun next to Tobias's head.

"I wouldn't," the man said.

Evelyn was mute with surprise. She looked at the man, struggling to figure out where she knew him. Recognition triggered and she spun on Carter.

"He's working for you!" she yelled. "He was that drunk who bumped into you."

The man, still focused on Tobias, reached out and grabbed the gun from Tobias's hand. "I don't work *for* him," the man said. "I work *with* him." Other men, a few wearing badges, ran into the alley, rifles and guns at the ready. The man in the black coat uncocked his pistol and returned it to his holster. He turned.

"Thomas Jackson," Carter said, "meet Evelyn Paige." He gave Jackson a sidelong glance. "Took you long enough."

Jackson nudged something on the ground beside the barrel. Evelyn and Carter peered over the side. The two large men that had dragged Jackson out of the saloon lay in a heap. "Had some trouble."

Carter clambered out of the barrel, turned, and offered a hand to Evelyn. Swatting it away, she sat on the edge, swiveled, and stepped down to the ground, using the unconscious men as a step.

Jackson chuckled. Carter shot him a disapproving look.

The clink of handcuffs sounded as the sheriff locked up Tobias. The captured man bolted and ran at Carter, eyes blazing, furious. With a casual sweep of his leg, Carter tripped Tobias, who went sprawling into the dirt.

The sheriff nodded and two deputies walked over and pulled Tobias to his feet. He struggled and kicked at them. "I know who you are, Calvin Carter!" Tobias yelled, spittle mixing with dirt in his moustache. "You can't pin this on me."

Carter tilted his head. "Perhaps not. But I'll sure have fun trying." He waved and the deputies carried the man away. "Jail ain't gonna hold me forever," Tobias snarled.

Evelyn looked at Carter. "He's right, you know. He'll come for you. One way or another, he'll come for you." She toed the dirt with her shoe. "Doesn't that scare you?"

Carter's heart pounded at the thought. He wasn't too far into this new job and he had already attracted some important enemies. Outwardly, he smiled and put his arm around Evelyn. "No, not really. What I'm more concerned about is finding a good place for you and me to have dinner since we shot up the best restaurant in town."

With dainty fingers, Evelyn uncurled herself from Carter's grasp. "Actually, I won't be having dinner with you. I'll be down at the courthouse taking credit for this little case of yours." She reached into the folds of her dress and withdrew a small, metal box. She unfastened the clasp and opened it.

Inside was a thick layer of dark wax. She moved it about, allowing the sun to glint off its edges. Carter and Jackson looked at it. Clearly visible were the impressions of various keys.

Reproachfully, Carter said, "Hey, now, I did all the thinking and leg work. You can't have all the credit."

Evelyn snapped the box shut and grinned. "Oh, but I can. You see, I have the only piece of physical evidence that will convict Tobias and his gang. Moreover, if Mark Twain is to be believed, you can identify a man by his fingerprints. One of them was stupid enough to leave a fingerprint on the wax. If I can tie that man to Tobias, I'll have him. Case closed." She turned and, gathering her skirt, strolled toward the main street and the courthouse.

Mute, Carter watched her leave. Jackson clapped Carter on the shoulder. "C'mon, Cal. I ain't as discriminating as she is. I'll join you for dinner." He sniffed his duster and grimaced. "But first, I need a bath."

Blood Trail to Dodge

A Talbot Roper Story

by Robert J. Randisi

Robert J. Randisi is the author of more than 540 books in the Western, Private Eye, Men's Adventure, and Horror genres. As J.R. Roberts he is the creator and author of the long running series "The Gunsmith." He also wrote and created the Tracker, Angel Eyes, Bounty Hunter, Mountain Jack Pike, Widowmaker, Gamblers, Sons of Daniel Shaye *and* Ryder *series. Born in Brooklyn, New York he currently resides in Clarksville, Missouri--a town of 500 people overlooking the Mississippi River--with writer "Christine Matthews".*

Intro

In the 30 years I've been writing the Gunsmith series as J.R. Roberts I've used many historical characters, such as Bat Masterson, Wyatt Earp and Mark Twain. One fictional character who has appeared in many of the books has been Talbot Roper, a former Pinkerton who eventually opened his own detective agency in Denver. He is also good friends with the Gunsmith, Clint Adams. Roper is generally considered to be the best detective in the country.

I've wanted to do a spin-off series about this character for a long time, and now I have the chance. I'm writing Roper books for Berkley, but they won't be Adult Westerns, so instead of appearing under the Roberts pseudonym, they'll be appearing under my own name. The character will also be slightly different, so I decided to introduce him in this, our first Western Fictioneers anthology.

Chapter 1

The hey-days of Dodge City were long gone by the time Talbot Roper rode into town. When the Atchison, Topeka & Santa Fe railroad came to Dodge in 1872 the town boomed. Many railroad cars a day filled with buffalo hides and meat left there, and just as many arrived carrying supplies. The streets – both Front Streets, one on each side of the railroad tracks – were lined with wagons and filled with people. But by 1878 the good times were over, and people started to leave. Now, almost eight years later, the town was quiet, almost dead.

These days Roper was a private investigator working out of Denver. His job took him to big cities, ghost towns and everything in between. And he adapted to his surroundings with equal comfort.

In Denver, New York, San Francisco he wore a fancy suit with a matching hat, carried a short-barreled .32 in a shoulder rig, a derringer in his vest pocket and a straight razor in his boot because it was more comfortable than a knife.

Out on the trail throughout the West, in towns or the Territories, he wore trail clothes and a worn Stetson, nothing that would make him stand out. He carried a Peacemaker in his holster, a second one in a holster affixed to the leather of his saddle with needle and heavy thread. The razor was still in his left boot, the derringer in his right, and a Winchester in a scabbard on his saddle. He had a third Peacemaker in his saddlebag. No matter what environment he was in, he was ready for action.

This case had started right there in his home city of Denver, and had taken him across the plains to Dodge City, with a lot of bloodshed in between. It seemed fitting that it should end here, where the blood of legends had soaked into the soil many years ago, and still resided there.

* * *

Roper followed the tracks he'd been tracking for miles right to the edge of Dodge City. There they mixed with others, but he was still able to make out a distinction he'd found in the right hind. They led right into town, and seemed fairly fresh.

Roper directed his horse to the livery, which was still where it had always been. He dismounted and collected his belongings before turning the animal over to the liveryman. It had been so long since he'd been there – or had paid any attention to the goings on in Dodge – that he did not know who was presently the law.

"Any strangers come to town in the past hour or so?"

"Not that I seen."

"Who's the law in Dodge, these days?" he asked the man.

The liveryman stroked the horse's damp neck as he said, "The sheriff is Pat Sughrue, the marshal is Bill Tilghman."

"Tilghman is here?" Roper asked.

"Yessir, been the marshal here for over two years," the man said.

"Well, that's good news," Roper said.

"You know the marshal?"

"I do, indeed. Thanks."

Roper carried his belongings to a nearby hotel – one of the few that were still open – got himself a room, and then left there to walk to the marshal's office.

Chapter 2

Bill Tilghman looked up from his desk as the door to his office opened. He frowned, seeming confused for a moment, the way you are when you see someone someplace you don't expect to see them.

"As I live and shit, Talbot Roper," he said, "what the hell . . ."

He stood up, his hand outstretched, but did not come out from behind the desk. Roper noticed that the experienced lawman was wearing an empty holster.

"It's good to see you," Tilghman said, pumping

Roper's hand.

"You, too, Bill," Roper said.

"What brings you to Dodge City?" Tilghman said, waving to a chair. "Coffee?"

"I could use a drink, but coffee will do."

Tilghman smiled and said, "I've got that."

He sat, opened a drawer and pulled out a bottle of whiskey. After pouring a generous dollop into two mugs he handed one to Roper.

"Thanks." The detective took a huge swallow. The heat warmed him.

"That do the trick?" Tighman asked.

"Oh, yeah."

The lawman sat back in his chair.

"What's goin' on, Roper?" he asked. "You're a long way from Denver. What brings you to a dead town like Dodge."

"Dead?" Roper asked. "Is that the right word?"

"Oh, yeah," Tilghman said. "This town is long dead."

"Why are you still here, then?"

"I won't be for much longer," Tilghman said. "I'm headin' out in a month or so when my term is over. Bought me a little place."

"A ranch?"

"Yep. Gonna raise some horses."

"Where?"

"Near here," the marshal said. "What the hell are you doin' here? This ain't the place to stop in for a visit."

"It's a long story," Roper said. "I started tracking a man from Denver, and I think he's here."

"What's his name?"

"Sender," Roper said, "John Sender."

"Should I know him?"

"I don't think so," Roper said. "Not yet, anyway. Maybe not if I can catch him and cut his killing spree short."

"What's he look like?"

"Tall, broad shouldered, black hair, about forty," Roper said. "Wears a silver plated Peacemaker, likes to use it."

"Far as I know, nobody like that's ridden into town," Tilghman said.

"His trail leads here."

"Could you have beat him here?"

Roper thought a moment, then said, "Could be. His trail led me this way, but I can't say he definitely rode in here."

"You huntin' bounty now?"

"Not exactly," Roper said. "I was hired by a man whose son Sender killed. They argued over a poker game, but everyone said it just looked like an excuse for Sender to gun the kid. I'm inclined to believe it, because he's killed three more men between there and here."

"What about the local law?"

"Once Sender left Denver the police there didn't much care," Roper explained. "The boy's father isn't a politician."

"But he had enough money to hire you."

"He did."

"You don't come cheap."

Roper didn't respond. His eyes moved around the room. The rifle rack was full, cell block keys were hanging on a wall peg. The door to the cell blocks was open. The shutters of the front window were closed. He looked at Tilghman again. The man was staring at him intently.

"No, I don't." Roper stood up. "Well, if you can't help me I'll check with the sheriff, and then have a look around town, myself."

"Good idea," Tilghman said. "Pat Sughrue's a good man."

Roper walked to the door, and Tilghman remained behind his desk.

"Stop back in before you leave, Roper."

"I'll do that, Bill."

He stepped out and closed the door behind him.

Chapter 3

Roper worked his way around to the back of the Marshal's office. He knew something was wrong in the office, but had no view from the front window, because the shutters were closed. His only chance was to try to get in through the back door – if there was one.

Before reaching the back he came to a barred window, decided to try to get a look through there. He looked around the alley, found a crate that would make a good step stool. He set it down beneath the window and climbed on. He was looking into a cell, and then beyond, through the bars, he could see the open door of the cell block.

Through the doorway he saw slivers – a piece of Bill Tilghman's desk with the marshal still seated there, and a partial view of a man standing next to him. Roper had never seen Sender. He had his description and wasn't sure this was him, but it didn't really matter. Whoever he was, he was holding a gun in his hand, pointed at Tilghman – and the gun was silver.

Roper got down from the crate and went to find the back door. When he got to the rear of the jail he found out there was none.

Now what?

He could bust through the front door and hope he could get to Sender before he shot Tilghman, but that didn't seem likely. Sender – or whoever it was – would likely pull the trigger at the first sight of Roper.

There was only one way to go.

He went back into the alley to his crate, climbed up again. Looking through the window he could see the hand holding the gun on Tilghman. Roper was a detective, not a sharpshooter. He used his brain more than he used his gun, but he didn't feel he had a choice.

He took the shot.

Chapter 4

Tilghman came out of the cell block, having just locked the wounded John Sender in a cell.

"How did you know?" Tilghman said. "I was tryin' to send you a mental message the whole time."

"I noticed a funny look on your face, but I just thought you had the trots, or something."

"Very funny."

"There were a few things," Roper said. "You'd never wear an empty holster. You either keep your gun on or take the whole rig off. I figured somebody had taken your gun. Also, you were calling me Roper, when you usually call me by my first name. And finally, you hate Pat Sughrue and would never call him a 'good man.'"

"If he wanted to take a lawman hostage because he knew you were right on his tail why didn't he pick the sheriff?" Tilghman wondered. "If he'd shot Pat it would have been no loss."

Roper knew Sughrue was a good lawman. He and Tilghman just didn't like each other.

"Maybe he recognized your name, but not Sughrue's," Roper suggested.

"That was a nice shot, by the way," Tilghman said, "but why did you decide to just shoot the gun out of his hand? If you'd missed he mighta killed me."

"I didn't have a choice," Roper said. "That was all I could see from the window."

"Jesus," Tilghman said, "if I knew my life depended on you makin' a shot like that, I mighta been nervous. I guess I'm just lucky you're a good detective, and a fair shot."

The Sin of Eli

by Troy D. Smith

Troy D. Smith hails from Sparta, Tennessee. His first Western story appeared in Louis L'Amour Western Magazine *in 1995; in 2001 his novel* Bound for the Promise-Land *won the Spur Award. He has written for several history magazines, and recently earned a history Ph.D from the University of Illinois, where he has taught the last few years. As a professional historian his primary fields are American Indians, slavery, and the South; as a historical novelist, his interests lie in the human beings at the heart of his stories. "I don't write about things that happen to people, I write about people that things happen to."*

Robert Darnell had always tried to be a good father. When his only son, Spence, was a child, Darnell had thought he was succeeding at that task. The boy's mother had died in childbirth, and Darnell had been father and mother alike to him. It had been hard, in some ways, but it had been easy in others. Little Spence had his mother Lorene's soft blue eyes and dark hair, and held his chin like her when he laughed. Lorene had been the love and light of Darnell's life. When Lorene's spirit fled to heaven, that love and light was transferred to the son she had given him with her last push of life.

He had doted on the boy. It was easy to do, and hard to avoid. Spence was so much the image of his mother —perhaps he, too, would be as fragile as her. What if the warmth of his smile, like that of his mother's, should blow away one day like dry leaves, leaving nothing behind except the sound of the wind? Robert Darnell could hear that wind every time he looked on his son's face. The pride and joy he felt was tinged by a sadness at the knowledge that the Lord was a Taker as well as a Giver. The pride and the joy and the sadness and the loss mixed so completely together that they all became the same thing, a bittersweet amalgamation which, if forced to put a name to it, Robert Darnell could only call love. At those moments, his heart swelled so great that he felt it would burst, but it never did.

As the years went by, however, Darnell was crowded in by the growing suspicion that he was not a good father after all. Good fathers produce good sons, and any claim to the word "good" seemed to wash out of Spence Darnell with each passing summer. It started when he was small, dominating his classmates and taking whatever he wanted with no regard to rights or propers.

Sometimes Darnell would thrash the boy with a strap, the way all fathers he knew did, but they were half-hearted and infrequent efforts. Darnell could not hold such a strap in his hand without remembering his own pa—a stern, implacable man—and how much, as a boy, he had hated the old man. He could not bear the thought of his own son hating him—of Lorene's sky blue eyes looking at him with tearful reproach—and so his hand wavered, when he raised it at all.

By the time Spence Darnell was seventeen, everyone in the valley knew him as a holy terror. No one was surprised when he shot down an unarmed man in the midst of a robbery—no one except Robert Darnell. The boy had come to him, pale-faced and desperate, begging for money and a fresh horse.

"I have to leave, Pa, or they'll hang me, sure."

"Where to, son?"

"Anywhere."

"When will you come back?"

The boy's face shined wet with tears.

"I can't never come back, Pa. Please, I have to hurry."

Robert Darnell had handed over all his money with numb fingers. He wanted to speak, but his throat constricted and no words could escape. *How can I live without you, boy?* he wanted to say. *Who will I be, if I'm all alone?*

"I'll send word soon as I can, Pa, I promise."

Spence embraced him, if only for a moment. Darnell channeled all his strength into his arms, all his life, pumping it like his heart was a bellows—and then his son was gone. His only son, and all that remained of the sweet woman he had loved. It was like Lorene's ghost withdrew her hand from Darnell's brow and followed behind their son, not even leaving the broken man the comfort of her haunting. He sank to his knees in the dirt and watched Spence ride away.

He was still on his knees when the posse arrived half-an-hour later. They did not even bother asking which direction the boy had gone, for Darnell's anguished face still stared after him, giving them their cue.

"I'm real sorry, Mister Darnell," the sheriff said, and several of his companions mumbled as well. He could feel their pity wash over him—and, beneath that, their contempt.

Robert Darnell was a God fearing man, and he knew that their contempt was deserved. He had sinned. He was like David of old, who refused to visit the full punishment on his son Absalom when he had murdered his own brother. The old king had even tried to spare the youth from harm when he plunged Israel into civil war—and when the rebel was killed in battle, David grieved beyond all comfort.

Oh Absalom, Absalom, my son, my son. Would that I could die for thee, my son.

Even more, Darnell realized as he sat in the dirt, he was like the high priest Eli. That old man's sons were cruel and wicked, stealing from God and abusing their power. Eli lectured them, but did not give them the punishment they deserved—and so shared in their guilt.

Finally God took action Himself and struck them dead. When Eli got word, his grief was so powerful that he fell from his seat and broke his neck.

Some could argue that Eli's swift demise was a blessing, in a way, for he did not long survive the sons he loved. But it was not a blessing. A single moment of knowing your child is dead while you live on—a single such moment was more profound a torture than all the fires of hell.

Robert Darnell was spared such a knowledge that day. Spence avoided the posse, and reached safety. That had been five years ago. In those five years, Spence Darnell managed to smuggle two letters home—they were short, and vague, but the old man treasured them. Beyond that, the only news of his son came in the reports of the crimes he had committed.

Until today.

Today the sheriff had arrived with a telegram. Spence Darnell, the notorious outlaw, had been captured, tried, and was sentenced to hang in three days in Wichita.

"I wish we'd have got word on this sooner," the sheriff said. "You could've had plenty of time to get there. If you was of a mind to. As it is, there ain't no train or stage due soon enough."

"I'll get there," Darnell said. "It'll be a hard ride, but I'll get there. I have to see my son."

The sheriff sighed. "I hope you make it in time."

Darnell did not respond. The sheriff no longer existed to him. He was walking to the stable to saddle his horse. The sheriff mounted his own animal and rode sadly away.

Darnell left his little ranch less than twenty minutes after the sheriff had arrived. He rode his chestnut mare, leading his blue roan—all the horseflesh he owned— with the aim of switching back and forth as each grew tired. Three days' rations were in the saddlebags—there would be no time for hunting. Darnell's Winchester was in the rifle scabbard, and his old Army Colt—well-oiled, caps set—was on his hip.

He rode until it was too dark to see, and made a dry

camp. He stared into the darkness for hours, and slept very little. There was a time, not long before, that he would have spent the time in prayer—but God had not made camp with him, he could feel it. God had no approval for what Robert Darnell planned to do—the rancher had cast his lot, once and for all, with his own flesh and blood over his God. This ride would be a journey to Hell. It was a hard choice, at first—not the choosing between God and Spence, but the deciding on whether to go to Heaven to be with his beloved Lorene or to follow their child to the devil. He knew she would understand his sacrifice. She would have the angels for company—Spence would be alone in perdition when he finally got there. Paradise would be no comfort, knowing his son was in the flames of damnation. The trail Robert Darnell rode now would surely take him there, as well.

On the second day he passed a young family on the road. Their wagon wheel had given out on them—the husband had been thrown from his seat and suffered a broken arm. He was gamely trying to fix his wheel with one arm, face white with pain, while his wife swayed back and forth with a screaming infant.

"Thank God you come by, mister," the young man said—then his mouth slowly fell open in shock as Darnell rode past him without a word.

"For God's sake, we need help!" the injured man cried out.

For God's sake. Any other day Darnell would have stopped to help, but there was no time. It was no longer God's sake that drove him on. Still, his face burned with shame. He half-turned in the saddle.

"I'm real sorry," he told them. "If I pass anybody, I'll send 'em back. But I can't stop." He almost added that he would pray for them—but he knew that, to them, it would seem like adding insult to injury. Besides, his prayers at this point might do a body more harm than good. He rode on, therefore, the injured man's impassioned curses following behind him.

That night he took the time to build a fire and cook up some bacon to go with his cold corn dodgers. It was almost done when his hobbled horses whinnied. Darnell was on his haunches, gloved hand on the handle of the skillet he was just about to draw out of the fire—his head jerked up at once, eyes alert. There'd been no Indian trouble in those parts for years, but it was still not beyond the realm of possibility.

It was no Indian voice that called out to him, though.

"Howdy, friend. That sure smells mighty good."

Two men rode near Darnell's camp and dismounted. They stepped out of the shadows—they were unshaven and trailworn.

"Mind if we warm up by your fire for a little spell, mister?"

"I don't mind," Darnell said. "Y'all can eat this bacon, if you want, I'll make more." He knew this would mean going hungry later, but he could not be inhospitable—especially after leaving the stranded family behind him earlier. That had been in the afternoon, though, and he could not afford to burn any daylight to help them. He was done riding for the night now, and could afford to be a good host.

"If you boys are headed north," he said, "there's a young family up the trail with a broke wagon wheel. Unless somebody else has come along to help 'em, I reckon they're in a bad way. Maybe you can help 'em out, if you come across 'em. I ain't got no plates or nothin', you might want to find somethin' to set this bacon on, it's hot as the dickens."

"Why, that's mighty kind of you, mister," the taller of the two said. He was apparently the leader, he seemed to do all the talking. "Offerin' to share your supper with a couple of total strangers, and worryin' about some poor travelers at the same time. That's plumb Christian."

"I try."

The other man spoke for the first time. "Seems like I remember the Lord said, if somebody was to ask you for your coat, give him your cloak as well."

"I recall that."

"Well," Number Two continued, "it don't seem

Christian, you havin' them two fine horses, and you just a useless old man."

Darnell's eyes narrowed. "What are you gettin' at."

The leader's hand dropped to his pistol. In a flash, Darnell tossed the pan of sizzling bacon grease at the leader's face with his left hand, while drawing his own pistol with his right. The leader screamed in agony—his gun had cleared leather, but he dropped it to clasp both hands to his burned face. His partner went for his own gun, but only after a moment of shocked hesitation. Darnell put two bullets into him, and the man's gun flew away as he spun and fell.

The leader was on his knees, feeling in the dirt for his lost weapon. Darnell put a bullet in his forehead, and he dropped like a wet sack.

Darnell stood silent, almost in shock himself, as the smoke curled from the barrel of his Colt. He had never killed a man—not even in the war, that he knew of—and was rather amazed that it had happened so quickly.

The second bandit moaned weakly. Darnell walked over to him. The man managed to roll over onto his back.

"You're—you're just a damned old farmer," he gasped. "We've shot our way through posses. This is crazy." He coughed, and frothy blood bubbled from his mouth.

"Holy God," the man said. "You've kilt me."

"When's the last time you seen your pa, boy."

"What?"

"Your pa. How long since you've seen your pa."

"Hell, I don't know."

"I reckon he loves you, son, even if you're a piece of shit."

"My pa's a ignorant old farmer like you, and a mean son of a bitch. I don't give a damn what he thinks, or you neither."

He coughed again, and moaned in pain. His fingers scratched the dirt as his arm swept up and down, trying desperately to find his own weapon, just as his partner had.

"I'll tell you the same thing I told that family back yonder," Darnell said. "I'm truly sorry, but I ain't got time to fool with you."

He shot the outlaw in the head, and cooked up some more bacon.

* * *

He was almost too late.

The whole town, it seemed, was gathered around the scaffold—and maybe folks from several towns close by. The preacher stood up there, Bible in hand, and a fat middle-aged man whose badge glinted in the afternoon sun.

There was only one other figure on the scaffold. A sack had been pulled over his head, and the noose was fitted around his neck. Robert Darnell did not need to see a face to recognize his only son. He dropped the lead rope of the chestnut which trailed behind him and spurred the flanks of the roan. He galloped straight into the gathered crowd. People scrambled out of his way to avoid being trampled—and trample them he would have. He reined in near the base of the structure and hopped out of the saddle. Two rangy men with rifles, deputies, stepped toward him.

"Spence!" he yelled up. "I'm here, Spence!"

"Pa!" the outlaw called back, his voice muffled by the sack. "Is that you, Pa?"

"It's me! I'm with you, son! I'm with you."

The sheriff looked flustered.

"I reckon it's Providence you made it here in time, mister," the sheriff said. "But we can't delay this none."

It was in that moment, while the deputies' eyes were on their speaking boss, that Robert Darnell put his desperate plan into action. The Army Colt seemed to leap into his hand, just as it had with the horse thieves—Darnell had never known, or even dreamed, that he was especially fast with a gun. He shot down both of the deputies in almost the same instant. Men shouted all around him, and women screamed. Darnell looked all around, desperate, scanning the crowd for more deputies. Hoping for them.

"Nobody expected this crazy old man to show up to rescue Spence Darnell from the gallows," folks said afterward. "That was a bold plan."

But they were mistaken. Such was not Robert Darnell's plan, and never had been. His first goal had been merely to lay eyes on his beloved son, to hear his voice one more time in this world. As for the rest of his plan—he had expected far more resistance, and a far better prepared constabulary. Like the horse thieves, they had not expected such deadly and efficient action from the frail-looking rancher. He had killed the two men almost before he himself had realized it, and before he realized there were no more deputies in sight.

Once he started shooting, Robert Darnell expected to be cut down by a hail of bullets. In fact, he had planned on it. His goal was two-fold—to see his living son, and never to spend a single instant knowing that son was dead. One such instant would be worse than an eternity in Hell—and he was willing to trade that eternity for avoiding the instant.

But no bullets came.

The sheriff, rather than drawing his own gun, stepped toward the lever which would open eternity beneath Spence's feet. Robert Darnell emptied his revolver rapidly into the lawman's large gut—the sheriff had reached the lever, though, and as he fell it went down with him. Spence dropped, then bounced at the end of the rope with a horrible snap.

"No!"

The snap signified not only the breaking of Spence Darnell's neck, but of his father's heart and soul. He sank to his knees in the dust—they were too weak to support the weight that was upon him. Rough hands grabbed at him and threw him to the ground. He was smothered by the weight of bodies. The townspeople had found their courage when Darnell ran out of bullets.

In the back of his mind he was dimly aware that he would be locked away until such time as a noose would be fitted for him. His own body would take the drop, and dance though it might, the soul would be ripped from it and continue its plummet straight into Hell, and to his son.

But it did not matter. He had not been spared. All the soothing flames of Hell could not strip away the awful pain of knowing that his son was dead before him. Like Eli, he could not escape God's punishment for his sin—not even by fleeing to the devil.

The bodies of his attackers bore ever harder upon him, until he could scarcely breathe.

My son.

My son. Would that I could die for thee, my son. My son.

The Way of the West

by Larry Jay Martin

L. J. Martin is the author of 27 fiction and non-fiction books, and has articles published in dozens of national publications. He lives in Montana with his wife, NYT bestselling romantic suspense author Kat Martin. Learn more about the Martins at www.ljmartin.com & www.katmartin.com.

"Aye, Mr. Hogart, I hear you perfectly well, and I understand you, but I still think it's about as good an idea as ticklin' a mule's heel to cure your toothache." Big John Newcomber spat a stream of tobacco juice in the dust to punctuate his point.

"Come on inside and let's gnaw a cup of coffee," Hogart said, trying his best to sound like the men who worked for him.

The owner of the recently renamed Bar H, Harold L. Hogart, reared back in his chair, stuffed his fat banker's cigar in his mouth, and narrowed his eyes. He wasn't a banker, but he was the next thing to it; he was an investor. And he had invested in the Bar H a year ago after old man Wells lost it to the Merchant's and Farmer's Bank – but then, old man Wells wasn't the only one to lose a ranch in 1886. All hoped this year would be a lot better.

The two men took a seat at the plank table that served the bunkhouse. And Hogart did his best to sound the empire builder. "You and I have gotten along fine so far, Newcomber, I hope to continue the relationship . . . But you've got to abide by my wishes, and his mother and I wish to have our son accompany you on this drive."

"I've already got a half dozen whelps green as gourds, Mr. Hogart – "

"Then another won't matter much. Wilbur will be ready and waiting at sun up. He's eighteen, older than some of your hands, and perfectly capable. We want him to have this experience before he leaves for college in the East."

So it was settled. John Newcomber had his back up over the whole affair, but he said nothing knowing from long experience as a *segundo*, foreman, that it was hard to put a foot in a shut mouth, and besides, it's usually your own throat you slice with a sharp tongue – and he wasn't about to walk away from a good job when even a poor one was nigh impossible to find. Still and all if he could change the man's mind, he'd give it a go, but he knew that trying to make a point when Hogart thought otherwise was like trying to measure water with a sieve. He'd end up all wet with nothing to show for it. Hogart was slick as calf slobber, but he was the boss.

Ah Choo, the cook, who was nicknamed Sneezy for obvious reasons, filled the two men's coffee cups, but was thinking of his honorable ancestors as he did so – which he had a tendency to do when he had to face unpleasant tasks. He was the bunkhouse cook at the Bar H, not the main house cook. That was Mrs. O'Malior's job. The two of them spatted like a pair of cats whose tails had been tied together before they were tossed over a clothesline. And this afternoon, Sneezy had to go to the main house to round out his chuck for the month-long trip ahead. He did not look forward to the afternoon's chore, nor to having John Newcomber, who he had to be as close to for the next month as a tick in a lamb's tail, start on a long drive with a burr already festerin' under his saddle.

Mr. Hogart finished the varnish Sneezy called coffee,

acted as if he enjoyed it, then rose and extended his hand to Newcomber. "You know how important this trip is to the Bar H, John. These cattle have to be in Mojave by the 16th of September in order to fulfill the contract with Harley Brothers Packing. A day late and those robber barons will want to renegotiate, and the price I have now will just barely cover this year's costs. Be there on time."

"God willin' and the creek don't rise...and some tenderfoot don't stampede the stock, we'll make it. Dry year or no." He couldn't help put the dig in to the boss's withers like a cocklebur, but it rolled off Hogart like rain off an oiled slicker, not that there'd been enough rain this year to test the theory.

Hogart left the bunkhouse, and John Newcomber stood at a window staring out through the dirty glass, shaking his head. "This is gonna be like startin' a long trip with a sore backed horse and hole in yer boot sole," he mumbled, more to himself than to Sneezy.

"Pardon, Mr. Maycom'er?" the little cook asked.

"Nothin', Sneezy. Pack a lot o' lineament and bandages, an' a Bible if you own one. I got a bad feelin' about this go."

"Yes, sir, Mr. Maycom'er, sir. Renament and ban'ages and the Christian book, snap snap."

Morning dawned fresh and breezy, with the Sierras at the ranch's back and the Whites, also the better part of 14,000 feet above sea level, between it and the rising sun – it took a while before the sun touched the Owen's Valley bottom with its warmth. It was the better part of two hundred fifty miles down the valley and across a piece of the Mojave Desert to reach the rail station at Mojave, and to be comfortable they'd have to average ten miles a day to keep the schedule. Ten miles should be easy, all things being equal. But John Newcomber had driven stock long enough to know that all things never stayed equal for long.

Sneezy had rung the chuck bell at 3:30 A.M., a half hour earlier than usual, so he could feed the men the last of the eggs and milk they'd see for a good while, and still get a jump on the herd. He wanted to stay ahead of them if he could, at least on this first day – for he'd be eating dust the rest of the drive. And the four-up of mules he had pulling the chuckwagon would keep ahead of the herd, given no major trouble.

True to his father's word, just as Sneezy whipped up the chuckwagon team to get a jump on the drovers, Wilbur Hogart pranced up on one of the Hogarts' blooded thoroughbreds, a dun colored horse with fine long bones that stood sixteen hands. It was a pleasurable animal to look at, but . . . Wilbur carried a quirt and wore a fine new Palo Alto fawn colored hat, twill pants, a starched city shirt, and English riding boots. On his hip gleamed a new Smith and Wesson chrome plated .38 in a polished black holster. The bedroll he had tied behind the saddle couldn't have carried more that one blanket and one change of clothes. John Newcomber stood cinching up his sorrel quarter horse as Wilbur's animal proudly single-stepped over to the hitching rail.

"John," the young man said, "I'm ready – "

"You'll call me Mr. Newcomber while you're working for me," the Bar H *segundo* said quietly, his voice matching the cold-granite of his chiseled face – but Wilbur heard him clearly enough. The young man's eyes and nostrils flared a little, but he said nothing in reply. "Understood?" Newcomber asked, unsatisfied with the boy's silence, his own voice a trifle louder.

"As you wish, Mr. Newcomber," the boy replied, stressing the mister in a manner that rang of sarcasm. John left it at that, knowing it would be a long trip and that time and the trail would work out most of Wilbur Hogart's kinks. Hard work had a way of doing that to a man, or breaking him, if he wasn't much of one to start with. John really had no way of knowing if Wilbur Hogart had any sand, but time and the trail would tell.

"Dad said I was to ride point," Wilbur added, rubbing salt in the spot Harold H. Hogart had already galled on John's back.

"You'll ride drag, like all new hands do, Mr. Hogart." John Newcomber swung up in the saddle, forking the sorrel and waiting for him to kick up his heels with the first saddle pressure of the morning – he didn't, but John knew the sorrel was saving it for later. He took the time to switch his attention and give Wilbur a hard look.

The boy glared at him. "Dad said – "

"Wilbur, let's get something straight right up front. Your daddy's not going on this trip, and if I hear you say one more time, 'daddy said,' I'll not take kindly to it and I might lose my temper. I've got a deep well of temper, Wilbur, and I can lose it every hour of every day and not run out. It's been tested. That's the kind of trip this might be, Wilbur, if you say 'daddy said' ever agin'."

"But – "

"There ain't no butts about it, Wilbur."

"Yes, sir," Wilbur said, to his credit, and reined the tall dun colored horse away.

Sally Fishbine had ridden for the Bar H for fourteen years, the first thirteen when it was the Lazy Loop, and the last one under John Newcomber. He reined his bandy legged gray over beside John and paced him out to what they called the creek pasture, where the eight hundred fifty seven head, by yesterday's count, of Hereford mix – with Mexican Brahma – were gathered. The rest of the hands, a dozen of them, were holding the cattle and getting their minds right for the drive.

"Salvatore," John said quietly as they gigged the horses toward the creek pasture, "is the weather a'gonna hold."

"Bones say it is," he said, stretching. About that time John's sorrel decided he was awake enough to shake loose, and began a bone-jarring humpbacked dance. "Step lively!" John shouted, giving the big horse his spurs and whipping him across the ears with the rein tails at the same time. The sorrel settled, and John knew from long experience that that was it for the rest of the day.

"I swear, you two are like an old married couple . . . got to have yer spat or you can't get the blood to pumpin'," Sally said, rolling a smoke with one hand as his own mount plodded along.

"Both of us got to show how young we still are," John said, reaching forward and patting the big horse on the neck. "If'n I didn't pop 'is ears ever' morning, he'd think I didn't care for 'im."

They picked the pace up to a cantor, with Wilbur Hogart keeping a respectful twenty paces behind. Wilbur had learned to ride English, in Oakland at the Hogarts' breeding ranch, across the bay from their home in San Francisco, and he could sit a saddle with the best of them by the time he was sixteen, and rode jumpers, but it was different from western riding – considerably different in that you handed the horse to a groom when finished for the day, and you finished for the day whenever you tired of the animal and the exercise. Still, he knew he was equal to anything the country and John Newcomber could throw at him – at least he was quite sure he was.

They crested a rise and looked down into creek canyon, and a thousand bald faced and mixed breed cattle lowed and grazed while a dozen cowhands waited the chance to earn their dollar a day and found.

Stub Jefferson had ridden in the year before, and John Newcomber had hired him on without so much as a second glance. His rig, and the way the black cowboy sat the saddle and kept his own council was enough of a resume for John.

Sergio and Hector Sanchez, a pair of young brothers up from San Diego were hired on just for the drive. John knew nothing about them, other than they rode fine stock and carried the woven leather reatas of the vaquero, and theirs were well tallowed and stretched to seventy feet with the weight of many a cow.

Old Tuck Holland had been working cattle on the east side of the Sierra for as long as John could remember. He had tales both older and taller than the Sierras and would tell 'em until they chopped ice in Death Valley, if you'd listen. His age was indeterminable but he had to be on the shady side of seventy. He looked so puny he'd have to lean against a post to spit to keep from blowing himself down; but he was tough as wang leather, had a face carved and etched like a peach pit by sun, sand, and wind, and spent most of his time looking back to see if the younger hands were keepin' up. And they were struggling along wondering why he made it all look so plum easy.

Colorado, which was the only name he gave and consequently was the only name used for him, was red-headed befittin' his name, bow legged enough that a pig could charge twixt his knees while he was clickin' his heels, and loud; but he pulled his own weight. He too had been hired on just for the duration of the drive.

Pudgy Dickerson was the last of the hands hired on, and John had to bail him out of the Bishop jail in order to do so, but he needed a hand and the rest of the able bodied men in the valley had run off to another silver strike in the high country – another whiff of bull dung as far as John Newcomber was concerned. But particularly when times were tough men seemed to jump at the chance for easy money. It normally turned out to be grit and grime and beans and backache, but still they chased the will o' the wisp.

The remuda man was Enrico Torres, as good a man with horses as John had ever seen. He pushed three dozen head of rank half-broke stock so the cowhands could trade off a couple of times a day. It was hard country between the north end of the Owens Valley and Mojave. Some spots of good grass and sweet water, but more than enough hard-as-the-hubs-of-hell ancient lava flows and flash floods, cactus and snakes, and heat if the weather decided it wanted to run late, or snow if it ran early. And it usually decided to do one or the other – and sometimes both – when a herd was being shoved to market. It was hard on horses and men, and hard as hell on a good attitude..

They pushed the herd out, jittery, but then all of them were when a drive began and before they settled into the routine. The men found their positions, all unassigned except for Stub Jefferson, the black cowhand who was riding point, and the Sanchez brothers, who were assigned drag with Wilbur Hogart and quickly took up positions flanking and staying out of the dust. The Sanchez boys had ridden enough drag to know they could stay out of the most of it on the flanks, and still do their job. So they gave Wilbur the position of honor . . . or so they told him . . . dead center trailing the herd.

John Newcomber floated from position to position, judging the men he didn't know, watching the herd, eyeballing the weather, and worrying – that was his job.

They hadn't gone three miles before Wilbur Hogart let his horse drift over close enough to Hector Sanchez so he could call out to him. "I'm Wil Hogart," he called.

Hector looked over and nodded, and touched the brim of his sweat soiled sombrero.

"What's a fella to do about the privy?" he shouted again.

Hector looked at him, a little confused.

"I need to pee," Wilbur said.

"Sí," Hector repeated, "the señor needs to pee.'" He reined over closer to the fancy looking gringo, who didn't look quite so fancy now that he was covered with a half-inch of dust. "Well, señor, you ride sidesaddle to accomplish that task."

"Sidesaddle?" Wilbur questioned. "You're funnin' me, *amigo*. I meant do you take the drag while I drop out, or just what?"

"Senor Newcomber will be very angry if you stop to water the sagebrush, señor. It is the tried and trusted sidesaddle method – "

"Fill in for me, señor," Wilbur said, and reined away to find a bush, which was no problem as the country was chaparral covered.

"Sidesaddle," Hector said to himself, then laughed aloud. He couldn't wait to tell his brother.

"Sidesaddle," Wilbur repeated to himself, pleased that he had not fallen for the obvious prank of the other rider. He knew he would be the butt of many attempts, but was wise to them.

He dismounted and unbuttoned his trousers and began to relieve himself, just as the grass under his attacking stream came alive in the most terrible buzzing and thrashing Wilbur had ever heard. He stumbled back and pawed at the Smith and Wesson when he realized it was a four foot rattler he had the misfortune to awaken from his repose in the sun.

Wilbur emptied the six shooter, managing to scare the snake into retreating even faster than he already was, but not managing to kill it.

Still, Wilbur was satisfied with himself – until he heard the men begin to yell, and felt the vibration of four thousand hooves begin to beat in rhythmic stampede.

"My God," Wilbur said aloud to himself. "Did I . . . ?"

He raced for the thoroughbred, mounted, and rode after the advancing wave of cattle and men, and into a wall of dust as he had never seen.

The cattle ran for three miles, then the heat and the sun dissuaded them and they slowed, and finally, no longer hearing the explosions that had set them off, stilled and grazed.

John Newcomber sent Stub and Sally back along the flanks to pick up any strays, and checked with each of his men to make sure they were present and accounted for.

Wilbur Hogart, who sat at the rear of the herd, catching his breath as the thoroughbred stood and hung his head sucking in wind, was the last man he approached.

"You managed to keep from getting ground up," Newcomber greeted him.

"Yes, sir."

"Let me see that firearm," Newcomber said, his face turning to granite.

"It was a snake, Mr. Newco – "

"You shot at some poor ol' snake who was trying his best to get the hell out of the way!"

"He was only a couple of feet away, makin' a terrible

noise."

"Give me that weapon."

"Dad said – "

"What did I tell you about that 'dad said'?" Newcomber snapped.

Wilbur looked red faced, but quieted and reached down and slipped the Smith and Wesson out of its holster and handed it over. Newcomber slipped it into his saddlebag. He eyed the boy up and down shaking his head. "Don't make any more trouble, Wilbur. You just cost the Bar H about a thousand dollars in lost weight. At a dollar and a half a day, not that you're worth that, it'd take you some time to pay it back should Mr. Hogart want his due."

"A thousand dollars?"

"A thousand dollars . . . that is if we get all the steers back."

John reined the sorrel away.

Wilbur sat chewing on that for a while, when Stub and Sally approached, pushing a half dozen head that had strayed during the stampede. They reined over next to him as the strays rejoined the herd, kicking up their heels like a reunion of old friends.

"You the *jefe*'s pup?" Sally asked.

Wil gigged his horse over and extended his hand. "I'm Wil Hogart." Sally shook with him, but Stub just touched his hat brim, and Wil said "Howdy."

"Did the boss tell you about Oscar?" Sally asked.

"Oscar?" Wilbur said.

"Oscar, the new hand with the six kids and the crippled wife."

"He didn't say – "

"Oscar got stomped under," Sally said, keeping a straight face. Stub eyed him but, as always, kept his own council.

"Stomped under?" Wilbur asked.

"Ain't enough of 'im left to bury," Sally said, shaking his head sadly.

"You mean – "

"Oscar's cold as a mother-in-law's kiss, boy." Sally looked as if he was about to break into tears.

"It's all my fault," Wilbur said, his face fallen.

"Don't know about that," Sally said. "It's the Lord's place to judge reckless behavior . . . the kind what causes the good to die young. Yer misbegotten ways will be laid out a'fore St. Peter soon enough. You may not even survive this drive. Many won't. Maybe you'll meet Oscar in heaven and can explain to him why you got him stomped into salsa. Well, it's nice to make yer acquaintance." He reined away. Both he and Stub were doing their best not to break into uproarious laughter, and in doing so, their shoulders quaked. Wilbur thought they were both in the throes of grief.

"Aren't we going to bury him?" Wilbur called after them.

Stub turned back, wiping the tears of laughter from his eyes. "He's already stomped so deep he'll take root and sprout." He turned away, and the shoulders shook again.

Wilbur Hogart had never felt so terrible. What kind of a man was John Newcomber to worry about running off a thousand dollars worth of fat, and not even mention a man who had been stomped to death?

The word traveled quickly among the men, and all stayed away from Wilbur for the rest of the afternoon – knowing they would break into laughter if they rode up beside the dejected boy, and give it away. Wilbur clomped along behind the herd, his eyes and ears filled with dust, his mind filled with remorse.

They caught up with where Sneezy had made camp, an agreed spot ten miles from the home place on the edge of Bar H property and on the bank of a fair cold creek, lined with willows, a couple of spreading sycamores, and a few Jeffery pines.

Wilbur was the last to the camp, and the men parted from a group as he rode in – Wilbur presumed it was because he was approaching, and that they didn't want to have anything to do with the man who'd caused Oscar's death. Not that he knew who Oscar was. He'd only met a couple of the men, and Oscar had not been one of them.

Wilbur dropped the saddle from the thoroughbred and turned him out with the remuda, then walked straight over to John Newcomber.

"They told me about Oscar," he said, his weight shifting from foot to foot. "I want to go back and pick up his body. A Christian – "

John Newcomber gave him a dubious look and started to say something, but was interrupted.

Sally stood nearby and offered quickly, "Oscar wanted the coyotes and other critters to have him, boy." Sally removed his hat and placed it across his heart, "It was his last wish. He always was a kind soul to the little critters. And it's the way of the west. We'll say a few words about him after we bean up."

Wilbur was still unsatisfied, but didn't know what to say. It was a custom he'd never heard off, but little would surprise him with what he knew of cattle drives and drovers.

"The coyotes?" he finally managed to mumble in amazement. His gaze wandered from man to man, but none would meet his and none offered to disagree with what he thought was a pagan practice.

"Oscar was a religious soul, but he was the outdoors type...thought these here mountains was his...what do ya call them fancy churches... his cathedral. He wanted to be spread all over these mountains," Sally added. "Nothing like a band of the Lord's scavengers to spread a body about. Crows and buzzards and such fly for miles doing their business and the coyotes and skunks and wolves'll deposit him in all the places he loved – not in exactly the way I'd personally favor it, but he'll get spread. Ashes to ashes, dirt to dirt, dung to dung, so to speak."

Wilbur thought he was going to be sick to his stomach. All the men turned away, and some were obviously overtaken with grief. They held hands to face and shook, or turned away. He walked away from the camp and into a clump of river willows and found a rock by the creek and sat, watching the water tumble by, wondering what would happen to "Oscar's" six starving children. He sat there until he heard Sneezy bang the bottom of an iron skillet, and hurried to get his beans – grief and remorse was one thing, hunger was another.

The men ate in relative silence. Once in a while, one would mention one or another of Oscar's children, or his crippled wife.

The men cleaned up the biscuits, bacon, and beans, and hauled their tins to Sneezy. Darkness was creeping over the camp, and chill setting in. The drive would take them from 5,500 feet elevation on the slopes of the Sierra that rose to 14,000 feet behind them, down to less than 2,000 feet at the railroad corrals at the town of Mojave.

"Time for the ceremony," Sally said. "Gather round, boys."

All the men gathered in a circle, standing, drinking their coffee, gnawin' chaw, smoking roll-your-owns. "Now, what do you remember about Oscar?" Sally said. "You start, Stub."

Stub removed his hat and scratched his woolly head. "Well, I ain't much on reminiscence, so to speak, but I might remember something, given as how Oscar was such a fine fella." He took a long draw on the tin cup then began. "You know that ol' Oscar used to run the Rocking W down near San Berdo. He was countin' cattle there for a buyer from San Francisco, and knew the W didn't have enough cattle to meet the contract, so ol' Oscar set his countin' chute up again' a small hill. The buyer set up on the top rail and went to markin' off the stock. Ol' Oscar had the boys drive those heifers and steers round and round that hill till the buyer counted what he needed, then drove the herd off to the yards. The W got paid for nigh 500 hundred head...twice. Oscar saved the Rocking W, which the bank was sure to grab."

The boys laughed at that, but Wilbur found it to be downright dishonest. He smiled tightly.

"How 'bout you, Tuck," Sally encouraged the old

cowhand.

"Well, Oscar was a tough ol' bird." Tuck scratched his wrinkled chin and it's stubble of a day's growth of beard. "One time the foreman of the Three Rivers Ranch bet him a season's pay that he couldn't make love to an Indian squaw, kill a grizzly bear, and drink a fifth of whisky in one day...and the foreman knew where the bear's den was and knew an ol' squaw who was a mite friendly to all the Three River's hands, were they to bring her a bag o' beans or sugar. Well, Oscar took that bet, but the thing was, he drank the fifth a' rye first, then . . . a little confused with the fire water an' all . . . he shot the ol' squaw dead as a stone. The hard part was holdin' that griz down . . . but he did an' that's why some bears here a'bout is such sons a' bitches."

The boys laughed and slapped their thighs.

Wilbur began to get a little suspicious.

"How about you, Colorado?" Sally asked the pock-faced redheaded cowhand. He sat away from the others, sharpening a ten inch knife on an Arkansas whet stone.

"I never much cared about tellin' tales," he said, and spit a mouthful of tobacco juice, then went back to his work on the blade.

"You, Pudgy," Sally asked the man John Newcomber had bailed out of the Bishop jail to join the drive.

"Nobody," Pudgy began, "could ever find his way home, good as old Oscar. One time over at the Whisky Holler saloon in Virginia City, old Oscar went up to the bar with a bunch of hands he'd just finished a drive with, and they got to drinkin' and drinkin'. A couple of the boys, realizing how drunk ol' Oscar was, went out to his nag and turned the saddle around – they didn't want him riding into trouble. Oscar, hanging onto that poor ol' nags tail, rode clean to Sacramento before he sobered up and realized he was facing backward. He never could find his way to Sacramento after that, unless he reversed his saddle. But he was always real good at knowin' where he'd been."

By this time Wilbur was red in the face.

"We need to cheer up," Hector Sanchez said, after he

quit holding his sides from laughing. "A little friendly competition. Who's the newest hombre to sign on?" Hector asked.

"Must be ol' snake killer," Sally said, putting an arm around Wilbur's shoulders. "You get to go first."

"Wait a minute," Wilbur said. "Did any of you fellas even know this Oscar fella? In fact, was there even any Oscar at all?"

"I've knowed a few Oscars in my day," Sally said. "How about you, Stub."

"Cain't say as how I ever knowed an Oscar."

All the men broke into laughter, slapping their thighs. Wilbur reddened again, and he felt the heat on the back of his neck. He didn't know whether to get angry and stomp away or offer to fight, so he just stood and got a silly grin on his face.

"Ain't you proud you didn't cause nobody to get hurt with that fool stunt?" Sally said, more serious than not.

Tuck cut in before Wilbur could answer. "Give the boy a chance to show he's as good as the rest a' ya," old Tuck looked serious. "Ya'll been funnin' him enough."

Hector stepped over in front of Wilbur. "Can you swing an ax, Señor Hogart?"

"I imagine."

"Good, then we have the notch cutting contest."

"Notch cutting?"

"Sure, every drive has the notch cuttin' contest."

John Newcomber walked away shaking his head, but was unseen by Wilbur who was anxious to redeem himself for being stupid enough to be taken in with the stomped rider story.

"Notch cutting," Hector said. "You go first, so the rest of us know what we have to beat."

Sneezy had already fetched the double bladed ax out of the chuckwagon and offered it to Hector. "Come on, over here," he led Wilbur to a fallen log, two foot in diameter.

"This is a good log for notch cutting," Hector said, and the other men agreed with him. He lined Wilbur up in front of the log. "Get your distance, *amigo*," he suggested, and Hector adjusted his distance from the log.

"Now, here is the rub, *amigo*." Hector stepped behind Wilbur and encircled his head with his red checkered bandanna.

"Hold on, now," Wilbur tried to protest.

"This is how it is done, *amigo*. Blindfolded. You can do it."

Wilbur allowed himself to have the blindfold put on.

"Wait until I give the signal," Hector said. "Your hat, *amigo*," he said, and removed Wilbur's new fawn colored, now dusty, wide brimmed hat. "You will do better without the hat."

"One, two, three, go," Hector called and, and the men yelled their encouragement.

Wilbur with vigor born of embarrassment and a desire to show these men he was equal to any of them, swung the ax five times before Hector yelled for him to stop. "Time is up, *amigo*."

Wilbur reached up and removed the blindfold, anxious to see how much of a notch he'd cut. And he'd cut three fine ones . . . in his hat. His new Palo Alto lay in front of the log, its crown split, its brim with two wide splits.

"*Carumba*," Hector said, a sorrowful look on his face, "you have cut the notch right where I put your *sombrero* for safe keeping."

The men roared with laughter.

"You win the contest, Wilber," Tuck said. "The prize is a free millinery re-design. That's now what's known as an Owens Valley special."

Wilbur's mother had bought him that hat, just for this trip. The anger began to crawl up Wilbur's backbone, and to the men's surprise, he cast the ax aside and went after Hector Sanchez with his fists. Hector was quick as a snake, and back peddled as Wilbur took four or five healthy swings, then charged in low and tackled him and drove him to his back. He got astride him and pinned him down. Wilbur was red in the face and spitin' mad, but he couldn't move.

"Hey, *amigo*, you can't take a joke?" Hector asked.

"Let me up and I'll show you."

"I think I hold you here a while until the pot she don't boil so much," Hector said.

"Let him up," John Newcomber said, crossing the clearing from where he'd been leaning against a log, taking it all in. "And Mr. Hogart, you will find your bedroll and a place to bed down. The fun is over."

"You might think it's fun."

"I notched my hat, as did most every man here. It'll pass and you'll see the humor in it."

"The hell I will."

Hector unloaded off of him, and Wilbur regained his feet, spun on his heel and stomped away.

"Remember the Alamo," he said under his breath, but no one heard.

He found a spot away from the others for his bedroll, and ignored the feigned compliments to his hat the next morning as the men ate beans and cornbread by the dawning light. He turned in his tin and got a handful of jerky and hard biscuits for his noon meal, and was the first to saddle up for the day's work.

The wrangler, Enrico Torres, cut out a new horse for him – ignoring Wilbur's suggestions that he ride his own thoroughbred with a terse, "Horse has to last the trip, and you will get a new *cabillo* at least twice a day, sometimes thrice, from here on."

The ragged looking buckskin selected by Torres stood and allowed the curry comb then the saddle and bridle, but went into a stiff legged bounce as soon as Wilbur forked him. As much as the boy fought to control the animal, he turned and bounced right through the middle of Sneezy's camp, kicking fire, and ash, and dust in every direction. The Chinese cook scattered for cover, cursing in Oriental jabber, then sailed a pot lid after the boy and high-jumping horse as they moved on into the chaparral.

But to the surprise of all who watched in amusement, Wilbur stuck in the saddle.

He tipped his hat after he got control of the animal, yelled, "Sorry, Sneezy," then gigged away the snorting horse, keeping the animal's chin pulled to it's chest, to take up his position riding drag.

"Not bad for a stall-fed tenderfoot," Enrico said to Sally and Stub, who were currying their animals nearby. "His ridin' ability is a bit better than his sense of humor."

"Spent his first day admiring his shadow, cause there was no mirror handy," Stub said, "I thought at first he might be studyin' to be a half-wit, but I believe he might just end this trip knowin' dung from wild honey. He's game enough, and has more sand than I figgered."

"I dunno," Sally offered. "He seems to me he's taken too much of a liking to thick tablecloths and thin soup, but we'll see . . . we will see. My bones is goin' to achin', weather's a' comin'."

Before noon, the sky turned from deep bright blue to flat pewter and the temperature plunged forty degrees. The wind whipped down out of the Sierra, and men pulled coats from rolls behind their saddles.

Wilbur Hogart had a coat, but a light one that served as little more than a windbreaker, and the gloves he pulled from his saddlebag were kid leather – not working gloves, nor warm. Before long, he was cold to the bone, hunkered over like a ninety year old man, and shivering in the saddle. To add injury to insult, the hole in the crown of his hat leaked water, and his head was soaked.

Hector Sanchez had kept his distance and the two young men had no more than exchanged glances.

By mid-morning, flakes of snow began to drift. Both Enrico and Hector Sanchez had pulled heavy *serapes* from the rolls at the back of their saddles, and their wide sombreros kept the snow from their shoulders. A steer began to fade back from a position between Hector and Wilbur, and both men moved to haze it back into the herd.

As they did so, Hector spoke for the first time that day. "You do not have a heavy coat?"

"I'm not cold," Wilbur managed through teeth gritted to keep them from chattering.

"I see that, *amigo*," Hector said, and smiled and reined away.

"Greaser," Wilbur said under his breath, and pulled the light jacket closer as he moved back to his position. At least the dust had stopped.

After a moment, Hector again moved closer and yelled to Wilbur. "I must leave for a *momentito*. Cover the flank."

Wilbur said nothing, even though he heard. He watched the Mexican gig his horse and lope away, then laughed to himself. If the herd did fade and stray on Hector's side, Hector would get a dressing down from Newcomber. He ignored the herd on Hector's flank and tended only those cattle directly ahead of him.

But as fate and the cold would have it, the herd did not stray but rather bunched closer, and Hector soon returned. He drifted over to Wilbur and tossed him a bundle. "It was Oscar's *serape*." He laughed and slapped his thighs. "He needs it no longer so he left it to me. It is not because I am generous, *amigo*. If you continue to knock your teeth together like the castinets, you will cause another stampede. And more work for us all."

Wilbur held the wool *serape* in his hands and stared at the young Mexican, saying nothing.

"Ayee! You stick your *cabaso*...your head through the slit, tenderfeets."

"Though the slit," Wilbur repeated. And without hesitation, learned the use of the *serape*. The same one he had seen Hector use as a blanket the night before.

"*Sí, amigo*," Hector said, and spun his horse to return to his position.

"*Gracias, amigo*," Wilbur called after him.

"*Da nada*, Wil," Hector said, and gave the spurs to his horse. "You have mastered the *serape*, a difficult task. Tomorrow, if the weather is better, I will teach you the use of the reata...it should be nothing for a man who can chop a notch as you can."

"Tomorrow, if the weather is better," Wil called after him, and wondered what new trick Hector had up his sleeve and he knew that if Hector was fresh out, the others weren't. He wondered if he could borrow a needle and thread from Sneezy to sew up his hat – if Sneezy wasn't still wanting to sail pot lids at him for riding thorugh the middle of camp.

But he was sure Sneezy had long forgotten the incident.

The wind picked up again. But he didn't care. He was warm, for the first time that day.

He removed his hat, eyed it skeptically, and began to chuckle.

The Great Texas Kapusta Incident

by James J. Griffin

James J. Griffin is a lifelong horseman, western enthusiast, and amateur historian of the Texas Rangers. He is the author of a series of Texas Ranger novels, and his extensive collection of Texas Ranger artifacts is now part of the permanent collections of the Texas Ranger Hall of Fame and Museum in Waco.

Chapter 1

Texas Ranger Sean Kennedy looped his horse's reins around the battered hitch rail in front of Ranger Headquarters in Austin.

"I won't be long, Ghost," he promised the blue roan, patting the gelding's velvety muzzle. "Just have to find out where we're headed."

Sean slipped his horse a piece of licorice, ducked under the railing, entered the headquarters building, and strode down a long corridor to the office of Captain Earl Storm.

"Sean, glad to see you here so early. Grab some coffee and take a seat," Storm greeted him. "How's Amy?"

"Amy's doin' right fine," Sean answered, as he took a cup from a shelf and filled it with the strong black coffee Storm always kept simmering on top of the corner stove. He settled into a worn leather chair. "Her ma's comin' down from Waco to visit for awhile. She's planning on stayin' with Amy until the baby comes. Sure hope I'll be home by then, too."

"When's Amy due? I can't quite recall," Storm asked.

"About two months, the doc says."

"Then you'll be back home in plenty of time for the blessed event," Storm assured him. "I don't imagine this assignment will last more'n two or three weeks at the most. Once it's finished, you can have the leave you're due. You'll be home to see your child born."

"That's what I wanted to hear," Sean replied. "So, what's the job you've got for me?"

Storm took a long drag on the cigarette dangling from his lips, then picked up a letter from his desk and passed it to Sean. "It's all in there, although you'll probably have a hard time deciphering that message," the captain said.

"As you'll see, it came from Panna Maria. That's a little settlement about fifty miles southeast of San Antonio."

"I've heard of it," Sean answered, as he glanced over the letter. "It's mostly a Polish town, I seem to recollect."

"That's right. Quite a few Poles emigrated to Texas startin' about 1854. Panna Maria was their first settlement. Now there's several others in the same area."

"Seems kind of strange there'd be trouble brewin' in a place like that," Sean noted. "It's not a cowtown, or near a cavalry post."

"I'd usually agree with you, Sean, but not this time," Storm explained. "You see, those folks never quite fit in with the rest of the settlers in that area. They're mostly farmers or laborers, while just about everyone else down that way raises cattle. In addition, most of the Polish favored the North durin' the War, so naturally that caused hard feelin's, some of which still linger. They've been easy prey for outlaws, and the story is lots of cowboys go outta their way to make fun of those people."

"Then why hasn't something been done about this

sooner?"

"We haven't had any formal complaints until now. The Poles are hard-working folks who pretty much keep to themselves, just like the Germans, Czechs, and others who've immigrated to Texas from Europe. All they want is to be left alone to tend to their farms and families, not stir up trouble. Most of what's happened previously hasn't been all that serious. There's been cowboys' pullin' pranks, verbal insults, things like that. However, as you can see from that letter, things have recently gotten to the point where something has to be done before someone gets hurt, or worse."

"I'm having a hard time decipherin' this, Cap'n" Sean admitted. "It's written as much in Polish as English, near as I can tell."

"I'll boil it down for you, Sean. Several of the farmers have had their fields trampled by cattle, ruinin' the crops. There's also been damage to buildings in town, and night riders shootin' up farmhouses and barns. We need to put a stop to that, right quick. It shouldn't take you long to root out the troublemakers and settle things down. That letter is signed by a Jan Kaminski. Since there's no town marshal in Panna Maria, look up Kaminski once you get there. Any questions?"

"Yeah, I've got a couple, Cap'n. Why not send Jim Blawcyzk instead of me? After all, he's Polish. His family arrived with the original bunch of Poles who settled in Bandera. He'd fit in with the folks in Panna Maria far better'n me."

"Two reasons. First, Jim doesn't speak Polish any more than you or I do, except for a few words. Second, he's way out somewhere in West Texas. Same with Cody Havlicek. He's up in the Panhandle. I need a Ranger in Panna Maria as quickly as possible. You're the only man who can be there in a few days. What else?"

"You have any clues as to who's behind all this trouble?"

"Not any names, no. Kaminski's letter says he'll provide more information to whoever I send to Panna Maria. I do have a feelin' the men responsible are comin'

113

over from Helena. They like to brag Helena's the toughest town on earth, and it sure lives up to its reputation. Since Helena's only about five miles from Panna Maria, it'd be real easy for an *hombre* bent on trouble to ride over, create a ruckus, then run back to Helena where no one'd dare bother him. It makes no never-mind to me if those ranahans want to shoot each other up, but I have to draw the line when they start botherin' decent folks. That's your job, to make sure they don't."

"Then I'd best get at it," Sean said, rising from the chair. "Ghost'n I'll be there in three days, tops."

"You be careful, Sean," Storm advised. "*Adios.*"

"*Adios*, Cap'n."

Chapter 2

Sean reached Panna Maria late in the evening three days later. Full dark had already fallen, so the streets of the small hamlet were deserted. Close by a huge live oak, the Immaculate Conception Catholic Church, the town's main structure, loomed darkly over the square. While a few lights glowed softly from behind windows, most of the houses were dark, their occupants having retired for the evening.

"Looks like we're gonna have to rouse someone to find a place to spend the night, Ghost," Sean spoke to his horse. "Good thing Kaminski's letter included directions."

Sean heeled the tired blue roan into a slow jogtrot, past the church, two story school, and rectory, reining up in front of a small house about three blocks south. He dismounted and dropped Ghost's reins to the ground.

"You wait here while I see if I can wake anyone up," he ordered the horse, with a pat to his nose. "I'll be right back."

Sean strode up the short walkway to the front door and knocked twice. After a moment, receiving no response, he knocked again, harder. Shortly, a dim light shone behind a curtained window.

"Who's there?" a sleepy voice called.

"Texas Ranger, here answerin' your letter," Sean replied.

"Be with you in a minute."

After a short wait, the latch rattled, and the door was partially opened, to reveal a stocky, barrel-chested individual, who held a lantern in one hand and a shotgun in the other. He held the lamp high to scrutinize Sean's face.

"You're a Ranger, you say?" he questioned, in heavily accented English.

"Texas Ranger Sean Kennedy. I have your letter in my shirt pocket, if you need proof."

"C'mon in. I'm Jan Kaminski."

The door swung wide, and Sean stepped into a cramped room.

"You said your name is Kennedy?" Kaminski repeated as he set the lantern on a table. Kaminski had a florid face, deep brown eyes, with thick brown hair and a huge mustache to match.

"That's right, Sean Kennedy. Most folks just call me Sean."

"All right, Sean it is. You must have had a hard ride from Austin, so I would guess you're starving. My wife's asleep, but I can round up something if you'd like."

"I ate some jerky and biscuits on the trail. I'm not all that hungry, but my horse sure needs feedin'. Where's the livery stable?"

"Panna Maria's too small for one, but you're welcome to put your animal in the corral out back," Kaminski offered. "I'll show you where to find grain and hay. Far as you, we don't have an extra bed, but you're welcome to sleep on the couch."

"I don't want to put you out," Sean answered. "Isn't there a hotel? If not, I can roll out my blankets in the barn."

"No, there's not. Jaksina Markewicz runs the only boarding house in town, but she's full. And don't even think about sleeping in the barn. My wife would have my *dupa* if I let you do that. Besides, if you stay here that will give us a chance to talk first thing in the morning."

"I sure wouldn't want you to lose your *dupa,* whatever that is," Sean chuckled. "Reckon I'll take you up on your offer."

"Good, that's settled," Kaminski answered. "Let's take care of your horse."

Ghost was soon curried, fed, and bedded down along with Kaminski's plow horse. Fifteen minutes later, Sean had pulled off his boots, Stetson, and gunbelt, and was stretched out on the couch, covered with a thick wool blanket. Five minutes after that, he was sound asleep.

* * *

Sean was awakened the next morning by the aroma of something unfamiliar, but appetizing, sizzling on the stove. He swung his feet over the edge of the couch, pulled on his boots, and headed for the kitchen.

"*Dzien dobry*, Sean. That means good morning. Did you sleep well?" Kaminski greeted him.

"I sure did," Sean answered. "Good mornin' to you, Jan. Somethin' sure smells good."

"Breakfast will be ready in a few minutes," the woman at the stove answered. She was blonde, blue-eyed, and petite.

"Sean, this is my wife, Maria. Maria, Ranger Sean Kennedy," Kaminski introduced.

"Pleased to meet you, ma'am," Sean said.

"You also, Sean; however, you must call me Maria. I hope you're hungry, although I have to apologize breakfast is mainly leftovers. When we have extra *kluski,* the next morning we mix them with eggs, sausage, and onions, then fry them up."

"*Kluski?*" Sean echoed.

"You'd call them noodles," Maria answered. "Jan, why don't you show Sean where to clean up? By the time you're finished, I'll have the food on the table."

"I need to care for my horse first," Sean noted.

"He's already been fed and watered," Kaminski

replied. "Come with me. Maria prefers not to have anyone underfoot while she's in the kitchen anyway."

After washing and shaving, Sean and Kaminski headed back inside, to where Maria had already set out plates heaped full. In the center of the table were several loaves of crusty rye bread, a crock of butter, and a pot of coffee.

"We always say Grace before we eat, Sean," Jan said. "Would you like to give the blessing?"

"Sure," Sean agreed. He blessed himself with the Sign of the Cross, as did the Kaminskis, then bowed his head and folded his hands.

"Bless us, O Lord, and these Thy gifts, which we are about to receive from Thy bounty, through Christ our Lord. Amen."

"Amen."

"I didn't imagine you were Catholic," Kaminski observed once the Grace was concluded.

"Sure am," Sean answered. "Although I don't get to church anywhere near as often as I should."

"Never mind talk, just eat," Maria ordered.

"I won't argue about that, Maria," Sean grinned. He took a forkful of *kluski*.

"Well, Sean?" Maria asked, as he chewed his first mouthful.

"It's delicious," Sean replied. "Like nothing else I've ever tasted."

"It sticks to your ribs, too," Kaminski observed. "You can go all day without getting hungry."

"There's plenty more, so don't be shy about asking," Maria added.

"All right," Sean agreed.

They ate in silence for a while, enjoying their meal, until Sean pressed for more details about the problems confronting Panna Maria.

"You may or may not be aware of this, but we Poles have been putting up with harassment almost from the day we settled here," Kaminski began. "Most of the cowboys and ranchers around here don't care for us.

They don't consider us true Texans, even though many of us have been here longer than they have. Our customs are different, our clothes are different, since we're Catholic our religion is different, and quite a few of us, especially the older folks, don't speak English. Also, even though we formed a cavalry unit, the Panna Maria Greys, which fought for the Confederacy during the War, that's pretty much been ignored. Quite a few of us were Northern sympathizers, which hasn't been forgotten by a lot of Texans. However, up until recently we only had to contend with minor episodes, cowboys shouting insults, ridiculing our dress or speech, things like that. Now, as you read in my letter, the problem has gotten much worse."

"So it would seem," Sean agreed. "You have any idea why?"

"I think at least one, possibly more, of the ranchers want to drive us off our lands," Kaminski answered.

"Can you give me a name?"

"I have no proof, but Ben Craddock would be my guess. His cowboys seem to be causing most of the trouble lately."

"Where's his spread located?"

"About six miles from here, about a mile north of Helena. It's the Rafter BC."

Sean stroked his jaw thoughtfully.

"Helena? Captain Storm seems to think that's where the troublemakers might be comin' from."

"I wouldn't be surprised," Kaminski agreed. "Lots of folks emphasize the 'Hell' in Helena. It's a place to stay away from, that's for certain."

"Decent women won't go within a mile of that town," Maria added. "They wouldn't be safe."

"Sounds like I need to pay Helena a visit," Sean said. "Anyone else besides you think Craddock's the main culprit, Jan?"

"Just about everyone around here," Kaminski answered.

"Does he seem to be after anyone's land in particular?"

"Yes, Anna Bialek's place. Anna's a widow who still runs the farm her husband's family settled. She lost her only son in the war, so her sole help is a neighbor's boy she hires as needed. Craddock probably feels she's an easy target, but he sure doesn't know Anna. She won't give up without a fight."

"Then my first order of business is to visit her," Sean answered. "Can you tell me how to get to her place?"

"Better than that, I'll take you," Kaminski offered. "That way I can show you the town, and perhaps introduce you to a few others."

"I appreciate that," Sean said. "I'd also like to meet with everyone I can before I see Craddock. Can you arrange that?"

"I'll call a meeting for tonight," Kaminski replied. "In a town this small, it doesn't take long to get everyone together. Will seven o'clock at the church hall do?"

"That'll be fine," Sean agreed.

"Good. I'll take you to Anna's, we'll talk with her, then we can make the rounds of town."

"You won't need to stay with me at Mrs. Bialek's," Sean said.

"Yes, I will," Kaminski differed. "Anna doesn't speak English, so you'll need me to translate. Besides, you being a stranger and looking like any other cowboy, Anna might stick you with a pitchfork before you could even say hello. You'll need me to smooth things over."

"Fine. How soon can we start?"

"Right now, if you're finished eating."

"I am. Maria, that was delicious. I can't eat another bite," Sean praised.

"*Dziekuje*, Sean."

Kaminski rose from the table and kissed his wife on the cheek.

"Maria, we'll be back in a few hours. *Pozegnanie.*"

"*Pozegnanie*, Jan."

Chapter 3

In the daylight, Sean was able to get a better look at

Panna Maria. The village had been settled on a small hill overlooking the junction of the San Antonio River and Cibolo Creek. With the exception of the church and school, most of the buildings were unassuming. Modest homes were scattered among the live oaks, with Pilarczyk's general store appearing to be the only business. While they rode along, Kaminski greeted several passersby, introducing Sean to them.

"Seem like real nice folks around here," Sean observed.

"They are, for the most part. Hard-working and honest, too. All we ask is to be left alone to tend our farms and businesses and raise our families," Kaminski answered.

"What about havin' fun? I didn't even see a saloon."

"Oh, we have one," Kaminski assured the Ranger. "Although we call it an *ogrodek piwny,* or beer garden. It's behind Stanley Piontek's place. We'll probably end up there after the meeting tonight. You can sample some Polish beer."

"I'll look forward to that," Sean said. "I get mighty thirsty. Now, how much farther to Mrs. Bialek's?"

"Another quarter-mile. It's just outside town."

A few minutes later, they rode up to a tidy whitewashed home.

"I don't see Anna," Kaminski said. "She's probably out in her fields."

They circled the house, to several fields planted in cabbage. Kaminski pointed to a diminutive figure hoeing between the rows.

"There's Anna. I'll call her."

"Anna!" he shouted, *"Czece!"*

The woman straightened and turned to face the arrivals.

"Jan! Dzien dobry!" she answered, continuing in Polish. "Who is that with you?"

Sean and Kaminski rode up to her.

"Anna, this is Texas *Lesniczy* Sean Kennedy," he introduced, using his native tongue. "He's come to help us. Sean, Anna Bialek."

"Ma'am." Sean touched two fingers to the brim of his Stetson in greeting.

Anna Bialek was tiny, no more than five feet tall, and very thin. The hair under her babushka was silvery-gray, her face wizened with age. Sean would guess she was in her mid-seventies. However, her brown eyes were clear and bright.

"Anna, I told Sean you were having most of the trouble from Ben Craddock's men," Kaminski explained.

"Jan, ask her exactly what those men have done," Sean requested.

Kaminski immediately translated Sean's question.

"Kowboje zachowac jazdy przez moje pola kapusty!" Anna answered.

"She says cowboys keep riding through her cabbage fields," Kaminski translated.

"Pola kapusty!" the widow repeated. She pointed to several rows where the plants had been trampled under horses' hooves.

"I can see that," Sean answered. "When were they here last?"

Kaminski repeated the question, then Anna's answer.

"She says three days ago. They come and go as they please. I try to stop them, but what can an old woman alone do against such men?"

"Does she think they'll return?"

Again, Kaminski translated the question and response.

"She says of course, it's just a question of when."

"Jan, I have an idea," Sean said. "Ask her if I can stay with her. I can act as a hired hand, mebbe give her some help with the work. Then, once those cowboys show up, they'll have a surprise waiting."

"That is a good idea," Kaminski agreed. He repeated Sean's request.

Anna's eyes seemed to blaze with determination while she studied the Ranger. Sean was a big man, just over six feet tall, huskily built, with wide shoulders and a broad chest. His dark brown, almost black, eyes were his most distinct feature, their gaze penetrating. Seated on his big blue roan, Sean presented an imposing picture.

"*Tak,*" Anna said, breaking into a smile.

"She says yes, Sean."

"Fine. Tell her thank you."

"You can say that, Sean. It's *dziekuje.*"

"*Dziekuje?*"

"That's right."

"*Dziekuje,* Anna," Sean returned.

Anna immediately broke into a rapid stream of Polish.

"She thanks you also, and says since it's almost dinnertime, she's inviting both of us to stay for the noon meal. There's *kielbasa* and *pierogies,*" Kaminski explained. "Polish sausage and stuffed dumplings."

"Never heard of those, but if Anna cooks like your wife, it'll be a mighty tasty meal," Sean answered.

"Good. Only problem I see is Anna not speaking English, and you not speaking Polish, but I'm certain you'll both manage," Kaminski replied. "I'll show you where to put your horse and clean up. Once we've eaten, I'll head back to town and start spreading the word about tonight's meeting."

* * *

About four that afternoon, Anna left the field where she and Sean had been working. She went inside a shed, retrieved a rope halter, lead rope, and bucket, then brought those to Sean.

"*Krowa*", she said, pointing to a fat cow in a small enclosure. She shook the bucket at Sean.

"Cow? You want me to milk the cow?" Sean asked.

"*Tak.*"

"All right," Sean nodded, took the bucket, then turned at the sound of approaching hoofbeats.

"Just a minute, Anna," he said, studying two approaching riders. "Let's see what these *hombres* want."

Sean dropped the bucket and loosened the Colt in his holster, waiting while the riders neared. They deliberately allowed their horses to trample some of the remaining undamaged cabbages.

"Hold it right there, you two!" Sean ordered, lifting his gun and pointing it at the nearest rider's stomach. Alongside him, Anna was wielding her hoe like a club.

"Keep your hands away from those guns," Sean added. "Now, you're gonna turn those horses around and head back where you came from. Don't, and you'll both have holes through your bellies. I'll also be expectin' you to pay for the lady's cabbages."

"Who do you think you are to be issuin' orders, Mister?" the first rider questioned. "We've been ridin' over this land for quite a spell."

"The name's Sean Kennedy, and you won't be trespassing on Mrs. Bialek's land, or anyone else's, from now on. *Comprende?*"

"You might wanna think twice about makin' threats like that," the second rider said. "You don't act like one of these thick Polacks. What interest do you have in them?"

"Let's just say I was hired to make sure snakes like you don't cause the Poles any more problems," Sean snapped.

"You a gunfighter?"

"You really want to find out?" Sean challenged, his gaze seeming to bore right through the two men. They saw death in those dark eyes.

"No, reckon we don't. But you ain't heard the last of this, Mister."

"Neither have you," Sean replied. "Not until you pay for the damages."

"You're welcome to come collect for those anytime. Just see Ben Craddock at the Rafter BC. Better yet, come over to Helena Saturday night, and you'll get paid then. We'll be at the Hell-Ena Saloon. C'mon, Bob, let's get outta here."

The men turned their horses and galloped off, trampling more cabbages.

"*Swinia!*" Anna called after them, shaking her hoe.

"Don't worry, Anna," Sean assured her, with a smile. "They've ruined the last of your *kapusta*. Those men won't bother you again."

He slid his gun back in the holster and picked up the bucket.

"Dziekuje." Anna bobbed her head and smiled.

"No *dziekuje* needed, Anna. Let's milk your *krowa.*"

Chapter 4

"Dunno how long I'll be, Ghost, so you just relax awhile," Sean told his horse after placing him in the carriage shed behind the church. He slid the bridle from the gelding's head and loosened his cinches. After giving Ghost a licorice, Sean headed for the church hall, where Jan Kaminski was waiting, along with Anna Bialek, who had insisted on accompanying Sean. To his surprise, the elderly widow had no problem riding double, balancing easily on Ghost's broad back.

"Dobry wieczor, Sean. Good evening."

"Good evenin' to you, Jan. Don't see anyone here yet. You expecting a good crowd?"

"Most of the men in Panna Maria, and quite a few of the women, too," Kaminski replied. "It's a bit early. They'll be along. Come inside."

The hall was brightly lit, pews from the old church, which had been destroyed by lightning, serving as seats. A battered table up front served as a podium. After a couple of moments, the first man arrived.

"Sean, this is Thomas Moczygemba," Kaminski introduced. "Thomas, *Lesniczy* Sean Kennedy."

Sean and Moczygemba shook hands and nodded.

"You'll meet quite a few Moczygemba's tonight," Kaminski explained. "Thomas's uncle Leopold was the priest who founded Panna Maria. Thomas himself will soon be studying for the priesthood. Leopold's father and brothers came over after him, so most of the people in this area are relatives. Father Moczygemba's no longer here, but up in Michigan. Father Jankowski, who took his place, is visiting San Antonio for a few days.

Ah, here's Stanley Piontek."

A steady stream of men and women soon filled the hall to near capacity. Once everyone was seated, Jan rapped on the table for order.

"Everyone," he began, "For those of you who haven't met him, this is Texas *Lesniczy* Sean Kennedy. Sean has been sent in answer to our plea for help. I don't need to explain again the trouble we have been having lately. Sean will be staying at Anna Bialek's until the problem has been solved. Sean..."

"*Czesc,*" Sean said. With Kaminski translating, he explained what steps would be taken to stop Ben Craddock and any others from bothering the Poles further.

"Let me assure you, first of all, that I will remain here as long as necessary. That said, I cannot stay indefinitely. Once I have taken care of the main troublemakers, you'll have to establish your own law and order. I suggest you consider appointing a town marshal as soon as possible."

"None of us are qualified to be a lawman," Anton Bish objected.

"Then you need to hire someone," Sean answered. "I've already confronted two of Ben Craddock's men. It appears Craddock won't give in easily. I'll ride over to Helena Saturday night, and with luck will be able to convince Craddock to stop hasslin' you folks, although I don't think that's likely. I hope it won't come to it, but there may well be gunplay before this is settled."

"Again, few of us can shoot very well," Bish answered.

"I'm aware of that. Taking care of Craddock and his men is my problem. What happens after that is yours."

For over an hour, Sean and Kaminski presided over the meeting, while questions were shouted and options discussed. Finally settling on the plan of action Sean recommended, that he meet with Ben Craddock in hopes of settling matters peacefully, the gathering was adjourned to Stanley Piontek's beer garden.

"This is mighty fine beer, Jan," Sean praised, taking a long swallow of the dark amber home brew. "Tell Stanley I said so."

"*Sean lubi piwo, Stanley,*" Kaminski told the bartender.

"*Dziekuje,*" Stanley answered, grinning. He placed another foaming pitcher in front of the Ranger. "Now I've got to get Anna another glass."

To Sean's surprise, the feisty widow also enjoyed her beer.

"Sean," Kaminski asked, his mood turning serious. "Do you really think you can stop Ben Craddock?"

"*Quien sabe?*" Sean answered. "Don't know how to say it in Polish, but that's Spanish for 'who knows'? More important question is, can your people handle any other trouble which comes along after I'm back in Austin?"

"As you said, Ranger, *kto wie?* Who knows?"

Chapter 5

"Ghost, you reckon I'm plumb loco, ridin' into a trap like this?" Sean asked his horse when they reached the outskirts of Helena. The blue roan merely shook his head and snorted.

"Guess you ain't talkin'," Sean chuckled. "Well, I'll find out soon enough."

In the gathering dusk, the self-proclaimed "toughest town on earth" looked downright peaceable. The streets were virtually deserted, and the outlines of two churches were silhouetted against the darkening sky. The sleepy appearance of the town belied its reputation . . . until Sean turned a corner and came to the Hell-Ena Saloon. Raucous shouts and curses from the rowdy crowd inside shattered the still night. Sean dismounted, looped Ghost's reins over a hitch rail two doors down from the saloon, and gave him a licorice. Sean loosened the Colt in his holster, climbed the stairs to the Hell-Ena, and stepped inside.

The two men he'd chased off the Bialek farm were

standing at the bar, along with several other cowboys. One shouted in recognition when he spotted the Ranger.

"Ben, there's the *hombre* we told you about. Sure didn't think he'd have the guts to show up," he said to the man at his side.

"Bob speakin' the truth? You're the one who pulled a gun on him and Jess?" that man challenged Sean. He was tall and thin, with dark eyes and a thin mustache.

"That's right," Sean answered. "Did they also tell you they destroyed much of an old woman's cabbage crop, and that I'd be comin' here to collect for the damages?"

"They did mention that, yeah."

"You Ben Craddock?"

"Yep, I'm Craddock."

"Good. I was lookin' for you too. Keep your riders out of Panna Maria."

"You think you can order me around, just because you're some kind of hired gunslinger?" Craddock retorted. "I want that land, and I'll get it. No bunch of dumb foreigners are gonna stay on good Texas soil."

"You a native Texan, Craddock?" Sean questioned.

"No. Came down here from Tennessee after the War," Craddock admitted.

"How about your family?" Sean continued.

"They're Scotch-Irish," Craddock answered.

"So you've got no more claim to that land than the Polish do, in fact less, since most of 'em have been here a lot longer than you have," Sean answered. "Far as why this is my business, I never claimed to be a gunslinger. I'm a Texas Ranger, sent down here in answer to a request for help. Anyone I find botherin' those folks in Panna Maria'll be arrested."

"Oh, you're a Ranger," Craddock sneered. "That's different. Reckon we'd better pay for that cabbage then. I've got the money right here."

Craddock pointed to a bank note lying on the bar, between two short-bladed knives and a length of rawhide.

"There's a hundred dollars. That's three or four times

what that cabbage is worth. It's yours for the taking, on one condition."

"You're in no position to be makin' demands, Craddock."

"Not to disagree, Ranger, but I figure I am. You try'n leave this saloon and you'll have seven or eight bullets in your back before you make the door. Either you try'n take that money by my rules or get gunned down where you stand. Your choice."

Sean realized the futility of his situation. Even if he managed to pull his gun and shoot Craddock, he'd also die this night.

"All right, Craddock. What's the condition?"

"It's been quite a while since we've had a good old Helena duel. We're gonna end that dry spell right now," Craddock answered.

"A Helena duel? What's that?" Sean asked.

"It's really pretty simple. Two men, in this case you and Jess, are tied together by their left hands. Both have a knife, and fight until one is dead. That's all there is to it."

Sean glanced at the weapons on the bar.

"Those knives? The blades can't be more'n three inches long. You can't kill a man with one of those."

"Not with one stab, no," Craddock conceded. "To win, you have to keep slashing and cutting until your opponent bleeds to death. So there's your choice, Ranger. If you fight Jess and win, the money's yours. Of course, I should mention Jess has already won four Helena duels."

"He's got to lose sometime," Sean answered. "I reckon tonight's the night."

"I wouldn't bet on that, Kennedy!" Jess shouted.

"I doubt anyone will bet on him, Jess," Craddock said. "However, if anyone does, we'll take his money. Meantime, you and the Ranger get ready, then we'll head outside. No one'll touch that hundred. It'll be waitin' on the bar for whoever's left standin'."

Sean and Jess removed their gunbelts, hats, bandannas and shirts, placing them on a table. They were led to the street, where their left hands were tightly bound together. While that was being done, the crowd placed bets on the fight's outcome. Comparing the husky Sean to the lanky Jess, they were confident of the result. Certain the big Ranger could not move fast enough to avoid the cowboy's blade, they bet heavily on Jess.

"We're ready, Ben," Bob stated, handing each fighter a knife.

"You have anything to say, Ranger?" Craddock asked.

"Not a thing," Sean answered.

"Good."

Sean and Jess were spun around several times. Once they were released, Jess quickly jabbed his knife into Sean's belly. When the Ranger buckled, Jess slashed him across his upper arm and chest, bringing a cheer from the spectators.

Sean shook his head to clear it and sidestepped Jess's next thrust. He knocked the cowboy's arm aside and stuck his knife into Jess's ribs. Sean's next slash opened Jess's left cheek, just under his eye.

Jess slashed Sean's chest again, but his next blow went wide when the Ranger yanked him around and stuck his knife into Jess's stomach. For a big man, Sean was surprisingly agile. He managed to keep Jess off-balance while slashing at his forearm and ribs. Jess finally recovered and slashed the side of Sean's neck, then across his belly. Both men were now bleeding profusely, gasping for breath.

"C'mon, Jess. Finish him," Craddock urged his tiring rider.

"I'm tryin'," Jess answered, swinging wildly at the Ranger.

Sean concentrated on Jess's middle, stabbing repeatedly at his belly. When the cowboy finally buckled, Sean plunged the short-bladed knife into the soft tissue at the base of his throat. With a gurgle, Jess collapsed.

Sean cut himself loose from the dying man and

staggered toward the saloon. When he did, Bob pulled his gun and leveled it at Sean's back.

"Not now," Craddock ordered. "Put up your gun."

"But he killed Jess," Bob protested.

"Think I can't see that?" Craddock answered. "We'll take care of the Ranger, but this ain't the time."

Sean stumbled up the steps and into the Hell-Ena. He retrieved his gunbelt, buckled it on, then threw on his shirt and hat. After shoving the banknote in his pocket, he headed to his waiting horse.

"You ain't heard the last of this, Ranger," Craddock shouted.

"Whenever you want to finish it," Sean replied. He untied the reins, pulled himself into the saddle and backed Ghost away from the rail. Slumped over the blue roan's neck, Sean rode out of Helena, ignoring the curses and shouts sent after him.

Chapter 6

Sean spent most of the next week in bed, recuperating while Anna Bialek fussed over him and ministered to his wounds. It was the following Friday before, over the old widow's objections, he decided enough time on his back was enough. He got up, redressed, and went outside to groom Ghost. While he was working on the gelding, Jan Kaminski drove up. He pulled his team to a halt alongside the Ranger.

"*Czesc*, Sean."

"*Czesc* yourself, Jan," Sean answered.

"You've been working on your Polish," Kaminski chuckled.

"Haven't been able to do much else the past few days," Sean said.

"I would imagine not. How are you feeling?"

"Stiff and sore, but not too bad, considering."

"That's good to hear. You think we'll have any more trouble from Ben Craddock?"

"To borrow Jim Blawcyzk's favorite expression, I'd bet a hat on it," Sean replied.

"Jim Blawcyzk?"

"He's a lieutenant in the Rangers, from up Bandera way," Sean explained. "And you're the first person I've ever heard get his name right on the first try."

"That means you haven't met very many Poles before," Kaminski laughed.

"You're right about that," Sean agreed. He gave Ghost a final swipe of the currycomb, slipped him a licorice, and with a fond slap on the neck sent him trotting off.

"*Masz piekny kon,*" Kaminski said, studying the blue roan. "That means you have a beautiful horse, Sean."

"*Dziekuje,* Jan," Sean replied. "I'm rather fond of him."

"And him you. It shows," Kaminski said.

"Reckon it does," Sean smiled. "What brings you by, Jan?"

"I'm dropping off this wagon. Tomorrow most of the people in town will be coming here to help Anna harvest what's left of her cabbage crop, then I'll haul it to town. We're all grateful for what you've done, getting that money out of Craddock."

"Don't mention it. All part of my job."

"Nonetheless, without your help Craddock would never have paid for the damages."

Their conversation was interrupted by a call from the house. Anna shouted rapidly to Kaminski, who answered her just as quickly.

"What'd she say?" Sean asked.

"She says supper's ready. You're havin' *kiszka* and *pierogi* tonight. Easier for you to say kishka and dumplings."

"She said more'n that," Sean protested.

"She also invited me to supper, but I told her I can't stay. Maria will have ours on the table by the time I get home. She then said you get up to the house before supper gets cold. She'll beat your *dupa* if you don't."

"It's about time someone told me what my *dupa* is, although I've got a pretty good idea," Sean replied.

"That's right. It's your backside, Ranger, to use the polite term. Unless you want a sore one, you'd better head up to the house. Anna means what she says."

"I don't doubt that," Sean laughed. *"Pezegnanie, Jan."*

"Dobranoc, Sean. I'll see you tomorrow."

* * *

By four o'clock the next afternoon almost all of Anna's cabbages had been gathered and loaded into Jan Kaminski's buckboard. Sean, still hampered by his wounds from the knife fight, helped as best he could, but spent most of the day keeping watch for riders from Helena. He was certain Ben Craddock would not let the matter drop.

The harvesters were gathered around a table, taking a break before collecting the few remaining cabbages. Sean was the first to notice a group of approaching cowboys.

"Jan, tell everyone to be careful, and let me handle this," he ordered.

"Trouble, Sean?"

"Without a doubt. That's Ben Craddock and his men."

Jan rapidly translated Sean's orders into Polish.

Craddock and his men rode to within twenty feet of Sean before halting.

"I thought I told you to stay away from Panna Maria, Craddock," Sean snapped.

"You did, just like I told you, Ranger, I had no intention of doing so. You must be as thick as these dumb Polacks, thinkin' I'm gonna let them have this land."

With that, Craddock drew his gun and fired, Sean's injured arm not allowing him to meet the rancher's draw. Craddock's bullet struck the Ranger in his left shoulder and spun him to the dirt. Sean lay helpless as Craddock stalked up to him and leveled his gun at the Ranger's chest.

"Now I'm gonna finish you, Ranger!" he snarled.

"Szalony swinia! Idz do diabla!"

With a curse, Anna Bialek picked up a large cabbage and hurled it at Craddock. The butt of the heavy vegetable caught Craddock squarely on his temple, cracking the bone and stunning the rancher. He dropped as if pole-axed.

"Przejdz do Pieklo!" Anna shouted, throwing another cabbage at the downed rancher.

Before Craddock's men could react, the rest of the harvesters grabbed cabbages from the buckboard, sending a veritable bombardment of leafy green globes at the startled cowboys. Several were knocked from their saddles, others thrown when their panicked horses bucked and whirled under the assault, spilling their riders. The few men who managed to keep their horses under control spun them and galloped away from the infuriated farmers' assault. The others came to their feet and ran after their companions as fast as they could move, hurried along by the barrage of cabbages.

"Swietzy Jacek z jego pierogani!" Anton Bish exclaimed, when the last of the cowboys disappeared over the horizon.

Jan Kaminski hurried over to Sean, and helped him up.

"Are you hurt badly, Ranger?" he asked.

"No, just need to have this bullet dug out of me," Sean answered. "That can wait until I get Craddock jailed."

Sean took out his Colt and walked to where Craddock lay, moaning. He pulled the rancher to his feet.

"C'mon, Craddock. You're under arrest."

Craddock placed a hand to his blood-trickling temple.

"I need to see the doc, Ranger," he said.

"He can visit you in jail. Get movin'," Sean ordered.

"You think the others will be back, Ranger?" Aaron Swintkowski questioned.

"Nie," Sean answered. "Not a chance."

Chapter 6

"Sean, if it weren't for you, those cowboys would have destroyed our community, so you get the first helping of *golabki*," Maria Kaminski told him. The entire town of Panna Maria had gathered at Stanley Piontek's beer garden to celebrate the routing of the cowboys from Helena.

"What's *golabki?*" Sean asked. His left are was still in a sling.

"It's stuffed cabbage, also called pigs in a blanket or piggies," Maria explained. "Cabbage leaves rolled around chopped up beef and rice or barley. It's usually called galumpkis in English. These were made with Anna's cabbages."

"Sure sound good, Maria," Sean said, taking the dish of *golabki* she handed him. He cut one in half and took a bite.

"Sure tastes good, too," he praised. "Soon as I've eaten, though, I've got to be on my way.

"*Dziekuje,* Sean," Maria answered. "However, we won't allow you to leave until the party's over."

"But my wife's going to have a baby in a week or two," Sean protested. "I need to get home before then."

"All the more reason to celebrate," Jan Kaminski said. "You're going to be a father, those cowboys won't bother us anymore, and we'll be hiring a town marshal, as you recommended. There's no reason for you to leave tonight. Besides, the band will start playing shortly. You can't leave without hearing a few polkas. Stay awhile, eat, drink, and enjoy yourself."

Sean took another mouthful of *golabki,* washing it down with a good-sized swallow of beer.

"I guess you're right," he conceded. "It won't make any difference if I wait until morning to leave."

"Now you're talking, Ranger," Kaminski grinned. "I'll tell the band to get started."

"Before you do, I've been meanin' to ask you what Anna yelled at Craddock just before she beaned him with that cabbage."

"First she called him a crazy pig, told him to go to the devil, then to Hell," Jan explained.

"How about what Anton yelled. *Swietzy Jac... Jac...*"

"*Swietzy Jacek z jego pierogani!* Saint Hyacinth and his pierogis. It's just an exclamation, kind of like a Frenchman saying *sacre bleu* or you saying what in blue blazes, Sean," Kaminski explained. "Now, let's get the music goin'."

A moment later, the musicians swung into a lively polka tune. Before Sean realized what was happening, Anna Bialek had grabbed his hand and pulled him onto the dance floor. Everyone surrounded the big Ranger and the diminutive widow while she whirled him around the floor.

"By the way, Sean, I forgot to mention, when we Poles party, we *party!*" Kaminski yelled to be heard over the band. "This celebration won't end for two or three days. Let's see if you're tough enough to handle that!"

The Death of Delgado

By Rod Miller

Rod Miller is author of two novels, The Assassination of Governor Boggs *and* Gallows for a Gunman, *two books of poetry,* Things a Cowboy Sees and Other Poems *and* Newe Dreams, *and two works of nonfiction,* Massacre at Bear River—First, Worst, Forgotten *and* John Muir: Magnificent Tramp. *He also writes short stories, essays, and magazine articles. Visit www.writerRodMiller.com*

I came face to face with my future the day Christian Delgado rode onto our ranch. At least I hoped—dreamed—I had.

Delgado was a cowboy.

Oh, there were plenty of cowboys in our part of the country. But Delgado was a different sort. Flashy isn't the right word, but there was a certain amount of sparkle to the man and his trappings. He was some strange crossbreed of what nowadays we'd call Californio, buckaroo, and vaquero. Heavy-roweled Mexican spurs, high-topped boots with tall, underslung heels, short chaps that covered his lower legs with nothing but leather fringe, wool vest up top.

His saddle was especially eye-catching. Unlike the plain and practical kacks around our place, his slickfork was silver mounted with conchos, buckles, and bands; his other tack and horse jewelry likewise festooned.

As I said, I was enthralled the minute I saw him. He

filled the dreamy eyes of this eleven-year-old Idaho ranch kid with a near-perfect vision of what a cowboy ought to look like.

Mind you, he wasn't anything outside of ordinary from a physical standpoint. He wasn't tall, maybe seven inches above five feet, hung on an average frame that was neither slender nor stocky. Not particularly handsome, I'd say, but neither was he hard to look at. His face, save for a sharp-trimmed mustache, was so clean-shaven it always looked as if he'd just now toweled off the last flecks of lather. He was, I suppose, in his twenty-third or -fourth year that summer.

Even though Christian Delgado had never seen the south side of the Rio Grande, he was, to folks hereabouts, a Mexican. (Some called him a greaser, but never within his hearing.) But he claimed descent direct from the Spaniards of old, and offered deep green eyes and the pale skin on the inside of his forearms as proof of his genealogy. And, to this fascinated boy, he did carry himself with the elegance of a conquistador, a caballero, a Don. There's no doubt he was the kind of man folks paid attention to—the focus of attention in most every crowd, with the quiet confidence of one accustomed to that attention.

He showed up in the Curlew Valley because he heard that Dad had horses that needed rode. He'd heard right.

Dad and Uncle Evan had a sizeable ranch and raised a good many horses for sale. Nothing fancy, mind you, just good solid cow horses and some heavier stock for driving. We also put up a considerable amount of winter feed cut from hay meadows, and ran cattle on range that required the beef to graze at a fast walk just to get to enough grass to work up a cud of a size worth chewing.

And so Delgado went to work. Most of the time he spent horseback, either tending the cow herd or breaking horses. His means of training was simple: a good horse is the result of a lot of wet saddle blankets. When he wasn't sweating the edge off green-broke colts on long trails up and down the hills and canyons of our rocky, brush-covered country, you'd find him starting even greener colts in the round pen. He'd sometimes have half a dozen tied up outside waiting their turn.

Every chance that summer, you'd find me hanging by my elbows from the top rail, eyeing his every move. On a lucky day, I'd ride beside him through the brush, doing my best to handle one of his graduating students like a real hand—like Delgado—would. While abroad on the range we'd see to the cattle; doctoring any that needed it and drifting them back toward home if they wandered too far. Lucky days, for sure, for a kid with cowboy dreams.

But I wasn't all that lucky all that often that summer.

Dad, you see, was digging a well up in the corner of the south pasture. Water was scarce in Curlew Valley, and the stream through that end of our place, while wet enough in springtime, flowed only shallow dust by late summer. A reliable water supply was always to be desired, and always to be realized when chance presented itself. So when Dad watched a forked willow stick in the hands of an itinerant water witch take a nosedive, he dedicated his summer to digging a well.

Digging a well in those days and in that place wasn't a complicated job—you just grabbed the handle of a shovel and put the business end of it to work. The only thing you needed to worry about, Dad always said, was to fill up the back half of the shovel—the front half would take care of itself, he said.

He also told me that when you stood in the deep bottom of the long hole the well was becoming, you could look up at the narrow opening and see stars shining in the middle of the brightest day.

But all I could see those long days helping out at the well was lost opportunities—squandered time, wasted time, time I wanted to be with Delgado.

Instead, I spent my time daydreaming about what I was missing. Now and then, in answer to Dad's call echoing up the hole, I'd pull the well rope off the stake it was anchored to and knot it to the clevis on the singletree, then kiss ol' Socks into a shuffling walk, watching the rope feed its way through the squeaky hand-carved wooden block lashed to the top of the cedar pole tripod over the hole. When the heavy bucket cleared the hole I'd whoa-up Socks, swing the laden tub over to solid ground and call the horse back to slack the rope until the bucket landed. Ol' Socks didn't even need a jerk line to control, just voice commands.

Bucket settled, I'd walk over to the horse, unhook the rope out of the clevis, walk back and two-hand-heft-and-grunt the bucket over to the pile and dump out the hole it held. Hand-over-hand all along the length of the rope, I'd lower the bucket back down the well, careful not to let it fall too fast for Dad to grab before it beaned him, then take another hitch to the anchor stake. As Dad commenced putting more of the hole in the bucket, I'd bring Socks around and back him up close to the hole so we'd be ready to haul up the next load.

Mostly, the big bucket would be heaped with dirt and rocks, but for a few days now it had been showing more and wetter mud so Dad was feeling like the bottom of the well couldn't be far off.

A couple of times a day, besides the trip up for dinner and the one at the end of the day, Dad would ride the bucket up for a rest and some fresh air. Sometimes the air down there would get pretty thick, he said, and that meant more trips up the hole and longer stretches in daylight before going back down.

From time to time he would fashion a bundle of grass hay about the size of the hole, tie it to the rope, and plunger it up and down the well to force the heavy air out. A trick he learned, he said, from an old Cousin Jack miner who lived in town.

Dad sensed my fascination with Christian Delgado, and knew I saw in the young man the realization of my cowboy yearnings. And, of a normal summer, he would not have objected to my making of myself a full-time apprentice to the horseman. But he needed my help at the well, what with Uncle Evan and the hired hands busy with haying from dark to dark those long hot days.

And he often enough made me to realize he appreciated my help, and promised there'd be a time for cowboying.

Truth be told, Dad wished he could be out cowboying too, for he was a man who loved horses and cattle. I knew, too, that he admired the touch Delgado had with horses. Not as much as I admired him, maybe, but even through eyes wrinkled with experience Dad saw something beyond the ordinary in that cowboy's ways.

The day Delgado died dawned like any other.

He haltered and tied that day's mounts to the rail outside the round corral.

Uncle Evan and the hay hands hitched up a team and hayrack and rolled out for the meadow.

And Dad and I and ol' Socks shuffled slow toward the hole in the far corner of the south pasture.

"It's getting pretty boggy down there, son," he said.

"How much deeper you gonna have to go," I asked through a wide yawn as I fisted some of the sleep out of my eyes.

"Can't say. The mud makes for a messier job, but the water does cool it down some."

The past day or two he'd been coming out of the hole muddy above his knees, and he'd said the bottom got softer with every shovelful he hefted out of it. We were threading a good sixty feet of rope down the hole by then.

"I hope, in another day or three, to have to tread water down there. Then I'll know it's a good well. If it draws water enough in the dead of summer, it ought to serve year round. And, near as I can tell after straining the mud through my teeth, it's going to be good, sweet water."

Being a kid, and lacking proper appreciation for such things, I answered with another yawn.

We soon settled into the day's routine, and it did not appear anything would be along to break it. As usual, a breeze kicked up as the day warmed then grew gusty and dusty as the air got hotter. A dust devil whipped up out on the flat and I watched tumbleweeds spin around and around and up and up and eventually peel off to roll back to earth.

"Up!" Dad hollered from down the hole, but his call didn't register.

"Up!" he said again, louder, jolting me back into the present.

I worked the rope off the stake, knotted it through the clevis, and kissed Socks into motion. Unlike me, he'd paid attention to Dad's call and was ready to lean into the harness. By now, the both of us could practically do the job in our sleep and I was soon back on the powder box I used for a seat with barely any recollection of having left it.

This time it was the wind that woke me from my daydreams—heavy, hot gusts peppering me with dirt and debris. I squinted over my shoulder to see that dust devil right there and bearing down on us. With arms wrapped around the top of my head, I fell to my knees and made myself small.

Through the blow I could hear, barely, rattling harness and ol' Socks snorting and blowing. I peeked past a bent elbow in time to see the horse sidestep then shy backward, haunches down and head up as he tried to back away from the swirling wind.

It was gone in an instant, but by then Socks was caving off the raw rim of the well, raining dirt and pebbles down the hole. Upset all the more, he kept snorting and shuffling until his hind legs slipped and he rolled onto his back and into the shaft.

He couldn't fall far—he wedged tight against the sides no more than six or eight feet down, all the while thrashing and screaming. He skidded another few feet and settled there.

"Dad?" I squawked with what little voice I could find. Socks blocked the echo I was used to hearing in the hole, and I thought maybe he blocked my voice as well. Beyond the horse there was nothing to see but darkness. The falling dirt must have broken Dad's coal oil lantern or knocked it into the slop.

"Dad?" again, louder this time.

I didn't even realize I'd been holding my breath until

it rushed out with relief when I heard Dad's reply.

"Honey?" he yelled. "What happened up there?"

"Socks fell in the well!"

"I see that. Think you can help him out?"

Our yelling upset the horse again, and his scratching and thrashing sent another rain of dirt and stones rattling down on Dad.

"I don't think so," I said. "He's too far down. And he's upside down."

"Damn!" I heard Dad say—the first foul word I'd ever heard out of his mouth, the hearing of which shocked me almost as much as the mess we were in.

"We'd best be quiet so's not to spook him any worse than he is," he said. "Check the rope, see that it's tied off tight."

I hustled over to the stake and took another double half hitch around it just to make sure.

"Is it all right?"

"I think so."

"Now, son, you just sit tight." I heard him working the shovel as he chinked a ledge in the shaft where he set the bucket to get it out of the way. "What I'm going to do is try to climb out of here. Think there's room for me to squeeze past ol' Socks if I can get up there?"

"Maybe," I said. "I don't think so."

The horse took another fit and in the squirming and straining slipped another foot or two. The block lashed to the tripod started to sway and rattle, the rope jerking rhythmically as Dad pulled himself steadily upward. Dirt and rocks splashing in the bottom said he was using his feet to help claw his way out of the well.

The rope stopped jerking from time to time as he wedged himself against the sides to rest. Soon, the pulse of his grasping hands would travel up the rope again and before long I could hear his breathing, and the strain in it.

Then the horse must have sensed Dad's presence beneath him, and not known what to make of it. In a renewed bout of heaving and clawing, twisting and straining, ol' Socks came loose of a sudden and slid

142

down the well scraping rocks, dirt, and Dad off the sides and taking it all down with him. They bottomed out with a thick splash and heavy thud that reverberated all the way to the surface. A few more pebbles and dirt clods trickled down, falling into silence along with the fading echo.

I wasn't there to hear the quiet.

After crossing the pasture at a dead run, I stumbled to a stop, the rails of the round corral the only thing keeping me from tumbling all the way down.

Delgado had seen me coming and waited quietly across the fence atop one of the colts, which shied and scrambled backward when I hit the fence. When the colt stopped, Delgado flexed his hips and kissed his lips to urge it forward, finally touching it with the spurs. A soft haul on the hackamore reins stopped the colt's sudden lunge and Delgado settled down into the saddle as I struggled for breath.

"It's, it's Daddy," I said. "He's down. The well. Socks fell in. On top. Of him."

The corral gate was already swinging open. Delgado had dismounted in an instant as soon as he and the colt were on my side of the fence. Without a word, he grabbed me by the waist and swung me aboard the skittish colt.

"You hurry. Tell Evan to bring the team and his men to the well. They are unloading. Tell him to bring the derrick cable. Hurry. I will go to your father."

That horse was only half under my control, if that, on the run to the hay yard. Once or twice he kicked up his heels and tried to bog his head, but by sawing on the reins I was able to prevent a come-apart or complete runaway.

He didn't want to stop when we tore out of the hay meadow and into the stackyard. I cranked his head to one side until it was practically in my lap and he finally came around in a circle and stopped as Uncle Evan and the three workers looked on.

Before the story was half told, Uncle Evan had scrambled down off the stack of loose hay, chopped the derrick cable in two with a hay knife and was pulling it screaming through the pulleys on the derrick. The hay hands lit into the load like windmills, forking it off every side of the wagon. They kept at it even as Uncle Evan heaved heavy coils of derrick cable over the rack on the front of the wagon then climbed up, hooked a leg over and whipped up the team with the lines.

As the haywagon clattered and bounced out of the stackyard, I tapped my heels to the colt's sides and hoped he'd do something other than go to pitching. He snorted some and flung his head around, but another soft kick in the belly convinced him to line out and walk. Once he settled in, I urged him into a long trot and figured to let it go at that.

Delgado was just clearing the lip of the well when I rode up. Any hope I had for Dad washed away in the tears streaming down his muddy face.

He'd stopped only long enough to grab a lantern from the milking stall and an ax and shovel from the tool shed. By the time Uncle Evan had arrived, Delgado was already at the bottom of the well, having slid down the rope with the lit lantern in his teeth. But all he could find to do was pull the bucket out of the mess, tie it to the rope, and ask Evan to haul him up—which he did, by hand, with help from the three men on his hay crew.

The cowboy stepped out of the bucket as it reached the surface and plopped down on my box.

"I cannot find him," he said as he absent-mindedly scratched with a fingernail at the mud that covered his chaps, then unbuckled and peeled them off. "The hole is full of nothing but broken horse and mud. I felt around as much as I could. Nothing." He unbuttoned and pulled of his vest then tugged his shirt over his head.

Delgado unsheathed his knife and went to whittling on the ax handle. It seemed a poor choice of activities in the circumstances. I said "What—"

"There is no room to work the ax in the hole," he said, cutting off my question. Although his voice was quiet, anger, frustration maybe, was as evident as if he had shouted. "It is too tight."

Still unsure what he was doing, I thought it best to keep my peace.

Snapping off the handle, he shaved the raw edge to smooth the splinters as best he could. To Uncle Evan, he said, "I guess we won't be needing that cable. There is no way we'll lift that horse out of there without caving in the sides. He will have to come up in the bucket. Lower me down, then get your team ready. It will be too much lifting to do by hand."

Evan and at least one of his hay hands were years older than Delgado. It didn't occur to me at the time, but I have since wondered why it was the younger man giving orders in that tense situation, and why the others complied without question or comment.

It did not dawn on me, either, what Delgado was doing down there until the first bucket came up. Blood sloshed over the sides as Uncle Evan swung it away from the well. The horse's head hung over the rim, muzzle stained scarlet and nostrils dripping gore.

I hit my knees as that red mess splashed to the ground and I heaved up what was left of breakfast and kept heaving until there was nothing left to come up and then I heaved some more. And even after that, the sound of Delgado and his ax at work down the well would set me to gagging all over again.

One front quarter, then another, came out of the hole in poorly butchered pieces. Then Delgado came up. Blood-spattered and gasping, he sat flat to the ground and sucked in air.

"Anything?" Evan asked.

"No. Nothing."

Uncle Evan asked no more questions, simply stared vacantly at the hired man on the ground.

"You're spent. I'll go down," he finally said.

"No. There is no room. I can hardly get any leverage myself, and I am smaller than you. I will finish the job."

He said the lantern kept flickering out from lack of air, so he gave up trying to keep it burning and did his awful work in the dark. Worst of all, worse than the dark, worse than the heat, worse than the mud, he told us, was the stink. Even in the open air the stench of blood and torn flesh was overpowering when the wind swirled it your direction. It got worse when broken entrails and smashed organs topped the pile.

Finally, the second hind leg, broken at an odd angle, plopped out of the bucket and onto the pile dripping mud and blood and that was the end of ol' Socks.

Standing with hands grasping spread knees, Uncle Evan bent over the lip of the well awaiting word from Delgado. From time to time he would hear him sloshing around down there, or the occasional splash.

Finally, "I have found a hand."

Later, "I have freed as much of him as I can, but he is stuck fast. You will have to send down the cable."

From the hay wagon, Uncle Evan fetched a steel pulley and short length of chain and hooked it to the tripod next to the wooden block through which the well rope was threaded. As he tested the strength of his work, his men stretched the kinks out of the cable. He threaded it through the pulley, quickly clamped a clevis to the end, and shoved the wire rope down the shaft an arm's length at a time.

It seemed an eternity until Delgado asked to be lifted up in the bucket. He stepped out, cut the well rope from the bail, then pulled the end through the block and tossed it out of the way so it would not tangle with the cable.

"I don't know. He is stuck pretty tight. I got a loop around him but I don't know," he told Evan as they watched the hands hitch the cable to the doubletree harnessed to the team. "I never could feel his feet. Too deep."

As the slack slowly came out of the cable he said, "I hope he doesn't come up like that horse."

Uncle Evan took over the team, and with his easy hands at the lines they leaned slowly into the load.

Nothing.

He urged the horses on—tugs creaked, singletrees cracked. The cable hummed, the pulley trembled. The heavy cedar posts in the tripod groaned and their thick bottoms pushed up ridges in the dirt as they tried to spread wider, threatening collapse.

The team grunted and strained and leaned harder into their collars as Uncle Evan, in desperation, slapped one horse then the other on the rump with the lines. Slowly, almost imperceptibly, they moved ahead. Half the length of a hoof. Another. And then, with a release felt deep in the belly of every one of us, the team was walking free.

The pulley from the hay derrick squealed as it slowly rotated. Uncle Evan handed the lines to another of the men as the team's distance from the hole increased and he quickly followed the cable back to the well to stand beside me and Delgado.

Dad came up belt buckle first. Uncle Evan collapsed in a heap when he saw his broken brother, bent double, backwards, swinging slowly from the derrick cable.

I stared, uncomprehending. I guess my day's ration of distress was long since used up, to be replaced by shock and resignation.

Like I had done so many times, Delgado swung the load away from the hole as the team backed slack into the cable and settled it to solid ground. He pulled the pin out of the clevis and cast it aside and carefully, gently, gathered Dad's limp body in his arms and carried him to the hay wagon. Then he turned for the house and walked away.

* * *

Delgado did not die that day.

At least not like Dad was dead.

But the spirit was gone out of him as surely as if it had been his body we pulled out of that temporary grave at the bottom of the well.

In a way, I guess it was.

He didn't stop at the bunkhouse any longer than it took to stuff his few belongings into his war bag. I don't know what he wore on his feet when he left our place. His soggy high-topped boots with the blood-and-mud-encrusted Mexican spurs still strapped to them were left standing outside the door, abandoned to the well as surely as Dad's were; his sucked off in the muck in the bottom of that hole where, I suppose, they still are.

So far as I know, ol' Socks was the last horse Delgado ever touched.

For years, he stayed around these parts setting his hand to a variety of jobs—sacking wheat at the feed and seed, clerking at a grocery store, tending bar, that sort of thing. Last I heard, he was somewhere off in Wyoming pushing folks around in wheelchairs in a convalescent hospital.

I led that green-broke colt he'd mounted me on that day back to the yard and pulled off Delgado's silver-mounted saddle and hauled it inside the tack shed. It has been there ever since, hanging from a rafter on a rawhide tether.

AUTHOR'S NOTE: Although the people and particulars in "The Death of Delgado" are imagined, the incident at the center of the story is real, as told in "The Land is Free," a September/October 1961 *True West* magazine article by Colen Sweeten as told to Colen Sweeten, Jr. My thanks and appreciation go to Colen Sweeten III for the use of the story, and to his father and grandfather for telling it.

Whiskey for Breakfast

by Jerry Guin

Jerry Guin is a member of Western Writers of America and Western Fictioneers. He authored a nature guidebook and has written many western short stories for various magazines and anthologies. His book Trail Dust *is a collection of twelve of his short stories. He lives in the rural northern California community of Salyer with his wife Ginny.*

Henry Wooster was awakened by blinding bright sunlight. He lay on his back next to a dead campfire. A raised hand, to his hatless head, produced a wince, to the touch, of an open wound and a knot on the back of his head. He had a booming headache and a pasty mouth, the product of last night's happenings. Henry heaved himself to a sitting position. A whiskey bottle, half empty, lay nearby. He reached for the bottle, uncorked it and took a swig. Slowly, his senses began to return and he became aware of the desert. He took another swallow of the whiskey then pushed the cork back into the bottle. With effort, he rolled over onto his hands and knees then stood on shaky legs. He stared miserably around looking for anything familiar. He was alone in a world of silent, almost barren, emptiness. He wanted coffee, but there was none to be had. They had taken everything, his horse, guns, provisions, even his hat, then had left him to his fate in the unchanging desert. Why had they left the whiskey, he wondered? "Punishment," he mused silently. "If you drink alcohol instead of water, the thirst will only increase." He looked at the bottle and almost tossed it away then thought better of it, he might need the bottle later for water.

Henry Wooster had come to this country looking for a new start. On the back side of fifty he was just shy of six feet tall, rangy and mustachioed. He had spent forty years working at whatever came to hand. Freight wagon driver, guard on a stage, two years as a deputy sheriff and a variety of other low paying jobs. Most of his working life was busied doing ranch work and trailing cattle to markets. There was a time when forty dollars a month seemed like fair pay. That had all changed now. Settlements, fenced land and railroad advancement had all but ended trailing herds to the northern railheads in Kansas and Missouri.

Henry knew that he needed to make a change. To find something to do in these last few years so that he could ease into retirement. He drew his time, spent half of it for a roan that he favored and pointed the horse west. He had ridden for days, taking his time, looking over familiar country and some that he had not seen before. Eventually he came to the little town of Wago, strung out on a flat spot near the San Pedro River in the Arizona desert.

Brad Wago owned most of the town which consisted of a hotel, three saloons, a livery, a freight company and several smaller businesses. All were dedicated to supplying the needs of the work force of a huge mine, just north of town, also owned by Brad Wago.

Henry spent the morning looking for work out at the mine. A look at the workforce of miners showed young men wearing scarred work boots, scruffy pants, and sweat stained shirts. The foreman said, "There's always a need for another pick ax." Henry knew, though, that physically he would not be able to stand up to the rigors of the twelve hour plus shifts of hard labor day after day. He thanked the man and left.

That afternoon he returned to Wiley's Saloon. Ben Horn, a burly saloon keeper at Wiley's, perhaps impressed with Henry's demeanor, mentioned that Brad

Wago was on the hunt for someone to be the town marshal. The job paid one hundred dollars a month, meals at Maggie's Café, and a shanty on the edge of town to call home.

Henry took the job. A good deal of his official time was spent in the evenings, breaking up fights among drunken mine workers. Most scuffles were brought on by gambling or the disaffections of wild-eyed women in the dim saloon lamps, of a night. Henry would haul the participants off to a cramped jail to sleep it off, then let them go the next morning.

Once a month, a payroll of twelve to fifteen thousand dollars was taken from the freight office in Wago to the mine site. The reason that Brad Wago had hired Henry on the spot was because Henry had experience as a guard on a stage and as a deputy sheriff.

"I need a man of experience to see that the payroll gets to the mine," Brad Wago had said. "The payroll comes in under heavy guard, but it becomes my responsibility once it is delivered to the freight company office. Until now, two men escorted the money out to the mine site, but I question their abilities."

Six months passed since then and all the payroll shipments had been delivered on time, all seemed well. Then, on a clear Friday morning, the tranquility of Wago was abruptly shattered when a single gunshot rang out. Henry had been up late the night before, quieting the usual nightly rowdiness. He had gotten up late and was still at his sleeping quarters, getting ready to go to breakfast at Maggie's, when he heard the shot.

Two men scrambled aboard their horses and kicked them into a run out of town. The freight office had been robbed of the payroll. The clerk, Wilbur Jakes, had been shot through the shoulder when he had tried to hoist a shotgun over the counter. Before others could respond, the robbers were gone. "It was the Munto brothers, Joaquin and Quinta," Jakes said while being cared for.

The Munto brothers were young rowdies, twenty-five and twenty-three, Joaquin being the oldest. Neither were large men, both being about five foot eight inches tall and light of weight but Joaquin, in particular, had a mean streak when drinking. He would confront normally mild-mannered miners, daring them to draw against his show of the fast draw. So far, no one had drunk enough courage to take the mouthy young man up on it.

Henry called for a posse to go after the bandits. Five men -- Randy Grimm, Jeff Ball, Willard Hayes, Bill Manner and Ben Horn -- responded. The bandits had a twenty minute head start before Henry and the posse were saddled and able to ride after them.

About thirty miles from town, the posse came upon two abandoned, thirsty horses and two empty canteens. Henry dismounted and pulled the saddle from his own sweaty mount. "We need to rest these animals," he advised.

"They'll get away!" Randy declared.

"They've got fresh horses. We don't!" Henry said.

"How long we gotta wait?" Ben asked.

"Until our horses are rested," Henry stated. "We'll see in a couple hours."

"They knew we'd be hot on their trail so they brought fresh horses out here," Willard said disgustedly. "Do you suppose that they stashed some more up ahead?" No one answered for all figured that the prospect was possible.

"You got any idea where they might be going, Marshal?" Jeff asked.

Henry thought it strange that back in town, everyone called him by name but now he was suddenly referred to by an official title.

He thought for a moment then said, "Whenever the Munto brothers come to town, on no set schedule, it's usually to get drunk and raise hell with the miners over the women at the saloons. They've never gone so far as to get arrested and they always seem to have money. Usually by the light of day they disappear for a while, sometimes for weeks at a time. This trail they have left is headed purposefully into the desert. They know we will follow but most likely have hopes that we'll give up and go away. Who knows what is on their minds. They won't be going back to Wago, that's for sure."

The posse began weaving their horses through draws and over rolling hillocks while mesquite scraped at their legs. When they trailed across the floor of the desert, dust lifted from the hooves of their horses, creating a choking dust cloud that covered horses and riders alike with a fine coating. Bandanas were pulled over noses but the pursuit was brought to a snail's pace. Henry pulled rein to a halt. He dismounted then took his bandana and wetted it from his canteen. Stepping forward, he held the bridle to his roan in one hand and used the other to swab out the animal's nostrils. "They'll breathe better after all that dust," he said. Soon others were swabbing their animals' nostrils as well as their own.

It was early in the afternoon when the grumbling began. Henry could hear the banter behind him among the posse members. "We're going on a wild goose chase! They've got fresh horses and water! We ain't never gonna catch up to them!" Henry appeared to ignore the complaints as he rode ahead silently, but he knew the gripes would intensify as the day wore on. When the sun hung on the distant horizon of purpled mountains then dipped out of sight, Henry called a halt. "We'll camp here." He had selected a dry creek bed that offered a little protection from wind and there was a generous amount of dead sagebrush nearby to use for a fire.

They unsaddled and ground staked the horses then made a small fire and coffee. Everyone was silent while eating their meager meal of hardtack and jerked beef.

When full darkness enveloped the campsite, a chill came into the thin air. Men turned up collars and stood near the fire. Jeff and Willard set to throwing more and more dead sagebrush on the fire only to have the flames flare up briefly and then die down again. They found a few sticks of anciently grayed mesquite that held the fire to a steady glow. The camp grew silent and everyone began to lie down and cover themselves with their coats and saddle blankets.

The posse lasted but another day, spent following tracks that had only led deeper into dry desolation. Grumbling had continued throughout the day but glum silence was the norm by nightfall. "This is a waste of time!" someone remarked before curling up for attempted sleep.

In the early morning, after they had all awakened from another chilled night on the desert, Randy and Jeff both approached to stand in front of Henry. "I'm heading back," Randy said while Jeff nodded that it was his intention also. "I like to froze last night. I didn't get a lick of sleep."

Willard's red-rimmed eyes showed the effect as did Ben Horn's. One mumbled, "Me neither," the other merely nodded.

Bill confirmed what the others were thinking. "I've got to get back to the business. We gave it a good try." He looked to the others for support but other than head nods in agreement they remained silent. He then turned to Henry and said, "It isn't like anybody got killed or anything. This is a job for the law. I've been happy to help out but I've done all I can. Brad will understand. I'm pulling out." The five men began saddling their horses.

Henry knew that no amount of talking would persuade any of the men to continue the pursuit. He did not blame them or feel any ill will toward any one of them. Bill was right when he said it was a job for the law. Henry was the one that wore the badge. He was angry with himself. It was his job to guard that payroll. He had gotten into a known routine, lax enough to allow the robbery to happen. His credibility was at stake. He could not draw another dollar of pay, even if Brad Wago saw fit to pay it, which he most likely wouldn't, unless the perpetrators were brought to justice. He would stay after the outlaws. Either he would hunt them down or he would die in this desert.

Ben stood nearby tightening his saddle cinch. "What little water we got left is warm and brackish. They got everything in their favor, horses, water, food and a good head start," Ben said. "They're just leading us around in circles until our horses give out!"

"You'd be smart to come with us, Marshal," Willard said, then mounted his horse.

"Nobody blames you, marshal, you done what you could," he soothed.

Henry watched as all five men turned their horses and one by one filed away.

Henry followed the bandits' tracks until nightfall then made a camp purposely behind a little knoll to shield any wind that came up in the night. He was tired and grimy, concerned that his horse needed more water but he could do nothing about finding some until daylight. He poured a little water for the horse into his hat. He made a small fire for coffee then chewed a little jerky before lying down for the night. Henry had always figured he slept light enough that he could detect any movement or sound that came near. He stayed awake until the moon was high in the Eastern sky then began to doze. When sleep took him, he must have been overly tired for he heard nothing and slept soundly.

Henry was awakened by a rough kick to his boot! He grabbed for his holstered pistol, but it was not there! He sat bolt upright. Above him stood a grinning Joaquin Munto. In his right hand he held Henry's own six-gun. He pointed it menacingly at Henry. "You sleep good, Marshal!" He laughed. Henry did not move, but he was aware that Quinta was behind him.

Joaquin was without scruples. He was cold and callous and had always been that way.

Quinta, the younger brother, was merely a pawn used and bullied by his brother his entire life. He would do whatever Joaquin told him to do. If there was any talking to do, Joaquin would do it. Quinta would maintain his usual silence.

"Why do you keep following us?" Joaquin asked in an ill-tempered way. "The others, they wisely gave up and went home."

"I came to arrest you," Henry said lowly.

"Ha, ha!" Joaquin smirked. "You are but a tired old

man with little food and water and a worn-out horse! What can you do?" He glanced behind Henry at Quinta then pushed Henry's six-gun into his waistband. "Do not try anything foolish, Marshal, Quinta is very good with his pistol." Joaquin reached down to pick up a bottle of whiskey that he had brought with him. He took a swig then tossed the bottle to Henry. "Have a drink with us, Marshal. We like to be friendly!"

Henry uncorked the bottle and took a drink.

Joaquin squatted in front of Henry. "You say you came to arrest us. We intend no harm. We needed some money and we found a way to have it. The clerk would not have been hurt but he drew a weapon on us. Brad Wago is a very rich man. He can afford to cover the loss. But you," he hesitated a moment then said, "you endanger your life by chasing after us."

"You broke the law!" Henry said sternly. "Stealing money and shooting a man is not to be taken lightly. If I don't bring you in, others will follow. They know who you are."

"If they know who we are, then they will not attempt to be as foolish as you. They will soon see, as others have, that we cannot be found."

"Does that mean that you are wanted, elsewhere?" Henry asked.

"Others have pursued us and failed," Joaquin quipped.

"I won't fail!" Henry said.

"We are tired of you dogging us!" Joaquin exclaimed loudly then quickly stood up. "We are ready to leave the desert, the game is over, but you, Mr. Marshal, you may stay!"

That was the last thing Henry remembered. Quinta had slugged him from behind, presumably with the butt of a six-gun.

* * *

So here he was, in the middle of nowhere, with neither a horse nor any sort of comforts. For some reason he thought of when he was a child and the words of his mother whenever he was hurt or ailing. "You just got to keep going." Determination gripped his mind. He wasn't about to give up now. Getting started took effort but he began to walk taking one shaky step at a time. The horse tracks were pointed straight away toward the blueish mountains in the distance. That part was good, he figured, to go in a straight line that is. A man is just as likely to strike water going in a straight line as going in a circle. There were fifty miles of desert behind him. He couldn't go back that way without water, he would surely die. He began to follow the tracks. Ahead in the mountains, maybe there was a spring. He had heard of water being pooled in rock crevices, unable to run off. Perhaps he could find a pocket of such.

Already the sun was beginning to heat the parched land. It was midmorning. It did not take long to understand that the boots he wore were not made for hiking. His feet rubbed inside the boots, creating friction and heat. By noon he could feel his feet swelling and he began to limp. He would need to stop and rest to conserve what energy he had and keep from sweating as much as possible. The conservation of body fluids was very much on his mind. Fortunately he observed an outcropping of rocks that would give enough shade to cover his head and shoulders. He crawled into the little shade to rest. He dozed fitfully during the hot afternoon, occasionally looking out to watch as the heat waves danced on the desert floor in an endless panorama.

Once sunset occurred the temperature began to drop and the nightly chill could be felt.

Henry knew that he could only travel in the cool of the evening and early mornings. He looked again at the distant mountains and estimated them to be twelve to fifteen miles away.

He felt lousy and his mouth was cottony and his tongue seemed to have grown in size. He uncorked the whiskey bottle and took a sip. He winced when the fire-like liquid touched his dried and cracked lips making him grit his teeth and grimace. He wasn't sure that taking the whiskey was better than not having anything, but at least it was wet.

He stood and tried to begin to walk. He found that he could hobble as his feet were swollen. At least he could move, and he was grateful for that. At his slowed pace, he figured it would take at least six to eight hours to reach the base of the mountains. There was no guarantee that he would find water, but he had no choice. At least there was a chance. He guarded against using up too much energy, knowing that a man will get a sudden burst of energy just before collapse.

It was past midnight and early in the moonlit morning when Henry smelled wood smoke. He strained to look in all directions then spotted a tiny glow of a campfire in the distance. If it were Joaquin and Quinta, he would be in grave danger should they spot him. He inched his way toward the glow, careful to circle downwind so as not to spook any horses by his scent. As he got closer, he could see two horses there, one being his own.

He approached cautiously and picked up a rock to use in defense, if need be. There was one prone figure lying near the fire but no sign of the other. Wary of ambush, Henry held the rock high and edged closer. It was Quinta laying face up and asleep. It was a fitful sleep, for the man moaned and moved his head from side to side as one does that is in severe pain.

A holstered six-gun lay near Quinta's right side, a whiskey bottle on the left side. Henry crept close and removed the pistol from the holster. Quinta remained asleep. A canteen was within arm's length. Henry lifted it up and took a small drink, taking care not to swallow too much at once. It had been more than thirty hours since he had any water and he knew if he drank too much too soon, he would become ill.

While keeping an eye on Quinta he rinsed his mouth then took another swallow. He moved a few feet away facing the still man. He put the gun in his waistband then took his bandana, wetted it and swabbed his face then winced again when he touched the wound on his head. It was apparent that Quinta was injured in some way and oblivious to his presence. He took another drink of water and moved closer to the glowing little fire. He helped himself to a coffee pot and a covered pan of beans and bread. Feeling revived, Henry scouted the camp, finding his own hat and six-gun. He strapped the six-gun on. He found his Winchester and Quinta's and moved them out of reach of the young man.

It was daylight before he tried to roust Quinta. He tried the customary boot kick to boot but got only a moan from the prone man. Henry wetted a bandana and swabbed the youth's face.

Quinta blinked awake. Henry poured water into a cup and held Quinta's head, allowing the young man to take a few sips. "What has happened here, Quinta?"

Quinta rolled his eyes then closed them. "My horse stepped in a hole," he said in faltered speech. "She fell on me," he said then grimaced and grunted in pain. A spittle of blood seeped from his mouth.

Henry removed the blanket covering Quinta and looked him over. "You're busted up inside. I won't ask you too much. I can see you're in no condition to do anything but rest."

Quinta nodded his head and seemed to go to sleep. Henry reached out to shake Quinta's shoulder lightly. Quinta's eyes fluttered open.

"Where's Joaquin?" Henry asked.

Quinta said in a strained voice, "He went for help. A travois." Then his eyes closed again and he lay still.

Henry was dog tired, but he knew it was no time for sleep. Joaquin had the right idea. Quinta was not able to sit astride a horse and would need to be hauled out of here. A travois would be the only way, since there were no wagons available. He needed poles for such so he went to the mountains to find some.

Henry thought about just waiting until Joaquin returned and then confronting him. That is, until he began to look the horses and camp over and determined that Joaquin had taken not only the money but whatever supplies they had as well. There was no food or water to be found except what was in the camp pots and Quinta's only canteen. Could it be that Joaquin, for love of money and convenience sake, had left his own brother here in the desert to a miserable fate? To die alone!

Henry saddled his horse, put a little water in his hat and put it under the animal's nose.

"Just enough to wake you up," he said. "We still have to find some water, somewhere."

He looked over to Quinta and wondered what he could do to give the unfortunate man some ease. He didn't want to leave the stricken youth in this condition but would have to, at some point, in order to find water. He walked over with the intent of giving Quinta a little water.

Henry was suddenly startled to see Quinta's eyes were wide open but sightless! Quinta had died!

There was no shovel so the best Henry could do was to move the body to an indented spot that run-off water had wallowed out. He placed Quinta into the spot, spread his blanket over him, then piled rocks over to discourage the scavengers.

Henry picked up what was left of the camp, saddled Quinta's horse then mounted his own.

He had two thirsty horses and only a half canteen of water. He nudged a heel to the roan and began following Joaquin's tracks straight away west toward the mountains.

Henry was in no shape to be walking but that is what he did, occasionally, to preserve the distressed horses. It was late afternoon when he topped a small knoll and looked into the distance. He was in the foothills. When he looked to the bottom of an arroyo his eyes were drawn to some greenery. He mounted up and headed the horses for that spot. There was a seepage of water there giving life to some plants. He jumped off the horse and began clawing at the dirt until he hollowed out a hat-sized hole that immediately began to fill with water. Using a knife he dug deeper and wider until the hole was about two feet square. The horses were fighting to drink the muddy water as fast as it filled the hole. He had to force the horses away and ground stake them to allow the hole to fill up and settle before taking each one individually to drink.

With water being there, it was the best campsite he had on the entire trip. He made a fire then led the horses again to the water hole to revive themselves. There was a little coffee and bread left from Quinta's camp. Afterward he stretched on the ground and was asleep almost instantly.

Henry awoke before first light and rekindled the fire. He got some water from the little reservoir for the coffee pot. The old grounds were still in the pot. After it boiled, he held a cup of the weakened brew then fished out the whiskey bottle that he had packed across the desert. The coffee spiked with a little whiskey made a fairly tolerable drink to get the day started.

He lay on the ground next to the water hole and drank his fill then filled the canteen. He watered the horses until they quit.

Henry doubled back to find Joaquin's horse tracks again, for he had not come this way. He wondered if the bandit had found water or had carried a great deal with him. He soon found that the tracks led to a water hole that Joaquin had dug out, most likely being of the same drainage that he had come upon. There was no evidence of a camp being made there.

After awhile Henry came to a spot clearly showing by the tracks that Joaquin had stopped here for a time, perhaps for a meal, then the tracks veered to the left, heading South. Henry surmised that perhaps Joaquin had intentions of getting some poles for a travois then changed his mind at this location. The tracks showed that he had left abruptly, likely spurring his mount to a run, for the tracks were much wider spaced.

Could be that he fought with himself as to whether to proceed and try to save his brother or forget it and go to Mexico. Was he angry with himself for thinking of an easy way out, and was thinking of himself only? But yet, he could not stop being the person he was. He took his anger out on the horse and forced it to a run. If this was true, Henry surmised, Joaquin had made a despicable decision that would haunt him for the rest of his days.

It was near nightfall when Henry spotted the campfire smoke at more than two miles distance. Henry rode as far as he dared without being spotted then halted the horses and waited until darkness covered all. He staked the horses then took a Winchester and jacked a shell into the chamber. On foot he crept to a point where he could make out the fire with Joaquin seated before it. Joaquin's horse was lying down with the saddle still on it.

Henry maneuvered stealthily to come in behind the seated man. He had never been a quick draw man, but could hit whatever he shot at with either rifle or pistol. He raised the rifle to shoulder height. When he was within thirty feet, he called out, "Don't move, Joaquin. I've got you covered!"

Joaquin did not move. Instead he answered, "Is this the marshal? I wondered when you would be along. I left you some whiskey so you could stay alive. Maybe you can return the favor now and let me go. I will give you half of the money!"

"Too thin, Joaquin, I'm taking all the money and you back to stand trial. Now get your hands up!"

For a moment Henry thought that Joaquin was going to comply for he did raise his left hand above his head. "Now the other one!" Henry commanded.

"Sure, sure, Marshal, just a moment, I am holding a coffee cup." Suddenly Joaquin sprang forward, rolling over the campfire and grabbing at his holstered six-gun at the same time.

It wasn't enough that Henry had him in the rifle sights. He did not want to shoot Joaquin. There was no time to try for a shot that would merely disarm the bandit. With no choice, he pulled the trigger. He saw dust puff from Joaquin's shirt where the bullet hit him below the breastbone. Joaquin attempted to bring his pistol around but it slipped from his hand as he fell over.

Henry walked up close and kicked the pistol away. Joaquin was conscious and a slobber of spittle and blood leaked from his mouth. He spat. "You won, Marshal!"

"I warned you!" Henry declared.

Joaquin coughed. "Did you find Quinta?"

"Yes, I did, Joaquin. He's dead, but not by my hand. He died this morning in his sleep."

"I knew he would not make it!" Joaquin managed.

"So you knew he wouldn't survive, yet you rode away without staying to give Quinta comfort in his last moments," Henry said.

Joaquin turned his head away without answering.

"Why didn't you take the saddle off of that horse?" Henry demanded.

"He became lame like Quinta," Joaquin said, pausing with a halting breath, "of no further use!"

"You left your own brother to die in the desert and then rode that horse to death! What kind of man are you?" Henry asked.

Joaquin did not answer, instead he attempted a grin. "The money is all yours now, Marshal, think of it!" He gasped. Henry kneeled to check Joaquin's wound. Joaquin rolled his head to one side then said, "Can I have a drink of whiskey now?" Henry nodded and went over near the fire and picked up the bottle Joaquin had been nursing. He knelt beside Joaquin and elevated his head so that he could take a drink. Joaquin opened his mouth to take the whiskey then stiffened. His breath could audibly be heard escaping his lungs as he died.

Henry went over to the downed horse and unsaddled it. The animal was in bad shape, abused beyond recovery. Henry hated to see the animal suffer so. Regretfully, he drew his six-gun and placed the muzzle close to the animal's head. A single shot ended the poor beast's misery. A lousy end, Henry figured, but at least his master had paid a like price.

He walked back and got the two horses and brought them to the camp. Along with the money he found plenty of provisions that Joaquin had been carrying. He made a meal and was going to attempt sleep, but he was too restless. He got up and gave Joaquin as good a burial as he had given Quinta. After some coffee and whiskey he was able to sleep.

At first light he stirred up the fire, made coffee and some fried bread. He found four canteens. Two were full. He gave each of the horses a little and broke camp.

He mounted and set there for a long moment. He had the fifteen thousand dollars of stolen money and both bandits were dead. Justice had been served. Still, Joaquin's words haunted him, "The money is all yours now, Marshal, think of it!"

He did think of it. Who would know if he just took off with it? Fifteen thousand would buy a nice little ranch back in Texas. He had never been to Mexico, but he could go down there himself and live his days in ease. Those back in Wago would most likely figure that he had succumbed in the desert while chasing the bandits. They would have a memory of him doing the job that he had taken. What would he gain by going back there? It would be seventy miles of gut busting traveling to re-cross that desert. The horses and he were in poor shape. Brad Wago would be grateful, but then Brad Wago would have expectations of him doing just that.

He recalled when he was twelve. He had fallen and broken the stock on a shotgun that he had borrowed from a neighbor. He soon learned that the repair would cost most of what he had earned the entire summer. His mother's words echoed, "It may be a hard thing to do, at times, but you can never go wrong by doing what your inner self tells you is right."

He took a last look at Joaquin's grave, a bleak reminder of what kind of man he had been. Henry would have a lot of time to think things out, but for now he needed to get the horses some more water. With no further thought he touched a heel to the roan's flank.

Rattler

by James Reasoner

A lifelong Texan, James Reasoner has been a professional writer for more than thirty years. In that time, he has authored several hundred novels and short stories in numerous genres. Best known for his Westerns, historical novels, and war novels, he is also the author of two mystery novels that have achieved cult classic status, Texas Wind *and* Dust Devils. *Writing under his own name and various pseudonyms, his novels have garnered praise from Publishers Weekly, Booklist, and the Los Angeles Times, as well as appearing on the New York Times and USA Today bestseller lists. He lives in a small town in Texas with his wife, award-winning fellow author Livia J. Washburn.*

Cobb had been holed up in the rocks for about an hour when the big diamondback rattler crawled over the back of his legs.

He felt it through his jeans and craned his neck to look over his shoulder. When he saw the fat, sinuous form slithering across his legs, his first instinct was to yell and fling himself up from the ground as hard as he could.

Luckily for him, he managed to suppress the impulse. If he hadn't, he might've gotten killed twice. Once by the snake sinking its fangs in him, and once by that human snake, Franklin Harmon, drilling him through the head with a .44-40 slug.

Harmon was about fifty yards away in a little dip in

the Texas prairie that was just large enough to shelter him. He couldn't go anywhere without Cobb dropping him. But Cobb, who had gone to ground in the rocks while trading shots with the outlaw, was pinned down, too.

The difference was that Harmon didn't have a big ol' rattlesnake sharing his shelter.

Cobb gritted his teeth. The snake's head had cleared his legs, but most of its body still lay across them. He felt the solid weight of it.

He had known the rocks looked snaky when he jumped into them, but he hadn't had much choice. Harmon was just too damned good with a rifle. He had already shot Cobb's horse out from under him.

Of course, Cobb had already shot Harmon's horse, so that score was even.

Cobb had been chasing Harmon around the Cross Timbers and the Palo Pinto Hills for three days now. He'd been sent out from the Ranger post at Veal Station when they got word that Harmon had robbed yet another bank, this one in Mineral Wells. Cobb was a big, ugly, rough man who didn't have much in his life other than chasing lawbreakers, but that was what he was good at. Once he was on an outlaw's trail, the miscreant seldom got away.

This time might be different, Cobb thought as he struggled to control the primitive part of him that reacted to the snake.

Finally . . . finally! . . . the rattler crawled off of him. But it didn't go very far, just a couple of feet, before it curled up in the shade of a rock like it intended to spend the rest of a lazy afternoon there.

The sun beat down fiercely. Cobb figured the temperature was probably over a hundred. He'd lost his hat when he took that tumble off his dying horse, so he didn't even have anything to shade his head.

He knew that he ought to keep quiet, but his frustration got the better of him anyway.

"Go home, you damn scaly bastard," he said.

The snake's tongue flicked out, tested the air. It lifted

its head a couple of inches. Dark, inhuman eyes seemed to fasten on him.

"This *is* my home," the snake said to Cobb.

Cobb's eyes widened in shock. His body stiffened even more than it already was.

"You're the one who bulled in here where you aren't wanted," the snake went on.

Well, this was it, thought Cobb. He'd gone completely loco. Years of chasing outlaws, guzzling rotgut whiskey, and consorting with soiled doves had addled his brain. Throw in the strain of being shot at by a cold-blooded killer and the heat frying his head, and he was hearing things.

"Don't just lay there," the snake said. "Vamoose."

Harmon's rifle cracked for the first time in several minutes, and a slug zinged overhead. He wasn't really trying to hit anything now, he was just keeping Cobb honest, the same way that Cobb took a potshot at him every now and then.

"I can't stand up," Cobb said. If he'd already lost his mind there was no point in worrying about it, so he figured he might as well answer the snake. "If I do that son of a bitch will drill me."

"That's not my problem," the snake said. "But I can tell you this: Franklin Harmon isn't going to kill you."

"Wait a minute. You know who Harmon is?"

"I know a lot of things, Cobb."

Cobb's memory went back to the brush arbor meetings his ma had dragged him to when he was a kid. He recalled the sin-shouters reading from the Book of Genesis about what happened in the Garden of Eden, and he said, "Are you . . . the Devil?"

"Just because I'm a serpent? Not all snakes are the Devil, you know. I'm sure he's capable of a lot of things, but do you know how many snakes there are in the world?"

"Well, then, who are you, damn it?"

"I'm the snake who lives in these rocks, and I'm not happy about having a man cluttering up the place."

Cobb still hadn't moved except to turn his head a little and look at the snake. He'd forgotten about shooting at Harmon.

"If you're not the Devil, how do you know Harmon's not gonna kill me? How can a damn snake tell the future?"

"How can a snake talk? And why is it always 'damn snake'? One serpent in one garden and after that it's always 'damn snake'." The wedge-shaped head lifted some more, and the rattle at the end of the thick body began to vibrate. "Here's what I know. Your name is Cobb. You're thirty-four years old. You've been a Texas Ranger for nine years. You've killed nine men . . . one for every year you've been a Ranger, but that's just a coincidence. You've been in love once, but she preferred another man. When you're not working, you drink too much and whore too much, and half the time you worry about who's going to take care of you when you're old and alone. The other half of the time you worry that you'll never get old because some outlaw will shoot you or stab you or you'll catch some terrible disease that will turn you into a drooling idiot before it finally ends your life. You don't think you'll ever have a wife, or children, or a real home. Am I right so far, Cobb?"

Cobb had started breathing harder. His chest heaved as he struggled to control what he was feeling. He burst out, "Why don't you shut your damned mouth, snake? I don't have to listen to this shit!"

"You asked," the snake said. "I'm just telling you what I know. And as for the future . . . maybe one of those things you worry about will come true. It could play out that way. But it won't unless you do something pretty soon, because Harmon thinks you're dead and he's sneaking up on you *right now!*"

Cobb jerked his head up and saw that it wasn't the middle of the afternoon anymore. Dusk was settling over the prairie. Hours had passed without him knowing it while he was talking to the snake. With no shots from the rocks in that amount of time, it was no wonder

Harmon thought he was dead. Cobb heaved himself up on his knees and saw Harmon standing arm's length away.

The buzzing of the snake's rattle got louder and louder until it seemed to fill the world, but even over that racket, Cobb heard the outlaw's startled yell. They were too close for rifles, but Harmon tried to use his anyway. Cobb dropped his Winchester and got his hands on the barrel of Harmon's rifle. It roared, so close that the report slammed against Cobb's ears and he felt the heat from the shot on his face. With a bellow of rage, he surged to his feet and twisted hard on the rifle. Harmon didn't let go of it, so he was slung off his feet. He tumbled to the ground among the rocks.

The rattler's thick body shot forward with blinding speed. Harmon screamed as the fangs sank deep in his throat. Even in that much pain and shock, instinct made him claw his revolver from its holster and try to lift it toward the Ranger.

Cobb drew a little faster. He thrust out the Colt and triggered a shot that sent a bullet exploding through Harmon's brain. Harmon wouldn't have a chance to die in agony from the snake bite. That was a shame, in a way.

Enough light remained in the sky for Cobb to see the rattler coiling again next to one of the rocks. He swung the gun toward it as it buzzed fiercely at him. His finger was taut on the trigger when he abruptly eased off the pressure.

"All right," he said. "All right. I reckon you've earned it. If you hadn't warned me, he would've come up and blasted the hell outta me." Cobb took a step back and shook his head as he realized what he had just said. He jabbed the revolver toward the snake and demanded, "Well? Are you gonna say anything or not?"

The snake just rattled at him.

Cobb snorted. "That's what I thought. Loco as a hydrophobia skunk. But I'm all right now."

He holstered his gun, reached down and grabbed the dead man's feet, and dragged Harmon away from the rocks. There was a little horse ranch about five miles from here, he recalled. It would be a long walk, especially in the dark, but he could get there, and when he did the rancher would loan him some horses or a wagon to come back here and fetch Harmon's corpse. Cobb's Ranger badge would see to that.

"Nobody's gonna disturb your home anymore," he called to the snake. "Just go on about your life . . . you damn snake."

He chuckled to himself as he turned and started walking. The red glow from the setting sun filled the western sky behind him. The air was still hot, but he caught a hint of a cool breeze stirring. Cobb took a deep breath. When he got back to Veal Station, he'd try not to drink so much. He'd make no promises about cavorting with the painted ladies, but at least he could cut back on the whiskey. Maybe. For a while.

Silence

by Ross Morton

Ross Morton has 4 westerns published by Robert Hale UK and his latest Old Guns *has just been accepted. As Nik Morton and other pen-names he is the author of eight more books and over 100 short stories in a variety of genres. He's been writing and editing for over thirty years. He's the Editor in Chief of Solstice Publishing, who also publishes Solstice Westerns.*

Joe watched the man as he entered his general store. The man's eyes narrowed, probably adjusting to the dim interior after the bright sunlight of the noisy street. Inside here, it was a complete contrast, silent, almost another world. The man was tall and lean, his features and complexion typical of the Mediterranean, which Joe could identify with ease. The stranger wore expensive clothes – a brocade vest, a crisp white shirt and a tailored jacket. A black hat cast a shadow over his face. The leather of his boots and gun-belt creaked slightly as he walked in, disturbing the silence. The two pearl-handled pistols at his hips signified he was comfortable with killing. Joe's stomach clenched in a familiar manner as the stranger strode over the dusty floorboards toward the counter.

"Good afternoon, sir," Joe said, resorting to his familiar welcome. "Joe Finzy's the name, glad to be of service."

"Afternoon." The stranger glanced left and right at the stacked shelves, the assorted barrels filled with grain and other foodstuff. Joe was proud of his inventory, among the items: baskets of eggs, jars of butter, strings of red peppers, crocks of honey, green Rio or Mocha coffee, tea, bottles of soda, cayenne pepper, catsup. Ham and bacon hung above the counter. "Quite a little empire you have here, Mr. Finzy."

Joe detected an Italian accent and he sensed the blood drain from his face. He hoped his eyes didn't give away anything. "Thank you, stranger," he said, his voice steady, belying the rising fear that threatened to constrict his chest. "I've spent many happy years building up my emporium." His fingers closed round the trigger of the shotgun; he'd learned from past experience and now the weapon was concealed behind the blue serge material that decorated the front of the counter.

The man thumbed over his shoulder. "Name on the sign, Finzy – sounds foreign."

"Yes, many years ago, my family came from Europe."

"Europe, eh? Fancy that." He grinned without mirth, his teeth small and yellow. "Small world."

"Why is that?" Joe croaked.

"I come from Europe as well – long time back." He sighed. "Ah, the old country still pulls at me."

"Indeed? It is a small world and it gets smaller, with the railroad and everything..." Joe coughed to cover the sound of the double hammers being cocked.

"I'm looking for an old family friend – maybe you know him?"

"I doubt it . . ."

"Take a look." The stranger's hand moved smoothly, unthreateningly inside his vest and pulled out a tintype photo. "Guy I'm looking for is on the right. His name is Giuseppe Finizzi."

His mouth suddenly very dry, Joe backed away and pulled both triggers.

The blast tore through the cloth that covered the gap beneath the counter. Buckshot discoloured the stranger's rich brocade vest and white shirt. The man jerked backward and thudded to the floor. The tintype fell out of his hand and clattered against the foot of an ornate mahogany table that displayed peppermint candy sticks, steel knives and forks and pewter spoons.

Fingers trembling, Joe lowered the greener and dabbed the sweat on his forehead with a bandana from his pocket. Without a sound, he moved round the counter and approached the dead man.

* * *

"Beats me, Joe," mused Sheriff Miller, pushing his Stetson back off his forehead. Sweat beaded on his furrowed black brow. The first time Joe saw the sheriff, the lawman's face had uncomfortably reminded him of the New York riots and it had taken a few meetings after that to shake the grim memory.

A small crowd of curious bystanders stood on the boardwalk at the doorway. Sheriff Miller chased them away.

"Your store seems to attract robbers like a honeypot draws bears." Miller's bright eyes levelled on Joe. "How many is that – four in the ten years I've been here, I reckon."

"Don't recollect exactly, Sheriff. It seems we still live in dangerous times, though." Guiltily, Joe felt the old tintype in his pants pocket.

Miller lowered on one knee to the floor, careful to avoid the blood, and picked up the pearl-handled Colt .45 near the dead man's outflung arm. "Left-handed gunny, I reckon."

"He's wearing two guns, Sheriff."

"Yeah, but his preference was for the left, obviously."

Joe shook his head. "I don't see the relevance."

"There ain't none. Just an observation."

"Left or right, his gun was a real threat, all the same."

"Sure. I can see that, Joe. You had no option."

* * *

No option. That's what Giuseppe told himself all those years ago. He'd been a brash, rather callow young man then. With his brother Vito, he'd thought himself invincible. Neither had any intention of following in their father's footsteps. Shoemaking wasn't for them. "Your mama and me come to this country with high hopes for you both, and you disappoint us," Papa said time and again.

The Finizzis landed at Castle Garden battery in the summer of 1858. He'd been eleven, his brother a year older. Their family possessions were few. But Papa had the tools of his trade and soon found enough work to feed them.

Giuseppe's emotions were mixed as they stepped ashore in New York. The smell of the place made his stomach squirm; it was even worse than the bowels of their ship. The air was thick with dust and both fresh and dried horse droppings, the sulphurous emissions of the gasworks along the river, and the rendering and hide-curing plants. A new world – yet it stank worse than the old one.

He was tall and strong for his age. For the first few months, he and Vito helped Papa with his shoemaking business, which thrived. But it was smelly, dreary work.

On their days off, they ventured into the city's warren of slum streets, fascinated by the breadth and complexity of the place and its strange mix of grand and ramshackle buildings, and the novelty of horse-drawn streetcars on rails.

Their family had ended up in Red Hook, one of several Italian quarters, filled with fellow countrymen. "They cling to the old world, afraid to change," Vito sneered. "Me, I will learn the American language. That is the route to success, little brother."

Giuseppe nodded. "I will learn also." True to their word, they quickly picked up the lingo, amazing and appalling their parents in equal measure.

"I'm not spending the rest of my life here in little Italy," Vito vowed. "I want to get out and see the world!"

"Me, too!" Giuseppe agreed with fervour.

Finally, Vito confronted their father. "Papa, we have signed up with the padroni, he has promised..."

"Silenzio! You have work here, boy. You will have a trade! Do not become simple low-paid labourers!"

"Maybe it is low pay, Papa, but at least we'll get

paid!"

Papa raised his hand to slap Vito, but Mama stepped in. "Rizzo, no! You promised, a new land, a new way for all of us!"

"So?"

"This new land calls for young strong workers to build it. Strong men like our sons."

Papa lowered his hand and scowled. "Very well. Your mother can help me, instead. Maybe a spell of hard work will make you boys appreciate your papa's trade the more."

For two years, the boys joined gangs of workmen hired out to construction sites. Besides learning about the building process, they found that their understanding of the American language improved. They lived cheek by jowl with their neighbours, people who worked as scavengers in the slum streets west of the Bowery, between Canal and Houston. These neighbours sold rags, bones and cans to nearby junk dealers. Little was wasted in this city, it seemed. And as the brothers mixed, their vocabulary grew.

One day, Giuseppe lowered himself to sit on a pile of bricks when the break whistle blasted off. His muscles ached, but they also bulged. He felt powerful and fit, in his prime. As he pulled out the makings and rolled a cigarette, he sensed he was being watched.

He looked up. A dark-haired girl – maybe ten or eleven years of age – studied him, her blue-gray eyes intent, unwavering. He was surprised to note that her clothes were not soiled rags like the others around here.

He flicked a match on his boot and lit the quirly. "What you looking at, little girl?"

"My name is Benedetta, and I'm not a little girl. I'm thirteen, as it happens." Same age as him, he thought. She spoke American with a very slight Italian accent. He'd like to speak like that one day.

"Really?"

"I was looking at your cigarette. Are you sure it is healthy to take smoke into your lungs?"

He laughed. "You're impertinent, I'll say that for you."

"Well, is it good, the smoke?"

"Aye." He nodded, puffed on the stub and flung it to the ground, where it glowed briefly. "It calms me."

"It is not opium, though?"

Giuseppe chuckled and shook his head. "No, it ain't a drug, Miss Benedetta."

"I think it is a drug, however."

"I don't care what you think."

"I've told you mine, so what's *your* name?"

He told her, and then added, "You ain't from around here, are you?"

"No, my father is the banchiere for this ward."

"Figures," he said, and nodded. That explained her clothes. Daughter to a moneylender, a man who greased the palms of business, kept it rolling.

"What do you mean, 'figures'?"

"Your pa, he works with figures, don't he?"

She smiled and her face lit up. "So he does!"

The whistle blast told him it was time to get off his butt and go back to work. He shrugged at her. "Nice talking to you, Benedetta."

All around them, the streets set up a raucous noise. Silence seemed a luxury. Yet as he looked at her in that instant, he didn't seem to hear a thing, save her hushed voice. "Call me Etta," she said.

"Sure. Call me Joe. See you around."

* * *

Joe's best friend was Giovanni, a lanky dark-eyed, thin-faced youth the same age as Vito. One evening, as the three lads went on their way home after work, Giovanni said, "There goes Falcone, the Moneyman." The man wore a stovepipe hat and baggy Oxford pants.

"Moneyman?" Vito queried. "He doesn't look too wealthy to me."

"He's a messenger," Giovanni replied, "one of many who carry money between banks and businesses all day."

"How do you know?" Vito asked.

"From my uncle, Columbo," said Giovanni. "He works

176

in a bank."

"How much money does he carry?"

"Enough, Vito."

"Enough to rob?"

Giovanni smiled and winked. "If we were dishonest, yes."

Vito shrugged. "Then the Moneyman is careless. He should have a protector."

Joe grinned. "Maybe we could hire out our services, offer protection?"

"Protection money." Vito chuckled. "Sometimes, little brother, I wonder where you live inside your head! That's an ancient racket already. Pays the gangs."

"Gangs?" Joe asked.

"Gangs like the Tenth Avenue, the Baxter Street Dudes..."

"...And the Nineteenth Street Gang and the Whos," supplemented Giovanni.

"How do you know about them, Vito?"

"I keep my eyes and ears open, that is why."

Flustered at not being knowledgeable about the gangs of New York, Joe said, "Let's get home, before Papa takes his belt to us."

"Sure. But soon we'll be too big for him to boss us around," Vito growled ominously.

* * *

Joe learned a lot in those years on the streets and when they lay in bed, he exchanged notes and thoughts with Vito about their day. Every day seemed filled with new discoveries, new fears, new hopes. "Vito, have you noticed there are tools for every kind of job?"

"So? That's no big deal."

"Yes, it is. When they started to build the railroad, they needed new tools, and the same goes for the streetcars."

"I still don't see what you're yapping on about."

"Vito, don't you see, if a new job needs a new tool, somebody invents it. America's full of inventors. America's going to be great, one day. These are exciting times!"

"Maybe. But inventors are rich guys. We're workies – and poor. We use the tools the rich inventors invent, that's all."

"Well, somebody has to supply all the tools, don't they?"

"Makes sense, I guess."

"Maybe one day, that's what I'll do – supply the tools."

Vito laughed. "You mean instead of working?"

Joe nodded and grinned. "Trade is where the money is. I've noticed that."

He was proved right when the Civil War started. The Finizzi Shoe Factory did a roaring trade, supplying boots for the army. It didn't matter that the material was of poor quality, so long as the orders were met. "I told you," Papa crowed, "this is the land of opportunity!"

Then, about ten days after the Union victory at Gettysburg, when so many soldiers were killed or maimed, there was an increased demand for conscription. The Draft Act passed in Congress earlier in March required all young men between the ages of eighteen and forty-five to sign up to fight for the Union. Giuseppe and Vito breathed a sigh of relief: they were too young, and their father was too old.

The draft riots in July 1863 devastated the city and marked Joe indelibly for life. Gangs of all kinds protested about the "rich man's war", referring to the ability of draftees to purchase substitutes for $300. Many rioters were Irish, Joe noted. They seemed the ideal "volunteers" for the army, since they spoke English. Recruiting Italians wasn't as vigorously pursued, it seemed. Briefly, he wondered that if the war endured until he was eligible by age, then perhaps he was foolish to learn to speak American. But no, he argued, success in trade required it.

During the riots, he witnessed several atrocities that turned his stomach against mob violence. Negroes were blamed for the war and also for taking valued work from others. Dead Rabbits and Plug Uglies and other gang members chanted the same litany: "Sold for $300! When a nigger goes for a thousand!" He watched as one poor soul was clubbed to death by a mob, strung up from a tree and set alight. This was the land of opportunity? He feared for his life – and his soul.

It was over in a week, though, and the stillness that briefly befell the city seemed like the aftermath of a natural disaster. Gradually, the pieces were picked up and Joe and Vito were required to work even harder as gangs of labourers reconstructed the many fire-ravaged buildings.

* * *

Toward the end of the war, Vito was drafted, but before he went off to fight, they had a tintype photograph taken of the pair of them, standing together and smiling. "I'll keep this with me while I fight," Vito said. "It'll remind me why I'm fighting, for home and family." He survived, and returned hard-bitten, his dark brown eyes cold.

By the time Joe was eligible for draft, the war was over. The influx of war-weary and battle-hardened men into the city transformed many neighbourhoods. The fights between gangs became bloodier, and seemed all pervading, and affected almost every strata of society.

Employers exploited their workforce without conscience. The denizens of the slums died mute and unmissed in their hundreds from malnutrition and disease. The foundations of the city were built upon money, and it seemed that the only way for the young poor to get any was to turn to crime. Giovanni joined an Italian gang who called themselves The Red Hooks and after a short while he talked Joe into it as well. It entailed taking an oath of allegiance to the gang members. Joe felt uncomfortable about that aspect, as the oath put the gang membership above family and friends, and any serious infraction was punishable by severe penalties, even death. Too late, however, he gave his oath and was a committed member.

He was twenty when he burgled his first house. The rush of fear, excitement and bravado was unlike anything he'd experienced before. He came away feeling like the king of the world, though the jewellery he got fenced didn't bring in that many dollars. He vowed to save as much as he could, hide the money away until he could marry Etta.

Before long, Joe was frequenting a number of fences. "Don't stick to one," Giovanni advised. "Spread your contacts wide – just in case the law closes one of them down. That way, you keep in business." One particular fence never seemed at risk, Joe observed. Fredericka "Marm" Mandelbaum employed the law firm Howe and Hummel on an annual retainer, rumoured to be $5,000. She was the queen of fences, a 250-pound matron who always wore a black bonnet. She ran her operation from a clapboarded wing behind her haberdashery store at Clinton Street on the corner of Rivington.

"You're smart, Joe," Marm told him more than once. "But your destiny ain't in crime. You're an honest worker, son, and if your ma could see the road you seem set on, she'd grieve mightily."

True enough, after the first excitement, Joe feared what his arrest might do to his parents, rather than what the subsequent punishment might be. And if he were caught, it would end his dreams of marrying Etta.

Yet he couldn't easily break away from the Red Hook Gang. Like many Italian gangs, it was cemented together by a code of honor. Once you joined, you never left alive. At nights he sweated and cursed Giovanni for suckering him, especially after that one night, when they met at Bill Varley's joint in the basement of a Bowery hardware store.

Joe said, "Why is everyone so miserable?" About twenty of the gang were present and there wasn't a straight face among them. A threatening hush pervaded the place. Word was out, the Torrio family – all three brothers – had taken over the Red Hooks.

"Gino Vitelli blabbed to the cops last night," Giovanni whispered.

"Blabbed? What about?"

"Last month's heist on the Hudson."

"But the code – the code of silence. What made him

break it?"

Giovanni laughed. "Some gal he was sparking. She told him – go straight or lose her."

Joe swallowed, speechless, thinking of Etta. If she ever found out he was involved with the gang and other criminals, his hopes would be forever dashed. He just knew it. "He should have told her to get lost," he said forcefully, not believing a word.

Giovanni clasped Joe's hand tightly. "That's what I said. We're brothers in crime. We can have any girl we want, so why settle on one, eh!"

* * *

"I've been hearing unsettling things about you and your brother," Etta whispered one night as they walked at the tail end of a procession through the streets. It was a fiesta day, in honour of the Madonna. Ahead, a team of men carried a large statue of the sainted woman, Mary. All around, fireworks whizzed and banged.

"What?" he said, pretending to be deafened by the noise.

"You heard," she said, clearly not fooled.

"What kind of unsettling things?"

"You're involved in one of those nasty gangs. They seem to be polluting the entire city, my father says. The prominenti come to him with worrying tales." She shrugged. "Not that I would know anything about it."

Joe laughed it off. "That's probably a fellow worker – I got him into trouble with the supervisor because he wasn't pulling his weight. He's just spreading untrue rumours about me." He nodded. "That'll be it."

She linked her arm in his and hugged close. "I thought it was something like that."

"Yeah. Let's get to the feast and eat!"

* * *

When Vito was arrested, there was hell to pay in the family. Papa bailed him, reluctantly. "For the sake of my business name, nothing else!" He wagged a finger at Vito. "You take the wicked path of your Uncle Giacomo." Papa crossed himself every time he mentioned his dishonoured brother and he did so now.

Some time ago they'd moved out of the tenement and lived in a separate apartment. It seemed soulless to Joe. And this night, it was filled with an oppressive silence that no family member dared break.

Later, as they lay in bed, Vito whispered, "Joe, I've had enough. I've heard from Uncle Giacomo. He wants me in his organisation."

"Chicago seems a long way off, Vito."

"A long train ride, is all." He leaned closer. "So, do you want to come with me?"

"When are you going?"

"Tonight."

Joe gasped at the suddenness of Vito's decision. He shook his head, thinking of Etta. "No, I can't."

"It's that girl, isn't it? She's got her hooks into you, I can tell. She'll be the ruin of you, God help you."

Joe didn't respond but clenched his fists and turned away.

That night, true to his word, Vito slipped out of their apartment and skipped the city. Papa lost his bail money. "He is disowned from this day forward. Never mention his name in this house or in my hearing!"

Silence was the only answer from Joe and his mother.

* * *

When by chance Joe got wind of a Red Hook bagman setting out for Chicago, he realised this might be his chance to finally break away from the city. He planned meticulously and when the moment came, he shadowed the man easily enough. He bought his ticket and boarded the train in the same car, finding a seat near the door to the next carriage. He waited till the station was behind them and they were well on the move.

Nerves on edge, he stood and walked along the aisle and then abruptly lurched and half-fell, half-sat in the seat across the aisle from the messenger.

"Mr. Falcone, what a surprise to meet you here!" Joe said, offering his hand.

"Do I know you?" Falcone's dark eyes were like

pebbles, without animation.

"Sure, I'm a member," he said, chuckling. "Well, you probably don't recognise all of us, it's a big gang – but I sure know you."

"Not so loud, man," Falcone seethed, his dark eyes intense, brows furrowed.

Joe nodded. "Discretion, yes, of course. Anyway, pleased to meet you, especially on this happy day!"

"What's so happy about today?"

"I'm on my way to fetch my bride-to-be!" Joe lied.

Falcone's lips twitched and he offered the semblance of a thin smile. "Congratulations, I guess, Mr....?"

"Torrio."

"Any relation to Tommaso Torrio?"

"Youngest brother." Joe smiled and they finally shook hands. Then Joe pulled out a hip flask. "Care to share a toast with the groom, sir?"

Falcone's swarthy face showed signs of reluctance.

"Please, just a gesture – it will make me exceedingly happy!"

"Very well." Falcone nodded and took the flask and sipped. He lowered the flask. "Hey, that's rather good bourbon, Mr. Torrio." Joe nodded, urging him to take another drink. Falcone flung his head back and gulped, then wiped his mouth.

"Especially for today," Joe said, taking the flask. He pretended to swig back a gulp, and then fitted the stopper and leaned back against the seat. After a moment or two, he feigned sleep.

Falcone's snoring alerted him and he opened his eyes. There were no nearby passengers, he noted, which was fortunate. He'd devised ways to hoodwink any witnesses, anyway, though they were not needed now.

The knockout drops he'd purchased from one of Diamond Charley's travelling salesmen had done the trick. "Chloral hydrate saves time and muscle," the man had explained glibly.

Now, Joe leaned over and tugged at the briefcase by Falcone's side, wedged between the carriage wall and his body. It came away – and it wasn't chained to

Falcone's wrist. His heart flipped. Maybe he'd wasted his time. Maybe there was nothing of worth inside?

He forced the lock with a small file – a tool for every job. Inside nestled bundles of dollar bills. He closed the case and smiled. Unhurriedly, he stood up and walked to the end of the carriage. He opened the interconnecting door and passed into the next passenger car. He went all the way to the baggage car and entered. The guard, he knew, was doing his rounds, at the far reaches of the train. Swiftly, Joe turned his jacket inside out, stuck a false beard and moustache on his face, and slipped on a pair of clear glass spectacles. When Falcone recovered, he wouldn't be able to identify Joe in his new disguise.

This, he silently vowed, was the last time he'd commit a crime.

* * *

He returned on next day's train and two days later, he eloped with Etta.

"We'll go west and carve out our own destiny," he told her. He knew that it meant never contacting his family or Giovanni again. But, as he looked at Etta, he felt that the price of silence was worth it.

As their journey progressed from train, to buggy, and finally prairie schooner, they got to know each other better. On their way, he explained that he wanted to change his name, to "become more of an American citizen."

"That sounds fine to me," she said, kissable lips curving. "I'd be real happy to be Mrs. Finzy."

He grinned. "Did you just propose to me?"

"It's the American way, didn't you know?"

The wagon train captain performed the wedding ceremony and the man's wife exclaimed, "It's so exciting and romantic, I bet they're eloping!"

* * *

Over the years, Joe worked hard and was true to his vow. He trod the straight and narrow path through life and remained silent about his youthful days of crime.

About two years after they'd settled in town, he'd

been delivering farm machinery to the Wilsons out at their ranch, when he pulled in his buggy as a stranger blocked the trail to town. Then he realised that maybe he'd forgotten his past, but others hadn't.

"Hey, mister," the stranger accosted, "sorry to bother you, but I'm new in these parts. Do you know if any Italians have settled hereabouts?"

"Italians?" Some sixth sense warned him not to be talkative. He was convinced that his accent was still very noticeable, unlike Etta's.

"Yeah, I'm looking for kin. The Finizzis."

"No," Joe said, and shook his head. "Sorry." He geed up his buggy and headed for town.

But the stranger wasn't so easily dismissed. He rode alongside the buggy. "Hey, wait up! What's got you so riled?"

Joe eased on the reins, halted the team and applied the brake. "I'm not riled," he said.

"Well, if you see the Finizzis, can you give them a message for me?"

"I don't know any Finnies or whatever you call them!"

"Hey, you sound like an Italian. Is that right?"

Sweat collected at the base of his spine, pooled at his waistband. "All right, let me get something to write with so you can deliver your message."

Stern now, the stranger said, "You ain't answered my question, mister. Are you Italian?"

Joe shrugged. "I am, as it happens. So what?" He rummaged in the well of the wagon, by his feet. "I have some paper here somewhere."

"You ain't levelling with me, mister."

Abruptly, Joe grabbed the .45 and aimed it at the stranger. He cocked the gun. "I'm levelling it on you right now, mister."

"Hey, don't shoot the messenger!" He raised his hands.

"What's the message?"

"Ain't you going to write it down – you know, for the Finizzis?"

"I've got a good memory."

"Yeah, Mr. Finizzi, and so has Tommaso Torrio."

Joe felt the blood drain from his face. He should never have used that surname.

"Torrio got some grief when you stole that money and used his name. He's been hunting for you all this time."

"How'd you find me?" He needed to know where he'd made a mistake, so if he and Etta upped and left, he wouldn't repeat the same error of judgment.

"Just pure luck. Torrio has hired ten men to search for you, and I got lucky, I reckon."

Ten! By the saints, there were nine more like this one, poking into people's business. He'd end up looking over his shoulder for years to come. For ever. He noticed his hand trembled. "What's the message?"

"Return the money and restore Torrio's name."

Joe let out a cold laugh. "How do I restore his name?"

"You face the Red Hook's tribunal."

"I don't think so," Joe said and fired. The buggy's horse bucked and whinnied. The man slumped forward over the pommel and his horse bolted back along the trail. Joe swore. There was no way he could catch up with the runaway horse now. The man seemed dead. He'd have to hope and pray that was the case.

His hands shook. He clasped them to his chest. Etta must never find out about this.

Then, like a hovering storm cloud, the thought occluded his mind: nine more men hunted him.

* * *

Despite two more strangers turning up out of the blue, the future looked good. At least he'd managed to misdirect those two, without having to kill them. When they were blessed with a son, Emilio, he felt he'd done the right thing. From time to time he regretted not being able to contact Vito and his parents, but he shrugged off such sentimentality.

He prided himself on being able to sell any tool for any job. If it wasn't in stock, he'd find it in a catalogue and get it shipped out. The Finzy Store empire would be big, one day; maybe not in his lifetime, but with Emilio to follow on, it boded well for the future.

Yet in the last ten years, like Sheriff Miller said, four would-be desperadoes had attempted to rob his store… That made seven of the ten had crossed his path, and five had died. He hated having their blood on his hands, but they'd been sent to kill him, after all. Surely no more would come this way. It was a big country, plenty of other places to search. So many years had passed. Surely Torrio had forgotten by now?

Emilio was fourteen when he left home.

There'd been no warning, save the usual bluster. "Pa, I want to make something of my life. I don't want to be beholden to you. I don't want to work in a general store!"

He could hear his own voice down the years, castigating the worthy yet unwanted trade of shoemaker.

* * *

"Joe, it's our anniversary in two months," Etta said.

"I know, dear. When have I ever forgotten?"

"I didn't imply that you had, dear. But I would like something special as twenty-one years of marriage is worth celebrating."

"You name it, and if I haven't got it, I'll get it."

"Even as a lover, you're always the salesman," she said with a chuckle.

Shamefaced, he held her hands, gently squeezed. "I know a good bargain when I see it, and that's why I chose you."

"Smooth talker!"

"So, what is this gift you want me to give you?"

"Our son."

He released her hands, let them drop.

"Advertise for him," she urged, breaking the charged lull. "He's been gone five years, without a word from him." She let out a sob. "I need to know he's all right."

Joe nodded. "Very well, I'll do this. Perhaps it's time to break the silence between father and son."

She embraced him, tears streaming down her cheeks. "Oh, thank you, Joe!"

He held her close, his heart hammering. "I can't promise he'll get in touch." He left unsaid that he didn't know if Emilio was alive, considering the path he'd chosen. A path he'd kept secret from Etta since he first learned about it some six years ago.

Emilio joined a gang, but this wasn't a typical gang of young men, simply having fun. There were four of them and they were hard men, all of them older than Emilio. Joe only found out by accident, when he unexpectedly visited the saloon to deliver merchandise that arrived on the stage late.

When he saw Emilio lounging at the table with those men, his stomach seemed to sink into his boots.

He drew his son to one side. "You bring shame on your ma by befriending these men!" he admonished.

"Befriending, Pa? Wake up!"

"They look like criminals to me, son. You–"

"Oh, Pa, we're a gang – and we rob stages!"

"Oh, Dio!" Joe wrung his hands, thinking about Etta. She mustn't know – ever.

"Yeah, Pa, we're desperadoes!" Emilio laughed and the sound seemed familiar, so much like Vito all that time ago.

"This path you've chosen will only lead to shame and probably disaster. Stop now, while you can." He was tempted to explain how he'd trodden that selfsame trail as a young man his age and turned away from it. But he remained silent. Perhaps he was still ashamed, as he rightly should be. If Etta ever found out, nothing would ever be the same again, that he knew.

"Don't hurt your ma like this, Emilio. She idolizes you!"

For a second, he thought he'd gotten through to the lad. Emilio's face clouded and his eyes dulled in thought. Then he shook his head. "You're right – better she don't know." He nodded to himself, twisted his mouth, fateful decision made. "I'll go somewhere else, so neither of you need be bothered about me again."

The weeks that followed Emilio's unexplained absence were some of the hardest times Joe had known.

He remained taciturn while Etta's muteness scourged his heart.

So for the next five years Joe read any newspaper he could lay his hands upon; in the saloon, the barber's, in the stage depot, even scraps that served for packing in delivered crates. Each time, he prayed that he wouldn't find a report about the death of a young man called Emilio Finzy. Though he realized that Emilio could have changed his name. After all, Giuseppe Finizzi had.

* * *

Reluctantly, Joe placed the advert far and wide, asking that Emilio Finzy return home, even if only for a brief stay, to celebrate his parents' silver wedding anniversary. And from that day on, he watched warily for the arrival not of his son, but unwelcome strangers brandishing guns.

Now, tonight, he lowered the newspaper and he allowed his heart to return to its normal beat. There wasn't any mention of Emilio, at least from what he could determine. The parlour was silent. Etta sat at the fireside, sewing. He'd been blessed to have her as his wife. He thought back to those old days in the slums, when the women who shared their cramped tenement had hired out their needlework, undercutting the charges of the Jewish seamstresses. A lifetime ago, a nightmare ago.

She'd taught him many things; among them, to be proud of his birthright. It began when they set out in their prairie schooner. "Don't ever complain about Little Italians again," she'd berated him. "Remember, the first opera house in America was opened in New York before we were born – all through the efforts of Lorenzo Da Ponte, Mozart's former librettist." Then she had to explain what a librettist did. Why she couldn't have said word-writer was beyond him, then.

There was a rapid knock on the front door, derailing his train of thought. "I'll get it," he whispered gently.

He got up, passed into the lobby and opened the door. "Hi, Marco, old friend," he said, greeting his elderly Italian neighbour on the porch. Dusk slithered through the town, relieved by the buttery glow from the streetlamps. "Come in."

"No, Joe, I'm not stopping." Marco shook his head. "It's about those rumours . . ."

Blood drained from Joe's face. His body seemed to seize up as he stood holding the door-handle.

"We've been good friends since you moved into this town all those years ago."

Numbly, Joe nodded.

"I got word from a cousin who passed through last night." Marco leaned forward and whispered, "There's a known hired killer in town. And the whispers are you're the mark . . ."

Cold fear seeped into Joe's chest. So, it had come to this, after all. There were too many of them. The cost of hiring a killer was nothing where the breaking of the silence was concerned. Torrio would pay whatever it took to regain his name and exact his revenge. Torrio had a long memory – and arm. Joe glanced over his shoulder at the lounge door, but it seemed that Etta hadn't moved to discover the identity of their caller.

Clammy hand gripping the handle, he whispered guardedly, "No, I can't believe that. Why me?"

"There isn't a one of us who hasn't heard the rumours, friend. Our letters from family always mention . . . well, you know . . .?"

"Silly rumours, they aren't true." He wondered if Etta had ever heard those same rumours. Surely, she'd have mentioned it? He forced an unconcerned chuckle and clapped a hand on Marco's shoulder. "You sure you won't come in?"

Marco raised a hand. "No, I best get back. Just thought I'd tell you . . ."

"Thanks, friend. But there's nothing to worry about."

He closed the door and noiselessly strode over to the lobby's window. Marco was alone in the street, hurrying across the hardpan with his awkward mincing gait. Nobody else stirred. The town was bathed in silence.

So, the vigil begins.

As he stepped into the parlour, he said, "That was

Marco."

"Oh?" She laid down her needlework and rubbed her eyes with her fingers.

"He was just passing, came by to see how we were, that's all."

"Odd," she said. "It isn't as though we don't see him and Maria most days."

Joe shrugged. "Just being neighborly."

"Yes, nice of him." She stood up. "It's getting late."

"I'll follow you in a while, dear. I think I'll have a nightcap and read the newspaper." A newspaper he'd already scanned from front to back.

"Well, don't stay up too late," she said and patted his cheek. "And..."

"I know. I'll only have a small glass." He kissed her forehead and watched her leave the room.

The staircase creaked under her tread.

And then he was alone, more alone than he'd ever been in his life. He rubbed a hand over his bristled chin and thrust out his jaw. He crossed over to the cabinet and opened the hood, poured two fingers of whiskey and gulped it down. His hands felt steadier already. He was tempted to drink the same again, but forced down that notion. Tonight, he might need his wits about him.

Careful not to make any sound, he moved the bottles aside and opened a deep-set drawer. He pulled out the tin-type, still puzzled by it. What was it doing in the hands of that stranger? He pushed it back inside and took out his Smith & Wesson .45 revolver and checked the cylinder. Still loaded. He spun it, then broke it open and removed the shells and reloaded them, his fingers quite steady. All in good order. He shoved the weapon into his tight waistband.

Moving his armchair over the rug, he placed it firmly to face the door that led into the lobby.

He turned down the light and sat waiting in the dark for his appointed executioner. Some years ago, he'd have ridden out to meet the man. Now, he was growing weary of it. Damn Torrio!

Dimly he recalled the other times he'd stayed up all

night like this, on heists in the Gotham streets. But then he'd been younger. Then, it seemed that he had no option.

He could hardly keep his eyes open and felt sure he dozed for odd minutes, only to be brought up with a start as the row house made its eerie night-sounds.

His heirloom fob watch said he'd been waiting two hours. He smiled. Etta hadn't bothered calling for him to come up to bed. Probably fallen straight to sleep, he thought, imagining her lying serenely.

Then he remembered he hadn't locked the back door after putting out the cat. Tiredly, he heaved himself from the chair.

He entered the compact kitchen, which still held the lingering smells of tonight's lamb dinner.

Harshly shattering the stillness, next door's tomcat screeched in sudden pain, as though it had been kicked downstairs. Joe's pulse raced. Maybe that was the killer?

Standing as if transfixed with one hand on the gun butt and the other steadying himself against the edge of the sink, he watched speechless as the brass door-handle slowly turned.

The door swung open on soundless hinges.

He pulled out the gun and his finger trembled on the trigger. Maybe the greener would have been a better weapon? No time to change his mind now, though.

In the doorway, tall, immaculately dressed, with lean tanned features shaded by a Stetson, the stranger stood half illuminated by next-door's rear porch light. The grim stubborn mouth twisted into a kind of ironic grin as the hidden eyes scoured the darkened kitchen. Long nimble fingers flashed inside his jacket and came away with a glint of metal.

Despite his fear, Joe moved with surprising speed. He raised the revolver and fired.

Almost in the same instant, two more shots rang out, the sound deafening, shattering the silence.

The man wheezed incredulously and doubled-up. He stumbled backward through the doorway and onto the porch. He tumbled down the three steps, arms and legs flailing. His shoulder bashed against a garbage bin. That damned tomcat screeched again.

The noise seemed sufficient to awaken the dead – though indeed the dead man caused it.

But had he killed him? He'd done for all the others, so maybe he'd done for this one too.

Tremulously, Joe took the kitchen lantern from the table, lit it and stepped to the doorway.

The shot man didn't move.

"Joe! I heard shooting – what's going on?" Etta's voice, strident, concerned, from the landing.

"Stay there, dear!" he shouted as the pungent cordite still blocked his nostrils.

He felt sick inside. The others had been secret or blamed on hoodlums and robbers, but he couldn't hide this deed from her. This killer wasn't dressed as a burglar. Slowly, he descended the steps, gun at the ready, just in case the man wasn't quite a corpse.

His heart wavered as he knelt by the twisted figure. He was too old for this sort of thing. But, by the Saints, still a match for their much younger executioners!

He turned the body over.

His head spun giddily. This killer wasn't younger – he was a year older. Joe stared unbelievingly into the tear-filled eyes of Vito, his brother. By Vito's hand was a gun, smoke curling from the barrel.

Abruptly, Vito grasped Joe's shirt and held tight. Through gritted teeth, he wheezed, "I'm sorry, Giuseppe, I had no choice..." His eyes closed and he relinquished his grip, his arm flopping limp to the floor. He'd been shot twice. Twice?

"I got him, Pa," said Emilio, emerging from the shadows of the back yard. In his hand he held a six-gun, its barrel smoking also.

His heart pounding, stomach churning, Joe straightened up and took a shaky step toward his son. "Emilio? What's going on?"

"I learned all about your past, Pa, from the Giacomo family. They heard that the Torrio family from New York recruited Vito to kill you. I followed Uncle Vito here." He shrugged.

"What did Vito mean, he had no choice?"

"Torrio threatened to kill Uncle Vito's family if he didn't do this job."

"O, Dio, a body!" wailed Etta in the doorway. Then she gasped, "Emilio, is that you?"

"Yes, Ma, I came home."

Joe gestured at his dead brother, his heart heavy at the tragic loss. "I'm glad you came – and sad it has ended like this."

"I've come to join your business, Pa – Finzy and Son, when you're ready – and I intend to put my past behind me, just like you."

"Past?" asked Etta. "What's Emilio talking about, Joe?"

Silence fell between them.

"Always so many questions," Joe finally bewailed. "The past's in the past, my dear. Think to the future – with our son." He hugged Emilio and exchanged a secret look with him, a conspiracy of silence.

Never Trust a Widder

by Phil Dunlap

Phil Dunlap is an award-winning author with seven published novels to his credit. He was a newspaper journalist and free-lance magazine writer for years, but a love of the old west inspired him to turn to Western fiction. The author's website is www.phildunlap.com. He lives near Indianapolis with his wife, Judy.

"I'm so damned hungry I could eat this ornery cayuse. We gotta do something, Huck, and soon, before we both drop from our saddles and go belly up." Trumble Barlow held his stomach as if it might just take a notion to fall out and leave him with nothing but a hole. The two out-of-work cowboys reined in and dismounted. Dust swirled around them from the severely dry ground. They'd been riding for several days and hadn't seen a hint of rain.

"Awww, Trumble, quit your bellyachin.' We been hungry before. We're still here, ain't we?"

"Dammit, Huck Bannister, I ain't foolin' this time. I'm thinkin' of takin' a chaw outta my saddle. It's bad, real bad."

"Okay. I'll come up with a plan. Sure as shootin' we'll find a ranch hereabouts that'll give us some grub."

"The last one we tried got us nothin' but a good run for our money to beat the lead shot from that scattergun."

"Yeah, thanks to you. Why the hell did you have to go stumblin' over everythin' in the yard on yer way back to the kitchen window whilst tryin' to filch them pies off the sill?"

"Well, they smelled so damned good, I was drawn to 'em like a bee to a posy. I was called to come sample their – "

"They was there 'cause they was hot, ya dern fool. Yer hollerin' when you burnt your hand give us away. That's what done it."

"I still got a blister." Trumble said, holding up his thumb.

"You'd a had more'n a blister if that old hag was a better shot."

"I'm still hungry. So what're we gonna do about it?"

"I'm thinkin' on it."

"We could shoot us one of them beeves we saw back about a mile."

"Uh-huh, and get invited to a necktie party for our trouble? Folks round here don't kin to rustlers, you know," Huck said.

"'Bout now I ain't sure I care. I'm wastin' away to nothin'. Hope it don't come up a blow or I could end up in the next county. Cain't hardly hold my britches up, now."

"Yeah, well, like I said, I'll come up with somethin'. You see if you can't find a few sticks to build up a fire over there by that creek, and I'll go find somethin' to shoot."

"How 'bout if we both go, different directions. That way, we're twice as likely to bag somethin'."

"You'd probably shoot yerself in the foot, again, Trumble."

"Aww, leave me alone about that, will ya. Anyone could shoot hisself in the foot if he was to drop his gun."

"You ever think maybe you shoulda stuck it in your belt instead of lettin' it dangle half outta yer pocket?"

"I cain't afford a holster. Lots of folks stick 'em in their pockets."

"I don't recollect seein' many folks got a limp like the one you come away with, though."

"I got other qualities, some I ain't never let on to no

196

one about."

"Just you never mind. Now git to gatherin' some sticks and be ready to start up a blaze when I get back. Think you can do that?"

"I reckon."

Huck Bannister climbed back into his saddle and slowly rode off across the grassy plain. The day was cloudy and a gusty wind swirled the tall grasses with a heat that drew sweat like a sponge draws water. He pulled off his scarf and wiped at his brow. Drops of moisture clung to the ends of a droopy, graying mustache. After having ridden for one outfit after another, twenty years of being a cowboy had left him as poor as when he left home right after the war to seek his fortune out west. He hooked up with Trumble Barlow somewhere in Kansas on a small ranch. He couldn't recall just why.

Misfortune seemed to cut his trail often soon after making friends with Trumble. After working only about three weeks, they were both let go because of a grass fire that nearly wiped out the whole ranch. Turns out Trumble had tossed a match on the ground after lighting a cigarillo. The match wasn't quite done burning. But Trumble and Huck were through with the ranching life. At least at that ranch. And broke. Again.

As Huck rode, his thoughts turned to the trouble upon trouble that had been visited on him ever since the two met. He liked the fellow, but damned if Trumble wasn't the dumbest cowpoke he'd ever met. Maybe he ought to just shed himself of this saddle bum. Then maybe his luck would turn around. Maybe, always maybe. If he could be sure of his luck turning around, it might be worth a try. He wasn't getting any younger, and if he was going to make any real money, he'd best be getting to it.

He rode due west until the land began to descend into a wide valley. A fast-flowing creek meandered through the grassy slopes, gouging a rocky-banked slit that deepened as it went. Stopping on a low hill beyond a sparse stand of trees, he made out a squatter's cabin made of mud bricks. Two horses stood in a crude corral behind the hut, and a milk cow grazed on the side of a hill. Out front an Indian pony switched flies with its tail, shifting its weight from one back leg to the other. Huck pulled up. He rubbed his chin as he tried to decide whether to ride on down to the soddy and ask for food. He didn't see any firewood cut and stacked for keeping the cooking fire going. Maybe he could volunteer to cut some wood, that way it wouldn't actually be begging. He'd earn whatever they could spare.

While the idea of working up a sweat chopping logs into splinters didn't really appeal to him, he figured that he'd rather work for a spell than starve to death. Besides, Trumble was back at camp expecting him to return with food, not excuses for why he was empty-handed.

Just then, a man backed out of the soddy with a gun in his hand. He backed away several steps then fired into the open door. Another man stumbled through the door and fell to the ground. A woman came screaming out of the house, waving her arms to prevent the man on the ground from being shot again. Without regard to the woman's protestations, he fired again at the writhing figure, then turned and pointed his revolver at the woman.

Huck knew he had to do something. And he had to do it quickly. He yanked his Sharps buffalo rifle from the saddle boot, a reliable and accurate weapon he'd been given by the railroad during his short-lived employment as a guard helping ward off Indian raiding parties. It also came in handy for shooting deer and the occasional buffalo needed to feed ravenous crews. He slipped from his saddle to steady his shot, lifted the rifle to his shoulder, slid the rear sight up a little to account for the distance and the wind, took aim and squeezed the trigger. The big rifle bucked like a startled mule; smoke swirled around him for a moment until the breeze carried it away. He lowered the Sharps to see if he'd hit what he was aiming at. On the ground, near the other fallen man, lay his quarry, unmoving. Suddenly it occurred to him that the law might question his judgment in shooting a man without really knowing what had happened in that cabin prior to the first shots. What if the couple in the cabin had tried to rob him, threatened him with his life if he didn't hand over his valuables? The distance from which he'd taken the shot prevented him from knowing any of those possibilities.

Damn, he thought. *What have I done?*

He climbed back atop his bay mare, slipped the Sharps back into its scabbard, and urged his mount down the hill toward the crude cabin. The woman was kneeling near her man, sobbing hysterically, and tugging at his bloody shirt to make him respond to her pleading for him not to die. When Huck reached her side, he could tell the man was finished. Two well-aimed bullets in his chest put a period to this poor squatter's life. The woman looked up at Huck through tear-filled eyes.

"Why? Why did that devil have to kill my dear Henry? We told him he could have whatever he wanted, to just go in peace." Her face bore the pain of loss, and years of hardship on the prairie.

Suddenly, as Huck Bannister turned his attention to the man he'd shot, a wave of near panic flooded over him. "Oh, my lord!"

"What? What's wrong?"

"This man, the man who shot your Henry, and darned near done you in, too, ma'am, is the outlaw, Dakota Joe! Why, this half-breed's been a scourge to the settlers all up and down the territory. Killed hisself a passel of 'em. Ain't none gonna be sad at his passin'." He shook his head and clucked his tongue. But the lady must not have heard him, for she was deep in grief.

Huck reached out to help her to her feet. At first, she resisted, then after one last look at her fallen husband, she hung her head and allowed him to lead her back inside. The place was dark and the dirt floor was scattered with shards of dishware probably busted up by the man lying outside, dead, who'd just destroyed their lives. She stumbled through the clutter toward a short bench that lay along a crude table. Huck bent down and yanked it upright, motioning for her to sit. She dropped onto it, put her head in her hands, and just moaned. Feeling her grief, Huck looked around for any hint of what he could do to help. He decided he had better get her dead husband put in the ground as quickly as possible. He went outside to search for a shovel, and, finding one leaning against the outhouse, he came back to ask where she might want her husband and his killer buried.

"You can put Henry alongside the house, over where the sun will find him every morning. He loved the mornin' sun." She got up and stood at the door, pointing to a grassy area between the house and a fenced-in patch with half a dozen chickens pecking at the dirt.

"Yes, ma'am, I'll put 'em both over there," Huck said, with a nod and a tip of his slouch hat, a habit his mother had pounded into him as a child. "Showin' respect is good manners and a Godly thing to do. And don't you forget it," she'd told him, time and time again.

But the lady hadn't paid any attention to his attempt at good manners, instead, she flew into hysterics at the very mention of the killer of her husband being laid to rest nearby.

"You take that heathen off our land and dispose of him somewhere else, far away from my sight. You understand?"

"But, ma'am, I can't–"

"Git him off my land, now!" she screamed.

"But–"

Wringing her hands over his inability to grasp her meaning, she calmed down enough to explain, "I appreciate what you done and all, savin' me from that awful, murderin' Injun, but can't you see the pain I'd have to endure, over and over, every time I laid eyes on my Henry's restin' place and knew that devil lay nearby?"

"I reckon so. I'll just plant, er, bury your husband, and be gone, then. Reckon I'll have to take him into

Russell Springs."

The lady stood by watching as he struggled to stab the shovel into the rock-hard ground. After he felt he had the hole as deep as any man could, solemnly dragging the body to the side of the excavation, he tried to place him in the hole with as gentle a touch as he could muster. Just then the lady whimpered something. He stopped shoveling dirt in over the corpse to cock his head to hear what she had said.

"I'm grateful for what you've done for me. I can never repay you, but I'd like to ask one more favor."

Huck removed his hat and mopped at his forehead with his sleeve. "Anything I can do, ma'am, before I go? Anything at all."

"Could I trouble you to hitch up the horses to the wagon? I don't think I can spend the night in this place, what with all that's happened, and my dearly departed Henry lyin' in the dirt, cold and stiff. I believe I'll stay in town for a day or two."

"Yes, ma'am. I'll do it as soon as I'm finished here." He patted the mound to tamp it down so critters wouldn't be able to dig the body up, at least not easily.

After he was done grappling with two uncooperative, sway-backed mares, getting them to back into the traces, Huck tipped his hat to the lady and returned to the task at hand, namely getting rid of a corpse that would soon start stiffening in the most expeditious manner. He rolled the man up in his own blanket, intent on securing him to his pony. As he was wrestling to get all that dead weight up and securely tied to the saddle, an ingenious plan came to him, one he figured Trumble would heartily approve. He had a slight grin on his weather-beaten face as he rode out, leading the Indian pony that bore the corpse.

He looked back as the lady stood at the doorway for a moment, then ran to where Huck had dug the grave, throwing herself on the mound of dirt. He couldn't bear to look at her any more. Her tears were too wrenching an experience, similar to what he'd seen his sister endure at their own mother's funeral. While he had been sad at his mother's passing, tears didn't come easy to him. His sister had accused him of being hard-hearted, but that wasn't it at all. He was a man, and men weren't supposed to show emotion, at least that was his excuse.

Huck had been so preoccupied with digging a hole and sliding Henry into it, then obliging the widow with harnessing up her team, he plumb forgot to ask the lady if she could spare some victuals. *Trumble's goin' to be madder'n a hornet when he finds out I came away without one tiny morsel to calm our aching bellies.*

Two hours later, he was in sight of Trumble, still piling sticks in preparation for one hellacious fire. When Trumble saw him approaching, he called out.

"What's that you're totin' in here? And where'd you come by that paint? You got a deer wrapped up in there? A fat venison steak sounds real fine, yessir."

Huck grinned as he reined in and dismounted. He stood staring at Trumble, trying to figure the best way to tell his friend that there not only wasn't any food, but that they would have to wait a spell before there was any.

"Well, what'cha got there? Come on, out with it. It ain't no secret, is it?" Trumble walked over to the pony to get a better look. He put his hand on top of the blanket, then yanked it back like he'd been bit by a rattler. "What the – ?"

Huck chewed on his lip for a minute, then said, "It's a long story. This here fella shot a man down and then was fixin' to plug the man's woman, and I, uh, just naturally couldn't let him do that."

"So you did what, exactly?" Trumble asked, his eyes narrowing, knowing full well what the answer was going to be. He just had to hear it from Huck's own lips.

"I plugged 'im," came Huck's words, almost in a whisper, "and it's the best thing I ever done."

"And the food you was goin' to bring back, where is that?"

"Don't you go getting' all righteous on me, Trumble. I was in a tight situation, and food wasn't at the top of my list. That poor woman come first, in my mind, at least."

"Well, I reckon I cain't fault you none for that. Let's have a look at this feller before we stick him in the ground." Trumble walked up to the Indian pony, and lifted the blanket enough to get a peek at the man's face.

"Sonofa – !" he jumped back, his face suddenly ashen. "You got any idea who you done plugged?"

"You bet I do. And we're just about a day's ride short of feedin' our bellies for a year."

"Why hell, yes, Huck, you just made us rich. This here fella is none other than Dakota Joe, the most ornery, lowdown, backshootin' half-breed Arapaho scoundrel what ever set foot on this godforsaken prairie. He's been on the wrong side of the law for a year because of murderin' a bunch of squatters, stealin' their belongings, and burnin' their homesteads."

"Yep. And there's a $500 reward on his head, dead or alive, Trumble."

"There sure is. And do you know what that means?"

"Means we better skedaddle our butts up to Russell Springs and turn him over to the sheriff before he gets too ripe."

"You're sure as hell right about that, partner," Trumble said, with the emphasis on *partner*. He swung the blanket and saddle back onto his horse, cinched up the strap, and was mounted before a man could spit tobacco juice in a bug's eye. "Let's get a move on."

On that warm, late summer day, Huck Bannister and Trumble Barlow struck out for Russell Springs, the closest town they knew might have a sheriff where they could collect enough bounty to keep them in spending money and as much food as they could ever hope to consume for quite a spell. The grin on Trumble's face was unmistakable by its recognition of a rosy future. Huck's expression, on the other hand, was dark and troubled. Trumble couldn't figure what could possibly be eating at his friend, but he wasn't about to spoil his own joy by asking. And Huck wasn't volunteering to explain.

Huck's internal turmoil centered mainly on his inability to get that poor widow out of his mind. She wasn't anything spectacular to gaze upon, rather skinny, with a figure that struggled to differentiate her from a young boy, but there was an undeniable plea for help in her defiant stance against any such proffered aid. Her toughness seemed masked by the thinnest of veils. What could he do? Trumble wouldn't understand his wanting to return to the tiny squatter's plot, and *he* wasn't even certain that he should go back. His mental gymnastics concerning the issue only served to drive his mood from dark to morose. Huck kept his thoughts to himself to avoid any speechifying from a man who was prone to giving unwanted advice at a moment's notice. He looked up at that moment, and seeing Trumble staring at him like a man watching a snake sneak up on a mouse, Huck got the sudden impression his quiet self-examination had given him away, and he was about to find himself on the receiving end of a flurry of inept prophesying.

"What's got you all twisted up, Huck? Bothered by killin' this justly deservin' owlhoot?"

"Naw. Just in a reflective sort of mind. Never you bother."

"Hmmm." The thought had occurred to Trumble that maybe his partner wasn't thinking on Dakota Joe as much as he might be dwelling on that little widow woman. "Say, you ain't goin' sweet on that lady you saved from Dakota Joe, are you?"

Huck sighed, hoping that Trumble would interpret it as a sign that he was barking up the wrong tree. It didn't work. Huck was a marked man, and destined to be the target of a heap of unsolicited advice, like it or not.

"That's okay. You don't have to say nothin'. I know when a man has a woman on his mind. Don't you think I don't. Why in my time, I've seen men driven to the most unspeakable horrors imaginable, even as downright disgusting as, well, as marriage." Trumble made a play of shaking all over at the thought of such a thing. His theatrics, however, weren't making the impression he'd hoped for on Huck. So he figured to continue, "Why I once knew a mountain of a man, a man of powerful strength, reduced to a snivelin' weakling by being tied to a woman's apron strings. Pitiful, just pitiful."

"Trumble, just leave a feller to his own thoughts, will you? If I want your lame advice, I'll up an' ask for it." Huck reached out with the lead rope and handed it to Trumble. "Here, time for you to take a turn at tugging this sorry carcass to Russell Springs for our reward." He let go and spurred his mare to take a more distant lead to give himself some relief from the odor, and to at least make Trumble shout if he was going to continue with his unwanted advice.

And shout Trumble did, for the next twenty miles.

After two days in the sun and heat, the anticipation of splitting $500 between the two down-on-their-luck cow punchers was giving way to something more unpalatable: the distinct odiferous perfume given off by Dakota Joe's bloating corpse. Huck tied three ropes together to allow leading the Indian pony at the greatest possible distance. It worked whenever they were upwind, but failed miserably whenever downwind. The good side of it all was that both Huck and Trumble had completely lost all desire for food of any kind. Any fear either might have had of dying from starvation was now but a distant memory.

Reaching Russell Springs turned out to be a most auspicious occasion, in that as soon as they hit the town limits sign, folks began scattering like chickens in the path of a runaway wagon. Folks were holding their noses and hollering at them like they were about to become the most unpopular drifters that ever set foot in the town. Huck spotted the sheriff's office by the sign hanging on a pole over the door. They dismounted out front, but before Huck could dismount, a portly man in a dirty cotton undershirt and suspenders yanked open the door.

"What in tarnation give you two idiots the idea to park that foul-smellin' thing in front of my office?" yelled the sheriff.

"We got ourselves a man wanted dead or alive," Huck blurted out, "and we come to collect the reward." Huck dismounted and strode up to the sheriff.

"Whooeee," he said, "that's got to be the godawfulest stench I ever did draw breath of. Get him down to the undertaker's, pronto. Tell him I'll be down directly." The sheriff went inside and closed the door before any more of the odiferous corpse could affect his surroundings further.

Huck turned to Trumble. "You take him on back down the street, while I go and arrange for our reward. I saw a sign in a window on our way into town. It said 'Undertaker and Tonsorial Parlor.'"

With no small amount of grumbling and muttering, Trumble led the horse carrying Dakota Joe using all three ropes tied together to keep as far away as possible from the deteriorating body.

Huck stomped up on the plank sidewalk and entered the sheriff's office. He removed his hat and stood in front of the desk, a makeshift contraption consisting of two barrels with a wide plank across them. The sheriff looked up from holding a handkerchief to his nose.

"Now what?"

"Well, sir, I was wonderin' if we could discuss the reward for the man we brung in. It's a feller called Dakota Joe, and I hear he's worth, uh, about five hundred dollars."

The sheriff picked up the top sheet off a pile of reward dodgers stacked on the end of his desk. He tossed it in front of Huck. "This the fella?"

"That's him, yessiree, in the flesh. He's the one I done plugged after he murdered some poor squatter out there 'bout twenty miles beyond them foothills."

"Can you prove it's him?"

"I knowed him on sight. You can have a look for yerself."

"Hmmm. Can't say as I, uh, favor visitin' with a rotting corpse."

"Can't you just take my word for it?"

"Oh, it ain't your word I'm bound to cogitate on. Fact is, we got ourselves a problem. It concerns the reward."

"Uh, what kind of problem you talkin' about?" Huck frowned suspiciously.

"The reward has already been claimed, and paid out."

"What! How can that be? My partner and I just brung in the body. How can you pay a reward before the corpse arrives?"

"I knew it was on its way. She said there'd be a drover bringin' ol' Dakota Joe in. She claimed the reward. Said it was her husband that was killed, therefore it was the just thing to do."

"She?"

"The widder woman. 'Course she tells a slightly different tale. Says she plugged him herself just as he was about to do to her what he'd done to her husband."

"Well, how'd you know we'd be bringin' in the right fella?"

"She pulled out that right distinctive Smith & Wesson of his with the silver snake on the grips. Half the country has seen him with it. Too often, up close. Never saw another'n like it."

Huck stood staring at the sheriff with a look that suggested he'd just consumed a bowl of persimmons. He swallowed hard. He'd just been bamboozled by a skinny little stick of a woman, and he wasn't quite sure what to do about it. And why the hell hadn't he thought of pickin' up that .44?

"But I – " Huck stammered.

"Aint no sense chewin' on it no more. There ain't nothin' I can do to change the circumstances. Sorry, son; better luck next time."

Huck slunk away to meet up with Trumble halfway between the sheriff's office and the undertaker's establishment. He was muttering to himself when Trumble came up looking like the cat that swallowed the canary.

"Let me see it. I ain't never seen five hundred dollars all in one place before."

"And you ain't goin' to now, either."

"Huh? What do you mean? You got the reward money, didn't you?"

"No."

"What! How come you don't have it? There was a reward. I know 'cause I saw the poster."

"It ain't that. The widder woman claimed the reward before we got here. She beat us to town. Said she'd shot him. She said a feller came along and offered to haul the corpse into town for her. The sheriff believed her and took her to the bank to get her the reward."

"How in tarnation could she have beat us here?"

"Someone musta hitched up her wagon."

"Now what lamebrain would do such a thing?"

"I reckon you know."

Trumble hung his head. "All that work and we still ain't even goin' to get a bite to eat for our efforts."

The two of them settled on the steps in front of the hotel. Both leaned on their knees, with chins buried in their cupped hands. Just then, the rattle of a wagon could be heard approaching. Huck looked up to see the widow holding the reins, sitting up straight and proud, with a peaceful look on her face. When the wagon was within a few feet of the boys, she pulled back hard on the reins, bringing the horses to a halt. She looked down at Huck with a smile, the first he'd seen after all the tragedy that had befallen her. *She's durn near pretty*, Huck thought. *Too bad she ain't a tad more honest.*

"I want to thank you for helpin' me. If it weren't for you, I'd be lying out there on the prairie cold as a stone. I feel bad for claiming the reward, but without the money, I'd have nothing. And with my poor husband dead and buried, what chance would a woman alone have in this godforsaken wilderness? "

"Reckon we know the feeling," grumbled Trumble.

"You boys work a ranch hereabouts?" she said.

"No, ma'am, we're out of work. I was on my way to ask for a handout when I saw that man shoot your Henry," Huck said.

"Got no jobs at all?"

"Nope."

"Well, I sure am sorry to hear that. But you'll come up with somethin' one of these days. Best of luck to you both." She clucked her tongue and slapped the reins against her team's rumps. She gave the boys a dispassionate nod as the wagon rumbled on out of town.

The boys watched it disappear in a dusty cloud. Huck looked at Trumble, and Trumble looked right back, his expression turning dark as a storm cloud.

"I don't like that look on your face. What's rattlin' around in that empty space where a brain ought to be, Trumble? C'mon, out with it."

"Maybe you shoulda let Dakota Joe do what he intended *before* you took yer shot."

Storm Damage

A Rome Warfield Frontier Mystery

by Pete Peterson

Pete Peterson, a member of Western Writers Of America and of Western Fictioneers, is the author of The Relentless Gun, Reckoning At Raindance, A Dark Trail Winding, Bloodbath At Picture Rock *and* Mark Of The Serpent, *which is also available as an audio book and an e-book under the title of* Black Clouds And Epitaphs, *plus an e-book novella,* Catch A Killer By The Toe.

Chapter 1

"You can see him now, but don't stay long. I gave him a hefty dose of laudanum, and he needs to get some sleep." Doc Blanchard dropped his stethoscope into his bag and snapped shut the clasp.

"What all did you find wrong with him, Doc?"

"Well, his right forearm is broken, as you know. You splinted it. ...Nice job, by the way... And he has a badly sprained ankle. Otherwise, just a few scrapes and bruises. What happened to him, anyhow? All he had to offer me were a few select cuss words."

Deputy Rome Warfield grinned. "Yeah, he's good at that. He was on his way back from a meeting in Climax with a group of mine owners and area lawmen about a rash of payroll robberies. Said a cougar spooked his horse, and he got tossed into a tangle of brush and downed trees off the side of the trail. When he wasn't back by dark, I took off looking. I ran into his horse, then backtracked it to the marshal. He'd dragged himself back up to the trail and was sitting there smoking his pipe."

Rome shook the doctor's hand and escorted him out, then entered Marshal Sam Catlin's bedroom. Ruth, Sam's wife, smiled at him and left them alone to talk.

"How you feeling?" Rome asked.

"Don't know. Doc's got me juiced up on that stuff he totes around in his little case. Thanks again, for coming out to get me." Rome nodded. "You're going to need to hire you some help 'til I'm back on my feet. We've been needing another man anyhow, what with all the drifters passing through since the end of the war."

"Any ideas on who we could get?"

"Maybe. There's a cowpoke from that ranch just over the mountain, name of Nick Hazard. He's a nice youngster, and gun handy. Had him with me on a posse or two a while back, before you hired on."

"I've met him," Rome said, "he courts that little waitress, Katy Nesbitt, who works with my girl, Janet, over at the restaurant in the Paragon Hotel. I'll give him a holler."

"Do that. But it's your call, Rome. If you take him on, be careful. He's fearless, and cocky. Doesn't have sense enough to be afraid when he ought to. Makes him reckless.

"Now, get out of here so I can get some rest."

* * *

It was Saturday, and the main street of Fairplay was clogged with traffic at this time of evening. Merchants closing up shop and headed for home, freight and ore wagons making their final runs of the day, early arrivals looking to make a long and lively night of it in the saloons. A plump crimson sun was just settling behind the jagged peaks of the Continental Divide, and already the air was filled with tinny piano music and the first awkward sounds of gritty laughter filtering into the street through batwing doors.

Knowing it would be a busy evening for him, Warfield headed for the Paragon to get a meal prior to having to deal with the night's celebrants, and, primarily, he wanted to see Janet Tinker, who managed the restaurant in the hotel. He and Janet had been keeping steady company since Rome captured the man who had killed her father. They were planning to marry soon, an event both anxiously anticipated. He peered between the shade and the painted lower section of the restaurant window. Only a few diners were in attendance. Maybe Janet could sit with him while he ate. Walking into the dining area, Rome spotted Katy Nesbitt. He motioned to her.

"Evening, Katy. Is Janet here?"

"In the kitchen. Want me to get her for you?"

"Please, in a bit. Have you seen Nick Hazard? I'd like to speak with him."

"We have a date tonight, after the restaurant closes. I'll tell him."

* * *

Nick Hazard was a dark, handsome young man, broad through the shoulders, with a ready smile and boundless energy. Rome figured him to be about his own age. Maybe a year or two older, an inch shorter. He held himself erect, and wore his sidearm low on his hip.

"Hazard, I've got a proposition for you. The marshal is going to be laid up for a while as a result of an accident he had . . ."

"Yeah, I heard. Too bad."

"Anyhow, he reckons we need another deputy until he's fit for duty again, and he suggested you. Are you interested?"

"Yer dern tootin', I am. When can I start?"

"Bring in what gear you need tomorrow morning. Find you a place to stay while you're in Fairplay. Then I'll take you over to the marshal's house and he can swear you in." Warfield stuck out his hand. "Glad to have you aboard."

* * *

The cowpoke enthusiastically accepted the deputy's badge that Marshal Catlin offered. Rome and he soon became friends. They worked well together, and Nick was a quick learner and a tireless worker. As Janet and Katy were also friends, the two young couples occasionally spent time together, riding, picnicking, just visiting... their opportunities limited by the opposing and alternating schedules of the two lawmen.

For weeks, the women of Fairplay, and some of the men, had been excitedly making preparations for the annual Spring Dance and Hoedown. People flocked to these annual affairs from miles in every direction, hungry for news, anxious to be among their friends and neighbors again after being cloistered inside by a long winter. Tables, chairs and benches were gleaned from kitchens, homes and businesses; bunting and banners were hauled out of storage; ladies were busily threading needles or pumping the treadles of their sewing machines, stitching, snipping and sewing on new and refurbished outfits for the anticipated gathering. Rome arranged for two of the townsmen who were not planning on attending the festivities to watch the office so that both he and Nick could squire their ladies to the dance.

Nick had taken a room at Miss Hazel's Bed & Board, but he had left many of his belongings at the ranch. The afternoon of the big dance, he told Rome that he was riding over to collect his dress clothes. Warfield cast a wary eye on the sky to the southwest where a dark cloud bank was building.

"You'd best take the long way 'round and stay off the summit, Nick. Looks like it's going to storm, and it'll get mighty hairy and dangerous on top."

Hazard raised an eyebrow and looked at Rome with a smirk on his face.

"Thanks for the advice, Mother Warfield. Meet you at the dance." He galloped off, waving his hat in the air and whooping it up like a school boy.

* * *

People poured into the Golden Egg Dance Hall and Saloon, greeting old friends, craning their necks as they entered to see who had arrived before them. Townsfolk, farmers, cattlemen, sheepherders, miners . . . men who were often at odds with one another during the normal course of their working lives . . . visited amiably in the convivial atmosphere. The ladies proudly carried their covered dishes to place them among others on the long tables, then circulated around the hall to see who was wearing what and who was with whom. The men greeted each other, passing sly winks as they showed the bottles hidden in their coats and boot tops. The musicians and callers milled around the band area under colorful bunting streamers, tuning their instruments and making preparations. It promised to be a gala evening.

Little square wooden tables, each covered with a cloth, were spread around the perimeter of the hall. An assortment of chairs were placed four to a table. Wooden benches were situated farther back against the walls. Rome, Janet and Katy had lingered at the door, waiting for Nick to join them, until it started to rain, then hustled inside and settled themselves at a table.

Rome reached beneath the tablecloth to clasp Janet's hand. She was dressed stunningly in an emerald green gown with white lace ruffles top and bottom. Her hair was pulled cleanly to one side, cascading in long, golden ringlets over her shoulder. He had been taken with her from that first glance; she had been one of the first faces he had noticed in the town of Fairplay as he was having coffee with Marshal Catlin in the restaurant. He'd been captivated then, by her large green eyes, her pert little button of a nose, sprinkled with freckles. He liked the way she allowed her blond hair to fall free over her shoulders, and the way her nose crinkled when she laughed. Most folks might not see her as beautiful, but to Rome she was the loveliest creature he had ever encountered. He felt that he was a most fortunate man.

Katy kept a worried watch on the entrance for Nick Hazard's arrival. Janet patted her hand, saying, "Don't worry. He'll be here. He was probably forced to take shelter from the rain."

The musicians raised their fiddles and bows, guitars and picks. The music began, and, as if in concert from above, a tremendous clap of thunder resounded through the hall. The walls shuddered. Windows rattled. Rain pounded the roof in a deluge. Undaunted by Nature's competition the callers cried out, the music continued and the floor filled with swirling skirts, stomping boots and smiling faces.

* * *

Earlier, Nick had agonized over his choice of wardrobe longer than planned. With a dubious glance at the darkening, boiling clouds that were beginning to block the mountaintop from view, he cinched up, donned his slicker and swung into leather. He patted his horse's neck.

"We're running late, ol' fella. But I'm figuring we can beat the storm to the top of that pass."

The absence of marmots, chipmunks, birds and squirrels along his route nagged at him. He had learned long ago to heed nature's warnings. Were the creatures seeking shelter from a serious storm? Picking his way up the trail through a light but steady rain, Nick topped out on a granite slab. His horse began sidestepping, eyes wide, searching for purchase on the slick surface. Dismounting, Nick tried to lead his frightened mount. Inch by inch they made their way toward firmer footing.

"Rome was right. Should have taken the longer trail downslope."

A crash of thunder startled them both and the reins were jerked free of his grasp. He lunged to catch up the reins as lightning danced all around them along the sodden ground. Spotting a slight overhang of rock, he huddled against the cliff face, fighting to keep a grip as the horse danced about in terror.

The blinding bolt of lightning unleashed from the heavens carried with it a momentous crash of thunder. Time seemed to stop as Nick watched the fiery shaft strike the horse, killing it instantly and sending a charge through the wet reins into Nick's body, robbing him immediately of consciousness and hurling him powerfully and roughly into a nest of boulders.

* * *

Rome and Janet danced a couple of times, then he

215

danced once with Katy, trying to take her mind off
Nick's absence, but she was preoccupied and they
returned to the table before the music stopped.

"Katy," Rome said, "You need to forget whether Nick
will show or not, and have some fun. If he doesn't get
here, I'll go find him when the storm's over. You are an
attractive girl, and there are plenty of young fellas here
that'd love to dance with you. This is a once-a-year
occasion... enjoy it!"

"I don't know. It just doesn't feel right... kind of like it
would be disloyal."

Janet took her hand. "Katy, Nick's the one that didn't
show. The bad weather is the only culprit here that I
can see. Now, I'm your boss. Have fun! That's an order."

Katy nodded and smiled as she became visibly more
relaxed. Shortly, a young cowboy came sidling shyly up
to the table. Hesitantly, he tapped her on the shoulder.
"'Scuse, me ma'am. Would you care to dance?"

Chapter 2

The storm lessened, then passed on to the east and
was replaced by the setting sun. It was too late to begin
his search for Nick Hazard by the time the dance ended;
he'd be apt to miss him in the dark. So, after he'd seen
the ladies home, Warfield went to the marshal's office to
relieve the men that had volunteered to hold down the
fort. They were playing a game of dominoes at the
marshal's desk.

"Thanks, Josh... Ed. I appreciate the favor. You can
leave any time."

"Can we finish our game first, Rome? We each won
three games," Ed told him, "and I'd like to break the tie
before we quit."

"By the way," Josh added, "you have a prisoner. Old
man Redding got so drunk he was afraid to ride home,
with it raining and all, so we let him use a bunk in the
first cell. You can kick him loose if you want."

Rome grinned. "Naw, let him sleep it off. While you
gents finish your game, I'm going to walk over and see if
the marshal's still awake. I gotta take a little trip in the

216

morning, and I need to tell him about it."

"Do you want we should come back and watch the office while you're gone? This beats working all ways from Sunday."

Rome smiled and waved away the comment as he went out the door.

* * *

He was up and saddled by dawn. Assuming that his missing deputy had taken the sensible, longer route around the base of the mountain, Warfield headed out. He rode slowly so that he wouldn't miss any sign that Nick had come this way. It was almost noon by the time he reached the Double D ranch. He rode up to an old cowpoke who was tossing hay into a muddy catch corral.

Introducing himself, Rome asked the man if he knew the whereabouts of Nick Hazard.

"Nope. Didn't he make it back to Fairplay?"

Rome shook his head, and said, "Thanks," starting to turn his horse. The cowpoke stopped him.

"Last I seen him, he was headed upslope to the pass."

"Dadgum it! I told him to take the long way 'round, that the summit is too dangerous in bad weather."

"Told him the exact same thing. But if you know Nick atall, you know he always figgers he knows best."

More worried than ever, Warfield headed slowly up the mountain trail, eyes to the ground, alert for signs of the deputy's passing. He topped out on the granite surface at the summit, glanced to his right and spied the carcass of the dead horse.

As he got nearer, he saw that the scavengers had already been at the animal's vitals, and when he smelled the fried meat aroma he was seized with fear for his young friend's safety.

"Nick! Nick Hazard!," he screamed out, his head on a swivel.

Climbing slowly from the nest of boulders where he'd been catapulted by the powerful thunderbolt, Nick stumbled into the clearing. His eyes were but pinpoints in their sockets, his hair and brows were singed and Rome could see that his left hand was red and angry. Bruises and scrapes covered his face, but otherwise he seemed in fair shape, physically. He wandered about in a daze, barely taking note of Rome.

"Nick . . . are you allright?"

He didn't answer, but stared blankly past Rome's shoulder.

Dismounting, Warfield walked up to his friend and gently led him by the arm to the big buckskin. After several tries and one slight mishap, Nick was sitting the saddle. Rome mounted behind him on the horse's wide haunches and they rode cautiously down the mountain toward Fairplay.

* * *

Doc Blanchard treated his burns, scrapes and bruises, pronounced him otherwise unharmed physically, gave him a dose of medicine to help him sleep and ordered him to bed. Nine hours later, Nick stirred and opened his eyes to find Katy and Rome at his bedside.

"Well . . . howdy, I guess. What are you two doing here? What happened? Am I sick . . . or hurt?"

"You don't know what happened to you?" Katy asked him, gently laying her hand atop his.

Nick frowned in concentration. "No, I reckon not. Last thing I recollect was heading out to get my fancy duds for the dance. Is the dance over?"

Katy shrugged, looked to Rome, and he explained what had happened.

"I went back up to get your saddle and tack off the horse. Some of it is pretty badly charred, but it will do to use until you can replace it. Thank heavens you're not bad hurt."

Nick sat up and swung his legs over the side of the bed. He looked woefully at Katy and said, "Sorry I missed the dance."

Katy laughed and gave him a hug.

* * *

The next day, Nick Hazard was up and dressed,

anxious to renew his duties. He walked downstairs to the dining room, ate a hearty breakfast, and then rushed out the door. Hesitantly, he looked up. The sun was shining brightly and a few puffy clouds floated across an azure sky, looking like biscuits spilled from a pan.

When he reached the marshal's office, Rome wasn't around, so he fetched some water, kindled a fire in the cast-iron stove and put a pot of coffee on to brew. Shortly, Rome walked in, a sheaf of papers in his hand.

"Nick. I didn't expect you in. Don't you think you ought to take a couple of days to get your strength back?"

"I'm not one for lyin' abed. I need to be doing something."

"Allright then, if you think you're feeling up to it. Why don't you walk over to Marshal Catlin's house. He's been concerned about you, and I know he'd appreciate the company. He's sitting up in a chair now, but he still can't get around much.

"Then we better decide what to do about getting you a horse. You can't pursue the forces of evil afoot."

Nick grinned. "Right. I can borrow a ride from the ranch. And I know they've got extra saddles and tack. After I see the marshal I'll hire a horse from the livery and ride over there."

"Tell the hostler that I said to bill the office," Warfield told him. "Then, when you get back, you'd best check in with Katy. She'll be happy to see you up and about."

Rome watched Nick out the door, then seated himself at the desk and gathered together the papers he'd picked up earlier at the Wells Fargo office. A fresh batch of wanted flyers. It seemed that most of the hombres walking outside the boundaries of the law of late were Southerners, disenfranchised by the war. He, himself, had not joined in the conflict. Being from Texas, he would have felt honor bound to cast his lot with the gray of the Confederacy, but he had disagreed with the entire concept of secession. And he didn't think he could have fired upon the Stars and Stripes. Luckily, being employed as a lawman in Colorado Territory, he had not been forced to a decision.

Rome was still fairly new at this law business. He had been riding the shotgun seat on the big ore wagons out of the Climax diggings when a half dozen hard-eyed highwaymen, bristling with hardware, stormed from the rocks at the top of a grade and opened fire on the train of three mule-drawn wagons. When the gunsmoke had cleared from the scene and the echoes of gunfire had stilled in the surrounding forest, Rome Warfield stood alone in the road, his shotgun and sidearm empty. Three of the bandits were dead. Another lay wounded, and two had crept off into the trees. The very day the story reached Fairplay, Marshal Catlin, needing a deputy, rode to Climax, sought young Warfield out and offered him the badge. Rome had always imagined that being a law dog would be an exciting, romantic, action-packed way of life, but he had discovered that it was more a matter of serving as combination night watchman, paper shuffler and nursemaid to drunks, even in a frontier town as unruly and unkempt as Fairplay. Still, if he hadn't taken the job, he would never have met Janet, and he could not imagine not having her in his life.

* * *

The distant roll of thunder from the peaks to the west caused Nick to toss restlessly in his bed. He opened his eyes, then rolled over, seeking sleep. A brilliant bolt of lightning outside his window lit up his room and pulled him erect as surely as a rope might do. He sat, his eyes wild, then arose and dressed. In a trance, he left the boarding house and walked the half block to the stable. Quickly saddling his horse, he rode away, toward the mountains, toward the storm.

Chapter 3

Nick Hazard awoke as false dawn came creeping into the town of Fairplay, a heavy cloud cover abetting the darkness in corners, cracks and crevices. His head was pounding. It felt as if it were about to split open. He raised a hand to his brow.

He sat bolt upright. There was blood on his hands. He looked down at his body. He was lying on top of the bed covers, fully dressed. His clothes were damp, there was mud on his boots. What the hell?!

Quickly he got to his feet. He washed off in the porcelain basin on the stand under the mirror, changed into dry clothes and wiped his boots free of mud. He stared at his image in the mirror. *What was happening to him?* He had no recollection of anything that may have occurred last night. Where had he been? What had he done? He remembered nothing after the startling lightning and thunder last night . . . not having gotten out of bed . . . not getting dressed . . . not going out. Was this some aftereffect of the incident of the storm on the mountaintop? Nick decided not to confide in anyone until he could figure out what was going on; what was happening to him.

Aware again of the throbbing pain in his head, he headed downstairs to rustle up a cup of coffee before breakfast. As he reached the portal to the dining room, Rome Warfield burst through the front door.

"Good. You're up. Come with me."

Nick had a sinking feeling of impending doom. "I haven't even had coffee, or breakfast," he complained.

"Eat later . . . there's been a killing!"

* * *

The lawmen rushed to an alley behind the Tenstrike Saloon. A small group of men, all huddled and bent at the waist, were staring at a large, rain-soaked mass on the ground. Warfield elbowed his way into the circle and ordered the men to stand back. A body lay in disarray, covered by mud and blood. It was one of the women that worked in the saloon and plied her trade in the rooms above the bar. She lay face up, her eyes bulged in their sockets. Doc Blanchard was squatted by the body, his weight resting on his heels. He was wiping eye make-up and splatter off the victim's face with his handkerchief. Stepping closer, Rome saw that a wire of some sort was deeply embedded in the woman's throat. The group of men had moved in closer again. The deputy waved them away.

"You two men stick around and carry the body to the casket maker. The rest, get out of the alley. Go home. Show a little respect."

One of the gawkers wisecracked, "Precious little . . . all she deserves."

Another added, "Damn sure won't help her, she's sure enough dead."

Rome, anger at their callous remarks showing in his eyes, glowered at them, stood and moved toward the men, who turned in unison and bolted for the street. He glanced around, looking for Nick, who was leaning weakly against the outer wall of the saloon, his face pale.

The doctor eased the wire from around the corpse's throat, wiped it with his kerchief and handed it to Deputy Warfield. He looked to the men that Rome had recruited to transport the body and stepped away from the dead woman.

"You can take her now."

Rome stepped up beside the doctor, saying, "Must have happened during or before the rain we had last night. Her clothes appear to be soaked through, but the ground under the body is fairly dry.

"Doc, could you tell if she'd been... you know... messed with?"

"Don't know for sure, seeing as what she did for a living, but her undergarments weren't torn or in disarray. I'd say no.

"Who do you figure could have done this brutal thing, deputy?"

"Hard to say, doc. Might have been a disappointed client, a drifter, someone from the mines . . . most anybody."

Rome turned to Nick, who was still leaned against the saloon wall. "You O.K.?"

Hazard nodded that he was. Rome stepped over and handed him the wire from the murdered woman's neck.

"Better get you some breakfast under your belt. You look a mite peaked. Then ask around... see if you can find out what sort of wire this is and where it came from. I'm going to talk to Mrs. Blessing and find out what this gal's name was, and see if she knows who she was keeping company with last night."

They left the alley, the doctor headed back toward his office. Rome knocked at the closed saloon door, trying to rouse the occupants.

Nick wandered down the street, inspecting the murder weapon in his hand. He lowered himself weakly to sit on the edge of the boardwalk. He pushed his hat back on his head and rubbed his forehead. He knew well what the wire was... a guitar string, like the ones he carried as replacements in his saddle bags. Why couldn't he remember where he was last night, what he'd done? The last he recalled was the blinding flash of lightning and the crash of thunder. Was his lack of awareness some aftereffect of that incident on the mountain top? Was the storm a trigger to his memory lapse?

Dreading what he might *not* find, Nick made his way to where his horse was stabled and where he stored his saddle and other tack. His horse was in its stall, still saddled! He *never* left a horse saddled! Warily, with the irresistible need to know, he lifted the flap of his saddlebag and withdrew a soft deerskin pouch. He peered inside... four guitar strings. The breath was pulled from his lungs, there was a ringing in his ears! *There should be five!*

Nick Hazard was stunned and frightened... or was it excitement instead of fright? Could he possibly have killed that woman and not remember doing it? Why would he kill her? He had never even seen her before that he recalled. Would it happen again? Of course he couldn't let Rome, or anyone else, know what he was thinking, or imagining. It was ridiculous, of course. Or was it?

Chapter 4

Nick kept a wary eye to the sky. It was spring, the season of thunderstorms. But fair weather reigned as the days and nights passed. The only new disturbances in the town of Fairplay were the normal fights and brawls sparked by women, cards and booze. Nick had told Rome that the wire that had strangled the soiled dove from the saloon was determined to be a guitar string, but *not* that it might have been one from his own saddlebag. When he had first discovered the string missing, he had started to discard those that remained in the pouch, but something stayed his hand. The shocking crime remained unsolved.

* * *

Dark clouds, laced with lightning, gathered over the western peaks, their bellies filled with rain. As they neared, Nick could feel his awareness slipping away, but he steeled himself, fighting it off, resolved to stay alert. The storm and the lightning grew closer. He raised his face to the skies. Pelted by raindrops, blinded by lightning, he felt suddenly obsessed to join the storm at the heights of the mountain. As he rushed toward the stable, he knew with a growing excitement that tonight he would kill!

* * *

He was standing over the body when Warfield arrived at the scene. He slipped his hands into his pockets.

"I just found her, Rome, while I was doing my rounds. Looks to be like the other killing . . . there's a wire around her neck, too."

The latest victim of the storm killer was an elderly Chinese woman who eked out a modest living taking in laundry, mending and tailoring clothes.

"Dammit!" Rome kicked at a whiskey bottle laying near the body. "It's old Miz Chen Li. Never bothered a soul.

"Well, go fetch the doc and send him over, then have the undertaker send someone for the body. I'll wait here until Doc Blanchard finishes, then I better go tell the marshal about it. Maybe he's got a notion on how to solve this thing."

It was lunchtime when Warfield left the Catlin house, so he headed for the Paragon dining room. Janet served him the special of the day, then joined him at the table. He filled her in on the latest murder in the streets of Fairplay.

"Trouble is," Rome was saying, "there's lots of cowpokes and such play the guitar, and anyone would have access to the strings. They got them on the shelf over at the Mercantile. Where do I even start?"

"You're right," agreed Janet. "I know of several who play. Two of the musicians in the band that played at the Spring Dance, for instance. Why, even Nick plays some."

"Huh? How do you know that?" Rome was frowning, looking thoughtful.

"Katy told me. She says when he first started courting her that he used to play for her. She said he plays well. But wait . . . surely you don't suspect Nick?"

"What? No . . . no, of course not. I just didn't realize he was musical. He never said"

He filed the thought away.

* * *

"Looks like rain again, Nick. Keep your slicker at hand. I want us both on the street tonight in case this madman tries to kill again."

Nick was staring into his coffee cup. He nodded his head, but didn't look up.

"Get yourself some supper," Rome added, "and meet me back here at dark."

The deputies of Fairplay, each armed with sixgun and rifle, patrolled the main street of town in a pouring rain, one on each side, peering into every darkened alley, corner, and alcove, alert to every movement and sound. Each man cast furtive glances at the other, watching his counterpart's progress. As Warfield neared the Tenstrike, a crashing of glass, a woman's scream and a shot pierced the night air. Rome pushed open the door and rushed inside, his rifle cocked and held at waist level. Nick, his eye on the action, leapt off the boardwalk into the mud of the street as rolling thunder filled his ears.

Inside the saloon, a cowhand and a miner were struggling in front of the bar, pounding on each other, the source of their disagreement watching from behind a support post with an expression of excitement evident on her painted features.

"Who fired that shot?" Rome yelled toward the barkeep.

"I did," he said, "the Cousin Jack pulled a knife."

A disgusted look on his face, Deputy Warfield stepped between the combatants.

"That's enough! Now break it up, or you are both going to jail!"

Grumbling to himself, Rome pushed through the door and into a driving rain. Squinting, attempting to spot Nick through the downpour, he plunged into the muck of the street. He roamed both sides of the street, looking for the missing deputy. A blinding flash of lightning made silhouettes of the buildings as crashing thunder rattled windows.

Warfield faltered, then headed swiftly toward Miss Hazel's Bed & Board. He checked to make sure that Nick was not in his room, then rushed to the stable where he kept his mount, a suspicion growing in his gut despite his wanting to reject it.

Nick's horse and saddle were missing. Hurrying home, Rome quickly saddled up, mounted and rode to the marshal's home. Seeing light at the rear of the house, he pounded on the door.

"Sorry to disturb you, Miz Catlin, but I really need to see the marshal."

"Ruth, what is it?" Sam Catlin called out from his bedroom.

Apologizing, Rome pushed past the marshal's wife and hurried into the bedroom, where he explained the events of the evening to the marshal, and told him of his growing suspicions.

"I'm going to follow him up the mountain. I needed

you to know, Sam, in case something happens up there."

"This is hard to believe, but yes, follow him. But you watch yourself. Go . . . git."

* * *

Cautiously, Warfield approached the spot near the summit of the mountain where he'd found Nick's dead horse upon the occasion of that earlier, fateful storm. The white, stripped bones of the carcass with the beast's staring skull were illuminated by a flash of lightning. Rome dismounted, tethering his horse, then drawing and cocking his sidearm. Rain pelted the brim of his hat. Every sense alert, he walked stealthily through and across the rain-slicked rocks and boulders of the summit. He was creeping through the belly of the storm.

To hell with this. I'm going to get myself killed. I'll wait him out at the base of the trail. Warfield turned to gather in his horse as a brilliant display of lightning danced around the mountaintop. His horse screamed in terror and reared up, pulling loose its tether. As Rome lunged for the reins his feet slipped on wet grass. His sixgun fell from his hand and tumbled out of reach. As he started to clamber to his feet, another lightning flash revealed Nick Hazard standing over him, rifle in hand, glaring at him with wild eyes.

"Nick, don't!"

But the man standing over him was no longer his friend, the Nick he knew. This was a fiend. A man possessed. Hazard pumped a cartridge into the chamber and took a bead on a spot on Rome Warfield's forehead between the eyes. His finger closed on the trigger of the gun.

"Nick . . . stop!"

Lightning now danced all around the drama playing out on the heights. Thunder was a constant, deafening roll. Then, as if in direct defiance of the powers of the storm, Nick Hazard raised his face to the sky, roared and stabbed the rifle in the air. *Fire danced down the barrel of the rifle, lighting up the gunman, encasing his body.* A sickening odor of burning flesh and brimstone filled the air.

Rome lay there, stunned and baffled, for what seemed a long while. The atmosphere calmed and the fury that had engulfed the mountain moved off, its damage wrought. Rome's heart slowed. His horse came up from behind and nuzzled him. He pushed to his feet, and, eyes filled with tears, bowed his head against the horse's long head to send a "thank you" heavenward.

* * *

When the charred corpse of the haywire killer cooled to the touch, Rome hefted the body to rest over the haunches of the dead man's horse. Using some guitar strings he found in Nick's saddlebag, he tied the blackened body securely. Then, mounting his own horse, he plodded slowly down the trail to Fairplay.

Epilog

The storm had passed, as storms do, when Deputy Warfield returned to town, shoulders slumped and hat hung low, with his grim cargo in tow. The stirrings of a community preparing to meet a new day told him how long he had spent on the mountaintop. He delivered his gruesome cargo to the undertaker, then rode on to the marshal's house.

Marshal Catlin had been unable to go back to sleep after Rome had left the previous night, and was awaiting his return in a chair in his living room. Deputy Warfield reported the happenings of the long night. Then, refusing Mrs. Catlin's kind offer of breakfast, he went to his quarters, where fatigue pressed him deep into his mattress. He slept past mid-day.

Now he sat at a table in the dining room of the Paragon Hotel across from Janet Tinker. Janet's arm was draped around the shoulders of a snuffling Katy Nesbitt. Rome was telling them of the entire progression of events, and of the harrowing episode on the mountain.

"Nick wasn't a bad person, really. When that earlier incident with the lightning occurred, it must have done something to his mind. He went haywire, and whenever it stormed again, he just snapped. We'll never know, I guess, if he'd have been all right in time. But the killing had to stop.

"Now, if one of you ladies can find me a waitress to take my order, I am famished."

Catch as Catch Can

A MAPLE JACK TALE

by Matthew P. Mayo

Matthew P. Mayo is a Spur Award and Peacemaker Award Finalist. His novels include the Westerns Winters' War, Wrong Town, *and* Hot Lead, Cold Heart, *and he contributes to several series of popular adventure novels. His short stories appear in numerous anthologies, and his non-fiction books include* Cowboys, Mountain Men & Grizzly Bears; Bootleggers, Lobstermen & Lumberjacks; *and* Sourdoughs, Claim Jumpers & Dry Gulchers. *Visit him at www.matthewmayo.com.*

I knew that leaving Mildred Tenterholden was the best thing to do. It was messy, what with all her crying and yelling and bouncing that two dollar china cup off my head, but it had to be done. I grunt, even now, when I think of that dainty cup. The lump from it's mostly gone, though if I probe the back of my pate, I can locate the sore spot.

I'm not sure what she was thinking, but as my eyes teared up from the pain, I watched that cup wobble then come to a stand-still, upright and unhurt on the polished floor beside my boots. I was ruminating on the fact that this woman wanted more than I was willing to part with. Like . . . my life, in a manner of speaking.

I plucked up my boots and took a last look at the woman who, for some crazy reason, had her flowery hat set on being my wife. I gave her a brief nod and slipped on out that door, clunked it shut behind me. She didn't follow. I let out a long breath and started legging it. Little did I know I may have been better off staying put in that fancy, powdery house. Well, maybe not. But before too long, I did have cause to reconsider my hasty departure.

Let me back up a bit and fill you in on who I am, what I do. It might help. My name is . . . well, never mind that. Folks call me Maple Jack. Have for as long as I can recall, on account of me coming out West from Vermont, the land of sugar maples, back when I was no taller than a tree stump. Back then I was long on possibilities and short on experience. I reckon I've tightened the distance between those two notions a good bit since then.

I have few talents, though I have acquired a good many skills in my time. I've been a fair hand at roundup, branding, castrating, the whole works — I can still put my shoulder to the wheel when I really need to. And though I prefer to keep a horse under me whenever possible, it's been a while since I've ridden anything but the aforementioned Miss Tenterholden. Come to think on it, she is a might long in the face.

Oh, I've also trapped beaver, skinned buffalo, and prospected some, and though the work was fine, the financial reward for each task was paltry. But I can, by God, catch a fish. Always could, and it's been a good talent to have through the years. Feels like money in the bank to me, though I'd never had enough cash at any one time to justify a bank account.

Heck, I've only ever been in a bank twice in my life, once to cash a check at the end of a short trail drive from Dios to San Juabel, and the last had been not long after I was "resurrected," as Miss Tenterholden called her rescue of me. She made a withdrawal to fund what she called my "requirements." Right about then I got the twitches deep down. Anyone other than me thinking they knew what I required was sorely mistaken or just plain wrong.

And not too long after the teacup incident, there I was, pretty near right back where she'd found me two weeks before — only this time I was awake and sober as a schoolmarm, though only because I was penniless. And fishing in the river instead of laying half in it, passed out and in danger of drowning, as she'd found me.

Under a gray rock by the riverbank, I found a fat, white grub, legs still raking the air like a machine, and speared him on one of the store-bought hooks I keep in my possibles bag, then swung-and-tossed my hand line in. Fishing's something anyone can do, though most people don't do it well.

As I overhanded that line back on in, then tossed it out again, I watched the little stick float I'd tied two feet above the hook to keep it up off the stony bottom, free from snags. And I thought back on this and that, nothing and everything, looked at the days as if I were seeing them through a stereopticon, some visions were clear as the water at the edge of the river, some were murky and full of motes, as if a detail I hadn't noticed before got startled and clouded the view as it left.

I wasn't even sure why — and I meant exactly pin-prick why — I stayed any longer than was necessary at Mildred's fancy little mansion. I'd recovered within a day or two, well enough for shuffling back out to the road. Could be the kindness she'd showed me. I guess I felt obliged to linger around the place for a spell, though there wasn't much for me to do. She had servants for near everything.

She'd found me on one of her Sunday buggy rides. Dragged me into her barouche and off we went. Course, this is what I've been told. I only remember waking up in a four-poster with clean duds and thick quilts. But do you know? There was not a drop of Who-Bit-Sam in the place. Dry as a landlocked boat. For two whole weeks. Twitchy? I guess to hell I was twitchy.

* * *

Everything I own is on my person or in my coat, so when I left there were no concerns about toting baggage. My possibles sack was looped about my neck on a leather thong and cinched at the mouth. In it I keep my money — when I have it — plus matches, flint and steel, fish hooks, and two small carvings, once richly colored in orange and blue and red. One is of a burro with full panniers looking down as if weighted by its flopped ears, and the other is a man, made to stand beside the beast, one hand out and looking up. He even has tiny notches like whiskers on his face. Just like me.

Whenever I shake them out of that old leather pouch to look them over, the colors are not like new and so always a bit of a disappointment — as with most things from the past, except maybe memories. And the memory of where they came from remains heartening.

They were given to me by the small, homely Mexican woman who carved them. I hadn't recalled her name in years. But I remember her hands — like worn leather, but always with a dusted look to them. From keeping them so often in water, she'd told me, they were always chapped and dry. She cleaned in the kitchens of three cookhouses and cafes in Santa Calla, where I had met her. In her spare time, since all of her money went to keeping her parents and nieces and nephews fed, she carved the little figures out of soft woods, and painted them with dyes she made herself from berries.

As I located the float bobbing in the current and twitched the line, her name popped into my head. Lucenza, the little carving woman. I wondered if she was still alive. Not any older than me, but she'd had a more difficult life, filled to brimming with worries and promises and disappointments. All from men who'd left plenty of seed but no roots. I supposed I'd been just another of those to her. As a whelp, I never set out to let anyone down, but over the years it always seemed to happen, just the same.

She carved each night, working away at the little figures so you could even see features like noses and cheekbones, little pokes for eyes. When I asked her one night why she did them, she'd just shrugged and dug at the little wooden creation, knife and figure each lost in the palms of her thick hands. I recall leaving her the next morning.

* * *

I feel like a preacher whose congregation's sprawled out snoring in front of him. Bear with me, I'm just getting to the meat of the matter — to the point, I've heard it called. And trust me, it's a sticker.

I tell you what, other than a different feeling I know of, a tight trembling on the fishing line has to be the best one going. That distinctive tug, like no other on earth, dragged me out of my musty old mind and told me I had a fish on.

I yarned him on in, steady and true. I had him hooked good, and he fought like he should, given that his life was on the line — which it was — and then there he was, twisting and flopping on the mud, a rainbow trout, thick in its sagging middle as my forearm used to be, back when I a mite taller. I rapped him on the bean pretty quick. No need for him to suffer because I wanted to admire his beauty.

I always regret taking the most valuable thing a creature has, its life, so I can fill my belly and not have to give up my own most valuable thing. It's a rough swap, but as the man said . . . you buy your ticket, you take your chances.

I will admit I was more than a little played out myself, not that it was hard work, but I hadn't had a proper feed yet that day, nor the day before. So I worked my way back to the edge of the mud, just onto the grass, where I'd probably get a little wet but not sopping, and was about to sit on down when I saw that log in the tall green grass, a little above me on the bank. I crawled up and over it, and laid down on the high side.

Just a quick wink, I told myself, and before I knew it, I was cutting wood. My fine fish was laid out waiting on the cool bank mud, line trailing from its mouth up to my hand, looped a few times around my wrist and forefinger, and tied in a light knot for safety's sake, the rest of it tucked in my breast pocket.

Well, sir, I've done a wagonload of fool things in my life, I'm here to tell you (which only shows how lucky I am), but grabbing winks behind that log ranks up there with the dooziest.

Some time later — how long I had no notion — I awoke, groggy and confused about why my arm was flopping and jerking like a fish itself. Then my arm whipped harder, almost pulled off of me.

It takes me longer than it ought to get my eyes open and clear the fuzziness from my brain. I sat up, pulling back on my arm, and heard a queer noise like gravel sliding or maybe drunkards belching. Or both. As I said I was a little groggy from sleep. I peeked through that tall grass and over the log, and what I saw made me want to close my eyes tight again and wait for the fever dream to pass.

But it was no dream. It was a mountain lion, one of the biggest I have ever seen, and it had my trout all but eaten. The only thing left was the head and I saw that disappointed, downturned mouth of the fish poking from the big cat's whiskered chops.

I watched that cat's head, some big when you're fifteen, twenty feet from it — the eyes in that head, I've never seen the like. A brown-gold with flecks of something even brighter in them, like seeing true gold glinting in the sun at the bottom of a shallow streambed. And they were fixed dead on me. I could not move. Look such a beast in the eye and tell me you ran from it — I won't believe you.

Its whiskers were as thick as that steel fishhook, and sticking straight out like porcupine quills. But the two things I noticed most of all were the yellow teeth that kept right on working that fish, even while that cat watched me, and the noises that bubbled up like coffee percolating from deep inside that animal, on up through its gizzard, and right out its mouth at me — even while I heard that fish snapping and cracking.

One of the cat's big bottom corner teeth was broken and jagged. I remember thinking a bone might have caused it, and immediately had thoughts of my own limbs snapping and cracking in that great maw.

I finally remembered to breathe, and it was then I noticed my arm, half-extended over the log, wagging in time with that cat's chewing. My fool limb was trying to conduct the cat like a bandmaster at a Sunday afternoon park concert. And then it occurred to me why — I was still what you might call attached to that fish. And if that fish went fully inside that lion's chops like it was fixing to do, then I would be attached to a mountain lion, too.

I reached with my free hand to loosen up the fish line and that lion's mouth, still gripping the fish, opened wide around my fish and shot a growl at me, warning like, and that free hand of mine slapped right back out of sight of its own accord. I don't think the cat could quite see all of me, but it doesn't matter. By then that light knot I'd tied on my hand to keep it safe had somehow ratcheted down on itself and welded into a hard knob. I felt it, but I couldn't quite see it, and I definitely couldn't reach for it. What a fix.

I figured at the rate that cat was dining on my fish that I had a good half-minute left before it was satisfied enough to leave. And then it would drag me with it. And it would also be in pain because of a certain fish hook it had just swallowed. And it would see that a man was following it. A man who it might associate with that pain it was feeling in its gut. Wouldn't take me long if I were in his shoes to turn on me and give me what-for. Then it came to me — my folding knife.

And just as fast as that thought came to me I remembered that the knife was in my coat pocket, along with my possibles bag, which I had taken off in case I had to go in after a fish. I'd laid the coat out away from the water, it being a hot day and the coat being the vehicle to carry all of my worldly goods. It was too far from my grasp. I could inch forward and nibble on that line. But it was newfangled and thick and truth be told not at all for fishing but more suited for cinching loads, it was that thick.

I wished for a gun. And wishing still didn't do any good. Several years before, I'd lost my sidearm to the threat of hunger. My old Texas Paterson had been with me since the war — I'd taken it off a dead Reb. He didn't need it and I did. Had to snap the fingers of that cold corpse to get it from his blue-skin grip — the holster slid out from under him easier. But in the end, after all those years, it bought more than a week's worth of tinned beef, peaches, and coffee. Kept body and soul together. And all to end up as a mountain lion's dinner. Strange world.

I lay there behind that log, my arm twitching with each bite, and it occurred to me: Just pull on it. I told you I was fuzzy when I first woke up. So I gave it a bit more tension. The chewing stopped and that cat made a sound I hope I never hear again in all my days: It sort of barked and coughed all at once. And then it growled. I gulped, but didn't let up on the pressure I had on the string.

Not that it would have mattered, because right about then it went slack. I peeked over the log and that thing was crouched down, shuffling toward me, in full kill stance, I'm sure of it.

I lowered my head and tried to flatten my tied hand down as close to the log as possible.

* * *

I'll always curse the fact that sound carries in that little river valley. From the narrow trail that runs alongside the stream, I heard the squeak and clatter of wheels on gravel — a work wagon, maybe. And so did the mountain lion. He spun and took off. My flopping arm nearly left me as that thing dug into the riverbank mud. The line connecting us zinged tight and that beast stopped short, confused and yowling again.

I couldn't take another wrenching like that so, keeping low, I skinned over that log and as soon as that cat felt slack in that line it cut loose again. Seconds passed before it winced and spun. I gave it slack and it took off. And this time, so did I. We made it across the river and well into the woods like that, stopping and staring at each other, then bolting. In my prime I couldn't keep up with a mountain lion, let alone now. But between that fetched up hook nagging him and being that they are ambush killers, I don't think he knew quite what to do with the man who trailed him so boldly. If he only knew how harmless I was to him, I feel sure I would have followed that fish in short order.

Finally, that cat made it past a big old oak and I happened to stumble 'round it the other way. Don't ask me how — to this day I cannot recall in much detail how we did it — but me and that cat whipped right around that tree, passing each other at least once as we ran. I think by that time we were both cinched tighter than Dick's hatband and twice as crazed, and were just looking to get away from each other.

I am still eternally grateful that the tree that chose to come between me and that mountain lion was thicker around than a fat man. We ended up on either side of it, me whining like a babe with colic, and that cat alternating between wincing at the sting of that hook in its jowl and swatting at me with paws the size of stove lids tipped with claws the like I've only seen hanging around the necks of Comanche braves who earned them in a way I wasn't prepared for at that moment.

At some point we both stopped and stood panting and staring at each other. I tugged at that damnable knot on my wrist. By then my hand was swelled up and throbbing like a bag of bees. But I did know that if I didn't do something soon, that cat would grow weary of this game and figure out a way around that tree and commence to tear me up. I did the only thing I could think to do: I muckled onto that knot with my teeth and, keeping my eyes on that cat, I chewed at the knot like I was starved and it was a two-dollar steak.

I may not have much in this world, but I do have a decent set of choppers — mostly still with me. I've taken care of them all these years. Always had a natural inclination to shy away from sweet foods — I'll take a cup of coffee and a wedge of cheddar over a slab of pie most days. If I've a hankering for a sweet flavor I'll tuck into a nice, crisp fall apple. Or maybe a can of peaches. But right then all I wanted was for them teeth to work double time on that blamed fishing string.

By that time we'd closed to within a man-length of

each other, I felt a couple of those strands pop, and I kept right on gnawing like a beaver in a brushfire. We made another turn around that tree, because that cat was too smart to stop, and I knew that if I didn't keep on moving, that thing would run into me from behind.

I don't know about you, but I'd rather face my end than have it sneak up on me all coward-like. Three feet now and that cat was yowling like his backside and his head were both on fire. There was another noise and I don't know but what it might have been me. It was a sort of high-pitched, girlish squeal. That's the last I'll speak of that.

As tough as that string was, it wasn't near tough enough to keep that cat from figuring out a different way around the tree in short order. I didn't waste any time in churning up sticks and leaves as soon as the last of that string snapped. I was halfway to China when something occurred to me that caught me up short.

Call it an attack of the guilties, call it humanity, call it what you will, but I stopped right there in that forest. I had been headed back the way we'd come, back toward my coat and the road. But that growling, coughing, barking, crying cougar pacing on a short tether, tight to that big old oak tree was pitiful, and I knew I couldn't leave him there.

What if he was too bothered by the pain that hook caused to ever free itself? What if it just stayed right there, whipped tight around that tree, getting more sore every day until that hook wound brought on a full-blowed body infection? What then? It would die. And all because of my store-bought fish hook.

I gulped then, I can tell you, as I turned back toward that mewling, yowling beast. But I knew what I had to do. Figured I was old anyway, and not much use to anyone anymore but maybe myself. Is that enough reason to keep on with it all? I still don't know the answer to that.

But I do know that a man, when hit hard enough just above the ear — don't even have to be all that hard — will drop like a sack of wet sand right where he stands, unconscious to the world. I reasoned that since that thing had ears and a head roughly the size of a man's, a few stout raps on the bean, just like I did with that fish, would soon render it pretty near unconscious. Enough for me to work that hook out of its jowl, anyhow.

Didn't take me long to find a short, thick club of an old branch. I snapped off the pokey bits and licked my lips a few times as I quivered my way closer to that beast, which of course had turned to face me. I made sure I came up to it from the proper side, just in case the thing lunged at me, I'd have an extra heartbeat or so to scamper backward before it mauled me.

The beast stood there, looking ready to pounce. It had stopped growling and whining and stared at me with those vivid gold eyes, its ears flat back to its head.

I commenced to whomping on that cat's head. Figured I wouldn't kill it — thing like that's too angry to kill, at least with a stick. But it kept jerking its head back and forth. I can tell you for a few brief moments there I was having myself a fine time. Been many a long year since I had the upper hand in a tense situation.

I could at one time hold my own in a saloon brawl, and I've tossed my share of men — some my friends — over poker tables. One even went through a front window. Spent half a year's wages paying that one off. I had the good dumb fortune to fall asleep in the alley beside the saloon shortly after the incident. Woke up to someone toeing my boot and a voice saying, "Yep, that's him alright."

As I would with a man, I was trying to land a quick, clean blow to just above the cat's ear. Problem with that is a cat's ears are already pretty near the top of its head. So I tried to wheedle my way to where I could whap him just behind the ear — figured that was where I might have the most luck.

"Stand still and take it!" I yelled, that great beast cowering before me, that fishing line tensed right out like piano wire. I tell you I was feeling more like a man than I had in a long time. And I liked the feeling. That cougar was confused more than anything, now that I think back on it. Sure, he kept on lashing out at me, but I kept right on handling him with that stick, up one side and down the other, working his head like a surly rock that won't pop loose from the middle of a prize corn patch.

I was beginning to think that maybe man is the only beast who will succumb to such a beating when I heard a noise behind me. It was a snort and a bawling, low and rough. I knew what it was before I turned my head. And that cat did, too. For the time it takes to blink, that cat and me shared a look, right into each others' eyes, like we did before, back at the log, only this time it was more like shared pity.

I spun my head and yep, big as a small horse and twice as fat and hairy, was a silvertip grizzly bear. He dropped to all fours and started swinging his head back and forth like he was saying no in a big way, his head a hairy pendulum. And that killer clock was telling me one thing: Time to run. But I knew enough to not turn my back on such a beast. I backed away, talking to it like it could understand English. If it did, it didn't tell me so.

Meanwhile the mountain lion had backed away as much as the string allowed and had also quieted down considerably. He was just showing his teeth and laying them ears back. I noticed I'd lumped his noggin up a bit. I felt bad about that. I only wanted to cold-conk it to get the hook out, then I planned on skedaddling before he came to.

Add a bear to the batter and I wasn't so sure I wanted anything to do with that batch of biscuits. I backed away, keeping one eye on the bear, one eye on the lion — no simple trick, since they were about forty yards apart. But a distance like that means little to a full-grown grizz on the gallop.

He came on, slow and steady, swinging his great shaggy head, his ears perked in curiosity, his front feet almost facing each other at the instep. But it was those curved claws I was more concerned with. Every time he

241

set a foot down those gleaming black knives shook, his shoulder hump wagged, and that head swung. And he bawled like an old range boss I once worked for.

I was the only one of the three of us to keep my peace. At one point I backed into a tree, then scooted around it right quick. Good thing to have between me and a bear. The club I'd used to button up that cat's head was still in my hand and I gripped it tighter. Then, right at that point where the bear had to make a choice between me and that mountain lion, when the bear was two loping strides from either of us, that cat growled and shrieked like a surprised woman and all at once — ping! went the fishing line back against the tree.

The lion let out a long, trailing sound like a cross between a curse and a growl and it wasted no time in turning tail. All I saw was a golden blur heading away. He was eating up the ground, stretching that long, muscular body full out, weaving through those trees like they weren't even there. It was enough to grab the bear's attention.

And I tell you what, that bear was no idle loafer. He hit the trail no more than a few bounds behind that cat. I watched, peeking around my tree, as that bear's rolling, wagging rump wobbled in a full-bore run on out of sight and into the forest, bawling and mewling, the pair of them.

Then I slipped on over to that string-wrapped tree, keeping an eye on the woods just in case, and what do you think I found? If you guessed a fish hook, you're only partly right. I also found a fingertip-size chunk of pink meat that could be but one thing—the inside of that lion's cheek. No wonder it howled like a knife was being twisted straight into its craw. The meat was speared neat as you please on that hook. I was about to wipe it off on the bark of that oak when I stopped myself and pondered, keeping an eye toward the trail.

That hunk of cheek was still wet with the cat's spittle and I said to myself, "Now, Maple Jack, doesn't that mountain lion owe you a fish supper after all?"

I unwrapped the line from the tree, quick like, and

stuffed it in my breast pocket. I held up the hook with my strange new bait and started back toward the river — keeping an eye behind me all the way. In my other hand I held my club, just in case. I had enough surprises for one day, thank you.

As I approached the river, my mouth commenced to water. Yes sir, I most definitely wanted to catch the fish that would be tempted by lion flesh. A big hog of a trout, to be sure, tucked under the bank, just waiting. As I thought on this, I must admit I felt closer than ever to that mountain lion. I fancy we were both masters of escape. Tired as I was, I had to smile.

Then I heard a god-awful roaring from deep in the woods — no telling which beast it was. And I'll be danged if it didn't sound like they'd turned around . . .

I hurried my pace and as I broke through the riverbank brush I saw, just across the river on the road above, a gleaming black barouche piloted by a scowling woman in a flowery hat.

Kataki

by Chuck Tyrell

Chuck Tyrell is the pen-name of Arizona native and international award-winning author Charles T. Whipple. Grandson of an Arizona pioneer and avid listener to the old timers as a lad, he began writing western novels as a way of keeping in touch with his roots and of helping revere the memories of the hardy people of the western frontier. See www.chucktyrell.com for details.

Chapter 1

The name he received at birth was Sojiro. The name he earned in the dark mountains of Hida was Kage, the shadow. The name he used when he came to El Paso was Kay, because it meant respect. And out of respect for his dead father, he meant to put Jason Peligross to death.

I met Kay at the King's Palace, one of El Paso's better saloons. I say met, but he came looking for me.

Our game of five-card draw was no more than three hours old when Kay pushed his way through the batwings. He was a odd-looking little man to our eyes, dressed in clothes the color of desert sand. Blousey trousers like the Turks wear with wrappings around the shins and the strangest moccasins I ever saw. They reached a hand span above his ankles and they were split so the big toe stood apart from the rest. The sash at his waist went around twice and the knot was at the small of his back. A knife about the size of a Bowie, but with what looked to be a straight blade, fit behind the sash on the left side, like it was ready for a cross draw.

His shirt looked a bit like one an Apache would wear, but its sleeves were long and floppy and came down halfway on his hands. It didn't have any buttons either. One side was crossed over the other and held in place by the sash. His hair was short, very short, like he'd shaved his head a couple of weeks ago and a stubble had grown out. He also wore a headband of cotton cloth the same desert color as his clothes. A few supplies, I found out later, hung in netting cattycorner across his back, and he carried a monster of a sword slung to his back, with its long handle sticking up above his head.

To say he was a strange sight would be entirely an understatement.

His dark face was expressionless as a rock. He walked to the bar, but he slid his feet instead of heel-and-toeing like most people, and his knees were slightly bent.

"Hey Chinaman. Getchor ass outta here."

Kay could have been deaf for all the reaction the rowdy's shout got from him.

"Hey, Chinaman. You got ears?"

The man doing the shouting pushed himself away from the bar and turned to face Kay. "I'm saying no one in this here saloon wants to drink with no Chinaman."

Kay came to a stop at the bar. He put both hands on the edge.

Charlie the bartender ambled over, his face none too welcoming.

Kay gave Charlie a short nod, a kind of a bowing of his head. "Sir," he said. "Looking for a man, I am."

Before Charlie could open his mouth, the rowdy who'd shouted at Kay strode over and put a hand on Kay's shoulder as if to turn him. "We — "

He started to give Kay what for, but that little man — he stood no more than about five six — that little man took the rowdy's hand and twisted it somehow and the rowdy went to his knees, howling in pain. "Quiet," Kay said, applying some pressure for emphasis.

The rowdy shut up. I guess he figured out that if he didn't move, it didn't hurt, because he was real careful.

Kay faced Charlie again. "Sir, looking for a man, I am. Is he here?"

"Who?" Charlie asked.

"Kensington St. George," Kay said, but it sounded like Ken Jing Tone San Joji.

"Who?" Charlie said.

Kay held the rowdy with one hand and fished a piece of paper from inside his shirt. He handed the paper over.

Charlie took a look at the paper and handed it back. He turned and pointed at our table. "Kensington St. George is right over there," he said. I scraped my chair back and stood.

Kay gave the rowdy's hand a tweak and he yowled. "Stay," Kay said. He let go of the hand and walked that smooth sliding stride toward our table. He came around until he was about six feet from me.

As he came, I turned to face him.

"Ken Jing Tone *sama*?" he said. The rise at the end made it sound like a question.

"Yes," I said. "My name is Kensington St. George."

Kay slapped his hands to his sides and gave me a stiff bow, bending at the waist but keeping his back and neck straight as the proverbial ramrod. "Pleasure," he said. "Buy you, I want. We talk?"

"Go ahead," I said.

Kay turned and started for the batwings. Two steps and he realized I hadn't moved. He stopped and faced me again. "Go ahead? You say, go ahead. I do. Not enough?"

The two steps separated Kay from the card players at the table. Far enough, the rowdy figured, I guess. "Goldam Chinaman," he hollered, scrambling to his feet.

Kay watched the rowdy, his eyes almost shut. I could only see about half of the irises. He seemed not to be breathing and stood as motionless as I've ever seen a man stand.

The rowdy scrabbled for his six-gun. "You're dead meat," he screamed.

Kay made a quick flicking motion with his right hand, and the rowdy howled. Something like a 4-pointed spur rowel stuck out of the rowdy's wrist, one of the points buried deep into the joint. He dropped to his knees again, his off hand supporting the wrist with the rowel sticking out of it. The fingers of his hand were splayed and he couldn't seem to close them. Kay walked over in the slip-slide stride and pulled the 4-point rowel out. At the same time, he snaked the rowdy's six-gun from its holster. I could tell Kay was no stranger to guns.

"King," I said to King Fisher. He sat in on card games of a time, even though he owned King's Palace.

"Yeah?"

"Lend me your office for a few minutes? I'm curious as to what this stranger thinks he can buy from me."

"Help yourself."

Kay dumped the bullets from the rowdy's Colt SAA onto the bar and handed the gun to Charlie.

The rowdy sat cross-legged, holding his wounded wrist to his chest.

"Stay," Kay said to him, and looked at me.

I waved at the door at the back of the saloon. "In there," I said. "Come on." I started for the office door, my boots clomping on the plank floor. I couldn't hear if Kay was following, so I looked over my shoulder. He could have reached out and touched me. He was that close.

I prided myself on being a man people couldn't sneak up on, but Kay could have had my bacon anytime. He'd been in King's Palace for going on a quarter of an hour, and the only sounds I'd heard from him were words, and the slick whistling sound the 4-pointed rowel made as it flew into the rowdy's wrist.

Grabbing the knob, I opened the door and motioned him in. He hesitated as if he wanted me to go in first. I motioned again. He gave me a little bow and entered the office. I followed him in and turned to shut the door. When I looked at him again, he was on the floor, sitting on his legs. He put his hands on the planking about shoulder-width apart and touched his forehead to the floor between his hands.

"Wha'?" I'd never seen anything like it.

"Ken Jing Tone *sama*. I name Kay. One name only."

"Kensington St. George," I said. "Friends call me Ken."

"Ken." He tasted the name. "Ken. Good. You Ken *sama*. I Kay. Buy you, I want. Can?"

"Why?"

"This man say buy Ken *sama*," Kay said. He fished a business card from the fold of his shirt and offered it to me. He still sat on his legs.

I took the card. It showed the silhouette of a chess knight and had three words on it. San Francisco and Paladin.

Of themselves, my eyebrows went up. "Paladin said to hire me?"

"Yes. Hire. Yes. Hire. Not buy. Very sorry." Kay put his forehead to the floor again.

"Okay. Okay. What is it you want to hire me for?"

Kay looked perplexed. He shook his head.

I tried again. "Why me? Why hire me?"

Kay nodded. "Yes. Hire Ken *sama*."

I had to sigh. "Why?"

"Oh. Ah-m. Man say you hunt other man," Kay said.

"I do."

"He say you hunt man for Kay." He pointed at his nose.

"Who should I hunt for?" I said.

"Kay."

"No. No. No." I tried another tack. "I hunt man for Kay. What man?"

"Ah. *Hai*. Hunt man name Jay Song Pelly Gross."

I tried the name out. Jay Song Pelly Gross. I tried stringing them all together. Jaysongpellygross. Wait. Two names. Jaysong. No. Jason. Jason Peligross. Shit. "You want me to find Jason Peligross?"

"*Hai*. Yes. Please." Again he pulled something from

the folds of his shirt and held it out to me.

I took it. A small package wrapped in some kind of purple paper and tied with a ribbon that looked like silk. I set it on King's desk and pulled at the tails of the bow in the ribbon. It came undone and the paper opened of its own accord.

"Jayzus." A stack of strange gold pieces, ten high. I picked one up. An oblong piece of gold about three inches long and one and a half wide. Felt like a couple or three ounces. Say two and a half. The packet was about eight hundred dollars in gold.

"Hunt Jay Song," Kay said. "I follow. You find. I kill." His face and his eyes said Jason Peligross was dead.

Anyone who hunted Jason Peligross hunted trouble. I picked up the pile of gold coins, the wrapping paper, and the silk ribbon and held them out to Kay. "Nope," I said. "No can do."

He sat there on his legs, his hands on his thighs. Tears welled in his eyes and threatened to spill over his lower lids. Once more placing his hands flat on the floor, he lowered his forehead slowly to touch the planking. "I'm so sorry," he said, his English suddenly more fluent. "It is very important to find this man Jason Peligross. He killed my father. Here. In El Paso. Almost twelve years ago."

Kay reached inside his loose shirt and came up with yet another item; a paper, rolled and flattened, with the ends folded over. It had something on it that looked to me like a turkey track. He pointed at the track. "In my language, this reads *KATAKI*. When word of my father's death reached us, my lord Asaharu gave me this *KATAKI* paper. It says I can kill Jay Song Pelly Gross. My right. Our justice says the second son must take the life of the one who robbed life from our father."

"That piece of paper doesn't make it legal to kill in Texas," I said.

Kay shrugged. "I must," he said. "It is my *sadame*, my fate. Will you assist? Will you find the man who killed my father?"

I didn't answer right away, and my indecision must have been written on my face.

Kay nodded. "*Ah so*," he said, and shifted so he was sitting cross-legged on the floor. He carefully took the knife from his sash and pulled it from its lacquered sheath. He laid the sheath on the floor pointing away from him, and placed the knife so the sheath held the blade off the floor. And what a blade! Polished to a mirror finish, it had some kind of pattern near the cutting edge. It looked like maybe the edge and the body of the blade were not the same kind of steel. If it could cut as good as it looked, that was one wicked knife.

He put the pile of gold coins off to the side, removed his sword and back packet and put them by the coins, then took a small sheaf of papers from the fold of his shirt, separated one sheet, and used it to wrap the blade, leaving about two inches at the point bare. He gave me a long look. "I see that you are not ready to help me find Jay Song Pelly Gross," he said. "If I cannot find and kill him, then I have no reason for life myself."

I had no idea what was going on and just stood there like a dumb ox, as the saying goes.

"Ken *sama*, I am very happy to know you," Kay said. "*Sayonara.*"

He slipped his shirt from his shoulders and pulled his arms from the sleeves so it fell away and left him bare to the waist. Whoever thought him a little man had another think coming. His stomach looked like knotted ropes, and muscles swam beneath the skin of his arms. His shoulders bulged, and if he'd not been a man, I would have wondered at the size of his chest.

"Stand to my left, please," he said.

Not knowing what else to do, I took the position he indicated.

Kay picked up the knife by the blade. The paper he'd wrapped around it kept the edge from cutting his hand. He put the fingers of his left hand at a point just under his ribs, and placed the point of the knife at the tip of his fingers. "I go now to comfort the spirit of my father," he said, and pushed the point of the knife into his belly.

Chapter 2

The instant I saw the blood, I jerked my 6-inch Colt Lightning from my own sash and lambasted Kay in the head hard enough to lay him out.

He came to at Doc Reynold's place, but he couldn't move because I'd tied him to the bed, wrists and ankles. The doc had placed an adhesive plaster over folded square of gauze on the puncture wound in Kay's belly. "Not serious," the doctor said.

When I saw Kay looking at me, I cocked my Lightning and let the muzzle wander in his direction.

He glared.

"Ease off," I said. "Jason Peligross may be easy enough to find. He's high on the Rangers' wanted list, and he's got a hideout in Chihuahua, across the border into Mexico."

Kay relaxed. "Take the ropes off, Ken *sama*."

"I don't want you trying to cut yourself open again," I said. "Or me either, for that matter."

"That I will not do," he said. "Now I know somewhere I can find Jay Song Pelly Gross." He paused. "Can you show me where he is?"

"We'll see."

"Will you?" Kay's face was no longer the slab of granite it had been in the office of the King's Palace. He had a relaxed maybe even pleasant expression. I untied him.

He bounded from the bed. "Can we go now?" He slipped into his loose-fitting shirt and tied it in place with the sash. He checked his carrying net, put it on over his shoulder, then slung his big sword. Kay stood in front of me, legs spread slightly apart, a deceptively small man with death in his eyes. "I am ready," he said.

I had to smile. "Not so fast. Let me talk to the Rangers. Maybe I can pinpoint Jason Peligross's hideout."

"Pinpoint?"

"Find out exactly where he is."

"Then we go?"

"When we're ready." Somehow it seemed that I'd agreed to go with Kay to find the killer of his father. So be it.

Doc Reynolds rapped on the doorframe. "Sounds like the patient can be released," he said.

"What do we owe you?" I said.

"A dollar would cover it," he said.

I paid him. "Come on, Kay."

"Do you have a place to stay?" I asked when we got outside.

"*Hai.*"

"Go get some rest, then," I said. "Come to the Regis Hotel tomorrow morning. Then we'll talk about going after Jason Peligross."

Jason Peligross made a name for himself in '68 when he and his gang held up an entourage of Japanese dignitaries headed for the west coast. Most stood by as Peligross's men ransacked the wagons. They left the paraphernalia and took only the gold. One of the Japanese objected when Peligross opened a lacquered box and found only a scroll, which he dumped on the ground.

The young man screamed at Peligross and charged him with a long knife.

Peligross shot him through the body but he kept coming. A second shot smashed the young man's left shoulder. He staggered, then straightened and took three more long steps toward Peligross, the knife outstretched and seeking blood. The tip barely reached Peligross's gunhand, which held a Colt Army 1861. Just the tip, but it was enough to sever his little finger between the first and second joints, and slash the ring finger above it.

The young man died.

The entourage, in flowing kimonos and hair bound in topknots, let the young man be buried in El Paso, though it was their custom to cremate the dead. They cut the topknot from his head and put it in a plain wooden box. This part of the young man thus returned to Japan.

Now Kay came to El Paso to claim a life for the one that was taken, as was his custom. And he hired me to find Jason Peligross. After he disappeared toward whatever lodgings he had, I went to Rosa's, which sits on the south bank of the Rio Grande, the river the Mexicans call *Rio Bravo del Norte*. The Rio is unruly at times and not always content to follow its usual course. Rosa's has been washed away twice that I know of, and owner Pedro Aguilar always builds another adobe structure in the same place. I never asked him why it's called Rosa's Cantina.

Funny, the town north of the river is just plain old El Paso, but the one south of it is El Paso del Norte. Don't ask me why.

I could hear the music from Rosa's as I rode across the bridge on Stanton Street. Hitching my roan Pete out front, I pushed my way through the men who stood with drinks in their hands, watching a young Mexican girl twirl to the music of a mariachi band. When she spun, her skirts flew out and up and the men shouted and whistled at the sight of her shapely legs.

Shapely legs had not drawn me to Rosa's, though I appreciate the female form as much as the next man. Vicente, the man behind the bar, came over when I beckoned. He put a hand behind one ear and leaned close to hear what I said.

"*¿El Señor Pedro está aquí?*" I asked.

"*Sí.*"

"*¿Puedo hablar con él?*"

"*Momento.*" Vicente disappeared through a door at the back of the room.

Pedro came out, both hands extended. "Kensington, *amigo. ¿Cómo está?*" Pedro Aguilar had the face of a choirboy, complete with cherub smile and dimpled cheek. He was probably the toughest, most dangerous man south of the Pecos.

After clasping my hands, he pulled me toward his office. "Come, come. We'll have some Cuervo together."

The mariachi music stopped. Men drifted to tables, and a young cowboy reached for the dancer's hand, probably asking her to sit and drink with him.

"Keep your filthy hands off my girl, cowboy!"

A way opened between the blocky red-faced man who'd called out and the cowboy. "Mister, I don't know who you are," the cowboy said, "but any girl working at Rosa's can drink with a customer. So back off."

People cleared out from behind the young man.

"You lay a hand on her and I'll kill you, cowboy."

"Move aside, Felina," the cowboy said. He touched the girl with his left hand, but never took his eyes off the man. "You're welcome to try, mister, but I'd rather buy you a drink than see you dead."

The man's face got even redder. "I said, don't touch her!"

The cowboy stood with his feet shoulder-width apart and his hands hanging naturally at his sides.

"How often men die over our tarts," Pedro said. "Such a shame."

The blocky man fumbled for his gun, which was shoved into his waistband.

The cowboy waited patiently until the barrel of the old Colt cleared the man's belt. Then, in a smooth, lightning-quick motion, his right hand snaked a Remington Army from its holster, the web of his thumb raking the hammer back as he drew. The six-gun pointed at the man's belly, cocked and ready to fire, before his gun even came level.

"That's it," the cowboy said. "It's over and you lost. Leave and you won't have to die."

Someone started to laugh. Then the whole room was laughing. The cowboy put his gun away and turned toward the girl he'd called Felina.

The man howled like a wounded beast. His trigger finger tightened and his gun belched smoke and flame, the explosion cutting the laughter off as neatly as snuffing out a candle. The bullet plowed into the floor.

The man dropped to his knees, sobbing. The cowboy didn't even bother to turn around.

Pedro signalled two men to take the sobbing would-be gunman out. "Come. Good tequila awaits," he said.

"Who's the cowboy?" I asked.

"I hear he is called Havelock. Johannes Havelock."

"Havelock. I've heard that name. Seems I remember a lawman in Arizona by that name. Half Cherokee. Garet. That's it. Garet Havelock."

"*Sí*. Johnny Havelock is Garet Havelock's younger brother."

I took another look at the young cowboy. He sat with Felina, his face animated as he regaled her with tall stories such as men tell, or so I supposed.

Pedro led me into his little cubbyhole of an office. Well, not an office in the Anglo meaning of the word, but the *jefe*'s room. "So, *amigo*. What brings you to El Paso del Norte?"

I told Pedro of Kay and why he'd come to El Paso. Then I said, "He's determined to find Jason Peligross. He hired me to point him in the right direction, but I'm no good in Mexico. Who do you suggest I get to help?"

Pedro chuckled. "*Amigo*, there is none better than the young cowboy you just saw refrain from killing another man. Johnny Havelock. *Yo no sé, amigo*, but the Yaquis of Sonora call him *El Invisible*, he who cannot be seen."

"Johnny Havelock." I chewed on the idea for a while. "Do you think he'd agree?"

"*¿Quién sabe?* You can ask. He sits in Rosa's with beautiful Felina. And he sips, he only sips at a little tequila, with many many limes. *Madre de Dios*, he will cost me *mucho dinero* for the limes. *Afortunadamente*, Feline consumes a great quantity of tea, which is also called whiskey, but does not get her stumbling drunk." Pedro smiled at his own humor.

"Could I talk to Johnny Havelock here in your room, *amigo*?"

"If he will come, *es possible*," Pedro said.

He went to the door, opened it, and signalled to the

man who stood nearby. He spoke quietly and quickly to him in Spanish too fast and too low for me to hear and understand.

"*Sí, jefe,*" the guard said.

In moments, a light knock at the door.

"*Adelante,*" Pedro said.

The door opened. The young cowboy came in, relaxed with a small smile on his dark face. "*¿Desea hablar conmigo, jefe?*" he said.

He stood relaxed, but he stood ready.

I got up.

"Johnny, this is my friend," Pedro said. "He wished to speak about some business with you."

Havelock gave me a sharp glance, no more. "Does your friend have a name?" He spoke to Pedro, who waved a hand at me.

Havelock turned slightly so both Pedro and I were in his field of vision.

"I'm Kensington St. George," I said. "I need your help. Or, should I say, the man who hired me needs your help."

"Kensington St. George, eh? Stomp Hale had good things to say about you."

"You know Stomp?"

"Worked as his deputy for a year in Grant's Crossing."

"Heard you ride the Outlaw Trail."

"Do. But I'm no outlaw. Don't like carpetbagger law, though. Lawyers and such change it every day, just to suit them."

"I could spin you a tale, Havelock, but you might not believe a word I say. But let me tell you this. The man who hired me's got good reason to go after Jason Peligross. Can you take us to him?"

"Him and me've crossed paths a time or two. I don't run with him."

"My man wants to hit Peligross in Mexico, and I reckon he can handle it."

Havelock turned to look at me straight on, an

incredulous expression on his face. "This man wants to face Jason Peligross alone?"

"He says it's got to be done one on one."

"Jayzus."

"Could I ask you to come over to El Paso to meet him? You can take the job on after that, if you've a mind to."

Havelock stared at me for a long time, his mind elsewhere, it seemed. I could see the wheels turning behind those dark eyes. Finally he gave me a short nod. "Alright. I'll come along. Take a looksee."

"Regis Hotel, then. Tomorrow. Come about noon and I'll buy you dinner."

Havelock almost smiled. "I could use a man-size steak," he said. "I'll be there." He stepped to the door. "*Con permiso, jefe,*" he said.

"*Por nada,*" Pedro replied. "*Hasta la vista.*"

"Tomorrow, then," Havelock said to me, and he was gone. Nor was he among the carousers in Rosa's Cantina when I left.

Chapter 3

Kay arrived at the Regis sometime before I even got up, not that I'm an early riser. He stood in front, straw basket on his head. He stood motionless. His eyes closed and his hands steepled before his chest. I could hear him mumbling some kind of prayer. He faced the sun, so maybe that had something to do with it.

"Good morning, Kay," I said.

He turned and bowed. "*Ohayo gozaimasu,* Ken *sama.* When do we go find Jay Song Pelly Gross?"

"A man named Havelock will come to speak with you about it."

"When?"

"At noon. We will eat together."

He nodded. "I understand. I will return then."

"Where are you going?"

Kay gave me his deadpan look. "Chinamen are okay only with Chinamen, even when they are from Japan."

He walked slowly up San Francisco Street, hands steepled, once more mumbling his prayer.

Everybody on San Francisco Street, walking, riding, or driving, craned their necks to watch Kay. Not often do you see a man with a straw basket on his head walking heel and toe down the street, ignoring traffic and mumbling to himself. More than one shook his head as if he thought Kay was crazy.

I stepped into Tully's, just to the side of the Regis, for breakfast.

Just as I got my second cup of coffee and was about to dig into scrambled eggs and bacon backed up with fried potatoes and onions, Buffalo Carter walked in. He took a quick look around and made straight for my table.

"Kensington," he said, leaning over so his voice didn't carry to the other three people breakfasting at Tully's. "Word's out that you're going into Mexico."

I raised my eyebrows and played ignorant. "Really? Wherever did you get that idea?"

Buffalo looked left and right, then leaned even closer. An inch and he'd have been whispering in my ear like a lover. I shifted away slightly.

"Someone seen you at Rosa's last night," he said. "That someone saw Johnny Havelock go into Pedro Aguilar's back room while you and Pedro was in there. And when Havelock come back, he wasn't in no mood to play with Felina. She asked him why. He looked at her kinda funny and told her he might be taking a little *paseo* into Mexico. Anyone could figure out the rest." Buffalo took a deep breath. "You'll need guns, Ken. I'd like to go along. Watch your back, kinda."

He stood back, an expectant look on his face.

"Don't know what you're talking about," I said.

"Shee-it. Don't know what I'm talking about my ass. Kensington kiss-my-ass St. George. Do I look dumb to you? Do you think I ain't seen that Chinaman? Do you think I don't know what kinda man Johnny Havelock is? Shee-it. You're headed into Mexico. No lie. What you

need is an army, but that ain't gonna happen. So if you
can't get an army, you'd better have some good guns.
I'm good. Not as good as Johnny, but good. Maybe
better'n you."

I had no reply.

Buffalo gave me a long look, then shrugged. He said
nothing more, just turned his back on me and left, his
displeasure plain in the set of his shoulders. Two men of
the ilk of Buffalo Carter were the equivalent of a dozen
horse soldiers. I wanted to call him back, but could do
nothing until Kay and Havelock met. Instead of brooding
about the situation, I ordered three eggs, scrambled,
sowbelly bacon, fried potatoes, and sourdough biscuits.
A man can't think properly when his stomach's empty.

Strictly speaking, I'd made no commitment to take
Kay into the wilds of Chihuahua. Strictly speaking, I'd
not taken even one of his oblong gold pieces, so I'd made
no promise. But we'd need to cross the Rio Grande and
get lost in the rough and tumble country south of the
border before the rumors reached the ears of Jason
Peligross.

By noon, I'd found no answers except to go, by God
and by golly. I sat on the porch of the Regis, chair
tipped back on two legs, contemplating the problem
when Johnny Havelock came around the corner of
Chiricahua and San Francisco Streets, and Kay
mumbled his way east on San Francisco, retracing the
course he'd taken away earlier. They reached the Regis
at almost the same time. Johnny Havelock climbed the
steps to the porch. Kay stayed in the street, watching.

"I'm here, Kensington St. George," Havelock said.
"What's to talk about?"

I waved a hand at Kay. "It's his *baile*. I'll let him talk
to you."

Havelock took a second look at Kay. "Him? A
Chinaman?"

Kay slowly mounted the steps, his upper face hidden
by the straw basket on his head.

"Kay is from Japan," I said. "Jason Peligross killed

his father in '68. He's got a license from Japan to kill Peligross."

"Easy to say, hard to do," Havelock said.

"You'd be surprised."

"Who is this man?" Kay said. He tipped the straw basket back, only now I could see it was made of thin strips of wood.

"His name is Johnny Havelock. He knows the way to Jason Peligross's hideout."

Havelock stood still while Kay examined him. I watched Kay's eyes flick from the light brown Stetson on Havelock's head to the off-white linen shirt to the faded canvas trousers stuffed into knee-high Apache moccasins.

Kay nodded. "He knows," he said. "I follow you, Johnny Havelock. Then kill Jason Peligross. We go." He looked at me. "When?"

"Wait up, now," Havelock said. "Why should I take you all into Mexico?"

"Jay Song Pelly Gross robbed my people. He threw our sacred scroll on the ground and killed my father who tried to keep the scroll from touching earth."

Havelock stood silent.

Kay's words were full of passion but his face was placid as if he were reciting his schoolwork. "My lord sent me to Hida to become, what do you say? Ninja. I trained for one cycle of years – one cycle is twelve. My father died twelve years ago. Pelly Gross must die now."

He spoke to Havelock directly. "You show me. I will kill. Me." Kay looked at me, then back at Havelock. "How much?" he said.

Havelock just stood there, his hard eyes on Kay.

Kay dropped to his knees like he had in King Fisher's office. He put the basket off to the side, placed both hands on the porch, and touched his forehead to the planking. "Please, Havelock *sama*. Please help me find Pelly Gross, who killed my father. If I cannot kill him, I must kill me."

"He will, too," I said. "He almost put that long knife of

his into his own gut a couple of nights ago. He's dead serious about this."

"Okay," Havelock said. "Two horses each. Two canteens. One day down, one day back, one day leeway. I'll get jerky. You get coffee, though fires may be a problem. Be a good idea to haul along some biscuits. We'll get whatever else we need on the trail."

"How much?" Kay asked.

Havelock didn't say anything for a long moment. "Mr. Kay," he said, "when and if we get back, we'll see how much the trip was worth to you."

To me he said, "Mr. St. George, you'll want to dress right. Red sashes are out and moccasins are always better than boots. Desert colors if you have them."

"I'm not a complete tenderfoot," I said.

"You're not used to the desert, sir, or you would not be asking me. No offense meant."

I shut up.

"We'll leave an hour before dawn," Havelock said. "Have your horses and supplies ready. I'll bring my own." He stepped down into the street. "Gentlemen, good day." He strode down the street, turned onto Chiricahua and disappeared. He didn't even eat that steak he'd wanted.

Kay nodded. "Very good," he said. "I will return tomorrow morning at the hour of the tiger. He went back the way he came, basket on his head, mumbling as he walked heel to toe, ignoring horses, riders, buggies, and pedestrians alike.

Chapter 4

Havelock rode a buckskin and led a lineback dun. I had Pete, my regular strawberry roan, and a grulla I'd rented at the livery. Kai showed up afoot.

"Horses?" Havelock said.

"No," Kay said.

"You'll never make it without horses."

"I do not ride. We go."

Kay had changed his head basket for a wide band of off-white cotton. The rest of his garb was exactly like when I'd first seen him. The big sword's handle stuck up over his shoulder, its hilt and hand guard covered with a brocaded silk sack.

Havelock shrugged. "We'll take Stanton to the bridge. On the Mexican side, we'll cut west into the mountains. Let's go."

He reined the buckskin around and started off, leading the dun. I followed. Kay walked, staying even with my stirrup, matching his stride to that of my roan. "It'll be a long walk," I said. He stared straight ahead like he was in a trance.

Havelock never looked back. Just past Rosa's Cantina, he took a narrow way that wound between adobe walls that protected the wealthier citizens in their compounds and jacals of sticks daubed with mud and topped with brush thatches where peons lived. Mangy dogs lay panting in the shadows of the walls and children in cotton shifts without pants or shoes stopped their games to watch the gringos ride by. What they thought, I have no idea. Strange to me, the scents rising from the poor section of the El Paso del Norte didn't have the pungent sewer smell of the poorer neighborhoods in Anglo areas of El Paso.

Beyond the city, Havelock took an eyebrow of a trail into the mountains. Almost like a runoff, but with occasional hoof prints of goats, or maybe mule deer. The horses humped upward, carrying our weight as they were trained to do, but laboring. Even the extra mounts we led breathed heavily as we topped out. Kay looked like he'd been on a stroll around some quiet park.

We pulled up at a wide place in the trail that gave us a view across a high plain at least twenty miles across. Octotillo and candelilla and paloverde dotted the flats while oaks and piñons and junipers climbed the hillsides beside us.

"A day down and a day back?" I said.

"We don't have to cross the flat," Havelock said. "Peligross's place is about 10 miles south long the foothills."

Kay sat cross-legged on a flat-topped hunk of

sandstone, his back held straight and stiff, his eyes closed, and his forearms on his thighs with his thumbs and forefingers forming circles and his other fingers held out straight. I took off my hat and wiped away the sweat. Kay's skin looked clean and free of any perspiration. He didn't seem to be breathing.

I took a pull from the four-quart canteen that hung from my saddle horn. "Kay," I said. "What's your plan?"

After a moment, he opened his eyes. "I will go to Pelly Gross in the night," he said. "In the night, even if he has many, I am but a shadow. I will kill him and we will return. Ken *sama*. Havelock *sama*. You will wait."

Simple as that.

We didn't push the horses and Kay had no trouble matching the pace.

Havelock called a rest stop just short of noon. He pulled some jerky from his saddlebags and offered me a piece. I took it. Kay sat cross-legged on the ground like he had on the sandstone earlier.

"Kay," Havelock said. "Jerky?"

Kay opened his eyes. "I cannot take food until Pelly Gross is dead," he said. He closed his eyes.

Havelock shrugged. We chewed the dried beef and swallowed tepid water. Kay remained completely motionless, as if he were some kind of carved statue.

As the sun dipped toward the jumble of mountains in the west, Havelock pulled up in a copse of oak and juniper. He pointed to a cut running into the eastern hills. "Jason Peligross has a hacienda up that draw," he said. "They'll be men on watch, and they'll spot us if we go any closer."

"How far?" Kay asked. He looked as fresh as the moment we left the Regis Hotel.

"Two miles. Maybe three," Havelock said.

"I must prepare," Kay said. "Then go kill Pelly Gross. You," he said, pointing at Havelock, "and you," pointing at me, "wait for me here. When the day comes, if I am not returned, go back to El Paso."

He put a hand into the fold of his shirt and brought

out a packet like the one he'd shown me at Rosa's. He handed it to me. "Pay Havelock *sama* for me, Ken *sama*, if I am not returned."

"Of course," I said, and accepted the packet of gold coins.

"I must prepare," he said again.

"No fire?" I said to Havelock.

"Not a good idea."

Pete took a healthy mouthful of chamise. Desert-bred, he was content to stay where he was. I loosened the cinch but left the saddle on him. I'd only use the extra horse if we had to run.

Kay separated himself from us a few feet and once again assumed the cross-legged position. He steepled his hands and said something that sounded like *namuamidabutsu*. He repeated it three times, then bowed until his forehead touched the ground.

A long moment later, he repeated the phrase and returned to his upright cross-legged position. He spent the remaining daylight sharpening his weapons. A half dozen of those rowel-like pointy things that he threw with such accuracy. Two little knives plucked from the tops of his split-toed moccasins. The long knife in his sash. Then he worked on the three-foot blade of the sword he'd carried slung to his back.

Finally, he stood. He shoved the long knife and the sword into the sash around his waist. The other weapons went back to their hiding places.

Standing with his feet splayed slightly and his hands clamped to his sides, Kai bowed first to me, then to Havelock. "I thank you, Ken *sama*, Havelock *sama*. I now go to kill Pelly Gross." He moved away toward the draw that led to the Peligross hacienda. He made no sound. Moments later, we could no longer see him.

"The man is somewhat better than good," Havelock said. I could only agree.

We waited through the night, Havelock and I, taking two-hour watches. The morning came, but Kay didn't show.

"He's not coming," I said.

"You don't know that," Havelock said.

So we stayed another night. Kay didn't show. There was nothing for us to do but return to El Paso.

Chapter 5

As soon as we reached El Paso, I gave the packet of gold coins to Havelock.

"Don't sit right," he said, "Kay not making it back and all. I shoulda known it was too easy. Coulda been someone waiting for him. Maybe they got news Kay was after Peligross."

"Not your fault, Havelock. Kay had to do it his way or die trying."

Havelock rode out a couple of days later. He didn't say where he was going.

I began to think it was time for me to move on as well. Maybe visit Paladin in San Fran. That afternoon a young Mexican boy showed up at the Regis, looking for me. "*Por favour*," he said. "*El jefe quiere que usted venga a verlo.*"

So I climbed on Pete and followed the boy across Stanton Bridge to El Paso del Norte. Pedro waited in the main room at Rosa's. "*Amigo, amigo.* Come. Come. I have something I thought you should hear." He ushered me into the back room. He waved at the rawhide chairs. "Sit down. Sit down," he said.

I sat.

"Tell me, have you tasted coffee from Chiapas? No? We'll have some." He sent the boy for coffee.

I waited. Pedro would tell me why he'd asked for me to come when the time was right.

The coffee came. Pedro filled his with goat's milk and great lumps of raw sugar. I drank mine black – rich, thick, and nutty with flavor.

"Aah. What's that wonderful English word you use for such as this?" Pedro lifted his pottery coffee mug. "Ambrosia. Yes. That's it. Ambrosia. Is this coffee not tasty?"

"*Delicioso.*" I couldn't resist using a word or two of my border Spanish. Pedro gave me a painful smile.

When the boy came to collect the coffee mugs, Pedro said, "*Traigo aquí al manco.*"

One-handed man!

"*Sí, jefe.*"

I didn't ask Pedro why. He'd called me for a reason. Perhaps the one-handed man was it.

Pedro did not explain. We waited, the silence hanging between us.

A tap came at the door.

"*Adelante,*" Pedro said.

The man wore a sling to support his right arm, which ended some three inches above where the wrist should be. The stump was properly bandaged and it seemed there was no putrification. Still, the wound was recent. Very recent. I looked at Pedro, the question plain on my face.

"Kensington, you must listen to this man," Pedro said. "What he has to say should interest you, I think."

"*Siéntese,*" he said. "*Cuente su historia.*"

The man with one hand sat on the remaining chair in Pedro's office, and began to speak:

The hacienda of Jason Peligross is a fortress. It stands on the hill above *el arroyo de Santiago.* Ten men guard the approaches. Five more watch from inside the hacienda walls. One walks the hallways to the south, one to the west, one to the north. Thus Jason Pelligross is safe. Thus no one holding evil intent can even come near *el jefe de los ladrones.* In the Hacienda de la Paloma, *el jefe* relaxes and drinks fine tequila and good wine. In the Hacienda de la Paloma, women and children laugh, and no harm ever befalls them. In the Hacienda de la Paloma, *el jefe* Pelligross is safe. Yet he always keeps a loaded pistol on his desk. The pistol that killed his first man. An ancient pistol made in *Bélgica* and used by men in New Orleans to settle quarrels in duels. But *el jefe* is safe . . . was safe.

Then he came. "I am the shadow," he said.

Ten men guarded the approaches. He found them all. They never saw him. They told me of a sudden pain in the neck, as if iron tongs had grasped them. Then blackness. They were still unconscious when I found them.

"I come to avenge my father," he said.

Four of the men guarding inside the hacienda fell to the shadow. He trussed them with strings of woven silk, tied their thumbs together and laced them to their ankles behind their backs. He tied sticks into their mouths so they could make no sound. He left them at their posts, and he came for *el jefe*.

"My name is Sojiro," he said. "The ninja call me Kage, the shadow. But for this task I take the name of Kay, which means respect in my language."

El jefe said nothing. I stood behind the draperies that cover the walls of *el jefe*'s room. He shot a glance at me. The shadow did nothing. But I think he knew I was there.

"Prepare to die, Jay Song Pelly Gross," he said. "Twelve years ago, you shot and killed my father as he tried to protect a sacred scroll. Now you forfeit your life for taking the life of my father."

I watched as he withdrew a roll of paper from his loose-fitting shirt. He shook the paper and it unrolled, showing lines of dark black writing of a peculiar type. He bowed to *el jefe*.

"This is the writing of my Lord Asaharu from Japan. This writing says I have the right to kill him who killed my father. That man is you, Jay Song Pelly Gross. This night you will die."

He took a cover from the handle of a long sword he carried thrust in his sash. He stood ready, one foot forward, knee bent; one leg back, knee bent. He placed his right hand on the handle of the sword and his left upon its scabbard. *El jefe* laughed, and I lunged from behind the tapestry, my pistol in my hand, cocked and ready to fire.

"You are foolish," the shadow said, and cut off my

arm. I did not even have time to pull the trigger. My arm and my pistol fell to the floor. The shadow shook my blood from his sword blade and returned it to its scabbard. I sank to the floor and bled.

El jefe no longer laughed. I tried to stop the bleeding by clutching my arm tightly. The bleeding slowed. *El jefe* snatched up the old pistol and cocked it. He stepped around the desk so there was nothing between him and the shadow, who shifted his stance slightly to confront *el jefe* directly. He stood like before, one hand on the hilt of his sword, one hand on the scabbard. The shadow and *el jefe* stood ten or twelve paces apart.

"I'm not gonna die!" *El jefe* snarled. "You are." He lifted the pistol, aimed and fired.

You will not believe what I have to say. I'm sure you will not believe it. But the shadow pulled his sword so fast that he was able to slice the leaden ball from the pistol in half. *El jefe* stood with his mouth open and eyes wide with shock. The shadow leaped high in the air with a fearsome scream, like a beast closing for the kill. He brought the blade of his sword precisely down on the top of *el jefe*'s head. It split as the leaden ball had split. *El jefe* dropped, his head hanging in two pieces from his neck. The shadow wiped the blade of his sword clean of blood with the paper that he said gave him the right to *el jefe*'s life. He returned the sword to its scabbard.

"It is finished," he said. Then he took his headband off and bound my arm. He cut a piece from a chair to make the binding into a tourniquet to stop my bleeding. "The women can help you," he said. He picked one half of a leaden ball from the floor and put it in my remaining hand. "Take this," he said. "Go to Rosa's Cantina and tell a man named Kensington St. George what has happened." Then he was gone.

In his left hand, the one-handed man held out half a neatly sliced .50 caliber musket ball. His story was true.

"Telegram for you, Mr. St. George," the front desk clerk said when I walked into the Regis. "From San Francisco, it says."

"Thank you." I took the yellow form.
KATAKI DONE KAY

When Was It Going to Rain?

by Dusty Richards

Dusty Richards is the past winner of two Spur Awards as well as the Cowboy Hall and Museum Wrangler Award. He will be the incoming president of WWA in 2012. When he's not out researching, he and Pat live on Beaver Lake in NW Arkansas.

When was it ever going to rain again? God must have forgot about the folks in western Arkansas needing water to exist. Even the big oak trees looked pale and their leaves about to crinkle up and it was only the end of July. With a red bandana, Ikert Holms mopped his sweaty face aboard his buckskin mule, Zarious, headed for Frog Holler. When he prepared to drop off Sunset Mountain, he nodded and waved when he passed a sweaty-faced man driving a team of lathered mules hauling a large load of hand-hewed ties to Winslow. He believed the driver's name was Swan Idles.

Being a U.S. Deputy Marshal for Judge Isaac Parker kept Ikert busy serving papers to individuals selected to be jurors on federal court cases in Fort Smith, besides running down outlaws and arresting illegal bootleggers. His job made him a less popular person to see on their doorstep. Such a jury notice to appear meant the citizen chosen had to go to Ft. Smith and stay there for ninety days for about a dollar a day to eat on and sleep in some bedbug-ridden flop house. Beside the sixty-mile trip, that meant nothing was done at home in their absence from the farm. Not to even think how it was over five degrees hotter down in the Arkansas River Valley than it was on Sunset Mountain where he came off the hilltop headed down into Frog Holler. A vast wide gorge forested in oaks, hickory, ash, and walnut to name a few of the hardwoods and postage stamp farms cleared out for agriculture on the slopes and benched land.

When he rode up the lane to the Willard place, several good bawl mouth hounds rose up in the dog trot like they were shocked anyone came and began to bark. The two long cabins were separated by the corridor that sheltered them. Wearing an apron and packing a homemade broom, Liz Willard came out to the top of the steps, hushing and swatting hounds to quiet them.

Hand beside her eyes to shut off the glare, she tried to see the invader. "My man ain't here."

"Ma'am, my name's Deputy Marshal Holms and I am here—"

"I knows why you're here. You've got a damn warrant for him to go to Fort Smith and be on a jury." She scowled. "He ain't here."

"When will he be here?" he asked, still mounted on his mule.

"I don't know." She spit tobacco off the deck, wiped her mouth of the back of her hand. "He ain't here."

"Mrs. Willard, Judge Parker sent me up here to serve these papers. If your man don't respect this call, I'll have to come up here and put him in chains and lead him down there."

"Don't that damn judge know how hard it is to farm and log up here making a living. Drought and all. We can't afford for him not to be here." Shy, thumb-sucking children began to gather around her skirt like chicks would an old hen.

"Judge Parker has to hold court and he needs jurors. This paper invites him to come willingly. Next trip I have to make up here it will be a warrant for his arrest for not showing up down there."

"Give me that damn paper. I don't know what he'll do about it. I'll tell him what you said."

He dismounted from his mule with a look about the place. Dogs had settled down to rest and sleep in the heat. A cow bawled for her calf and some pigs had a nasty squealing fight in a log pen. The chest-high corn crop had already turned brittle tan and rustled in the wind. She came half way down and took the paper.

"If you can't read do you still have to serve?"

"Yes."

"When's he got to be down there?"

"August First. Two weeks from last Monday. Good day," he said to her and doffed his wide-brimmed straw hat, taking a seat on his mule.

"You kids go play. Marlee Ann, come get these younguns. Marshal Holms, this ain't no good day. We all may starve this winter on account of you and that damn judge."

He nodded he understood, only thing bothering him was he hoped Willard would be down there and him not have to arrest him. Zarious headed out the dusty ruts through the trees for the road. Two hounds sat up and bawled goodbye. His next stop was in Hazel Valley back over the mountain to the north. The notice called for a man named Carl Vance.

Late afternoon, he found the red-faced farmer in his forties and his two teenage boys in a field loading dry corn stalks on a hay rack for winter fodder. Two mules hitched to it stood sleeping hip shot in the afternoon heat.

Vance took off his straw hat and wiped his wet face on the sleeve of the pullover shirt all dark with his sweat. "You're a marshal, ain't yeah?"

"Yes, a Deputy U.S. marshal, my name's Holms." He dismounted and the boys leaned on their pitch fork handles waiting for his words.

He found the paper for Vance in his saddle bags. "This is a summons, Mr. Vance, for you to appear in Judge Parker's federal courtroom on August First to serve ninety days as a juror."

His sons began to laugh at their father's plight. He frowned at them and said, "Well, you boys will have to handle this place." Then he asked Ikert, "Did you stop by the house?"

Ikert nodded.

"You tell her what you had for me?"

"Yes, I did. She asked."

"Fine. Boys, drive these mules up to the shed and unhitch them. We can unload this in the morning. Deputy. Did she invite you to supper?"

"No, sir. I think she was taken back by the news."

"No doubt, no doubt, but I'll ask you to stay for the meal. You ain't seen any rain hiding anywhere you've been?" He grinned at his own words.

"No, not this week." Vance was like most of the folks that he served juror summons to, they accepted it. "And I sure appreciate you offering to feed me."

"I'm not happy about this summons, but I don't aim to kill the messenger." They both laughed.

Later, Ikert rode toward home under the stars, the day's temperature dropping as he climbed out of the Middle Fork Valley. Both he and his mule were bone tired when he arrived at home. His wife woke at the stock dog's barking and came wrapped in a robe.

"Did we wake you up?" he asked her, stripping the saddle off the mule. He meant the dog who was anxious to see his master.

"No, I never sleep good when you aren't home." She swept her hair from her face.

"Sorry, but I served two court summons today and they were way up the Middle Fork and the other was over on the Frog side."

"I guess you had no place to stay?"

He turned the mule loose in the lot and then he hugged her. "No. I wanted to be back here with you."

"Oh, I'm glad. Have you eaten?"

"Yes." He checked the starry night skies. No clouds, no sign of rain.

They soon were in each others' arms on top of the sheet. It wasn't that cool, but he was glad to be back with her. He squeezed her hard and closed his eyes.

Dawn came early and he rose. His wife had left him earlier to milk the cow and handle chores. He found her in the kitchen and she set a fresh, steaming cup of coffee before him.

'What are your plans today?" she asked.

He shook his head, still hung over from the day before's long haul. "I guess split some stove wood for you. I'm not going far from the house today."

She came over and kissed him on the face. "Good, you need to rest some time."

Mid-morning, a boy brought him a telegram from Fort Smith. In the shade of the spreading walnut tree, he wiped his forehead on his sleeve and set down the ax to read the wire.

"How are you today, John Stone?" he asked the familiar delivery boy.

"Fine, Marshal. Do you have a reply?"

"Wait till I read it?"

"Yes, sir."

Marshal Holmes—a bank robber Floyd Sams is headed north by horse back for Prairie Grove—has kin folk in the area—age 27—5-10—blond hair—blue eyes — armed and dangerous—Chief Marshal Thames

He took a stub of pencil from his pocket and wrote a reply on the back of his yellow sheet to send to Chief Marshal Thames. *Will ride over there and look for Sams ––Holmes.* He gave John two dimes. One for him and one to pay for the message.

"Thanks, good messenger," he said and the barefoot boy shot off like a race horse for the railroad depot down on the Frisco tracks, the new paper message secure in his fist.

"You get a message?" his wife asked, coming out on the porch.

"Yes. There's a bank robber named Sams headed for Prairie Grove. They want me to go look for him."

"You know him?"

"I know some Sams from down by Mountainburg." He drove the axe in the chopping block and gathered her a big armful of stove wood for her box beside the wood range. "He may have a lady friend over there."

"Oh, honey draws flies," she teased.

"Yes." It was another hot dry day. He put the wood in the box and then kissed her on the mouth.

"I guess you won't be back today?"

"Probably not. Don't wait up."

"Oh, I will. You know me."

He hugged her shoulders, then put on his vest and the badge. He took the six-gun and holster off the wall peg and strapped the belt on. Then he checked the gun's cylinders to be certain they were loaded and ready to use. They went hand in hand to the pen and she watched him saddle Zarious. When he finished, the mule shook until the stirrups rattled when he led him out of the pen by the reins.

"Even the mule doesn't want to go."

"He never wants to go,' he said and kissed her goodbye.

His one regret was they'd never had any children in their seven years of marriage. A child would have made a perfect circle for them. He never complained, knowing that was not worth upsetting her over since he knew it was on her mind a lot. Even Doc Hamilton had no answer for them. So he smiled at her, mounted his mule, and waved goodbye.

The town marshal in Prairie Grove was Mark Paterson, he found him about sundown at his shotgun shack and they talked about Sams' possible place to land in the small community.

"I heard that he once lived with a Filly Kern woman," Ikert said.

"Yes, they lived together down by Mountainburg. They never were married," Paterson said as they sat on his back steps.

"This Filly lives up here with another guy, doesn't she?"

Paterson agreed. "Fred Graves."

"You think she'd meet Sams somewhere if he sent her word?"

Paterson nodded.

"Then I better watch that place. She might lead me to him."

"Could be dangerous. Sams might shoot you. He knows the law wants him."

"I'll try to duck."

Paterson laughed. "I simply wanted to warn you. You want some help?"

Ikert shook his head. "If I can't handle him, I'll come get you."

Paterson shook his head at his joking. "You know where she lives?"

"I think so. Just past the strawberry fields?"

"That's Graves's house on the south side of those patches over on the Illinois River Road. Want something to eat?"

"No, I'll eat some of Maude's chili. Maybe she knows something that we don't."

Paterson agreed the café owner might have heard gossip about Sams and his once woman. They shook hands and Ikert left on his mule for the café on Main Street. He had a nice visit with the friendly Maude Shores, a chubby woman who ran the town restaurant and who had heard little about Sams coming to see her former lover.

"But I wouldn't doubt she'd go meet him if he sent word for her. She's still in love with him."

After he finished his chili and coffee, he offered to pay her, but she shooed him away. "You be careful, he can be a very tough person."

He waited till sundown and then took up a place where he had a good view of the strawberry fields that were flat, open land. If she left Graves's house and went about any direction he should be able to see her crossing the wide open country. Then he hoped he could follow her.

About midnight, a figure moved across the fields and he watched where she went. Good, it was probably her. He rode Zarious around to the east in a gallop where the river road went southeast and he hoped to intercept

276

them. If Sams was close by, this was his chance.

He was grateful for the stars and wished he had some moon light, but he knew it would not be up until late. His mule reined up, he listened, but heard nothing beside Zarious's hard breathing. Then he pushed on south.

She tried to hide but he spotted her. In a short run, he was riding beside her and reached out to catch her shoulder. "Whoa!"

"What are you doing?" she said. "Who are you?"

"I'm a U.S. Deputy Marshal, my name's Ikert Holmes." He dismounted. "Where is he?"

"Who?" She was hardly out of her teens, her hair uncombed and dressed in rags. She stood trembling under the stars.

"Floyd Sams."

"I ain't seen him."

"Then where were you running to?"

"I'm—I'm—"

"Where is he waiting for you?"

"I'm not sure. He said he would come for me and to be on the Illinois River Road."

"All right. We'll wait for him here."

"You won't kill him, will you?" He could see her hugging her arms and shaking.

"Sit down, I won't hurt you. And I won't hurt him if he surrenders. Why do you even mess with him?"

She broke down and bawled. "Because I love him. You ever love someone a lot?"

"Yes, my wife."

"You got any kids?"

"No, we don't. Why?"

She shook her head and sniffled. "You two been married long?"

"Seven years. And I reckon we just won't have any." That silenced him. He put his mule aside and wondered if her man was still coming. Their conversation might have warned him and chased him away. No telling where he might be. So they sat on the ground beside the road and listened for a horse coming. But dawn finally came in a faint pink and still no Sams.

"He ain't coming." Crestfallen, she finally rose and without a word went back toward where she came from. He rode over to the Butterfield stage line road and no one he spoke to on the way had seen the fugitive. By mid morning, he rode Zarious in the yard and dropped heavily from the saddle.

"Do any good?" his wife asked, meeting him.

"No, he didn't meet her last night."

"I wonder why?"

"Oh, he may have stopped and been with his friends along the way."

"What now?"

A good question, but he had no answer for her. "Did I ever tell you I loved you?"

"Yes. Several times."

"Good, then let me wash up."

"Have you eaten anything today?"

"No."

"Was she pretty?"

"Who?"

"That woman of his?" Her hand held the crook of his arm and her dress hem in the other one as they headed for the back porch.

"She was a teenager, unwashed and her hair uncombed. Last time she saw bath water I'd bet was a considerable long time ago and her clothes were hand-me-downs."

"I'm glad you didn't run off with her."

He stopped in his tracks. "Do you really believe I'd do that to you?"

"No, but I'm still glad anyway." She gouged him in the ribs and chuckled at his upset. "Come on, Ikert, I know you're tired."

After eating, he slept until the day's heat awoke him sweating. Something was different. He pulled on his pants and put up his suspenders. On the back porch he could hear her rocking and talking to someone. Maybe a neighbor lady was out there. He decided he should dress better, so he put on his shirt and buttoned it to walk outside and see what was happening.

"Ikert, Phyllis is here."

He blinked and looked at the girl from the night before. He knew they called her Filly. "Good day, ma'am."

"Sams is here too," she said, looking downcast.

He searched around with no sight of him.

"Oh, he's sleeping in the barn. He ain't armed. I promised him you wouldn't shoot him if he surrendered."

"Phyllis wants to make us a deal," his wife said.

"Oh?"

"She's going to have their baby this fall and wants us to raise it for our own."

That was real serious. More so than even the fugitive's surrender. "Do you want to do that?"

She was rocking harder and faster. "Yes, you know I do."

He nodded. "Then we should do that." His wife jumped up and hugged him, so excited he thought she'd burst. Then she dropped back and looked at the porch floor. "Thank you, but she needs a place to live."

"If it suits you she can stay here and live with us."

"Oh, Ikert, I'm so happy."

He looked out to discover the rolling dark clouds overhead through the walnut tree's canopy. Then the low growl of a storm coming up the West Fork Valley quickened his already hard beating heart. Drops big as hands full began to beat down on them, the trees, and everything. A cold rain with even some hail dropped the temperature. He stood back from the edge of the porch's eve runoff and protectively hugged both women around the shoulders.

God brought him lots of things that day. Later a boy to be his son. Phyllis who became a much cleaner, better person under his wife's tutorage. A reformed outlaw who served his time and became a real man, who upon his release married Phyllis.

And enough rain fell to quench the earth's desperate thirst—August 3rd, 1882.

New Dog, Old Tricks

by Edward A. Grainger

Edward A. Grainger, aka David Cranmer, is editor and publisher of BEAT to a PULP. He lives in Maine with his wife and daughter.

Marshal Gideon Miles hoped the Maryland Rye would help wash away the memory of the grimace on the wanted man's face when the slug shredded the owlhoot's throat. He also wanted to drown out the screeches of the man's wife as she held her dying husband in her arms. As much as Miles knew the hard case deserved to die for drawing on him, he still hated killing, and the woman's screams when Miles draped the corpse over his pinto for the long trek back to Cheyenne were just as difficult to stomach.

Leaning into the wooden bar, Miles reached for his drink then stopped. A pair of spurs that had been jangling toward the bar halted behind him. His shoulders slumped at the clearing of a throat — so much for a moment's peace.

"Artimisia may be a little more open-minded," the voice behind him seethed, "but that doesn't mean the rest of us are going to tolerate you sidling up to our well here, Negro."

"Now, Pete—" Artimisia chimed in.

"Shut your cock-holster." Pete raised a hand at the diminutive blonde barkeep. She recoiled, shifting her eyes to the floor.

Miles whirled around to confront Pete whose hand

was readied over the butt of a Remington hanging low on his right side. His eyes bored through the callow youth. "That's no way to talk to a lady, Petey."

"Name's Pete." A sly grin plastered the young man's ferret like face.

Miles sized up the combatant in front of him and then scoured the run-down bar filled with mostly whites and a few Indians scattered about, all immobilized waiting for the ensuing clash. He thought about revealing his badge but another idea struck him.

The marshal noted the cowpokes at the table where Pete had been when Miles had walked in the bar. The way the men were now averting their stares and squirming in their seats, Miles knew they would pose no trouble.

He raised his voice, addressing the man who looked like an older version of the foul-mouthed youth. "Is this little button here yours?"

"Yes, mister, he is." Miles detected a tinge of embarrassment in the senior man's reply.

"Well, maybe I can help you teach him some manners."

Pete stepped back. "You best draw."

"I have something else in mind." Miles flicked a tired smile. He turned to Artimisia whose concern was ruining her plain but pleasing features. "Miss, if you could hand us three shot glasses and three pint glasses."

"I'm not sure I have exact pint glasses, sir."

Miles spotted several glass pitchers along the wall. "Three of those pitchers will do."

"Those are much larger than a pint."

"They'll do. Please fill them up, ma'am."

He turned back to Pete who was still preparing to fight though the muscles in his hand had relaxed.

A few bar patrons had gathered closer for a better view of what Miles was up to.

"I've had enough shooting for one week, so I have a challenge for you, Petey—excuse me, I mean Peter."

"Name's Pete." He dropped his hand, swaggered up to

the counter, and stood left of Miles, leering at him. His father joined them at the bar with the rest of the saloon's clientele crowding about.

"Well, son, I'm challenging you that I can drink these three pitchers of beer Artimisia has filled up before you can finish those three shots of whiskey." A rumble swept across the throng with lots of chuckles and hecklers yelling, "Impossible!"

Miles ignored the ringside taunts. "But, there are some rules."

"Rules? I don't play by nobody else's rules!" Pete scoffed.

"Well, these rules are simple enough, even for the likes of you. One," Miles held up a finger, "since I have an awful lot of beer to drink, I get to down my first pitcher before you begin."

Pete snickered. "Sure. And?"

"And, no touching the other man's glasses."

"How come?"

Miles leveled his eyes. "Because I don't trust a no-good, shit for brains, upstart like you!"

Pete's face burned red as a roar of support went up for Miles.

"I accept." Pete gritted his teeth.

"Son, let me talk to you first," Pete's father spoke up.

"Nothing doing, Pa. I'm gonna teach this loud-mouthed buck a lesson."

Frowning, the father looked over at Miles and said, "Yes, a lesson seems in order."

Miles grinned and turned to Pete. "Good. There's one last thing."

"What?"

"If I win, you buy these drinks and every other fella in this bar a drink and leave me to finish mine in peace."

"And when I win?" Pete asked.

"I'll do the paying and leave."

"Agreed," Pete said.

Miles gripped the handle of the glass pitcher and lifted it to his lips, gulping down the refreshing hoppy brew. He peripherally eyed Pete whose hand twitched within a nose hair of his first drink just as it had over his gun moments earlier.

As Miles neared the bottom of the pitcher, folks began clapping in unison and money swiftly changed hands.

Miles finished the last drop of suds, pitcher still in hand, when Pete hauled the first shot of whiskey to his mouth, downed it, and slammed the empty glass on the bar, reaching for the second.

While Pete worked on his second, Miles smirked and turned the empty pitcher upside down over Pete's third drink.

Laughter filled the saloon as the oblivious youth slammed his second shot glass on the counter and grabbed for the third.

"What the … what?" Pete eyed the last shot of whiskey under the pitcher. "You dirty cheatin' son-of-a-bitch!"

Pete lunged but Miles stepped out of the way, tossing a leg to the side, and with his left arm drove Pete to the ground. The defeated youth landed on his face, spread eagled. Pete rolled over coming up with the Remington but his father slapped the gun from his son's grasp.

"He beat you fair and square. I tried to warn you. That challenge is older than Methuselah's beard. Don't embarrass yourself, or me, any longer."

Pete stood, looking around at the revelers still guffawing, and stormed out onto the street. His father bent down and picked up the Remington then lumbered over to Miles. Extending his hand, he said, "I'm sorry. The boy has been hard to handle. The name is Simmons."

Miles ignored the hand and reached for his drink.

"I guess I deserve that," Simmons said. "Listen, I'm in good with the foreman for The Big D spread and they could use good men like you."

Miles turned to Simmons and pulled his duster back revealing the U.S. Marshal badge pinned to his shirt. "No, thanks. Already have a job."

Nodding, Simmons let out a chortle and moved away. "Good day, marshal." He then looked to Artimisia, yelling out, "Drinks are on me," as he tossed some coins on the bar top. The crowd roared again and flooded the bar with empty glasses for Artimisia to fill. She glanced over at Miles and winked.

The lawman touched the corner of his Stetson, smiling, and turned back to his drink, almost forgetting the wailing of the widow he'd made.

The Redemption of Cade Beauchard

by Kit Prate

I grew up at a time when Westerns reigned supreme; in the book stores, in film, and on TV. My playground was a working stockyards, populated by real cowboys, all of whom were great teachers and even greater story-tellers. My love affair with the West and things Cowboy continues still; but bear in mind -- I write fiction, not history.

Vince Walker took his time paring a small plug of tobacco from the lint-specked wad he hoarded in the old Bull Durham sack he always carried in his inside vest pocket. There was an artistry in his careful trimming, and he cocked an eye, measuring what he knew would be the proper amount. Closing the blade of the small pen knife, he worked the gob of tar between his fingers, waiting until the consistency was just right before placing the foul-smelling mess into his mouth. It took another long, leisurely minute before he had it settled in the right spot between his jaw and his teeth and finally began to chew; and then he spoke. "Only two things I've ever been afraid of, boy," he drawled, his voice deceptively soft, almost a whisper. "A decent woman and bein' left afoot in the desert." And then he spat.

His next move was to strike out at the young boy who was standing before him. Habit prevented him from pounding the youth's face – the boy's physical attractiveness had always been an asset in their trade, one way or the other. Instead, he planted a vicious blow to the young man's stomach. It was enough the kid doubled over and collapsed to the ground. The kicking began in earnest; the strikes measured, punctuated with bitter words. "Decent . . . woman . . . saddled . . . me . . . with . . . you . . ." This kick was particularly savage, aimed at the youth's groin, " . . . and *you*," the big man grunted as he circled the prone body, ". . . *you* . . . just . . . left . . . me . . . afoot . . . in . . . the . . . desert!" The final strike was aimed low, at the long muscles in the boy's right leg. He was aiming another kick to the kidneys when Jess Kennedy grabbed his arm.

"Let him be," the man said. The fact the fingers of his right hand were coiled around the butt of his pistol was more than enough to stay Walker's foot mid-strike.

Not that the subtle threat did anything to temper the man's foul mood. "You'd best keep your nose outta my business," Walker growled. Kennedy, his second-in-command, was the only man on the crew who had the *cajones* to ever challenge him. "And that kid . . ." he nodded at the prone figure on the ground, ". . . is my business."

Holstering his pistol, Kennedy shook his head. "Not anymore." He took a breath. Behind him, he was aware of the seven other men who rode with them. "We got a posse behind us, Vince; ten, maybe fifteen miles between them and us. We ain't got time for this. Just take the kid's horse and be done with it."

Walker lifted his right hand to his mouth, wiping the spittle away from the two-day old beard. He shrugged. "Why the hell not." And then he drew his revolver.

Again, Kennedy's good sense prevailed. "You fire that thing even once," he breathed, "you'll give us away for sure." He gestured at the expanse of dry desert surrounding them. "The Devil'll hear it in Hell, Vince; posse will hear it even sooner."

Still, Walker wasn't quite convinced. "But the kid. They'll find the kid . . ."

Kennedy's jaws tensed. "He won't talk, Vince. If you taught him nothin' else, you taught him that." His voice lowered. There was no way in Hell it could look like he was giving Walker orders. *Not in front of the others.* "Go on, take his horse," he urged, making it sound like a suggestion. "I'll see to the boy."

Walker gave a curt nod. "You can cut his fuckin' throat for all I care." He took a step forward, pausing just long enough to kick out at the boy one last time. "Dumb as dirt," he declared. "The little shit was always dumb as dirt."

Waiting until Walker was out of hearing, Kennedy reached up and removed the canteen that had been hanging from his saddle. Dropping down to one knee, he shoved the canvas covered tin into the dirt, right next to the boy's clenched fingers. He knew the kid, now huddled in a fetal position, was conscious. "That'll hold you until help comes, boy." There was something apologetic in his tone. Reaching into his vest pocket, he withdrew a neatly folded bill. "This is a hundred dollar gold note," he said, tucking the bill into the youth's waistband. "It isn't much, kid, but it'll give you a start.

"You need to get out of this business, boy. You need to forget Walker and all the rest of us." There was a soft chuffing sound as he let out a short, humorless chuckle. "'*Robin Hood of the West*'", he scoffed, recalling a recent article in *Harper's Weekly* Walker had delighted in reading just before their last job. With that, he gave the injured boy a final pat and stood up.

* * *

He came awake slowly, aware of the fact someone was bathing his face. Cold water was dribbling across his forehead, its flow following the natural curvature of his skull, seeming to waterfall behind his ears. What should have been a relief became instant terror. The sensation was like maggots squirming across his flesh. He bolted upright, shoving the hand and the cloth away.

"Calm down," the voice ordered.

A flat palm against his chest was the real deterrent.

He eased back down against the sheetless mattress. "Where?" he croaked out, instantly wetting his lips with his tongue. It felt like it was going to hurt to open his eyes, so he didn't even try.

"Jail." Levi Macklin, Cooperville's town marshal, was a man known for his brevity. *That and his tall stature, his pig-headed devotion to the law, and his iron will.*

The youth bit back the panic that was pawing at his chest. "How long I been here?" he asked.

"Three days," Macklin answered, levering himself up from the edge of the cot. He was careful not tip over the enamel basin of water that was right next to his left foot. "You got a name, kid?" he asked.

Instinctively, the boy's right hand went beneath the thin blanket to his hip; to the place where his pants pockets should have been. He felt nothing but bare skin; bare skin and the soreness of the bruise knotted on his right buttock. "Need my pants," he declared.

"Why?" Macklin snorted. "You aren't going anywhere." He waited a heartbeat. "Name?" This time it was a demand.

The kid's eyes closed and then just as quickly opened; black eyelashes fluttering like moth wings as he fought the pain. His entire body ached from the beating he had received, but there was a deeper ache in his soul. *He was tired. He was so damned tired of all of it. Of life.* "Cade," he said, hesitating. "Cade Beauchard."

Macklin studied the boy's profile, his gaze settling on the youth's pale orbs. *It wasn't just physical pain he was seeing; no, there was something else . . .* He pulled himself to his full six-foot-four. Using his size to intimidate was another trait he had used to advantage in his long career as a lawman. "You were with Walker and his bunch," he accused. Reaching down, he cupped the boy's chin against his palm and gave him the once over. *Fourteen, maybe fifteen,* he reckoned; compact enough he could pass for even younger. The thick black hair, curled and framing fair skin and striking blue eyes, gave the youth the look of a Botticelli cherub.

"Pretty young to be running with those yahoos."

Cade pulled away from the man's touch. "Who said I was runnin' with 'em?"

The lawman stretched, his fingers kneading the soreness at the small of his back. The long days in the saddle pursuing the outlaws had taken its toll, but he knew he wasn't anywhere near as sore as the kid. "Someone gave you a hell of a beating, boy," he observed. *He hadn't missed how there wasn't a mark on the kid's face. The rest of the boy's body was testimony enough to what had occurred.* "They kick the shit out of you and tell you to keep your mouth shut?" He didn't wait for an answer. "This is what I know. Ten riders came into town, *my* town." He held up both hands, spreading his fingers. "Ten men robbed the bank and shot the hell out of a lot of innocent people.

"I followed those men into the desert and I found *you* and a horse with a broken leg. Rotten thing, letting that animal suffer," he finished. The horse had worked itself into a frenzy attempting to get up; its heart rupturing after repeated hard falls.

Cade blinked, just once. "I didn't shoot anybody," he murmured. *That part was the truth, and he was grateful he didn't need to lie. Vince had never allowed him to carry a loaded weapon; at least not after that time he'd caught him sneaking up from behind.* "And I wasn't ridin' with *'those yahoos'*." It was a bad lie, poorly told.

Macklin grinned, the warmth failing to reach his pale eyes. "You better practice that story, sonny." He shook his head. "No way in Hell a jury's goin' to believe you." He bent over and picked up the basin of water, retrieving the discarded wash cloth from the cot. "In about twenty minutes, the girl from the hotel is going to be bringing you supper. Last time she came in to feed the others, she took a peek under that blanket." This time the smile was real.

The youth bolted upright in the bed, clutching the flannel blanket and bunching the fabric at his waist. Thoroughly flustered, he'd almost missed the part about *'the others'*. "What others?" he demanded.

The lawman had just shut the cell door and was locking it. "The ones I got out back," he answered. "This is the holding cell, button," he said, nodding at the barren space the younger man occupied. "The one I use for Saturday night drunks and kids who play hooky. I got better . . ." he paused, " . . . *accommodations* for the hardcases." He nodded to the heavy door that led to the back rooms. There was a small, barred window at the top of the steel-banded oak portal, just big enough to allow a view of the cell area.

Cade eased himself back against the cold brick wall, framing the question in his head before voicing the words. "How many others?"

"Three," Macklin answered. "And, no, Walker isn't one of them." Then, seeing the question in the younger man's eyes – *the regret?* – he continued. "And he wasn't one of the four we planted in the desert, either."

* * *

Supper arrived. Cade kept a tight hold on the blanket that was tucked around his lower torso; his back pressed against the rough adobe wall. For good measure, he'd also put the blue-ticked pillow across his lap.

He figured the girl was pretty close to his own age – sixteen – soft and round and smooth of skin. She had auburn hair that had a mind of its own; curls that broke free from the pins and combs she used to pull it back from her face. *And she had green eyes*. She stood behind Macklin, playing coy as she waited for him to open the door.

Cade was actually disappointed when Macklin took the tray from the girl and carried it across the cell's threshold. The lawman was balancing the tray atop his inner left forearm; his right hand hovering comfortably just above the butt of his pistol. "No free show tonight, Lily," he scolded. He nodded towards the door leading to the street, grinning when the girl flounced out. She had spun quickly on her heel, intentionally; her skirt swirling to display a goodly portion of her trim legs almost to her thighs before disappearing out the door.

"I'm not standing here all day," Macklin said, nodding towards the tray he was still holding in his left arm.

The lawman's voice cut into Cade Beauchard's lustful reverie. He lifted his head, catching the sly grin on the older man's face and felt his face coloring. Reaching out, he took the tray and settled it against his knees. "What about the others?" he asked, removing the checkered napkin and scoping out the food. It reminded him of the table scraps that had ended up in the slop bucket on a pig farm where Walker had bonded him out to work for awhile when he was twelve. *At least long enough to find out where the old Kraut stashed his money.*

Macklin had returned to his desk. "It's damned near seven o'clock," he answered. "Your friends ate two hours ago."

Cade shifted on the cot, casting a look out the barred window. The sky was a muddy grey, that peculiar color that could be either dawn or twilight. "Didn't say they were my friends," he groused. "And I wasn't ridin' with them." This time the words were accompanied with a petulant frown.

His stomach was growling, and the food was beginning to look better. He poked a finger into what passed for mashed potatoes, sucking the gook into his mouth. *At least the shit had been salted.* "When am I gettin' my pants back?"

The lawman was stacking papers; tapping them against the top of the desk to line up the edges. He answered without looking up. "About the same time you get back that hundred dollar bill that was shoved into your waistband," he answered. He raised his head. "Some things, kid, you should just throw away." The smile came then, creeping up to crease the skin at the corners of his eyes. "That C-note was part of the mine payroll that was shipped in from Phoenix," he said. "Same payroll that was heisted from the bank."

That got some reaction from the kid. Macklin

watched as the youth immediately stopped eating and put the tray down on the floor.

* * *

Jess Kennedy heard the clank of the keys and pushed himself up into a sitting position; not the easiest thing to do with his right wrist shackled to the cot frame. His left shoulder hurt like all holy hell, too; no big surprise considering the sawbones had taken considerable delight in digging out the bullet fragments without the benefit of a painkiller. Steeling himself, his jaw set, he faced the door and waited.

It didn't take long. Levi Macklin shoved open the oak door and stepped down into the corridor.

"Don't suppose you brought tobacco, Levi?" Kennedy drawled amicably. *Twenty years before, he and Macklin had fought on the same side, Texas boys rallying around the Bonnie Blue Flag.* He was leaning forward, his elbows resting on his knees, fingers tented. The wrist chain was taut.

The corner of Macklin's mouth twitched. He was playing with the key ring, sorting through the keys as if he wasn't sure which one opened the cell door. "How bad you craving that smoke?"

Kennedy's right eyebrow arched. He cast a quick glance over his shoulder at the two men in the adjoining cage. Tibbons was out, his breath coming in ragged gasps; wet-sounding. The half-breed was pretending to sleep. "Depends," he said. *The lawman,* he knew, *was there to barter.*

Macklin had opened the door, and was just coming across the threshold. "I want to know about the kid. What can you tell me about that boy?"

There was a soft *whoosh* as Kennedy inhaled. That wasn't the question he anticipated. "What boy?" he shrugged.

The lawman was rolling a smoke; taking his time. It had been three days since Kennedy had had a smoke. "The one that's going to hang if he doesn't come up with a better story than the one he's telling." Using the tip of his tongue, he sealed the tissue and twisted the ends.

"You make it sound like there's going to be a trial," Kennedy smiled. He reached out, taking the proffered smoke.

Macklin dug into his shirt pocket for a match, striking it against his thumbnail and cupping his hand as he offered the light. "Oh, there's going to be a trial," he breathed. "Right before they hang your sorry asses."

Kennedy exhaled, twin tendrils of blue smoke coming from his nose. "No shit," he muttered. He was quiet for a time, mulling the thing over in his mind. At his back, he heard the 'breed shifting on the metal bunk. He laughed, softly. He didn't even know the man's name. *Hell, out of the seven men who had been riding with them the past six months, Tibbons was the only one he could call by a proper moniker. Far cry from what it had been in the beginning, when he knew them all.* "This wasn't personal, Levi." he announced suddenly. "Walker comin' into your town."

Macklin toed out the wooden stool from its place in the corner and sat down. "Don't try bullshitting me, Jess," he countered. "Walker knows this is my town; he knows I report to the Territorial marshal once a month. He's been working his way in this direction steady for the past eight months, closing the circle. That makes it look pretty damned personal to me." He was quiet a moment, and then leaned forward, keeping the words private. "I asked you about the boy. Your initials were carved into the canteen the kid had; the one you stashed beside him when you left him in the dirt with the downed horse." His hands were clasped together now, his thumbs twirling. "You leave him that bank note, too?"

The outlaw was debating his response. "He didn't talk, did he?" It was a rhetorical question. There was a long pause before he spoke again. "He's Vince's kid," he said finally.

Macklin's face momentarily betrayed him, the surprise showing, then as quickly fading. "He told me his name," he replied. "And it wasn't Walker."

Kennedy shrugged. "Beauchard," he breathed. He

canted his head, studying Macklin's face and then continued. *Funny how knowing you were a dead man made it easier to spill your guts.* "His mother's name," he said. "She married Vince just before the kid was born, but it didn't take her long to figure out she'd made a big mistake. She went back to using her own name, hung it on the boy, too."

Macklin's butt was getting tired. He levered himself up from the stool and stretched. "How'd he end up with Walker?"

"Lizzie died," Kennedy answered. "We showed up at her farm looking for a place to lay low for awhile, and the kid was just there. Her kin couldn't get rid of him fast enough." He took a final drag on the cigarette and then ground it out between his thumb and forefinger before tossing the butt to the floor. A wry grin touched his lips. "Hell, he was ten years old. Smart enough to build a fire, make a pot of coffee; big enough to hold the horses for us outside a bank." He raked his fingers through his hair. "Vince took him in hand, and . . ."

Macklin's jaws tensed, his grey eyes becoming gun metal grey; the pupils dilating and looking as deadly as the twin barrels of a pair .44's. "I saw how Vince '*took him in hand*'," he snapped. "That kid had the shit beat out of him, and more than once from what the Doc said. Probably for a long time." He bit back the words he wanted to say, tempering the next. "Never knew you to stand back and watch something like that happen, Jess, and not step in."

Kennedy laughed. There was no humor in the sound. "Maybe in the beginning, Levi; when we were fighting that damned war, and we were lookin' out for each other." He raised his right hand, shaking his fist in frustration at the chain that bound him to the cot; wishing there was enough slack so he could stand up. "You remember how it was. When the army paid us to cut through the supply lines, sack the towns? Hell, we took everything that wasn't nailed down and never looked back!" More cold laughter, filled with bitter irony.

294

"We got medals, commendations, for what we did, Levi. And we were damned good at it!"

The lawman was pacing. Out the corner of his eye, he saw the half-breed rise up on his knees on the cot. With the suddenness of a snake, the breed reached through the bars with one arm, grabbing Kennedy around the neck; choking him and pulling his head against the steel cross bars. "You shut the fuck up, Kennedy!" he snarled. "Vince ain't gonna leave us here to die!"

Macklin's pistol was out faster than a greased shoat out of a deballing pen. He thumbed back the hammer, leaning across Kennedy's shoulder to jam the barrel between the other man's eyes. "You let him go, you bastard, or I'll blow your head off!" The words were whisper soft, but like steel. He kept applying pressure, hard enough there was a dark indentation in the soft flesh above the bridge of the *mestizo*'s nose.

So intent was the pressure from the barrel of the gun, the 'breed's dark eyes crossed as he stared hard at the weapon. He lifted his hands away from Kennedy's throat, wetting himself as he fell back on the cot. The pungent scent of strong urine seemed to fill the entire cell block. Macklin withdrew the piece, but he didn't release the hammer; nor did he holster the weapon.

Kennedy was rubbing at his throat, clawing at the soreness in his windpipe. "You move him to another cell, Levi. And then we'll talk."

It didn't take the lawman long to accomplish the deed. Knowing Kennedy was secure, he entered the second cell, pulled the *mestizo* to his feet and dragged him bodily to the last cell at the end of the hallway. To make the humiliation complete, he delivered a swift kick to the man's ass, knocking him clear across the stone floor. He secured the man's wrist to the iron bed frame; and then shackled the man's legs.

His mood was only slightly improved when he returned to Kennedy's cell. Macklin started right in. "There was a woman coming out of the mercantile when you jackasses backed out of the bank. She was carrying a baby in her arms," he continued. He held up his hand, his fingers forming a 'V'. "Two lives, one bullet," he intoned. "Four more were wounded."

Kennedy drew in a long breath that ended in a quavering sigh. "I didn't shoot that woman, Levi. Swear to God, I didn't shoot at anyone who wasn't shooting back at me."

Macklin snorted. "That isn't going to make one damned bit of difference, Jess. Jesus Christ could walk in here tomorrow with a full pardon from God, and the town is still going to hang the three of you."

Kennedy's hands were trembling. "I could use another smoke," he murmured.

The lawman nodded. This time he produced a tin of ready-rolleds and handed them off to his one time friend and comrade-at-arms. He handed him the box of matches as well. "How old is the kid?" he asked.

Kennedy's hands were steady now as he lit the smoke. "Sixteen. He's been with us six years," he breathed. "Vince wouldn't let him carry a loaded piece." He took a long drag on the cigarette, holding the smoke in his mouth, rolling it around before expelling it through his nose. "All the kid did was hold the horses and watch the street." *That would have changed when the boy got older.*

Macklin nodded. "He's never done a robbery?" he asked.

Kennedy shook his head. "Scouted for us; kept track of who came and who went. Watched out for us when we were inside." *There was no point in telling about the times the kid was used as bait in their smaller cons.*

"This is how it's going to be, Jess," Macklin started, his voice lowering. "You're going to write all that out for me. You're going to put it down on paper the boy didn't have a part in any of it. Nothing about him being Walker's kid either; just that he was some stray you picked up somewhere to do the grunt jobs in camp. And then you're going to sign it."

There was a soft *phhtt* sound as Kennedy spit out a stray piece of tobacco. "And why would I do that?" he asked. His eyes narrowed as he canted his head, staring up at the man. "What's in it for me?"

Macklin thought about it for awhile, but not too long. "A little something in your coffee to take the edge off before they haul you out of here to hang," he answered. He thumped his broad chest with his bent forefinger. "*Me* putting the noose around your neck for a nice, clean break when you take the tumble."

Kennedy laughed; forcing a humor he didn't feel, but appreciating the honesty. *It wasn't as though he had expected Macklin to show him the front door, put him on a horse and point him south.* "They'll still put him in jail," he said. He turned to face his companion. "Hell, they got a fourteen year old white boy over in Yuma doin' time for stealin' a greaser's mule." Mouth dry, he spat out a second flake of tobacco. "They'll put that kid in prison just for bein' with us when we rode in. You know that, Mac."

Macklin was shaking his head. "He isn't going to prison," he announced.

The outlaw's eyes narrowed. "You got that much pull with the judge? With the town?"

"I got that much pull," Macklin answered. *Not that he'd talked to anyone yet.*

Kennedy's head was rocking back and forth against the bars. He had already started a second cigarette. "Walker thought you were a fool when you walked away from him," he murmured.

Macklin's shoulders lifted in a noncommittal shrug. "The war was over, Jess. We should have all walked away."

The small cell was heavy with blue smoke now. "When?" Kennedy asked, done with the reminiscing.

There was, Macklin knew, no point in sugar-coating the truth. "The judge is already here. He's got the trial set for one o'clock tomorrow afternoon."

Kennedy was surprised and it showed on his face. "Why so late?" he asked, not sure he wanted the answer.

Macklin's face was devoid of any emotion. "Because the jury will be burying the woman and her baby at ten."

* * *

Macklin sat at his desk, the cigar he had been smoking already gone cold between his fingers. He sighed. The Regulator clock on the wall to his right was poised to strike the hour; the gears grinding as the chiming mechanism engaged. *Midnight,* he mused, *the bewitching hour.* He wondered where the hell the time was going.

He had just turned twenty-five when the War ended and he had ridden away from Walker; four years of rough soldiering behind him, four years that had seemed like an eternity. *And now the years seemed to be fluttering by like the pages of a book beneath an open window; picking up speed as they flipped with increasing velocity as his hair went grey and his body soft.*

In the twenty years that had passed, he had become town marshal; had married and fathered a child. Had watched his marriage disintegrate, his wife wither, and had buried his son. And then he was alone.

His job – which had too often taken him away from his family – had been his only constant. In the end, the job was the only thing that had endured.

His gaze drifted to the holding cell, coming to rest on the still form of the young boy. The kid was quiet now; out cold from the laudanum he had been given when the doctor was called to attend to his pain, the drug strong enough to stop the nightmares.

The lawman's jaws tightened. It had been like a kick in the gut, finding the boy in the desert. Everything about the kid was a reminder of what had once been; the slim build and the dark hair. The blue eyes, though, were what had done him in. *Matthew had had blue eyes; blue eyes as brilliant as sapphires in a bed of snow.*

He shook his head. He was being a fool; an old fool. *Still, if it was true the eyes were the windows to the soul* . . .

298

Restless, he rose to his feet, seeking out first the pot of coffee, and then the bottle of whisky he kept stashed in the bottom desk drawer. He dosed the java with a healthy shot, staying on his feet as he stared out the window into the darkness. It was too late to turn back now. He'd already spoken to Judge Hastings; had already cut the deal. Good or bad, he had made the decision. The why of it still mystified him. But, God help him, he had seen something in Cade Beauchard's eyes that had filled him with a renewed sense of hope.

* * *

Dawn came, ushered in by a clap of thunder that shook the adobe brick jail house to its foundations; a sudden bolt of sky-to-earth lightning illuminating the holding cell and the office beyond. The rain came then; sheets of water sweeping across the landscape pushed by a fierce wind carrying tumbleweeds and debris that pelted against the side of the building. Somewhere, a shutter banged against an exterior wall. And then the storm ceased.

It was deathly still now. *A good day for a hanging.*

Trembling, Cade Beauchard levered himself up from the narrow cot, gathering the blanket at his waist as he sat up. He was drenched in sweat, shivering as much from the early morning cold as from the memories of the recurrent nightmares. His father haunted his dreams, filling him with night terrors that mirrored the reality of his days.

Once, when he was twelve, he had tried to run away. Walker had pursued him with the ferocity and dedication of a blood hound. The beating he received after he was caught left him with a dislocated shoulder that plagued him still; a perfect ploy in some of his father's more resourceful cons when the man needed to gain access to an isolated ranch or a solitary house just at the edge of town. *"Nothin' better than a bawlin' kid to get you where you need to be . . ."*

The sound of a key in the heavy lock roused the young man from his grim musings. He turned to face his jailer.

Macklin swung open the cell door. He stood for a time, his grey eyes probing the dim interior before settling on his youth. Hefting the parcel he held in his right hand he addressed the boy. "Get dressed," he ordered, tossing the bundle toward the couch.

Instinct prompted the catch. Cade felt the brown paper crumple beneath his fingers. "What's this?"

"Something decent to wear that fits," the lawman answered.

Cade's eyes dropped to the package, which bound with coarse twine. He didn't bother to untie the knot, tearing the paper, somehow sensing his carelessness would rile the older man. *Everything about the lawman reeked thrift.* Showing no emotion, he shook out the clothing: an entire outfit from the skin out. "Don't much care for blue," he said, fingering the chambray shirt.

"Well, isn't that too damned bad," Macklin shot back. *Cocky little bastard*, he thought. *I'll be nipping that in the bud.* "You are old enough to dress yourself?" He took a single step forward.

"Yeah," Cade answered. "I can drink outta a cup, too." He slipped into the shirt, grinning inwardly when he saw the older man's right eyebrow arch at his failure to put on the summer-weight union suit. He climbed into the pants next, tucking in the shirt tails. *If the old buzzard was expecting gratitude, he'd have a long wait.*

Surprisingly, Macklin was amused by the boy's blatant bravado, recognizing it for what it was. He was about to speak when the front door opened and Lily, the little piece of fluff from the hotel stepped into the room. She was carrying a large, enamel ware coffee pot. "Caleb said you didn't order breakfast," she pouted. It sounded like an accusation. "You goin' to feed 'em before they hang, or what?"

Macklin heard the sharp intake of breath from the youth inside the cage and ignored it. Without looking around, he kicked the cell door shut. "You tell Caleb I've arranged for Sarah Tuckerman to bring them a proper meal," he ground out. "And, Lily, if I catch you within ten feet of here this afternoon," he pointed at the floor with his right forefinger, "I'll blister your behind." He reached out, taking the coffee pot.

* * *

The long morning stretched into high noon without much activity. Breakfast had come and gone, and it was pretty apparent there wasn't going to be any lunch. Other than Macklin's trips to the back cell area – he'd gone through the heavy oak door twice, both times carrying full bottles of whisky – there wasn't much happening.

Cade Beauchard found the wait unnerving, worse than the times he had spent dreading the arrival of his father after a Saturday night bender. He rose up from the cot, padding across the stone floor and moving close to the door. It occurred to him Macklin had not given him back his boots. "So, now what, Old Man?" he called. His throat was dry, and he was grateful his voice didn't crack.

Macklin was studiously writing in a large ledger. He didn't even look up. "I wait until my deputy gets here, and then I take those yahoos," he gestured towards the door leading to the cellblock with his pencil, "over to the court house."

Cade laughed, softly; no humor in the sound. "Oh, yeah. The trial."

The lawman shrugged. "That's how it's done."

Christ, he's a cold bastard. "So when do I get my boots?"

"Later," Macklin answered. He stood up just as his deputy came through the door.

The man, Fred Evans, was in his thirties; and he was carrying a greener. A part-time lawman, he worked a quarter-section just outside of Cooperville, a small patch of green with good water. Already, he had coaxed his first crop of alfalfa out of the acreage, something that had made him a bit of a local celebrity. "Judge says he's ready, Levi." He was quiet a moment. "Him first?" he asked, nodding at the youth.

Macklin was already shaking his head. He tapped his shirt pocket, indicating the piece of paper that was folded against his right breast. "Got a statement from Walker's man, Kennedy. The kid is just some stray they picked up last town they went through." He turned slightly, silently daring the boy to speak; a smug grin coming when the youth's mouth remained shut.

Beauchard watched as Macklin and his deputy both headed for the back corridor. It didn't take them long. There was the clatter of chains rattling; the shuffling of booted feet. Macklin reappeared first, his right hand firmly gripping Jess Kennedy's left arm. Tibbons was next, with the half-breed dragging along behind. Evans followed close behind. All three outlaws were handcuffed and shackled.

"Jess . . ." The whispered word was out before the youth could stop it.

Kennedy's head stopped mid turn. He quickly corrected the mistake and stared straight ahead.

The half-breed hadn't missed the blunder. He pulled up short; not giving a damn when Evan's poked him with the shotgun. "What about that little bastard?" he snarled. "He's . . ."

Macklin's right fist slammed into the *mestizo*'s mouth.

* * *

The waiting was even worse now. Cade Beauchard was sitting hunkered down on the narrow cot, his back against the walls, his knees drawn up to his chest. He didn't understand one thing that was happening; not one. At least when he was with his father, he knew the boundaries. There was a strange security in that; a simplicity. The experience had, for the most part, honed his survival skills. He'd sure in Hell – until this last time – gotten pretty damned good at ducking, at avoiding confrontation. *But this shit!* One thing about his father; he had never played head games.

Macklin was – *what did his mother used to call it? –* a conundrum, a riddle. *How the Hell did you figure a man who was a law unto himself?*

Picking at the threads on his shirt cuff, the youth pondered everything that had occurred the past few days. Nothing made any sense. His ass was still in jail. Jess and the others . . .

Jess. He thought about the man; what he had seen in his eyes when Macklin had been leading him out of the back cell area. And then there was that brief glance, just before the lawman had punched the half-breed. Kennedy had looked like a man who knew he was already dead, and yet he was strangely calm.

It hit him then. *Drugged.* Kennedy's eyes had had the same glazed look as the whores his father played with; the flat look that came with too much laudanum, or the opium they smoked in their cribs.

The sound of the front door opening was a welcome intrusion into the myriad of confused thoughts that were tumbling through the youth's head. He looked up to see Macklin cross the threshold, his eyes tracking the lawman's movements as he prowled about the room.

Macklin had picked up a pair of boots from beneath his desk. He clutched them in his left hand as he approached the cell door and fit the key into the lock. The lawman tossed the boots into the cage. "Put them on," he ordered. "You're coming with me."

It was a short walk. Out the front door, down the boardwalk; a right turn at the corner. Evans was waiting at the end of the alleyway; Evans and a dozen or so grim-faced men. There was a preacher.

A flat-bed hay wagon was sitting in the back alley, parked between the livery barn and the back side of jail house; a matching pair of Belgium draft horses – flaxen-maned sorrels – dancing in the traces. Above the wagon, a twelve-by-twelve rough hewn timber had been secured to the jail house roof; the opposite end – at a slight angle – disappearing into dark interior of the hayloft. Three ropes were coiled and knotted around the crossbeam.

Jess Kennedy, Tibbons, and the half-breed were standing atop the wagon bed, the ropes already around their necks. Flour sacks had been placed over their heads; the tempo of their breathing causing a quick in-and-out flutter of the soft muslin. *The material was patterned, tiny flowers dancing in the man-made breeze.*

Without any direct order from Macklin, Fred Evans turned and climbed aboard the wagon, gingerly hoisting himself up by stepping first onto the front wheel hub before swinging into the bench seat.

Cade Beauchard felt his knees give. *This isn't happening, this isn't happening.* But it was.

Macklin leaned into the boy, his strong right arm keeping the young man on his feet. He was whispering. "This is how it is, boy." He nodded towards the wagon, his grip increasing as Evans expertly used his whip to urge the team forward. A tumult of diverse sounds cut into the afternoon quiet; the jangle of trace chains, the scrape of leather-soled boots against the straw littered wagon bed, the sudden slip of hemp across timber, the sway and creak of stretching rope. "Life," the lawman continued. "It's about choices. Waste or redemption.

"That's waste," he murmured. "What I'm offering you, son, is redemption."

* * *

It had been five years. Cade Beauchard's lips parted in a lop-sided grin. The comforting, familiar creak of leather came as he shifted slightly in the saddle and he thought back on what his life had been. *Pretty damned good*, he reckoned, the grin blossoming into a full-blown smile.

Lifting his right hand from where it had been resting atop the saddle horn, he used the fleshy part of his palm to swipe at the tin star pinned to his vest pocket. Levi Macklin had worked hard to get him raised right; giving him not only a home and an education, but so much more. The lawman had given him a trade.

And he was good at it, too. At twenty-one,

Beauchard's own reputation was growing. He'd been a reluctant student at first, another man's shadow; but once Macklin had put him on the straight and narrow, it had all changed. He'd been schooled by the master; taught how to track, how to remain relentless when on the hunt. *How to use the Colt.*

Absently, the young man's left hand dropped to his hip; the feel of the walnut grip filling him with satisfaction. The weapon was almost a living thing; an extension of his arm that became a part of him as easily as slipping on a glove. He was fast -- there was no question of that -- but even more important, he was deadly accurate.

They made quite a pair, him and the Old Man. That single thought caused the youth to take a deep breath. He was alone this time; his first solo hunt. There was no way in hell he was going to screw this up.

* * *

Vince Walker cursed. Life, his bone-tired ass, the full bladder that had required yet another stop to relieve himself. Vindictive, he shot a stream of hot urine at the small mound of sand and gravel just to the right of the toe of his boot; a dry chuckle coming as he watched the piss-ants scatter. "Piss on *you*, you little bastards," he muttered. Shaking the last dribbles free, he tucked himself in.

He stood for a time, surveying the hostile terrain; shading his eyes as he noted the position of the sun, his gaze shifting to the southern mountains. Mexico was a good two days off, and that was with hard travel. But he had no choice. He'd run his string of luck north of the border. Civilization had spread her ugly tentacles across the face of the country, bringing the law and the military. The old cons weren't working anymore, and pickings were slim.

It didn't help that the nearest lawman was as close as the next telegraph office.

Rubbing at the ache in his back, the old outlaw stretched. Well, he had one thing going for him, he mused. Levi Macklin was no longer on his tail. They were no longer playing their little game.

He laughed, wincing at the sound of his own voice as it echoed back to him from walls of the arroyo. A whore in Sonoita had given him the news. Macklin had been thrown when his gelding took exception to a bunch of kids tossing Fourth of July firecrackers; and was stove up real bad, maybe even dying. *Independence Day*, Walker snickered. *His Independence Day.* He had celebrated with a two day *fandango*.

Sobering, Walker turned back to the matters at hand. *Damned if he didn't have to piss again.*

* * *

Cade Beauchard was sprawled out flat on his belly. He reached up, removing his Stetson and carefully placing it on the ground next to his right thigh; keeping his head low as he watched the scene below. Anticipation clawed at his gut; that and the hatred that had niggled at him for as long as he could remember. Both emotions, he knew, had to be held in check; not the easiest thing. His temper had always been a problem, something Macklin had worked hard to correct. *Not that it had been an easy task to accomplish.*

Absently, the young man dusted off the seat of his britches. He smiled. Macklin had blistered his ass on more than one occasion. Nothing like the beatings he had endured from his own father; no, Macklin would simply pop him hard enough to get his attention. *And it had worked.*

The noise from the small clearing below roused the young man from his quiet ruminations. He shifted slightly, taking advantage of narrow gap between two fair-sized boulders, peering down into the gathering shadows. A grim smile touched his lips. That was twice now Walker had had to relieve himself in the span of less than a half-hour.

Levering himself up from his perch, the young man cat-pawed his way down the shallow embankment. He was wearing moccasins now, another trick Macklin had taught him in the early days; moving as stealthily as a young buck in pursuit of game. The distance between him and his quarry had narrowed to a matter of yards, and then feet.

Cade pulled himself up short. He stood for a time, watching as Walker squirted the last of his water onto the thirsty desert floor. The smile came then, the one that crawled across the boy's face to crinkle the skin behind his ears. His stance changed, his right hip cocked. And then he called out.

"Been a long time, Pa," he drawled.

Walker's shoulders bunched, his right hand instinctively closing around his dick. The absurdity of his position didn't escape him; but it was the words and the voice that garnered his immediate attention. His head cocked to the right -- his good ear -- but he didn't turn around. *Not just yet.*

"Lose something?" the voice taunted. "Or just can't find it anymore?"

The old man's eyes closed, and just as quickly re-opened. "Thought you were dead, boy," he breathed. Carefully, he raised both hands away from his body.

"Nope," Cade responded, "not that you didn't try."

Walker's hands were even with his shoulders when he made the about face. His eyes narrowed. The sun was just setting; long fingers of hazy golden light holding back the shadows. There was more than enough light to bathe the younger man's countenance, but not so much as to put him at a disadvantage. *No*, Walker observed wryly. *The kid was on full alert.*

He saw it then, the shimmer of silver on the boy's chest. "What the hell?"

Cade laughed. The old man's fly was still open, his cock hanging limp and exposed. "Not quite how I pictured it all these years," he crowed, "but it'll do."

Walker's right hand dropped. He was still clawing for his pistol when the bullet tore into his lower abdomen, just to the right. The impact caused him to take a full step backwards. Then, his head tilting forward as he attempted to check the wound, he dropped to his knees.

Instinct prompted his next move as he finally succeeded in pulling the pistol; his fingers growing numb. The Remington thudded into the dirt.

In less than a heartbeat, Cade Beauchard was beside Walker, kicking the pistol away from the man's groping fingers. "Who's dumb as dirt now, old man?" he hissed. He watched as Walker fell face forward onto the desert floor.

Cade stood for a time, taking several deep breaths before he holstered his pistol. *Redemption,* he thought, remembering. Macklin had sure been right about that one; it was indeed a fine thing. Then, looking down at the man who lay slowly dying at his feet, he reconsidered. *Retribution was a hell of a lot more satisfying.*

Boot Hill Neighbors

by Clay More

Clay More is the western pen-name of Keith Souter - doctor, medical journalist and novelist. He lives in England within arrow-shot of a medieval castle, where he writes articles, non-fiction books and novels in a variety of genres. His favorite genre has always been the western. Learn more about him at www.keithsouter.co.uk

Chapter 1

From his vantage point in the alleyway between Hans Larsen's Emporium and The Painted Lady Saloon Skeeter Mills chewed his wad of tobacco with studied precision, working it round his mouth so that he gave each of his remaining five yellow teeth a fair piece of the action. Yet it was not as studied an action as usual for he was a man preoccupied. There was something about the two fellers that he had been watching for the past hour, ever since they independently arrived in Hagsville.

Skeeter was the town's grave digger, a role that he had held for ten years and which he took mighty seriously. After all, he had buried all of the town folks that passed away naturally in that time, as well as quite a few who had gone unnaturally.

He tugged at his straggly grey moustache then pulled his misshapen hat down a mite on his forehead.

"Something ain't right here, Skeeter. I sense trouble," he mused to himself as he watched the two fellers independently make their way along Main Street towards the church and Boot Hill beyond.

Satisfied in his own mind that the two men were headed to the same place he shoved himself away from the clapboard wall of the saloon and ambled after them, hands thrust deep in his pockets like any regular loafer.

The tall older feller in the fancy suit and black silk hat had the look of a gambling man. He had alighted from the morning Concord from Silver City, a fancy leather tooled bag in one hand and a silver topped cane in the other. Dark haired and hawk featured he didn't give anything away with his stone-walled expression. Skeeter had followed him into The Painted Lady and ordered his first dose of tonsil paint of the day, which he downed straight back as was his way.

"Is there much action here?" he heard the dude ask Gomez the bartender, who nodded in the affirmative in his usual surly manner. Clearly the dude intended playing a little poker and probably planned to fleece one or two folk who were ready to part with their money.

Then he had asked for directions to the town's Boot Hill. Skeeter grinned at the way that had made Gomez stare anxiously at him, as though he had plans to send one of his customers there if his game didn't go well. But then the stranger had just taken his drink to the end of the long bar and nursed it awhiles.

His own thirst momentarily slaked, Skeeter had taken his leave and gone over to Jenkin's livery and carpentry yard to see whether Doc Brady had given old Ben the nod to get a coffin ready for any of his ailing patients. It had been almost two weeks since he had planted the last two in the cemetery and his muscles ached for a little exertion. He had smiled ruefully when old Ben told him that the doc appeared to be looking after his patients as if they was kin of his.

It was as he was meandering back towards The Painted Lady that he saw the kid ride down the street on a horse that looked as if it was lucky not to have dropped and become buzzard-bait days ago. He hitched it in front of the sheriff's office and for a moment just stood as if he was in some sort of trance.

310

To Skeeter, he looked like a kid that was hurting inside, as if he had been crying fit to bust, his eyes all puffed up and red. Yeah, red just like his hair. He was a big strong youngster but probably not yet fully growed, Skeeter reckoned. Good looking with wide shoulders and thick wrists suggested that he had toiled hard all his young life. The peacemaker stuffed into an aged holster looked a tad out of place at his side, like he had borrowed it from his old man and as though he hadn't used it much. All in all Skeeter placed him as being some sort of homesteader. And he looked hot tempered too, judging by the way he finally stomped onto the boardwalk, shook off a patina of dust from all over hisself, and then hammered on the sheriff's door.

Not the sort of thing you do to Walt Ryker's office door, unless you want a slapping down. It was the kid's good fortune that the sheriff and Emmet Dubbs his deputy were meeting with Judge Gantry over at the courthouse.

Skeeter had waited a while then followed him across the dirt road to The Painted Lady. There Skeeter ordered another tonsil paint and watched the kid down two of Gomez's lukewarm beers in quick succession before asking the way to Boot Hill.

That caught the other feller's attention. He had looked up through a haze of swirling blue smoke from a long slim cigar. Skeeter spat nonchalantly in the direction of the spittoon in an attempt to show he was just minding his own business. Then he grunted at Gomez and left, taking up a place in the shade between the Emporium and The Painted Lady.

He didn't have long to wait before they both came out. The kid first, then the gambling man. And sure enough they both walked right on past the church, through the wrought iron gate into Boot Hill.

He followed at a distance.

Straight to the two new graves, one bedecked with several bunches of flowers, the other just a heap of dirt with a single flower laid on it. It was only when they stood over the two graves, the gambling man by the dirt pile, the kid by the heap of flowers, that they seemed to pay any attention to each other.

It was then that Skeeter thought it might be a good time to get the preacher or maybe even risk Sheriff Walt Ryker's wrath. He didn't want any trouble. Not in his Boot Hill.

Chapter 2

Jethro Dury was a couple of weeks short of his twentieth birthday and was bursting with rage and grief. He stared down at the grave with the simple wooden cross and the name Cindy-May Dury written in paint across it.

He looked at the smoothly dressed older man standing at the other grave then sniffed and wiped the back of his hand across his nose. He knelt down and read the message that someone had written on a card attached to one of the bunches of flowers.

We miss you Cindy-May. Love, Betsy.

Then he saw another written in a different hand: You shouldn't be there next to that dog!

Jethro felt a lump threaten to close up his throat and he screwed up his eyes to force away the tears that had welled up.

A couple of paces away Zeke Kincaid laid his bag down beside the grave and took his hat off. He sighed as he gently straightened the single flower on the grave mound with the end of his cane. Then his eye fell on the cross and his jaw muscles tightened as he read the brief message on the roughly tacked on piece of wood.

HERE LIES WILLIAM KINCAID

A MURDERING DOG HANGED

ROT IN HELL!

With a curse he bent down and wrenched the wood from the cross then tossed it down and smashed it with his heel.

Jethro had looked up at the sudden burst of activity and stared at the angry countenance of the man standing by the other grave. He read the words on the smashed wooden sign.

"Do you know the dog in that grave?" he asked, straightening up and pointing an accusing finger at the grave.

"He was my kid brother," returned the other in a deadpan voice. "I can see that you are grieving, boy, that's why I'll let that remark about him pass – once!"

"That dog murdered my sister," Jethro said heatedly. "The sheriff of this forsaken place wrote to me explaining it all." He drew out a crumpled blue envelope from his breast pocket. "He strangled her."

"And the town lynched him!" The voice had an edge this time. "I got a letter, too. But my Billy didn't kill any two-bit whore."

Jethro's eyes widened in horror, then immediately narrowed as rage started to rise within him. He reached for and drew out his old peacemaker, swinging it round to take aim at the grave.

As if by magic a double-barreled Derringer appeared in Zeke Kincaid's hand. There was a double click as the hammers were ratcheted back. "Drop it!" he snapped.

"You go to hell!" cried Jethro as he discharged a shot into the grave, inches from Kincaid's foot.

A split second later Zeke Kincaid shot the bottom off Jethro's right ear lobe."I said drop that weapon or the next will be between the eyes."

Jethro's left hand went to his ear, which was already trickling blood down his neck. Apart from that he didn't so much as flinch.

There was the explosion of a sawn-off shotgun being discharged into the air, just feet from the two men as they stared at each other with hate-filled eyes.

"Both of you drop your weapons or Skeeter here will be planting two more bodies next to these graves."

Another voice chipped in. Higher in tone, pleadingly: "No violence, I beseech you. This is hallowed ground. No more deaths, please."

Both hesitated then in unison they complied.

An instant later two guns rose and fell, knocking both men unconscious.

They fell towards each other, landing spread-eagled

across the graves that they had come to pay their respects to.

Chapter 3

Jethro came back to consciousness and was immediately aware of a thundering pain in the back of his head. Yet it was as nothing compared with the sharp stabbing pain in his ear. Involuntarily he screwed his eyes shut and clenched his jaw.

"God dammit! Hold his head still," he heard someone snap.

Immediately, strong hands grabbed his head in a vice-like grip.

Then the voice went on reassuringly: "Easy son, I've just a couple more stitches to do then I'm through. Your friend there gouged a fair chunk of your ear out with that Derringer slug. I've closed the wound pretty well, if I say so myself, but the ear will always be a mite smaller than the other one."

Jethro blinked several times and slowly his vision became less blurred. He saw a middle aged man with wire-framed spectacles just a few inches from his face. In his hands he was wielding forceps and catgut, tying a knot with trained dexterity. He was also conscious of two others; one pinning his shoulders down and one holding his head. As he attempted to move his arms he realized that he was handcuffed.

"Why have you got me trussed up like a hog?" he demanded.

The man snipped catgut with a scissors then grinned. "You could say thanks, first, son. Ain't many folks could patch you up as well as this, or stop you bleeding like a stuck hog. My name is Brady. Doc Brady everyone calls me."

"I am obliged, Doc Brady," Jethro replied. "But I'd be even more obliged if whoever is holding my head could just ease off a tad."

There was a snort from close by then a voice like a bullfrog, a voice he had heard before, at the grave of his sister. "There you go, boy. We was just holding you so the doc could work on that ear."

At the remark there was a throaty laugh from the man holding his shoulders.

Jethro turned his head as the two straightened up and stood either side of Doc Brady who had begun putting his surgical instruments into a metal tray. One was a well built, useful looking man with gimlet eyes and with a thick pepper and salt moustache. The badge pinned to his vest proclaimed that he was in charge. The other was a younger man of about twenty-five with bad teeth and a lazy eye. Like the sheriff he had a badge pinned on his vest

"I'm Sheriff Ryker," the older man announced in his bullfrog voice. "What's your name, boy? I guess I don't have to tell you that you're in big trouble. We don't take kindly to gunplay in Hagsville."

Someone coughed behind the sheriff and a moment later a tall gangly man in a frock coat and with a shirt buttoned up to his throat appeared. "And The Lord most certainly would disapprove of the desecration of a grave," he intoned in a voice that fairly rose and fell like he was on the verge of committing Jethro to damnation. He sounded just like the preacher man back home, who only smiled and eased off the brimstone and fire warnings when folk started dropping money into his box at the end of Sunday service.

"My name is Jethro Dury and I didn't intend any harm. I was just angry. I paid you a visit, Sheriff, but you wasn't in. You wrote to me."

"I figured as much," Sheriff Ryker grunted. He turned to the preacher. "What you reckon, Reverend Brown? It's still a crime in my book."

"Ah!" The preacher exclaimed. "So he's a relative of the – er – the dead woman." He pursed his lips. "I agree, it is a crime, but the young man may have had some excuse. Maybe Judge Gantry will take that into account when you talk to him. The Lord only knows what may have happened if Skeeter Mills hadn't sought us out to warn us about these two."

"Cindy-May was my big sister," Jethro said, to no one

in particular. "And she was an angel."

The deputy snorted. "She warn't no angel, boy." He grinned, exhibiting his yellow heavily tobacco stained teeth. "But there's plenty folks around here would tell that she was good." His face fell into a leer. "Real good!"

"Shut up, Emmet!" Sheriff Ryker snapped at him. "The girl is dead. Show some respect."

Jethro glared at the deputy. "Mister if you mean anything bad about –"

They were interrupted by a drawn out groan from the cot-bed next to Jethro. He looked round and saw the man who had blown part of his ear away slowly and painfully raised himself on his elbows.

Zeke Kincaid stared bemusedly about him.

"Why the hell have I got these damned bracelets on?" he demanded of the sheriff.

"They're on you because you shot this kid – and you resisted arrest," replied Sheriff Ryker.

Zeke Kincaid shook his head and blinked as he tried to clear his head. "I guess you're the Sheriff Ryker that wrote me a letter to tell me about my kid brother's death. Well, I admit that I trimmed the youngster's ear, but that was because he had just shot my brother. Or shot his grave at any rate. I sort of saw red."

Jethro looked at Zeke and nodded his head. "I was angry too, Mister. It was when you called Cindy-May a whore."

Zeke stared at him for a few seconds. "I apologize for that. Heat of the moment."

Jethro considered the remark then nodded. "I'm sorry, too, Mister. I reckon we both acted in temper."

"I'd shake your hand if I could, son," Zeke said. Then turning back to the sheriff. "So now that's all cleared up, suppose you take these cuffs off us both."

Sheriff Ryker raised an eyebrow. "Not sure that I can do that. Gunplay in the cemetery is a public disorder issue. That's up to Judge Gantry. The fact is that if we hadn't stopped you, one of you, maybe both, would be waiting to take a place beside your relatives on Boot Hill. Either that or we might have hanged one of you for murder."

"You mean the town might have lynched one of us?" Zeke asked. "Like this town murdered my brother? Guess that tells us a lot about you, Sheriff. There can't be any effective law round here."

Ryker's face turned purple and his hand hovered near his gun-butt.

"Easy Sheriff," the Reverend Matthew Brown said quickly, as he grabbed the lawman's arm.

Doc Brady stood up and put a hand on the sheriff's shoulder. "That's right, Sheriff. Keep calm. You need to make sure that everything that happens is strictly legal."

Chapter 4

A couple of hours later Zeke and Jethro had been released, following Sheriff Ryker's consultation with the judge. They had been told that they were free to go, on three conditions. First, that they would collect their weapons minus ammunition when they left town. Secondly, that they both left by sundown the next day. Lastly, they both had to stay at The Painted Lady saloon so that the sheriff knew where they were.

Ryker made them all too aware that if there was any trouble between them he would have them both behind bars as soon as spit.

Skeeter Mills self-appointed himself as their guardian busybody, since he kind of felt that it had been his interest and intervention that had kept them both alive this far. It was a fact that he acquainted them of when he joined them as they sat at a table eating in the back of The Painted Lady.

"Yes gents, I sort of felt that we all have a connection, account of me having buried your folks. I was glad that you didn't shoot each other."

"Reckon that deserves a drink at least," said Zeke.

"Don't mind if I do," Skeeter replied, catching the eye of one of the girls and raising three fingers, then nodding at Zeke to indicate who was paying.

They chatted for a few moments before Zeke changed

the conversation. "The sheriff told us all about the two murders, but neither Jethro nor I believe a word of it."

Skeeter swallowed hard, as if his mouth had suddenly dried up. His Adam's apple slowly rose and fell to mirror his discomfiture.

"You said t...two murders?"

"That's right," Jethro said, pushing his plate aside and clasping his hands on the table. "My sister Cindy-May and then Zeke's brother. We both reckon that a lynching is murder in any decent folk's reckoning."

Skeeter tugged his moustache. "The whole thing brung shame on the town."

He pushed his chair back slightly and beamed as a pretty auburn haired saloon girl arrived with a tray, a bottle and three glasses. "Why thank you, Betsy," he enthused. "This here is Mr. Kincaid, Billy Kincaid's brother and this is Mr. Dury, Cindy-May's brother."

Betsy's eyes widened and she pointed to the dressing on Jethro's ear through which blood had oozed. "I heard about the fracas and heard the shots. Is your ear paining you?"

Jethro darted a glance at Zeke before shaking his head. "It smarts a bit, but it'll heal. It's the least of my concerns right now." He pointed to a spare chair. "Will you have a drink with us?"

Betsy glanced backwards through the now crowded saloon. "It's a little early for me, thank you, but I'll sit awhile. Cindy-May was my friend. And so was Billy."

Her face had colored as she mentioned Billy Kincaid's name and she dropped her gaze on the table.

Skeeter poured drinks. "I told them a lot of us were ashamed of what happened, Betsy."

"It was horrible. And I know that Billy didn't kill her. That's why I...I..."

"That's why you left a flower on his grave?" Zeke suggested.

Betsy nodded. "I hated the message that they wrote on it. I wanted to tear it down."

"He was my kid brother, Betsy," Zeke said. "I appreciated the gesture."

Jethro smiled ruefully. "We don't believe it neither, Betsy. Can you tell us anything about it all?"

Betsy cast another glance over her shoulder and saw Gomez the barkeeper glower suspiciously across the crowded saloon.

"Not here. Not now," she whispered. "One of you meet me outside in the alley between the saloon and the Emporium in half an hour."

And so saying she laughed as if at some joke, gathered up her tray and returned to the bar.

Zeke reached into a pocket of his coat and drew out a deck of cards. He shuffled them then set them down on the table. "I suggest we cut for who goes to see her. High card wins."

Jethro cut and revealed the Ace of Hearts.

"Looks like you win the lady, Jethro," Zeke said with a smile. He shuffled the deck. "How about if we all have a couple of hands to make it look casual, then you head off."

Chapter 5

Betsy was waiting in the shadows of the alley when Jethro came out.

"Let's walk away from here," she said. "Just let me take your arm so no one thinks anything about us. I can only be a few minutes."

They went down the alley and emerged into a dingy back street.

"Why don't you believe that Zeke's brother strangled my sister?"

Betsy hesitated for a minute. "Because he was in love with me. He was going to take me away from all this."

"So he didn't go with Cindy-May?"

He could feel Betsy's arm trembling in his. "Look Jethro, Cindy-May was a good girl, she worked hard, if you know what I mean, but she was a good girl."

"I know that. She sent money home to my ma and me."

"And you...you know that..."

"I guess I know now. She – looked after men."

"Just like I do. So if anyone passes us, take me in your arms and kiss me."

It was Jethro's turn to tremble. He was glad it was dark because he felt his cheeks redden and despite himself he felt his heart quicken.

"The preacher found Cindy-May's body behind the church. He went screaming out into the street and they started a search. They found Billy collapsed in a heap behind the livery. Drunk they said, with a great gash on his head where he'd fallen over." She trembled again. "But I...I don't believe that. I think he was attacked and knocked out. He would never have done anything to Cindy-May."

"So how come the sheriff didn't stop the lynching?"

"He wasn't about. Neither him nor Emmet Dubbs, the deputy. They didn't come along until it was all over. Folks said it was because they were up at Judge Gantry's place drinking whiskey and playing poker. They do that a lot.

"But it was horrible, the town heard about Cindy-May being strangled and it took the law into its own hands. I think some men stirred them all up. It was just a mob!"

She stifled a sob. "They murdered my Billy," she whispered.

Jethro felt awkward and wanted to comfort her. She was maybe a year or two older than him, that was all, and clearly her life had been hard. Harder than any young girl's life should have been. He patted her hand then they walked on in the moonlight.

After a few moments he felt her arm tighten and she let out a slight gasp. She whispered: "I think I heard someone behind us. Kiss me, Jethro."

Before he could react, never having kissed a girl properly, she had turned, snaked an arm about his neck and started to kiss him. Startled by it, he was overcome by her scent and the touch of her body and her lips against his. Then all too soon, she broke away.

"I think I may have been mistaken," she whispered. "I can't see anyone, but I thought I heard something, like a boot scuffing the ground behind us."

Jethro suddenly felt used. He had been angry at hearing Betsy's account of the discovery of his sister's body and the lynching, and now he felt kind of cheated that his first real kiss had been nothing but a cover-up.

He suddenly felt a spasm of pain in his ear as if something had burst. He instinctively raised a hand to it and felt that the dressing was soaking with blood. It had started to trickle down his neck.

"Damn!" he cursed. "With one thing and another, I reckon it made my blood boil. It must have just burst through the doc's stitching."

In the moonlight Betsy winced at the sight of the blood oozing down over his neck and shoulder.

"Oh! It looks bad. Come on, I think we'd better get you over to see the doc right away."

Chapter 6

Zeke and Skeeter had been joined by a couple of other men and soon they had a lively game going. They played for small stuff at first, each player taking a pot. Then the two new players urged upping the ante. That was more than Skeeter was prepared to go, so he cashed in and wandered off to the bar to chat with Gomez.

Zeke played on, aware that all was not right. Although the two men seemed to be ordinary players, yet his gambler's sixth sense told him that they were working together. Soon, as was the way of things at poker games when the pots started to grow, and as Zeke's pile rose while the others' diminished, they attracted a sizeable crowd. Although he gave nothing away, Zeke had noted that hovering on the edge of his vision at opposite ends of the saloon, Sheriff Ryker and Deputy Dubbs were watching. Not just watching, he reckoned, but waiting.

He glanced at the large wall clock at the far end of the saloon. He figured that Jethro and Betsy would be coming back any time soon.

Then it happened. One of the men tossed down his

cards and stood up sharply, shoving his chair back as he drew his gun and leveled it at Zeke's head.

"You four-flushing dog!"

Chapter 7

Doc Brady opened the door of his place and squinted through his wire-framed spectacles at his visitors.

"Ah, the young man with the wounded ear!" he exclaimed. "And Betsy," he added with a curious smile. He ushered them in.

"Look's like I somehow undid your handiwork, Doc," Jethro said, doffing his hat and removing his balled up neckerchief from his ear.

"Durn it! I hate to see my needlework come undone," Doc Brady mused. He grabbed a towel and applied it to Jethro's ear. "Keep that pressed tight against your ear and sit down, son. I'll have a look, then clean you up and do some more stitching."

Betsy had gone pale at the sight of the blood and grabbed for the edge of the doctor's desk. "Do you mind if I sit, too, Doc? I feel like I'm going pass out."

Jethro quickly moved a chair and helped her to sit down.

"Seems like I got me two patients. I reckon some brandy will help you both." He went through the curtain that separated his consulting room from his living quarters, then returned after a few moments with glasses and a bottle of brandy. He poured them each a hefty measure. "Get these down you then tell me how you opened up this wound, while I get my instruments ready."

"Betsy told me about how my sister died and how the town lynched Zeke's brother Billy."

Betsy drained her glass and let out a deep breath as the fiery liquor hit her stomach. "Billy didn't kill Cindy-May. He was a gentleman. He was my man, Doc."

Doc Brady raised his eyebrows in surprise. "Really? So who do you think killed her?"

"From all that Betsy told me, I have an idea. I reckon I need you to stitch me up again, Doc, then I need to have a word with the preacher man."

Doc Brady spun round, astonishment written across his face. "The Reverend Brown? Are you serious? You think the preacher strangled Cindy-May?"

"He found the body and set the whole town on fire."

Betsy started to feel dizzy, as if the alcohol had really gone to her head. Her throat started to burn and she coughed. "That's strong brandy, Doc."

Jethro stared at the doctor, suddenly finding his vision had gone blurred. Then he heard Betsy slump back in her chair and her glass fell from her hand and rolled across the floor.

He tried to sit forward, meaning to reach for it, but found he couldn't move a muscle. Then he felt himself sinking into a deep pool of unconsciousness.

Chapter 8

Zeke slowly raised his hands above his head. The man facing him was wearing range clothes, although they were devoid of any sign of dust or travel. The way he held the gun it was clear that he knew exactly how to use it.

"Easy, mister!"

"You've been cheating us for several hands, you worthless tinhorn."

Zeke spotted the clock and despite his predicament wondered where Jethro and Betsy had gotten to.

Then he heard Skeeter's voice. "Settle down there feller. I was playing with you. Zeke here is a straight gambler. He's no cheat."

The other man, a rangy looking type in a crumpled suit also took to his feet and was pointing a finger at Zeke. "I thought so, too. The two of them were in it together." He reached for his gun. "A man who cheats at cards don't deserve to breathe long. That's my opinion."

Zeke chanced a glance sideways and saw Sheriff Ryker smile.

Chapter 9

Jethro came slowly back to consciousness. His ear

throbbed and his head hurt. Yet it was the discomfort of some sort of rag that had been stuffed in his mouth that worried him most. He tried unsuccessfully to push it out with his tongue and gagged in the process. He blinked as he struggled to move. It was immediately clear that he was tied to the chair.

The cruel laugh made him look up in alarm to see Doc Brady finish tying a gag on a similarly trussed up Betsy.

"It all worked like a charm," the doctor said, peering at him over the top of his spectacles. "I knew those stitches wouldn't hold and you'd have to come back to me to have them re-done. I guessed you'd be on your own, but I see you didn't waste any time and found yourself a whore."

Jethro fought against his bonds.

"Looks like history is going to be replaying itself. In the morning they're going to find another slut strangled to death in an alleyway. Then they'll find you, drunk as a skunk, drunk and knocked out cold." He cackled in a near maniacal manner. "Guess they'll lynch you."

Jethro shook his head fervently.

"What's that?" Doc Brady asked. "Maybe you think that your new found friend, the one that trimmed your ear will help?" He shook his head. "I sent a couple of boys to settle him. He's maybe bleeding his last right now. A bullet in his head or a knife in his chest, it doesn't matter which."

He clicked his teeth and looked regretful. "Although maybe I should have thought harder. It would have been good to have the mob lynch him as well. It's still a thought, if he's still alive by morning."

Betsy stirred and slowly came round, her eyes registering panic when she saw Jethro and the doc and realized their predicament.

Doc Brady beamed at her. "No need to look so scared my little soiled dove," he said, gently caressing her cheek. "I never did have the pleasure of you, did I? Not like I did with Cindy-May." He crinkled his nose at her and reached for a glass of brandy by his side. "A man in my position can't be seen visiting a cat-house. No, she was my special little whore. I paid her extra to come visit me. No one thought there was anything odd about her going to see the doc. Guess you didn't know that, did you?"

Betsy's eyes widened in alarm.

Brady sipped his drink and sighed with satisfaction. "But I didn't like it when that bastard Billy Kincaid came and consulted me about his blamed toothache. He had the nerve to tell me he was taking one of the girls away from The Painted Lady. Then when I saw Cindy-May she told me she was leaving soon and I just saw red." He slammed the glass down and clenched his fists.

"I strangled the bitch right then and there and hid her body through there. When he came knocking on the door when his pain killing remedy had worn off I sat him down in that chair where you're sitting, son. Gave him some of my special brandy and talked until he passed out. Then it was easy. I waited until dark then carried them out one at a time. Left them so that they'd be found and the alarms would go off."

He looked from one to the other and laughed at their looks of horror at his confession. "I hated them both for their deceit. He thought he could take her away from me!"

His eyes seemed to grow large behind his spectacles. "Bates and Milton were easy to work up. They'll do just about anything I ask, on account of how I give them so much business and tell them which folks are ready to be robbed and where they can find the valuables. Call it a perk of being the local doc. Everyone trusts you. Anyways, they whipped folks into the mood for a neck-tie party."

He grinned and picked up his stethoscope, grasping it in two hands as he approached Betsy. "Now it's your turn, whore."

Jethro struggled with all his might, but to no avail.

Betsy tried to move, but couldn't.

The doctor laughed as he suddenly coiled the rubber tubes of his stethoscope about her neck and started to pull hard.

Her face quickly turned purple and her eyes started to bulge.

Suddenly, the door burst open and Zeke Kincaid rushed in. He swung his silver topped cane and caught Brady in the throat. Then as the doctor staggered back he took a step forward and delivered an uppercut that caught the doctor's jaw and lifted him off his feet to land in a crumpled heap on the floor.

Chapter 10

"I've a good mind to let the mob string him up!" growled Sheriff Ryker.

The Reverend Matthew Brown laid a hand on his arm. "Remember Sheriff, the doctor himself said that you must do everything legally. We have all been – surprised by this revelation of a devil in our midst."

Jethro stood with his arm about Betsy's shoulders as they, Zeke, and the others waited for the doctor to regain consciousness. It was clear that Zeke had hit him with considerable force.

Then he slowly blinked his eyes open. Eyes that were full of anger and hate. He attempted to rise, but was hampered by the handcuffs on his wrists. He looked down at them, then at Jethro and Betsy. Then he inexplicably tossed back his head and laughed.

"So there's no repeat of history?" he said. Then he saw Zeke and raised his eyebrows. "And how come you are still alive, may I ask?"

"Because me and Deputy Dubbs had been watching those two mongrels that you sent to set Kincaid up. We know that you got them to whip the town into a hanging frenzy in our absence last week. They've been – cooperative!"

"And it was lucky that the preacher saw Betsy and Jethro high-tailing it over here to see you," Zeke explained.

"I followed and listened at the door," the Reverend Brown added. "I heard you, Doc. Then I ran back and got the sheriff and Mr. Kincaid."

"You...you monster!" exclaimed Betsy. "You killed Cindy-May and all because you thought she was going to run away with Billy? It was me that was going to go with him."

Zeke glared at the crumpled doctor. "You are a sad excuse for a person. You had my brother murdered."

"My sister was coming home to my ma and me," said Jethro. "She didn't deserve to die."

Doc Brady was silent for a moment then once more he erupted in a fit of high-pitched hysterical laughter. "So it was all a mistake! A simple, honest mistake!"

The Reverend Brown bent his head. "I am afraid that the only honest thing I can tell you, doctor, is that for your sins you will surely face a reckoning."

"Amen, preacher!" the doctor giggled. "Amen!"

Chapter 11

The trial was held a week later, that being the time it had taken to bring in another doctor to examine Doc Brady.

Judge Gantry, a wizened old nut of a man with the sourest of mouths found the defendant insane and arrangements were started to have him admitted to an asylum. Both Zeke and Jethro were relieved in a strange way, since neither had any desire to see the man hanged, despite the awful crimes he had committed. There had been enough death.

They met to have a last drink together with Skeeter in The Painted Lady Saloon before they went their separate ways.

"I feel bad to leave Betsy here," Zeke said as he leaned against the bar nursing his whiskey. "Especially when my little brother was going to take her away from this place."

Skeeter tugged his straggly moustache. "I can keep an eye on her, if you like."

"That won't be necessary. She's coming home with me," Jethro announced to both Skeeter's and Zeke's surprise.

"We've become close," he needlessly explained.

They all turned at the sound of footsteps on the board floor behind them. It was Betsy herself, dressed in a smart feathered toque hat and carrying a large case.

"I'm ready. All packed with all my worldly possessions."

Jethro kissed her chastely on the cheek and took the bag. "Then we'll go." He held out his hand towards Zeke.

"There's just one thing I'd like to do first," Betsy said hurriedly before they shook hands. "I'd like to pay my respects to...to...them."

Skeeter drained his glass and stood away from the bar. "Then I'd appreciate it if you'd follow me, folks. I've tidied their graves already."

He gave a rueful smile. "I've taken to you all and you can all rest easy. I'll tend their little part of Boot Hill." He grinned. "At least until I become their next neighbor, myself."

The Kindness of Strangers

by Cheryl Pierson

Cheryl Pierson was born in Duncan, OK, and grew up in Seminole, OK. She graduated from the University of Oklahoma, and holds a B.A. in English. She writes historical western and contemporary romantic suspense short stories and novels. Cheryl lives with her husband in Oklahoma City, OK, where she has been for the past 27 years. She has two grown children, ages 21 and 24. Visit her website at http://www.cherylpierson.com. You can e-mail her at fabkat_edit@yahoo.com. Visit her Amazon author page for a complete list of all work at:http://www.amazon.com/-/e/B002JV8GUE.

Jericho Dean was closing in on the bastards. Within the next twenty-four hours, thirty at the most, he intended to have killed the entire band of Tidwell's Comancheros, putting an end to their misery – and his – once and for all.

He was damn tired of running a cold camp every night. Was it so much to ask—a pot of coffee? He shouldn't care. He should enjoy the cool breeze against his face. This would be the last night he'd go without a fire. By this time tomorrow, he'd be roasting in hell alongside the bastards he was chasing. He wouldn't be safe in God's heavenly arms, but he'd be at rest. At peace. And quite warm and satisfied. It would be over, and it would be enough.

Right now, he needed to sleep. His butt was melded to the saddle, and he was bone weary. Even so, an odd exhilaration rushed through him as he thought of his journey—his mission—being so close to the end. It wasn't smart, though, to keep pushing.

Reluctantly, he drew rein and dismounted, the painful stiffness in his joints surprising him. He'd gotten old over the past two weeks. Ever since it had happened. Ever since he'd decided on his course of action, and set out to see the job finished and done proper.

Methodically, he went about seeing to the big animal that had been his constant companion. The only friend he had left in this world, now that his woman was gone. Deliberately, he turned his thoughts away from Elena, and what those bastards had done to her, and to his two young daughters. It was all he had thought of for two weeks, and it had worn a long, raw groove in his brain and his heart. Revenge had ridden with him every mile he'd covered. Soon, it would be done, and relief would be his.

The small clearing where he'd stopped for the night was serene in the evening shadows. Not quite fully dark, the inky spots of undergrowth held woodland secrets, but nothing dangerous. His senses would have given him full warning had that been the case. A small creek trickled nearby and the horse moved restively, his nostrils flaring in hopeful anticipation.

A rare smile touched Jericho's lips as he patted the big bay. "Yes, I know. We could both use a long, cool drink, Dan. Let's go see about it." And that was the first order of business for this, his last night on earth.

The water was just as cold as any mountain stream he'd ever drank from, even though he was not in the mountains now, and never would be again. There was beauty in this flat country, just as there was in the grandeur of the distant Rockies farther north.

Indian Territory was his home, and he knew it in his mind as if a map was imprinted there. He drew his sleeve across his mouth as he stood from the creek bank, wiping away the droplets of excess water. His eyes constantly narrowed as he scanned his surroundings for anything out of the ordinary.

Dan finally lifted his head from the stream and turned, as if he knew the way back to the clearing where Jericho planned to sleep that night.

For the second time, Jericho smiled, and it felt just as odd as it had earlier. He'd thought he'd never smile again when he'd made the gruesome discovery of the bodies. The world he'd worked so hard to build had been stolen from him in a matter of hours that day. He'd gone out to hunt that morning, and come home in the afternoon to find his wife and children murdered. He'd thought of it so often in the time since that the dawning horror of it had been steadily replaced with something else. The burning need for revenge, no matter what the cost. He had nothing left to lose.

After the initial shock of the discovery of the slaughter, after the mind-numbing grief of digging the grave to bury them in, a blackness had overcome him. He had tried to say a prayer over the bodies as he knew would be proper, but no words would come.

He wouldn't ask God for anything—not even a paltry blessing. That way, they would owe each other nothing. There would be no bargain struck. When he found the men who had done the unspeakable, he would feel no obligation to turn the other cheek, or to follow any other direction but his own.

He led Dan back to the clearing and unsaddled him, putting the saddle on the ground along with his bedroll, his back to the creek. He took the brush from his saddlebag and walked over to where he'd left Dan in the fading light of the late afternoon. No reason why he shouldn't give the animal a good brushing before he bedded down. He deserved it, after the long days they'd put in, and most likely it would be the last time Jericho would ever do it.

His neck prickled as the horse's head lifted. Dan whickered softly and in the next moment, a twig snapped. Jericho's hand went to his gun. He drew the revolver and held it steady, dropping the brush to the ground.

"State your business," he called.

"Just lookin' for water and place to bed down for the night," a deep voice answered. A nearby tree branch was pushed aside and a slight, wiry cowboy appeared, leading a dark horse with a white star marking his forehead behind him.

The man grinned and put out a friendly hand. "Name's Freeman Hart."

Jericho didn't put the gun away. He nodded. "Jericho Dean."

"You after Tidwell's gang, by any chance?"

"What if I am?"

Hart glanced toward the gun. "You can put that away, Jericho. I ain't your enemy."

Still, Jericho hesitated. The prickling wouldn't go away. He'd learned to listen to it—it was how he'd managed to stay alive. Though Freeman Hart was friendly enough, something warned Jericho the newcomer was not what he seemed. He didn't holster the pistol, and Hart nodded.

"I ain't one of them, son. I'm after 'em too."

"Why's that?"

"They . . . took something—something very dear to me." He didn't elaborate and Jericho understood that it was a subject the other man didn't want to discuss. He respected that.

"They took something mighty precious from me, too," he said quietly.

It wasn't the shared loss that prompted him to put away the pistol as much as it was Freeman Hart's disregard of it. He came forward, ground-pegging his big black beside Dan. He stooped down and picked up the brush Jericho had dropped.

"Here's your brush. 'Magine ol' Dan'll be awful glad of a good brushing tonight."

Jericho's pulse quickened. "How did you know his name?"

For an instant, Hart looked startled, then he just laughed. "Heard you talkin' to him earlier when I was comin' through the thicket just over yonder."

Jericho took the brush and began to curry the horse, but he kept a wary eye on his unexpected guest. Something wasn't right. He knew his 6'3" frame could most probably win any hand-to-hand battle he might engage in with the smaller man, but a gun was the great equalizer. And though Freeman Hart hadn't shown any sign of throwing down on him, he was too close to his quarry to risk defeat now. He meant to see Tidwell's gang dead, no matter what else came.

But Hart didn't seem to notice how Jericho charted his every move. If he did, he didn't seem to care.

"No fire tonight?" Hart began gathering wood, even as he asked the question.

"No. We're too close. One of 'em may double back to make sure they aren't being followed."

Hart smiled as if at some inner joke. "Nah. You got no worries there. They're at least a day and a half ahead of you. I 'magine they figger they don't have a care in the world."

Jericho stopped brushing Dan, turning his full attention to the other man. "Well, that's where they're wrong, Mister Hart. *Dead* wrong. Every last stinkin' one of 'em's got more'n a '*care*' in this world. They've got me, hot on their asses and once I catch up to 'em, they'll realize that mistake in judgment—if they truly are thinking the way you say."

"What do you intend to do, son?" Hart carried the wood he held to the pyre he'd begun to build in the center of the small clearing. "There's gotta be at the least six of 'em—probably ten at the most, but still—you're just one man."

Jericho's irritation boiled over. "I know how many of 'em there are. They rode onto my land while I was away hunting for the day. They raped my two little girls and my wife, and then they murdered them. It doesn't matter to me if there's six or six hundred, Mr. Hart. When I catch up, I plan to kill as many of 'em as I can before they get me."

Hart gave a low whistle, turning back to his wood

gathering. "You got some balls, I'll say that for you, Jericho. There ain't many men who'd take on what you're aiming to do, and not give a damn if they live to see the next sunrise."

Jericho gave Dan one final pat. "Ain't many men lost as much as I did on that day, Freeman. My wife, my daughters, and my desire to exist in this world without them." He pointed at the growing pile of wood. "No fire."

Hart gave a sage nod. "I see. You're expecting to be reunited once you complete your mission—kill the Comancheros. Once you die, you think you and Elena will be together again, along with Maria and Ana."

Jericho stood completely still. How did this stranger know the names of his family? How did he know Jericho's own heart and purpose so clearly?

Hart dropped the last two pieces of wood on top of the pile, then dusted his hands. "We need to have a talk, Jericho. A good long visit about things. I don't aim to do it in the cold. And make no mistake, this night'll be an icy one—way too cold to spend without a fire. Trust me, boy. They ain't gonna know—or care—if you spend it warm or freezin'. Got a match on you?"

Jericho sized up the other man once more, a shiver running up his spine. No, things were not what they seemed, but whether for good or evil, he didn't know. He cursed his luck, either way. He didn't want to be burdened with whatever it was this Freeman Hart brought to the table. He hadn't asked for it, either way. He remembered that he had deliberately not prayed, carefully refrained from asking God for any favors, so he wouldn't have to be in His debt. Well, he still didn't plan on owing Him anything, no matter how this all worked out.

He finally forced his legs to move, walking stiffly to his saddlebags. He put the brush away, and drew out the box of matches wrapped in oilskin.

Hart caught them when Jericho tossed them over, opened the box and struck one of them on the bottom of his boot. The match head flared in the gathering semi-darkness and Hart hunkered down, cupping his hand around the flame as it caught the base kindling of the pyre and the wood above it began to burn.

Jericho stood watching as the fire flared to life, remembering how he'd burned the cabin. After he'd buried Elena, Maria and little Ana, he'd poured kerosene throughout their home. The smell of it had made his stomach twist and roll over. He'd poured it over the cabinetry he'd built so lovingly for Elena, remembering how proud she'd been to have a pantry in her kitchen. He'd poured it across the bed where they'd made love. Made children. Made a family together.

He'd opened up the old trunk that had been Elena's, full of her keepsake treasures. He had taken only one thing from the chest before he'd saturated the rest of the contents with the kerosene remaining in the can. He'd stood at the door and tossed in the match, watching as the trail of fire raced across the dirt floor of the cabin and began to eat the furniture, the woodwork, and finally the walls.

Then, he had turned his back on the entire dream he'd created and then destroyed, riding away from it as it burned. It may be burning still, he mused. That entire northern part of Indian Territory could be nothing but acres of smoldering blackness destroyed by his hand. Right now, if he could, he'd set the entire world ablaze.

Yes. A fire *would* be good to have tonight.

"Say, Jericho. You hungry? Me, I'm so hungry my stomach thinks my throat's been cut. I've got some tins of beans and peaches we can open up." Hart rose and crossed to where his saddlebags lay, rummaging for the tins of food. He pulled them out and came back toward Jericho, who stood rooted to the spot where he'd gone moments earlier to get the matches.

Hart nodded toward the fire. "C'mon. Let's get some grub. Talk a spell. I can see you've got some questions."

"Who are you?" Jericho's voice was hoarse.

Hart laughed. "I knew that'd be the first one."

* * *

They ate in silence, spooning out beans from the two

tins Freeman Hart had opened along with the last of the jerky Jericho carried. Jericho discovered he was as hungry as he was curious, so he was well able to hold his questions while he sated his physical hunger. Freeman was organized, Jericho thought grudgingly. Seemed to have everything, and everything in its place. He'd thought, these last few days, he didn't care if he ever saw food again. But the beans had been welcome fare, and he was actually looking forward to the peaches, along with a cup of the coffee that Freeman had put on to brew.

Freeman gave him a sidelong glance as they opened the peaches. "Reckon there ain't another thing on this earth sweet as these peaches."

Jericho nodded after a moment. "I reckon you're right." When he took the first bite, he knew Freeman had worked some kind of magic. Nothing had ever tasted better. The fruit was succulent, and he tried to eat slowly, but it was a lost cause. He sipped a little of the syrup from the can, and then finished the fruit, unable to take it slow and savor the goodness.

Freeman smiled at him, his eyes crinkling at the corners. "Good?"

Jericho didn't answer. He hadn't wanted to enjoy the peaches so much. Or the beans. It was unnatural to think that much of food when he'd lost everything else. "Yes. It was good," he said finally, speculation clear in his tone.

The other man didn't seem to take offense. He laughed aloud as he tipped his own can up and drained the last of the peach juice.

"Who are you?" Jericho asked again. There was no rancor in him. Only determination to find some answers.

"You're direct, Jericho Dean. I like that."

"How did you know about—about Elena and my girls? Don't deny it, Freeman. You already knew who I was when you came into my camp. Have you been following me?"

The smile slowly left Freeman's face as he regarded

Jericho. "No. I ain't been following you, Jericho. Not like you mean, anyhow."

Anger surged through him. "What the hell does that mean, Hart? Talk straight to me. I deserve at least that much."

"It's . . . kind of like a job I gotta see done, Jericho." He seemed to choose his words carefully, and that irritated Jericho. Reading it in his impatience, Hart continued. "You must've figured it out by now. I'm here to see it all ended proper, one way or the other."

Realization at his meaning flooded over Jericho, and he sat up straight, looking directly into Hart's blue eyes. "What in the cornbread hell are you talking about?"

Hart began to clean his knife with the water left in his canteen, then took time to dry it on his shirt sleeve before he answered. "It's what I have to do."

"You sayin' you're some kind of *angel* or somethin'?" *Dear God. As if things weren't bad enough.* He was out here looking for the bastards that had murdered his wife, his children, his *dream*—and had run into a crazy man who, he couldn't determine yet, either planned to help him or stop him. He couldn't allow either. His hand moved down toward his gun.

Freeman shook his head. "You don't need that. Not yet. Not until you meet up with Tidwell's bunch."

"I don't want any help from you," Jericho told him bluntly. "This, I gotta do on my own."

Freeman's eyes filled with sympathy before he looked away. "You don't need to worry."

"You said you were after 'em too," Jericho remembered. "What for? What'd they do to you?"

"They set it all in motion, Jericho. I just have to see it end."

* * *

Jericho was oddly comforted by the fact that the "angel"—as he'd come to think of Freeman—had been the one to suggest a fire. If he was supposed to see it all ended proper, as he claimed, then they'd be safe with a fire blazing tonight. And he would sleep well, this last night on earth. *What could harm him, if the angel was with him?*

Jericho pulled his saddle and bedroll a little closer to the welcome warmth of the fire and lay down. He had to admit, even though he found the other man's presence unsettling in some ways, he'd also brought a heap of comfort with him. Thanks to Freeman Hart, Jericho had a full belly for the first time in days, and the fire was the thing he was most grateful for. The cold had seeped into his bones until he'd begun to think he'd never be warm again. The fire seemed to work a magic all its own—a seductive dance of flame and warmth that let his mind relax and go back to happier times.

He hadn't allowed himself to think of Elena and the girls much since that day—since he'd come home with fresh game for the pot that evening two weeks past; a day of hunting that had cost him his family. He had not been able to allow his thoughts to settle on what he'd had before then. It hurt too much. When he pictured Ana's sweet gap-toothed grin, Maria's dark eyes so full of mischief, and the soothing sound of Elena's voice, the bond that held them all together, it made his heart break all over again. He'd thought he would lose his mind with grief. The first three nights had been the worst. He awoke from a broken sleep, singing an old lullaby through a throat full of tears—a song he'd sung to his beautiful daughters when they were babies. When he'd come fully awake and realized the precipice of madness he stood upon, he'd wiped away the tracks of wetness and vowed that was the end of sorrow for him. Regret was a waste of energy. His thoughts would be better spent on hate and revenge—and after that, indifference as to what his own fate might be.

But God, it was so hard to push those sweet memories aside and not think of the only goodness he'd ever known in this world.

Now, sleep began to steal over him, and he almost hated himself for his weakness. He wanted to see this done, and an end to everything. Sleep only prolonged the hunt. Before it completely stole his reasoning, another thought came to him. What if he was being taken for a fool by Freeman Hart?

It could well be that he was not heaven sent, but had a different purpose, indeed. Was Hart here to keep him from his new reason for living? To renew his will to have some kind of real future and put off killing the scum he was set to ride after, come hell or high water?

The warmth of the magical fire seeped into him, working with the up-to-now forgotten comfort of a full belly, and his memories dulled to a bearable ache rather than the raw, gaping wound he'd carried for the last two weeks. Sleep claimed him at last, and he slipped into the welcoming, hollow arms of the night. It felt like heaven.

* * *

The next morning, Jericho awoke to the smell of brewing coffee. He stood slowly, nodding at Freeman who stood beside the fire, warming his hands around a steaming cup.

"Mornin', Jericho. Sleep well?"

Jericho eyed him narrowly. "I reckon. You know, I expect every night when I lay down, it'll be my last time to go to sleep. Every mornin' when I get up, I figure that'll be my last day to do what I gotta do before I die."

"Helluva way to live."

"It's the only way I know, now, Freeman. Ain't no other way." Jericho walked away a few feet to relieve himself. Grimly, he wondered if it would be the last time he took a piss, too.

When he came back close to the fire again, Freeman handed him a cup of coffee. "What, exactly, do you intend to do?"

Jericho arched a brow. "Thought you understood. I'm gonna kill Tidwell's bunch. Won't have time to make it slow and painful, but by God, I'll be thorough. That's all that counts."

Freeman gave him a faint smile. "Oh, I know that much, Jericho. What I meant was, what do you intend to do—should you survive?"

Jericho shook his head and laughed shortly. "I don't see that happenin', Freeman. There are six or more of those bastards, like you said. I just hope to take most of 'em with me when I go."

"Can't plan for everything." Freeman turned and paced away a few steps. "You've got to consider the alternative. Living may be something you're . . . stuck with."

Jericho scowled. "Listen, angel. Demon. Whatever you are . . . I don't want you interferin' in my business. You understand? I don't want your help."

Freeman nodded solemnly. "I know. I'm not going to help you, Jericho. I'm only here to show you the way."

"The way? What're you talkin' about?"

"When it's all over. If . . . your time is up today, then it's up to me to show you the way to go."

"Damn it, I don't *need* you!"

Freeman shook his head sadly. "Oh, but you do. You're the one who doesn't understand, Jericho."

Jericho took a sip of his coffee, his angry gaze boring into Freeman's steady, unperturbed look over the rim of his cup. He hated the damn winter. He hated the fact that he had to stand here in the cold and debate his uncertain future. In that moment, he hated Freeman Hart more than about anything—except for Tidwell's bunch.

"You don't get to choose your own end," Freeman went on, the hardness of his own determination evident to Jericho. It wasn't often Jericho Dean mistook a man's character. He couldn't determine what Freeman's purpose was, nor which side had sent him. There was so much about this unusual stranger that he probably would never know. But one thing was certain—Freeman wasn't afraid of him. Nor, Jericho thought, did he seem to be worried about Tidwell and his gang of cutthroats.

"I wish . . . I could have ended it that same day, Freeman. If I'd only come home earlier—"

"You wouldn't have been in time. It . . . happened not long after you left that morning."

"*How do you know these things*?" Jericho dropped the cup and lunged at Freeman. Freeman was ready for him, moving with unnatural speed to sidestep him.

Jericho sprawled in the leaves and bracken of the forest floor. When he looked up, there was nothing but pity in Freeman's blue eyes, with not even the barest hint of anger.

"Son, you aren't angry at me, you know. You're angry at Tidwell and his bunch. At what they did. At circumstances."

Jericho stood up quickly. "You're damn right!" His fists clenched, and the strain was harsh in his voice. "What kind of a God lets women and children be murdered, Freeman? Huh? My woman and my little girls were wiped out—butchered—in the blink of an eye. I'm pissed as hell at God for that. Anyone would be."

"There are injustices all over the world. God doesn't personally go about correcting all the wrongs at the time they happen. But in the end, it will all come right."

Jericho snorted rudely. "How in the cornbread hell can anything happen that will make this right?" He drew a fist across his mouth. "I know only one way this can end *right*, Freeman. That'll be with Tidwell and his gang turnin' the ground red with their life's blood. If my life is forfeit, so be it. I only hope that I kill Tidwell and as many of the others as I can."

"Thou shalt not kill."

"You're laughable. Don't even try to preach to me. I'll do what I want."

Freeman only smiled. "No, Jericho. You'll do what's *right*, in the end, for everyone."

* * *

They rode in silence for the first two hours. The winter wind had gotten up and whipped around their heads. Jericho's ears felt frozen. The cold blast sank down inside his coat, through the two layers of shirts he wore beneath, biting his flesh as he and Freeman leaned into the gale blowing around them.

"If this wind gets much stronger, we may have to

stop," Freeman yelled, drawing abreast of Jericho.

"I ain't stoppin'," Jericho said shortly. "You do what you will."

"Ridin' these poor beasts into the ground isn't going to help you."

Jericho started to answer, but at Freeman's knowing look, he kept quiet. It was damned strange riding with an angel. He'd given up on trying to glean the answers he so badly needed. Freeman wasn't going to give him any peace in that direction. Jericho's resentment was eating him alive. How could any of this be fair? Freeman could probably tell him everything, if he only *would*.

Jericho threw him a narrow glance as they rode on. Hell, he probably knew how many of Tidwell's band Jericho would manage to kill—

Maybe that's why he was so quiet and tight lipped. Jericho's heart stuttered. What if he failed? Did Freeman know the answer to that question? Would he tell him, if he asked? He drew up, coming to a halt.

"I *am* going to kill Tidwell. Right?"

Freeman drew up slowly and smiled. "Do you doubt it?"

"No. I sure as hell don't."

"It's never good to doubt."

"I said I didn't," Jericho snapped. "Can't you tell me . . . anything? I just want to know if I'm going to get those bastards."

Freeman's face became expressionless. "By this time tomorrow, you'll know everything."

Jericho's lips thinned in disgust. "Thanks, Freeman. Thanks for nothing." He kneed his bay and rode on once more. He couldn't wait to see the life gutter and die in Tidwell's eyes. He wanted to be done with everything, and to be shed of his odd companion one way or the other.

Dying would take care of that, he imagined. And that was just what he intended to do.

* * *

The fight began before he was ready for it. A bullet

sang by his ear so close he felt the warm hiss of it beside his cheek.

It was mid-afternoon, and the first thought that entered Jericho's mind was that Freeman had given him no warning whatsoever. He'd even had the balls to look startled, as if it were a surprise to him, too.

"I see smoke up ahead!" Freeman yelled as their horses pounded down the stretch of open range they'd been forced into.

Jericho had seen it, too. He supposed he'd tried to just block it out of his thoughts. The smoke rose like an evil cloud, billowing in the wind in the distance, an uncanny reminder of the last time he'd seen such a plume—when he'd set his own cabin ablaze.

His stomach flipped over, and his breathing became shallow. He cursed and gave himself a good set-down as he pounded ever closer to the now-visible fire in the distance. Behind them, he heard a horse and rider. Another shot sounded, but flew overhead wildly. By the echoing crack of it on the winter air, the rider was gaining on them. Jericho was about to see his revenge go undone. If the rider behind them managed to get close enough to aim true, Jericho would be dead before he ever laid eyes on Tidwell.

Veer off.

Though Freeman hadn't spoken aloud, Jericho heard his voice clearly in his mind. He shot the angel a glance. Freeman nodded at him, acknowledging the unasked question. Just then, he turned his mount toward the east and a small copse of trees a hundred yards away.

Jericho didn't let himself think. He followed Freeman's suggestion, turning the bay west to the shelter of a ridge in the distance that would give him the advantage of higher ground.

The burning cabin lay to the south along with, Jericho suspected, Tidwell and his gang. His palms tingled with dreadful anticipation. He wanted to kill Tidwell with his hands, not with a gun. He wanted to be able to see him realize his life was leaving him, and to know it was Jericho Dean who was taking it from him.

But he couldn't go rushing down to the cabin in the open and risk getting shot in the back. He rode Dan up the steeper ground of the ridge until he gained the top, guiding him behind a large boulder. From there, he was able to see everything.

Before the cabin had been set ablaze, Tidwell and two other men had carried out the provisions they could use and were divvying them up, distributing them amongst themselves, and tying them to their horses.

The man who had been on guard behind Jericho and Freeman came into Jericho's view, veering off toward the trees where Freeman had disappeared. Freeman was on his own, but he could handle himself. Jericho had vowed to kill Tidwell, and that was the business he needed to be about right now.

From somewhere behind the cabin, he heard a man's shout, a plea, then a single rifle shot. A woman screamed and wailed, the sound tearing into Jericho's heart as no piece of lead ever could, wounding him all over again. That sound she made was the way he'd felt when he'd made the horrible discovery of his own shattered world just days ago. It was despair, in its purest form, and he knew just how terrible a wound that could be.

He rode carefully along the top of the ridgeline, keeping a constant eye on the plundering going on at the front of the cabin.

His hand went to the delicate cross on the length of rawhide string around his neck—Elena's cross he'd fashioned from two of the nails he'd used to put the roof on their small cabin. They'd just been starting out together, full of love for one another, hope for the future, and faith that God would help them through anything they might face. Well, Jericho thought grimly, two out of three ain't bad.

That had been before they'd made a family together, when their home was as new as their love, and hope had seemed boundless. Now, this cross was all that was left of everything. He would be wearing it when he died—a symbol of salvation that would never be his.

He'd worked his way steadily around 'til he could see what lay behind the cabin. There were two more men there, rifling the bodies of the homesteader and his wife. Jericho's gut clenched at the sight. Evidently, the woman had been killed quickly, most likely accidentally. He was certain it wasn't because either of the outlaws had shown mercy.

"Hey, Gene," one of the men called from the front of the house, "let's go have a look in the barn. Could be this sodbuster had a horse or two."

"What are you waiting for?" Freeman's voice came from behind Jericho. He jerked around, startled by the angel's silent, sudden appearance.

"The right moment," he answered, pulling his Winchester from his saddle scabbard. "What happened to your company?"

"He's . . . chasing a mirage over yonder." Freeman nodded across the clearing to the stand of trees where he'd ridden earlier. "Better take care of business down there, Jericho."

There was an edge to Freeman's tone that hadn't been there before as the man approached the barn.

Jericho was well aware that shooting the man headed for the barn would alert the others. "They've got nowhere to run, son," Freeman said aloud in answer to his thoughts.

Jericho raised the rifle and aimed, pulled the trigger and hit the outlaw in the back of the head. "Gene," who followed a few paces behind, was next, dead before he could take the steps he needed to get inside the shelter of the barn.

The other man from behind the cabin ran around toward the front, yelling for Burk Tidwell. The burning cabin was no protection for him, and Jericho sighted down the barrel once more, dropping him before he cleared the corner of the fiery structure.

The two outlaws left in the front yard had drawn their pistols and had turned toward where Jericho sat astride Dan, firing off shots as they ran toward where the horses had scattered.

"Don't let them get out of range," Freeman said, and for a moment, Jericho wasn't sure if he'd heard it, or thought it himself.

He squeezed off another shot, missing just as Tidwell ducked. Tidwell grabbed the reins of one of the mounts and tried to fling himself to its back. Jericho's next bullet caught him in the leg, and he yelped in pain.

"You bastard," Jericho muttered, as he shot once more and Burk Tidwell fell to the ground, dead. The last man had managed to mount up, but Jericho's next shot sent him arcing from the saddle to sprawl in the dirt below.

There was another one to deal with out there somewhere. It occurred to Jericho that he himself wasn't dead yet. Maybe the last of Tidwell's men would be the one to finish him. He only hoped they went out together. Jericho didn't want to leave this business unfinished. He'd made a promise to Elena to see them dead—or as many of them as he could kill before they got him.

Now, he must hunt down the last of them. But first, he needed to ride down and make sure none of the Tidwell's gang had managed to survive. He didn't think it was possible, but he aimed to be certain of it.

The horses milled restively, unsettled by the proximity of the blazing cabin, the recent gunshots and the smell of fresh blood.

Jericho felt an odd sense of calmness wash over him. Soon, it would be over. He'd be with Elena and his girls once more. For some reason, there was a feeling of apprehension when that thought came to him this time.

Up to this point, he'd looked forward to seeing this job done, and getting on with his own death. But now, there was a sense of separation that he hadn't expected. He looked around quickly at the angel, who rode beside him with an air of secret knowing.

"Don't double cross me, Freeman."

The angel's lips curved faintly. "I never agreed to anything."

"You agreed not to help me. To let things happen as they would."

Freeman raised his hands in a gesture of helplessness. "I've done just that, son. I haven't influenced anything at all."

"Keep it that way, angel," Jericho growled. He couldn't get past the feeling that Freeman had done something to the other rider who'd come after them. Why hadn't he showed up at the cabin yet? "Is he in the barn?"

Freeman shook his head. "No."

Jericho didn't ask any more questions. As they approached the nearest of the bodies, those of Burk Tidwell and the other man who tried to escape on horseback, it was obvious that they were both dead. Tidwell's sightless gray eyes stared heavenward. Jericho fought down the revulsion that tried to claw its way up from his gut.

He and Freeman made the rounds of the bodies wordlessly, until they reached the owners of the cabin, a couple who looked to be in their late twenties.

"Poor young'uns. They never had a chance," Freeman said quietly.

"At least they went together," Jericho said. Suddenly, he turned to look at Freeman. "There weren't any kids in the cabin were there?"

Freeman started to say something, then stopped. "No."

Jericho nodded. "I'm gonna head over to the barn. Make sure that last one of the gang didn't somehow manage to get around and hide in there with all the commotion going on."

Freeman nodded. "He's not there. But I'll tag along, anyhow."

"Suit yourself."

They rode the last few yards together, dismounting at the barn and slipping inside the door that hadn't been latched. The wind banged it shut behind them, then open again.

A lantern hung on a nail just inside the door, a box

of matches in a cut out notch above it. Jericho reached for the lantern and matches, and lit the wick, giving him and Freeman a bit more light to see what lay in the dim recesses of the building. "I'll hold that," Freeman said, taking it from him.

Jericho stood still, listening for any sound form within. A horse whickered in the stall nearest to the door. He reached to pat him absently as his eyes searched the dim interior, then he moved on.

A quick assessment showed nothing more than the animals that might be found on any farm of this size—a couple of plow horses and a milk cow. Still, a feeling nagged at him; the thought that there was something or someone else hiding in the dark interior of the structure.

As Jericho turned to go, a muffled cough sounded from the back corner where some old canvas feedbags lay. He stopped and whirled, his gun ready, held steady at the feedbags that shifted, then just as quickly stilled.

"Come out of there, whoever you are," he ordered, taking a step back toward the corner.

"Jericho—" Freeman began but broke off as Jericho ignored him and closed the distance between where they stood and the back corner.

Freeman stepped close to him with the lantern just as Jericho reached down to jerk the feed sacks aside.

"No, mister!" A boy of no more than ten flung himself over two younger children, covering them with his own body as he looked up at Jericho, terrified.

A soft choking sob came from under the boy. Jericho looked down into the three children's faces—two boys and a girl, a near-baby. She wasn't old enough to be afraid of him, but the two boys made up for it.

Jericho wondered how much they had seen. "Anyone else in here?" he asked.

The oldest boy shook his head. "No. Just me an' Willie and Mary."

Mary . . . Maria . . .

He was scaring these children, and looking at their

faces made him think about his own two angels and how afraid they must have been when Tidwell's men came riding in to wreck their world.

"Don't be afraid," he said gruffly. "I'm Jericho Dean and this is Mr. Hart. You're safe with us, now."

Still, the oldest boy looked at him with distrustful eyes the color of heaven, so different than his Maria's brown ones had been, though they were close to the same age, he figured.

"I give you my word, boy. No one'll hurt you."

"Those men—"

"I know." Jericho would hear him out later, but for now, he still had one more of Tidwell's gang to see to before these children's safety could be assured. "They won't bother you again."

The boy shuddered, and moved off of his brother and sister.

"They killed our Pa," Willie announced, struggling to stand as he disentangled himself from the others and the mountain of feedbags.

"And ma, too, I reckon," the oldest boy said softly.

Jericho sighed, thinking of all the other dead bodies that lay strewn about the little clearing as well. He didn't know how to answer. They were in shock, he knew, and the tears would come later, once they understood their ma and pa were gone for good. He swallowed hard and looked at Freeman, who remained silent.

Damn him. He'd had plenty of opinions and thoughts to offer all this time. What was stopping him now?

As if Freeman read every black idea that flitted through his head, the angel's lips turned upward in a faint, knowing smile.

"Yeah. They killed your pa. And . . . I think you're right," he said, looking at the oldest boy, who nodded at the confirmation. "What's your name, son?"

"Arthur."

"A king's name."

"Ma said so, too." His chin trembled, but there was pride in his voice, and Jericho smiled kindly at him.

He crouched down, eye level, as the boy stood up. "Arthur, I want you to stay here in the barn with Mary and Willie. I've got some business to finish up out yonder. Can I count on you?"

"Yes, sir. How will we know when to come out?"

Jericho looked at Freeman. "Mr. Hart will come back for you."

"But . . . what about you? Maybe you could come back for us."

He feels safe with you, Jericho.

Jericho knew Freeman had shoved the thought into his brain. It was true. But he was getting ready to die. As soon as he found the last of Tidwell's men, he figured that'd be when it happened for him. A piece of lead between the eyes; or, most likely, in the back. He couldn't promise to come back for them.

"We'll see what happens," Freeman put in smoothly. "Oh, will you look at that?" He stepped aside as a brown puppy with a white spot on its tail bounded past him. "Looks like this little rascal sure is happy he came upon you kids. Poor little fella probably needs a good meal and a warm bed." Freeman just smiled at Jericho's surprised look, quelling the protest that rose to his lips. Jericho would have sworn that Freeman had somehow conjured the stray puppy out of thin air. But he was here now, and the children gathered around him, petting him in gentle wonder. "Now don't let him outside. Just pet him a while and we'll be back soon as we can."

"Thanks, mister!" Arthur exclaimed. The children had been immediately occupied with the little mutt and Freeman walked away with a curt nod toward the door. Jericho followed, an odd, unfamiliar sense of regret in his heart as he left the children behind in the safety of the barn.

"What now, Freeman?" he asked, as soon as they'd gotten to the door. He put a hand on the angel's shoulder, a tingle running through his body at the contact. "Just exactly where did you leave Tidwell's guard?"

"Dead." Freeman turned to face Jericho, all traces of the smiling countenance he'd presented to the children gone. Jericho noted the hard somberness of his face, his blue eyes like glass.

"I thought you said—"

"I didn't kill him. Damn fool was so intent on shooting me he completely ignored a low-hanging tree limb. He rode right into it."

"I thought . . . this was *my* time. Wasn't that why you showed up?"

"Disappointed, Jericho?"

He shook his head, forming a careful answer. "No. I thought it was what I wanted. To kill this bunch of bastards and die in the process. But . . . now I wonder— Freeman, what's gonna happen to these kids?"

Freeman lifted his chin a notch, his stare boring into Jericho. "I guess that depends solely on you. Most men would think they'd been spared for a reason. But knowing how angry and bitter you've been I'm not sure if you'll see it that way or not."

He wasn't sure how he saw it. It had been like the angel figured it, of course. No way he could be wrong. But things seemed to be changing.

"They . . . don't have any other family?"

Freeman's lips pursed. "If you mean 'blood relatives'—yes."

Jericho's heart plummeted. *It's for the best.*

Freeman continued. "They have an aunt and uncle who've never seen them, but would be glad to have the labor of the three of them. A more uncharitable pair of people I don't believe I've ever known."

"Do they . . . have to go? Isn't there someone else?"

Freeman shrugged. "Where else would they go? They can't stay here, obviously." He watched Jericho for a moment. "That's always the way of it, isn't it? Hoping that someone else will step in and take care of things we don't want to do."

Jericho's lips thinned in a set line. These children

weren't his responsibility, damn it. He didn't want anything to do with them—not really. He'd had two beautiful daughters who he'd loved, a wife he'd treasured. The cross felt as if it were burning a hole in his skin beneath his shirt.

"It's your conscience, Jericho," Freeman said very quietly. "Nothing more, nothing less."

"I don't want this!" He tried to keep his voice low, but his anger at the entire situation couldn't be held back. He'd thought he knew what he wanted. Death was the best answer. No more hunger, thirst or weariness. No more sadness or worry. Only peace, and the calm that would settle upon him forevermore. He'd lost everything. And he'd made the men who'd taken his world from him pay with their lives.

Freeman slowly looked over to where the children petted the puppy, adoration on their faces. "They've lost everything, too, Jericho. A new puppy is a good start at reminding them of what love is, but—" he shook his head, turning back to Jericho. "Once they go to live with their Aunt Nell and Uncle Roscoe, they won't be able to keep him."

Jericho's eyes narrowed. "Why not?"

"Because," Freeman answered patiently, "Aunt Nell 'don't like dogs.'"

"Well, I sure as hell ain't stayin' just so they can keep this—this *magic puppy* you pulled out of thin air. I had plans, too, you know."

"Are you really that anxious to die, Jericho? Do you really want to so much to take your last breath? To say goodbye to the feel of the wind in your face and the warmth of the fire on a cold night? Even the ache in your back after a hard day's work? Can you turn away from these children that need you so desperately? You have a chance to make a difference in three lives, Jericho."

Jericho felt his resolve crumbling. "I want my girls back! And Elena!"

"That can never be. But you could help these

children—well, never mind."

Why was Freeman arguing so hard for these children?

"I'm not arguing for *them*, Jericho," he murmured, answering Jericho's unasked question. "Don't you see? I'm arguing for *you*. Don't be afraid to live—and love—again. You fought so hard to rid the world of Tidwell and his men. You almost gave up everything."

"I *did* give up everything, Freeman." *How could he think otherwise?*

But the angel smiled. "Not quite. I think there's still a tiny spark of humanity left in you. And I think these children—"

"That wasn't the deal. You let me believe you were here to help me find my way to Elena."

"There are many ways to do that." But at Jericho's look, Freeman's shoulders slumped in defeat. "You're sure? Because, once it's done, it's final."

Jericho took a deep breath, uncertainty settling around him like a shroud. Just then, Arthur looked up and met his eyes, and in that instant, Jericho saw that the boy realized he was leaving them for good. He rose and walked toward where Jericho and Freeman stood near the door. There was no censure in his eyes, but an abiding sadness that Jericho felt must mirror his own. He'd suffered losses too . . . more than he even knew, yet, Jericho thought, remembering what Freeman had told him about the inhospitable conditions that awaited him at his aunt and uncle's home.

Arthur would have to try to make the best of things for Willie and Mary. Regret sliced through Jericho. He should be there, so Arthur could have someone to lean on. He was too young to shoulder such responsibility and sorrow.

"You leavin' now, Mr. Dean?"

Jericho was frozen for an instant. The boy seemed to be asking him to stay by asking if he were leaving. The puppy ran over to follow him, and he reached down to pet him.

"Oh, what a good boy." He raised his eyes back up to

Jericho. "Look here, Mr. Dean. This puppy you brung us, little Rascal, he's already part of the family. He loves us. We'll take good care of him, too. Don't you worry none about Rascal, once you're gone."

Jericho swallowed past the hard lump in his throat. Of everything that had happened over the course of the past two weeks, he'd congratulated himself on holding his emotions in check well. If Freeman hadn't produced that damn puppy with his magic, or however he did it, everything might have been fine. But to see the children who had been thrust into a world of loss, of having everything stripped from them, just as he had, rally around the little dog and make him their focus . . . it made him feel small with his thoughts of giving up.

"Best be on your way." Freeman's tone was frosty.

Jericho glanced at him. "You're . . . not coming?"

"No. This is a journey you'll have to make alone. One way or the other."

Just then, Mary wrapped her arms around Jericho's leg to keep her balance, and he bent to pick her up.

"Do you have to go, Mr. Dean?" Willie asked plaintively.

"Sure he does, Willie," Arthur answered. "Mr. Dean has to go do important things."

Mary pulled at the leather string around Jericho's neck. Her chubby fingers settled around the cross he had fashioned so long ago. He remembered his own daughters doing that very thing. Life went on. Who would care for these children if he did not? Wouldn't he hope for the kindness of a stranger for his girls if he'd been killed alongside Elena?

"No," he murmured, watching Mary's bright, inquisitive expression. "I don't. Not anymore. There's nothing more important than you."

"And Rascal," Willie said, matter-of-factly.

Jericho looked at Freeman, who stood, scrutinizing him in silent approval. "Uh . . . kids, we need to go bury the dead, Mr. Hart and I—"

"I'll take care of that," Freeman stated, taking a step toward the door. "If you'll give me a few minutes? Maybe long enough to tell them a story?"

Magic again. Or heavenly intervention. But Jericho was relieved for it, this time. He was ready to move on, to take Arthur, Willie and Mary somewhere new and start over.

"Freeman?"

The angel turned, his hand on the barn door.

"Will I—will we be seeing you again?"

"Not likely. I think . . . you'll be able to find your way from here on out, don't you, Jericho?"

Jericho nodded. "Much obliged. For everything. All that help I didn't want." At Freeman's odd smile, Jericho asked, "What was it they took from you? Tidwell's gang? When we first met, you told me they had taken something 'very dear' from you, too."

"Don't you know, Jericho?" he asked. "It was your soul. I'd thought for a while . . . we'd lost you for good. When you believed there was no good left in the world. Now," he nodded at the children and continued softly, "you only have to look into their faces to see what you mean to them. Right now, you're everything. *You* are the only good left, in their eyes." Freeman touched his hat brim in salute. "Just give me few, will you?" He opened the door, then pulled it shut behind him to keep out the cold wind. Inside the barn, the lantern cast a soft glow, and Jericho felt the remains of the ice that had encased his heart melt and slip away in the warmth of the expectant anticipation in the eyes of the children.

"Sit down here, boys," Jericho said, seating himself on the floor with Mary still in his arms. "I think I've got a story you might like to hear."

Willie and Arthur settled onto the floor in front of him, their legs crossed, elbows on their knees as they leaned forward intently. Mary held up the cross, the light catching it for a moment like a distant star.

"Once, there was a king whose name was Arthur Pendragon . . ."

And the world was his.

Wire

by C. Courtney Joyner

Courtney Joyner has written the screenplays for more than 25 movies, including THE OFFSPRING *starring Vincent Price, and the new telefilm,* RETURN OF CAPT. NEMO. *His fiction has been anthologized in* A Fistful Of Legends, Law Or The Gun *and the new* Beat To A Pulp, Round Two. *Courtney lives in Los Angeles with his fiancé and a ton of movie posters.*

My hands are shaking, but I feel I can still get off a good shot if need be.

I am Jonas Terill, Jr., son of Jonas and Sara, and I will be fifteen years tomorrow. I was hoping for lemon pie and a baseball, but will likely be hanged instead. Whoever you are, you think my ending was deserved, as I have bloodied people in the past and this latest kill is my undoing.

Things wasn't supposed to go in this way.

The body lying by the wire moved a little when I rode up, but that was after the kill shot, and I've seen that before. There was a little sound, like a baby's voice, and then nothing. I have pushed the hair out of the eyes and adjusted the hat, but blood is everywhere. The face is like a red Halloween mask.

There has been gun fire, I'd judge, a few miles away. I think this was a signal. I fired back, but I am expecting riders to see what's happened, so I will put down my confessing.

I was born in a dugout outside Rawlins, where Pa

was holed up with two other men and my mother. One of the men was a lay minister who married my parents while Ma was birthing me. I wouldn't have known this, except that after my father was shot, I found a letter recounting this among his things Ma had kept dear.

We was hiding at the farm of a dead man when my father told me that if you want to make it in the world, you have to be willing to go all the way. Do what the other fellow won't. It was near Christmas when he advised me, and was showing how to chop wood. He wanted me to swing a double-blade ax, when my hands could barely get around the handle. He held the blade off my shoulder, and guided it down against a frozen rail, but it bounced off. I cried and he laughed from the belly, and cut the rail with less than four strokes, clean through.

This was the same ax he used to kill one of the deputies who came to take him for robbing a mail hack near Jackson Hole. They said they was with Joe LeFors. That was Christmas Eve when they rode in, not letting my family alone. We never had any peace that I recall.

The deputies fired into the house, and one bullet nicked the top of my ear. Pa screamed, and grabbed the shotgun from behind the stove and fired out the door, killing a horse. To me it looked like summer lightning. One of the deputies ran for the house and Pa put the ax in his chest before the others started shooting, while my Mother curled herself around me, and used her nightgown to soak the blood. This is why I only have half an ear on my left side.

That was the last time I saw Pa, and I might have dreamed some of the things he said, but they seem real to me at this moment.

I am hearing something like shouting bouncing off the far hills, but I haven't seen riders. I could ride out but my legs feel like they are tied to the ground. Or maybe the hands of the dead are holding me. That is what my mother would call my fanciful thinking. For everything my Pa told me about what it meant to deal with the other fellow before he deals with you, my mother's ways seem to have more value now. I wish I could go back and follow them better.

Pa had been outlawed for a year when he met my mother. She knew what he was, but understood who he was inside, and had faith that he would mend his ways. She became his woman, and then his wife and talked about this freely, without a hint of shame. She believed in my father's soul because we all have a past, but she knew that when he fell in with a bad lot, he would follow their trail rather than cut one of his own. It was his failing. She called him, "The weakest man-of-strength God ever made."

Like many things she said, she made me write them down and read them back, to check my writing and spelling. She couldn't read numbers, but could add any sum in her head and I have the same talent. When I have gone to school at different times, the teachers always said I had had some fine education, and I thank my Ma for that.

It was three years ago that we rode to the prison at Rawlins, and I waited while Ma signed a paper for Pa's body. He had been shot while fighting with another prisoner, and buried in the common yard. We went to see the grave, but left him with the other plain crosses.

She died six months later in the backroom of the boarding house where she was cooking. She told me she was happy to see I had grown into my Pa's face, but not to follow that path. She left me with a ring and forty dollars.

I confess now that I lost the forty dollars playing faro and the ring was the cause of my killing a man.

There has been a shot. I can see something moving, a group of riders, in the far distance. The sea of grass makes it hard to focus beyond it, but they are there and coming for me. If they are men like me, I know what will happen. Somehow, I am writing with a steadier hand.

I am hours away from being fifteen, but I know what it is to ride beyond the law. After the undertaker and I buried Ma, I rode alone from town to farm, looking for work. Some folks were generous, others were not. I stopped by a schoolhouse and asked the Master about chores, hoping I could stay on. Ma would embrace that. He refused me nastily, so I stole his grey mare and sold her to a ne'er do well. I am not proud of this, but sometimes we do things we don't expect.

The night I got the money for the horse, I slept in a rooming house, and a man claiming to be a trail boss took exception to Ma's ring that I wore on my smallest finger. You can't explain anything to a drunk, so he was deaf to my words, and swung a whiskey a bottle.

I reacted the way Pa would have wanted me to, and the gun was in my hand, but I didn't feel it. The sound was louder than anything, and he flew back down the stairs. Because I was thirteen, and there were people in the house, I was let go. The law was also a drunkard and didn't wish to be bothered with this killing.

Now I had my father's name and a reputation following it. I didn't know what I wanted, but it wasn't this, although work now seemed to come a little easier from cowboys who had heard the story. And a few strangers bought me meals if I would re-tell it.

That's how I came to this war.

I was leaving a dogtrot when a man named Caleb rode in with some cowboys, but he wasn't covered in mud and hair. He had a new shave and a gold watch fob. We talked and he told me about The Newbridge Cattle Co. and asked if I wanted to be a Range Protector. I wouldn't get my hands dirty and I'd draw more pay than the cowboys, if I could handle a gun and was willing to use it. He heard the tale about me, and thought I'd be a good one. I had less than a dollar in my jeans, and had to listen.

I can hear voices and shouts. The riders are closer now, and I can't make out any of them, but in a war, you don't know the guy who's going to take your life. An enemy is an enemy. That's what Mr. Newbridge told me when I signed on for the job. It was his range and his wire, and I was one of his soldiers. He shook my hand, telling me what a pleasure it was I was riding for him.

Ma and Pa would have been proud of that, because I was drawing real pay. I was loaned a Winchester, and practiced with it when I wasn't riding the fences. Truth be told, I stood back while the other boys beat the homesteaders who were cutting through our range. No one challenged us, they were just folks, and my finger never came close to the trigger. Caleb shot an old man through the eye who'd swung at him with an ax just like my Pa did only now I was one of those deputies.

If Caleb reads this, he will think me a coward, but I was sick after this incident. I should have ridden out of Wyoming and never looked back. I didn't have what my Pa had. I have been a thief, and a killer by chance, but not for wages. This wasn't how things were supposed to go, not the way Ma had wanted. I don't know why, but I needed to prove myself to the men I was riding with. That's my failing.

This morning all I was thinking of was my birthday, and lemon pie. If I did a good job today, then Caleb and the others might celebrate me, and I could move on without shame. That is what was in my mind when I was riding along the miles of Mr. Newbridge's barbed wire.

That is what was in my mind when I saw the fence cutter. There was nothing for miles, except someone in hat and coat, bending by the wire with a cutting tool. That's a concealed weapon, and if you shoot, then you're defending yourself. I dropped to the ground and fired the Winchester once, trying for a wing. But my aim was poor, and I struck the cutter in the head.

When I rode up and saw the cutter, I thought I screamed, but I became light in the head and fell from my saddle. I woke up lying by the wire, the cutter next to me. Her face was covered with blood, but she was pretty with yellow hair and blue eyes, and close to me in years. I imagine she was helping her folks, who wanted to come through our range. She didn't have a gun, and her horse had bolted.

I have tried to be gentle with her, and started to put down my thoughts so people will know that it was just chance that this happened, like anything else in this life. She made the choice to cut, and I chose to shoot. I wish we had done neither. Instead, we might have met in town, and I want to think of what that might have been like.

The riders are not far off, and their curses and screams are quite clear. I think the one in front is her Pa. I don't know if this letter will give them any peace, but it has helped me. One rider has pulled up, and is taking aim.

I am not going to move. I can't. I can only pray to God that I -

Panhandle Freight

by L. J. Washburn

L. J. Washburn received the Private Eye Writers of America Award and the American Mystery Award for the first Lucas Hallam mystery, Wild Night. *She has been writing both mystery and western stories with the Lucas Hallam character for almost 30 years, and has been happily married to author James Reasoner for even longer. Her website can be found at www.liviawashburn.com, and she blogs when she can find the time at http://liviajwashburn.blogspot.com.*

"Close the damn door!" the station agent yelled at Lucas Hallam. "You're lettin' all the warm air out!"

And all the cold air in, Hallam thought as he shoved the depot's front door closed behind him. People sometimes said there was nothing between the Canadian River and the North Pole except a barbed wire fence, and on a night like tonight, when a blue norther swept down over the plains, it sure felt like that old saying was right.

Hallam was a big, rugged man in a sheepskin coat, with his hat pulled down tight on his head so the wind wouldn't blow it off. He tugged his gloves from his hands and stuck them in a coat pocket as he crossed the spacious waiting room toward the ticket window.

"I hope you ain't here to buy a ticket," the agent said from the other side of the counter. "No passenger trains comin' through tonight, only a freight that's due in about an hour."

"No, I don't need a ticket," Hallam told the man, who looked like he wanted to just close up and go home for the night. "I'm here because of that freight."

He unbuttoned the coat and slipped a hand inside it.

The agent dropped a hand below the counter.

"You'd better not be reachin' for a gun, mister," he warned. "I got a .45 here, and I know how to use it."

Hallam grunted and shook his head.

"Take it easy," he told the man. Moving deliberately so as not to spook the trigger-happy agent, he brought out a leather folder and opened it so the man could see the badge and identification papers inside. "I'm a Pinkerton agent, working for the railroad."

The man relaxed and blew out his breath.

"Well, why didn't you say so?" he demanded irritably.

"Thought I just did," Hallam said as he put away the folder. "I'm here about that freight. Rode all the way from Lubbock in the teeth of that gale to get here in time."

He was half frozen to prove it, too.

The station agent shook his head in confusion. "What about that freight?"

Hallam rubbed his hands together and blew on them.

"Somebody's going to hold it up when it gets here."

That just confused the agent even more.

"How do you know that . . . and who'd bother holding up a freight train, anyway?"

"The telegram I got from my bosses back in Chicago didn't explain that. It just said they'd gotten a tip that Seth Brackett was gonna stop the freight here and take something off of it."

"Brackett!" the agent repeated. "Why, he's raised hell all over this part of the country! He must've held up half a dozen express cars."

"And killed a dozen messengers and guards," Hallam said with a bleak nod. "Nobody knows how he gets on board, and he never leaves any witnesses. That's why we don't know what he looks like. Wouldn't even know his name if he didn't leave those notes braggin' about what he's done."

"And you say he's comin' here?" The agent's voice quavered a little.

"So I'm told," Hallam said. "My job's to stop him."

"How are you gonna do that when you don't know what he looks like?"

"That makes it a challenge, all right," Hallam said.

The station door swung open again, letting cold air swirl through the waiting room. The agent's head jerked in that direction. His eyes widened.

"Blast it, don't act like that!" Hallam said quietly. "We don't want Brackett to know we're waitin' for him. A killer like that, best to take him by surprise."

The agent swallowed and nodded.

"Yeah. Sorry, Mister . . . what was your name again."

"Hallam."

The man who had just come into the depot pushed the door closed behind him, appearing to struggle a little against the wind as he did so. He had a large box wrapped with paper and tied with twine hanging from one hand and wore city duds. He looked to Hallam like a drummer of some sort, middle-aged, with fair hair under a derby and a long, hangdog face.

"Evening," the man said as he came over to the window. He nodded friendly-like to Hallam and the agent. "Colder than a witch's tit out there . . . although I have no personal experience on exactly how cold that is, never having made the close acquaintance of a witch. Bitches are a different story." He paused, then asked Hallam, "Were you conducting business here, friend? I don't want to interrupt."

Hallam shook his head and said, "Nope, just passing the time of day with my amigo here."

The man lifted the package. "In that case . . . ."

Hallam moved aside so the man could set the bundle on the counter. "Sure, go ahead."

"I need to ship this," the man said. "There's a train coming through tonight, isn't there?"

The agent nodded and said, "Yeah, but this ain't a scheduled stop on tonight's run. I'd have to lower the signal."

"But you can do that, can't you?" the man insisted. "The sooner this package gets back to St. Louis, the better."

Hallam had heard a faint clank from inside the package when the man set it on the counter. He gestured toward it and asked, "What is it?"

"I'm not sure what business that is of yours." The man shrugged. "But it's no secret. I travel in kitchen appliances, and that's some defective merchandise I've accumulated from the past few shipments my company has sent me. I need to return it so it won't count against my balance sheets."

"Don't seem like that's urgent enough for the train to make a special stop," the agent said. "There's a regular freight comin' through tomorrow. It can go out then."

"I'd just as soon not wait." A sheepish smile appeared on the man's face. "My account's not in the best shape. I need the credit for these returns as soon as I can get it." He lowered his voice to a conspiratorial tone. "I'm willing to pay a mite extra."

"Thought you were havin' money trouble," the agent said.

"You've got to spend money to make money, as the old saying goes."

"All right. No extra charge," the agent grumbled. "Lemme weigh this and figure it up."

The transaction took a few minutes. Hallam stood off to the side in apparent disinterest as it went on. The drummer paid the charges as if it hurt him physically to hand over the bills, and then the agent said, "I'll take care of it from here, mister. You can go on back to the hotel."

There was no need to mention which hotel. In a settlement of this size, there was only one.

The drummer shook his head dubiously. "I think I'll wait here until the train comes in, just to be sure that the package goes out all right."

"I told you I'd take care of it," the agent said, not bothering to hide his irritation. He seemed to have forgotten his earlier nervousness. Doing business had settled him down.

"I'll just sit over there," the drummer said, waving a hand toward the empty benches where passengers waited for their trains. He walked over, took a seat, picked up a two-week-old copy of the Fort Worth Star-Telegram that somebody had left there, and started leafing through it.

The agent leaned forward through the ticket window and cut his eyes toward the drummer as he whispered, "That's a mighty thin story. You think he's – "

Hallam lifted a hand to stop the man before he mentioned Seth Brackett's name.

"He could be tellin' the truth," Hallam said. "I'll keep an eye on him."

The agent looked pretty doubtful, but he nodded.

The minute hand on the big clock on the wall ticked over with an audible sound every sixty seconds. Each one of those minutes seemed to take at least five times that long as Hallam, the station agent, and the traveling salesman waited for the train.

So it seemed like quite a while but really wasn't when the door opened again. The cold wind brought two people in this time, a man and a woman. He wore work clothes and a battered old hat, and the woman was bundled up not only in a thick coat but also a blanket. She walked delicately, like there was something wrong with her. The man helped her over to one of the benches. The drummer watched them curiously as the woman sat down.

The man hurried over to the window and asked, "Has the train come through already?" He was somewhere between thirty and forty. The lines of strain and hard work on his face made it hard to be sure of his age.

The agent shook his head. "No, it's not due for a little while yet. What do you need, mister?"

"I have to get my wife to Lubbock tonight."

The agent shook his head and said, "You're outta luck, mister. No passenger trains tonight, just a freight."

"But it's headed that way, isn't it? They could take us in the caboose, couldn't they?" the man insisted. "It's an emergency."

"What sort of emergency?"

The man turned to look toward the woman who sat huddled in the blanket on the bench.

"My wife's going to have a baby."

"Why, Doc Spurgeon here in town can handle that. He's delivered plenty of babies."

"Not like this one. There's something wrong. The doc said I need to get Sara Beth to the hospital in Lubbock as soon as possible. If I don't . . ." The man's face, tanned and seamed by working outside, turned pale. "If I don't, could be neither her nor the baby will make it."

"Well, if that don't beat all. I dunno. The railroad's got rules . . ."

Hallam said, "I'll bet the conductor would be willin' to make an exception to the rules in a case like this."

The agent's fingers rasped over the beard stubble on his chin as he frowned in thought. "I reckon since I got to stop the train anyway, I could at least ask the conductor."

The man reached through the window to grab the agent's hand and pump it. "Thanks, mister, thanks so much! This means the world to me."

"Why don't you go sit with your wife?" the agent suggested. "You'll know when the train gets here."

The man nodded and hurried over to the benches. He sat down beside the woman and put an arm around her shoulders.

"I don't believe it for a second," the agent told Hallam. "Why, the way she's bundled up, there ain't no way of tellin' for sure if she's even in the family way!"

"I never heard anything about the fella we're lookin' for havin' a female accomplice," Hallam said.

"Yeah, but we can't be sure that he don't!"

Hallam nodded. "I guess that's true."

The agent ran his fingers through his thinning brown hair and said, "Lord, who knew the place would get so busy, tonight of all nights! Ain't that always the way!"

They resumed their wait. The drummer rattled the newspaper, the man and the woman talked quietly with each other, the blue norther howled outside, and the clock on the wall continued its ticking. Hallam had warmed up enough now in the heat that came from a pot-bellied stove in a corner of the waiting room that he took off the sheepskin coat and draped it over the back of the nearest bench.

When the door opened again a while later, the agent muttered, "Lord have mercy! Now what?"

The man who came in on the cold air was tall and lean and dressed mostly in black, from his Stetson to his frock coat to his high-topped boots. The only bits of color about him were the diamond stickpin he wore in his fancy cravat and the ivory grips on the handles of the twin Colts he wore belted around his hips.

The agent swallowed hard and bit back a moan.

"That's gotta be him," he said in an urgent whisper to Hallam. "Look at him! You can tell he's an outlaw!"

"Or a gambler," Hallam said. "Looks more like that to me."

"Get ready! He's comin' this way!"

The stranger walked up to the window and asked, "Has tonight's freight arrived?"

The agent pointed a shaking finger at the board where the schedule was chalked and managed to say, "Not yet. Soon, I reckon."

The man smiled. "You look like you could use some nerve tonic, friend. I have a package coming in on the train."

"A package . . . comin' in?"

"That's right. It's being shipped special to me from New York. Will the train stop, or will someone just toss the package onto the platform as it goes past?"

"Oh, the train's stoppin' tonight," the agent said. "Freight or not, it's stoppin'. Which reminds me, I got to go lower the signal."

He came out of the door next to the ticket window shrugging into a coat.

"Why don't you come with me, amigo?" he said to Hallam. "It's a cold, dark night for a man to be out all by his lonesome."

368

"Sure," Hallam said. He reached for his sheepskin coat.

They went out through the door that led to the platform. The building blocked some of the wind's force, but the way it was whipping around, the bone-chilling cold it carried penetrated the men's coats anyway.

"Which one do you think it is?" the agent asked as he went over to the lever that raised and lowered the signal beam on a post next to the platform. "One of 'em's got to be Seth Brackett."

"Seems that way," Hallam agreed with a nod. He hadn't put his gloves back on, but he had his hands stuck in the coat pockets to keep them out of the wind.

The agent shoved the lever over and lowered the beam. A new-fangled electric light glowed redly on it. The engineer would see it far enough back along the track to bring the train to a stop as it rolled up to the station.

"Tell you what," the agent said. He pulled his coat back to reveal the butt of a pistol stuck behind his belt. "Let's go back in there and throw down on the whole bunch of 'em. We'll herd 'em into the storeroom and lock 'em up until the train's come and gone."

"What about that pregnant woman?" Hallam asked.

"Oh, yeah." The agent frowned in thought. "I guess if she can prove that she's really pregnant, we'll let her and her husband stay out so they can get on the train. But we'll lock up the other two."

"If we do that, they're liable to file a lawsuit against the railroad. Your bosses won't like that, and mine won't either." Hallam added wryly, "And I doubt that the lady will want to show you her belly to prove she's with child."

"Then what are we supposed to do?" the agent asked in exasperation. "Just wait?"

Hallam glanced at the signal. "It shouldn't be much longer."

The agent sighed and led the way back inside. The man in black had taken a seat on one of the benches, too.

"Gettin' damned crowded in here," the agent muttered.

The man who looked like a farmer told the woman, "Don't worry, honey. I'm sure the train will be here soon."

"I hope so, Henry," she said in a voice tight with strain. "I sure hope so."

Hallam took off his coat and wandered over toward them. He lifted a finger to his hat brim, nodded, and said, "Ma'am." Then he turned to the man and asked, "You have a place somewhere around here, mister?"

"Yeah," the man said with a nod. "Fifty acres about five miles west of town. It's a nice little farm. Won't mean much, though, if . . ."

He stopped, obviously unwilling to go on with that thought.

The woman squeezed his hand and said, "It'll be all right, Henry. I'm sure it will."

Hallam touched his hat brim again and said, "Best of luck to you, ma'am."

He moved over and sat down next to the drummer.

"Cold night out there, isn't it?"

The man nodded and said, "Cold as a . . . Wait a minute. We did that before, didn't we?"

"I reckon we did," Hallam said with a grin. Since most drummers were talkative sorts, he primed the pump. "You like bein' a salesman?"

"Oh, I used to. I enjoyed the traveling, even though these trains aren't the most comfortable conveyances in the world. And to be honest with you, the necessity of being away from the little woman back in Dallas most of the time didn't particularly bother me, either." The drummer shrugged. "But the miles are starting to pile up, and so are the years. It's getting harder and harder to make a living, too. Merchants buy from the bigger outfits now, and hell, you can't sell to individuals anymore. Everybody's got a Sears Roebuck catalog or a Monkey Wards catalog, and they just send off for what they want. Time for men like me to pack it in."

"That's a shame," Hallam said.

"What about you? What line of work are you in? You look like a cowboy, if you don't mind my saying so."

Hallam nodded. "I've done some cowboying in my time." He didn't say anything else. Manhunting was his line these days, and he didn't figure that business would ever dry up. There would always be outlaws.

The man in black was sitting close enough to eavesdrop on the conversation. He leaned toward them and said, "Pardon the interruption, but you look like a gunfighter to me."

"Me?" Hallam said in apparent wonderment.

As a matter of fact, when he was younger . . . when he was tracking down the men responsible for his father's death and for a few wild years after that . . . he'd been getting a reputation as a fast gun. It would have been easy enough for him to wind up like John Wesley Hardin or one of the other infamous pistoleers.

But then he'd pinned on the silver star-in-a-circle of the Texas Rangers and gone down that road instead, a road that had now led him to the Pinkertons. He shook his head and told the man in black, "No, I'm no gunfighter."

"You have the look about you," the man insisted. "I know it well. I've made a study of shootists."

"Is that so?"

"Indeed. They're my bread and butter, you see."

Hallam didn't see at all. But before he could say that, the man in black went on, "I'll show you, when the train gets here."

The station agent had gone back into his office. He was at the ticket window, close enough to hear what the man in black said. The agent cleared his throat and tried to catch Hallam's eye. Hallam saw him but pretended not to.

When Hallam first heard the locomotive's whistle a few minutes later, he thought it was that blue norther keening and shrieking. Then the sound came again and he recognized it for what it was. He put his hands on his knees, pushed himself to his feet with a faint protest from muscles starting to grow stiffer with age, and said,

"Train's comin'."

The other three men stood up. The woman remained seated on the bench. Her husband told her, "You just stay there and rest until we find out for sure they'll let us on this train."

"All right," she said. She sounded tired and weak.

The train's rumble reached into the station. The agent came out of his office and headed for the platform. The drummer, the farmer, and the man in black followed him. Hallam brought up the rear, keeping a close eye on the three men in case one of them them tried anything.

It occurred to him that the woman could easily have a sawed-off shotgun or a hogleg under that blanket, and the skin on the back of his neck crawled at the thought that she was behind him.

But when he glanced over his shoulder, she hadn't budged, and she looked as weary and miserable as ever. Hallam was convinced she didn't have anything to do with that train-robbing Seth Brackett.

With a squeal of brakes and a hiss of steam billowing from the engine into the frigid air, the train came to a stop with the caboose alongside the platform. The conductor, wrapping himself in a blue greatcoat, hopped down to the platform and demanded of the station agent, "Why's the signal down, Grady?"

"Got a shipment goin' out," the agent said, hefting the box the drummer had brought in. "And you're supposed to have a special shipment for this fella here." He jerked his head toward the man in black.

"What's your name?" the conductor asked.

"Boothe, with an 'e'," the man said. "John B. Boothe."

"Yeah, sure," the conductor said. "I forgot about that. It's in the caboose. I'll fetch it for you."

Before the conductor could turn around, the farmer stepped forward and raised his voice to be heard over the wind.

"Mister, I've got to get to Lubbock tonight!" he said. "My wife's fixin' to have a baby, and she's in a bad way. The local doc says she needs to get to the hospital. Can you take us in the caboose?"

The conductor frowned at the agent. "Is this true, Grady?"

"All I know is what he's told me," the agent answered. "Far as I know it's the truth."

The conductor frowned. "The line has rules against carrying passengers on freight trains. However, in the case of a medical emergency, I have some leeway. Is your wife here? I've got a schedule to keep, you know."

"She's right inside," the farmer said eagerly. "I'll go get her."

"Fine. We'll have you to Lubbock in an hour or so." The conductor took the drummer's bundle from the station agent, then turned to the man in black. "I'll get your package."

He climbed back into the caboose while the farmer hurried into the station to fetch his wife. The couple came back, the man holding an arm protectively around his wife's shoulders again. The conductor met them at the steps and helped the woman up into the warmth of the caboose. Once they had disappeared inside, the conductor came over to the man in black and handed him a cardboard box tied with twine, much like the one the drummer was shipping back to St. Louis only smaller.

"Here you go, Mr. Boothe."

"Thank you very much, sir."

"Grady, we're pulling out in five minutes. You got anything else for us?"

The agent glanced at Hallam, then said, "Not a thing. I'm gonna lock up and go home."

"It's a good night for it," the conductor agreed.

While the conductor returned to the caboose, the man in black took out a penknife, cut the twine, and opened the box enough to reach inside it. Hallam watched him closely in case it was a trick. The only thing the man took out of the box, though, was a thin, yellow-backed book.

"For you, sir," he said as he extended the book toward Hallam. "A complimentary copy of my latest masterpiece.”

Hallam took the book and read the title aloud. “‘The Brazos Kid vs. the Blacksnake Gang’.” He looked up. “You're a writer?”

The man in black nodded. “John B. Boothe, sir, at your service. Just as it says there.” He pointed to the author's name on the garish yellow cover. “This is my first effort for Beadle & Adams. I'm justifiably proud.”

Hallam chuckled. “Well, good for you, I reckon. I wouldn't want to sit down and make up a lot of words, but I guess if it's what you want to do . . .”

Boothe tucked the box under his arm. “I hope you enjoy it,” he said. He turned to leave the platform. The drummer was already gone. Hallam had noticed him walking away, head bent against the wind, as soon as the package he was shipping was on board the train.

That left Hallam and the station agent alone on the platform.

“I don't understand,” the agent said. “You got that tip – ”

Hallam shrugged. “Tips are wrong sometimes. So long.”

“Good night! And no offense, Mr. Pinkerton man, but I hope I never see you again.”

Hallam laughed. He walked back through the waiting room and out the front door to where his horse was tied. He felt bad about leaving the animal out in the weather for the past hour. But the horse would be in a warm stall at the livery barn soon enough.

Not quite yet, though, Hallam thought. Not quite yet.

He swung up into the saddle and rode toward the hotel. When he looked back over his shoulder, he saw the lamps in the station go out. The agent was done for the night.

The engineer pulled the whistle cord, sending another shriek through the night. The train lurched ahead, then smoothed out as it began to roll faster.

Hallam sent his horse galloping down an alley.

He swung back toward the railroad tracks, angling toward the steel rails. The train was picking up speed.

He urged his mount on, knowing that lives depended on him intercepting it.

He'd had a pretty good idea what he was going to find here tonight, but he had been willing to be proven wrong. Everything had worked out pretty much the way he thought it would, though.

The horse was big and strong and had a good burst. It drew even with the caboose. Hallam reached over, grabbed the railing around the rear platform, and left the saddle. He swung onto the platform and drew his gun as he carefully tried the doorknob with his left hand. Locked.

Of course it was. Seth Brackett didn't want to be disturbed while he was at his work.

Hallam leaned back, raised his right leg, and drove his boot heel against the door with all his considerable strength and weight behind it. The door crashed open, and Hallam went through it in a rush.

Taken by surprise, the station agent whirled toward him. The gun in the man's hand spouted noise and flame. Hallam felt as much as heard the bullet rip past his ear. His long-barreled Colt .45 roared. The slug tore through the agent's right shoulder, rending flesh and shattering bone. The impact threw the man back against the conductor's desk.

But he was too stubborn to quit. He reached across his body, grabbed the gun from the hand that no longer worked, and started to raise it.

"Drop it, Brackett!" Hallam shouted.

The outlaw ignored him. Hallam couldn't wait any longer. The conductor, along with the farmer and his pregnant wife, were huddled on the other side of the caboose, wide-eyed and terrified. With every second that went by, their lives were at risk from a stray bullet.

Hallam triggered twice more, driving both slugs into Brackett's chest. This time Brackett dropped the gun as he rocked back. He started to slide down the front of the desk, then lost his balance and pitched forward on his face.

"My God!" the conductor exclaimed. "He was going to

kill us! Phil Grady was going to kill us all!"

"He's not Phil Grady," Hallam said. "Or maybe he is, I don't know. But he's Seth Brackett, the train robber, that's for damned sure. He locked up the station, slipped onto the caboose platform, and waited until the train was movin' to bust in here and get the drop on you. I reckon he's got a horse stashed up the line four or five miles. All he had to do was kill the three of you, take what he wanted, drop off the train where he could pick up the horse, and ride back to town. Then he could go to bed and act just as shocked as everybody else tomorrow when the news came about there bein' three dead folks in this car when the train got to Lubbock. He's done it half a dozen times before. What I want to know is what he was after."

The conductor pulled out a bandanna, wiped sweat from his face, and said, "There's a special shipment of money in the safe. Upwards of fifty thousand dollars in cash from a bank in Denver bound for one of those big Panhandle ranchers. The bank made special arrangements with the railroad to ship it like this. They're sending another package with half a dozen guards, but it's just a dummy. Nobody on this train even knows about it except me. I didn't think anybody knew about it!"

"Somebody did," Hallam said. "Brackett, or Grady, had a partner somewhere along the line tipping him off. But somebody tipped off the Pinkertons, too, because I work for them and they knew something was gonna happen on this train tonight." Hallam's eyes narrowed in thought. "Brackett thought he was mighty smart, workin' out this scheme. Maybe *he* sent that warning to the agency, just to rub our noses in it, like he did with those notes he left after the other robberies. He seemed to be taking a lot of pleasure in his play-actin' tonight."

"Well, you're a better detective than I am, mister, because I never would have figured that out," the conductor said. "But I reckon that's why you work for the Pinks and I don't. Now what? Are you gonna try to find Grady's partner?"

Hallam shook his head. "Somebody else can do that. I'm ridin' on to Lubbock with you so this lady can get to where she needs to go, and then schedule or no schedule, this train's backin' up until I find my horse. I'm sure as hell not leavin' him out all night with a blue norther blowin'!"

Penance

by Kerry Newcomb

A boy in Texas sets aside his Roy Rogers Ranch set, arms himself with his Fanner Fifty Colt, his Red Ryder Winchester cap gun, loads his Hopalong Cassidy lunchbox with pb&j sandwiches and a thermos of milk and sets out to right the wrongs of the neighborhood. That's me, Kerry Newcomb. I grow up to write some novels, including a NY Times bestseller, and several westerns. The lunchbox is dented now and I'm out of caps, the neighborhood is plowed under, but I know the way home, by heart.

<u>San Antonio. November 11. 1918.</u>
She kicks him in the kneecap and almost breaks free. He barely manages to catch her ankle and wrestles her down on to her belly. Then his slender hands circle her throat.

See him there beneath the platinum moon, how he rolls her slender brown body down the muddy bank and into the river. The meandering current tucks her corpse beneath the shadow of a limestone bridge, a place where lovers come to tryst.

* * *

"Bless me Father for I have sinned . . ." Geoffrey Duncan shifted his weight, swayed from side to side, and winced at the pain in his left knee where, the night before, the young whore had kicked him as she struggled to break free of his grasp. Where's the cushion on this damn kneeler? he thought. Is there not enough suffering in the world?   The nephew of the State Representative from Bexar County, Judge T. C. Duncan, was accustomed to more comfortable perches.

"Bless me . . ." Geoffrey repeated, pausing again to consider his choice of words. A bemused smile lit his features as he appraised the dimly illuminated silhouette of the priest on the other side of the confessional screen. Thunder rumbled and beyond the foot thick adobe walls of the Mission San José, roiling clouds gathered to block the morning light and prepared to unleash their burden of rain. Lightning seared the menacing sky as the lumbering storms threatened to ruin the Armistice parade scheduled for later in the afternoon.

Geoffrey Duncan stared at the woven cane façade a few inches from his nose. Concealed like this, the two men confronted one another; one sinful, one absolving, both participants in a sociopath's ritualistic contest.

Duncan gingerly probed the streaks of scabbed flesh. His forearm was tender from where the hot-tempered puta sank her teeth into him, just before he crushed her windpipe. His chums back at medical school found it odd that such a slightly built, effeminate wag should have the powerful grip of a journeyman. Geoffrey Duncan liked to quip that it helped him keep a tight grip on his beloved uncle's money. But this visit to the confessional had nothing to do with the family fortune. The nephew sighed and massaged his bruised arm. Last night, the vixen had fought longer and harder than the previous two. But her struggles had only fueled his lust.

"Bless me father for I have sinned. My last confession was . . . ah . . ." Geoffrey pretended not to remember.

"Two weeks ago?" A dry, muffled voice filtered through the screen. Again the thunder punctuated his reply.

"Yes," Geoffrey said. Good, for a second there he had begun to wonder if anyone was awake on the other side of the confessional. Duncan ran a finger under his own stiff collar, brushed some errant threads from his coat sleeve. He took pride in being well groomed, handsomely tailored, as befit a man of breeding. Two weeks to the day. You do remember. I am flattered.

"I know you, Geoffrey Duncan."

"Then you know why I have come," Geoffrey softly laughed. "I have been a bit of a wag, yet again." The killer talked freely, excitement in his voice. The sanctity of the confessional was his protection, that and his uncle's wealth and prestige. The Old Judge was being groomed for the governorship of the Lone Star State and he had powerful friends who would protect the family name and never abide a scandal.

"If you seek forgiveness, you will find no absolution here." The priest had an edge to his voice this morning. He sounded different. Not nearly as distraught as he had been on Duncan's previous visits. Perhaps, Geoffrey thought, I have pushed him too far, too fast with my little revelations. The game would not be near as fun if the priest had lost his sense of moral indignation.

"Absolution?" Geoffrey mocked him. "That's what you think I am after? Come now, Father Baltasar, what's a few less whores in the cantinas?" He shook his head. "We have a deeper bond then that."

"What do you want?"

"Do not think to judge me, less you pass judgment on yourself. You have kept your vow of silence and it has made you my accomplice."

The nephew fished in his pocket for a handkerchief and dabbed the perspiration from his brow, then wiped his mouth. His oiled and neatly parted hair glistened in the glare of the votive light. Another volley of thunder sounded beyond the walls.

"They are whores. Where's the harm?" Duncan wondered if a priest knew anything about such passions. "Come now, *padre*, you have the same feelings below your belt as any man. You should be grateful I share my lark with you. Don't tell me you are not thrilled. Remember that *sheba* from off the Via Dolorosa, the one who took me to bed beneath the statue of Our Blessed Mother. What a shameless slut?

Isabel was her name, Our Lady of the Whores . . . !"

Duncan lowered his gaze to the candle on the shelf near his clasped hands. The flame was pure, encased in a slender chimney of ruby glass. Firelight flickered across his pale fleshy features. "Thanks to me, these trollops have answered for their sins. Think of me as being an instrument of the Lord." He could see his reflection in the crimson glass. The slut had been so willing and afterwards, she even followed him to the riverbank like some stupid cow, so trusting, right up to the moment when Duncan snapped her neck.

It heightened his pleasure, to share his secret with one who could not break the sanctity of the confessional at the risk of disgrace and condemnation. And yet, this morning, the priest just did not seem to have his heart in the game. Father Baltasar had become boring.

Geoffrey shook his head and sighed. "No one will miss them." Duncan checked his pocket watch. His stomach growled and he patted his thickening paunch. Too many breakfasts of biscuits and red eye gravy, he sighed, a thought in mind, I'll pop the buttons off my coat if I'm not careful. Well, a few extra inches around his middle didn't change the fact that he still had his looks, his finely sculpted almost feminine features. A pretty man . . . but slowly falling prey to his decadent lifestyle. Still a man had to sew his wild oats, that's what the Judge said.

Back in their suite at the Menger Hotel, Auntie would have cast a warning glance at the threatening gray clouds to the west, then hoped for the best and have his younger cousins up and dressing for the parade. The Judge, driving over from the ranch in his Model T, was not a man to keep waiting. Geoffrey Duncan and uncle T.C., Maynard Castleberry the mayor of San Antone, and a few of the Councilmen were to inspect the floats; the Bexar

Chapter of the Red Cross, the Ladies Auxilliary of the American Legion, the Daughters of the Texas Revolution, the Delphian Club, the Woman's Progressive Society, the Knights of Columbus, even the Boy Scouts had prepared a display. It would be a promising parade, if only the elements permitted.

Geoffrey Duncan tapped the confessional screen. So much for ritual, he thought. "Time to take my leave." The young medical student grinned, trusting in the power of the sacrament he had debased. "What would you have me do for my penance?" He suffered through another long silent pause. Then he heard the priest's low, menacing reply.

"This day we will both be beyond forgiveness."

"What the devil?" The Judge's nephew glanced hard at the vague silhouette behind the woven screen. Was the man holding a bible? He tried to peer through the lattice work. By heaven it was a Colt revolver.

"What the hell are you getting at, *Padre*? If you have something to say, then spit it out. Just remember this is a confessional and you're the priest."

The priest cocked the weapon in his hand.

Duncan's reaction was instantaneous. He reached inside his own coat pocket, his fingers closed around the reassuring grip of the .38 caliber revolver he had kept concealed.

"Now just hold it right there," he nervously blurted out, stalling for time. "You would not desecrate the house of God . . ." Duncan grabbed for his revolver, tried to pull the weapon clear, but the hammer caught on the lining of his coat and caused him to inadvertently squeeze off a round, blasting a hole through his pocket and into the floor of the confessional. He tore the weapon free, determined not to waste a second shot but the cane screen exploded in his face. A forty-five caliber slug vaporized his front teeth and shattered his jaw. The impact sent a shock upward to follow the path of the bullet as it plowed through the temporal lobe of his brain. The back of his head exploded back against the wooden paneling. Duncan reeled on impact, twisted a quarter of the way around. His stocky frame and sloping shoulders slammed back against the wall in a spray of blood.

Stunned, slipping into the blackness of his own eternal night, Geoffrey Duncan's last sight was the dark of his attacker's eyes and his vaguely glimpsed features, menacing, behind the tendril of powder smoke that curled serpentine from the muzzle of the revolver and slithered through the shattered lattice work. Duncan's pocket pistol slipped from his grasp and clattered to the floor.

The priest, Father Baltasar Ramos, emerged from the confessional; gunsmoke clung to his vestments. Deafened by the report, he was unresponsive to the startled reactions from the Mestizo laborers and townspeople who had entered the Mission chapel to escape the threatening weather and light candles for their departed loved ones. His right hand slowly lowered. He tucked the Colt into a pocket beneath his cassock as the penitents drew back from this unholy apparition.

Ramos' cheek was bleeding. He shed the cassock, removed his stole and dabbed the cut, then realizing what he held, dropped the sacred, stained cloth. It draped itself across Duncan's outstretched legs. Ramos stared down at the Judge's nephew. The murderous bastard wasn't so pretty anymore. Collapsed, bloodied, he looked like a fancy sack of watery fat someone had dropped off in the confessional. He'd popped two buttons off his elegant satin vest.

"Isabel was my sister."

He glanced down at the man crumpled at his feet then lifted his gaze as if appealing to the solemn statues of the saints for a mercy beyond their stone walled expressions. He'd been a bad man once, but he had tried to leave it behind him. And for a while . . .

Ramos could feel the watchful eyes of the peons where they huddled against the chapel walls. The next few moments would haunt him down the labyrinth of his days. He averted his gaze from the man he had just killed, from the images of the tortured Christ pitying him from the icon covered wall above the altar. He shrugged off his robes, adjusted his gun belt. That was the way with weapons. Some men are called to the cloth, others . . . he contemplated the pistol in his hand; it had the old familiar feel of a deadly companion.

There was no going back from the killing, no matter how well deserved. Old Judge Duncan would vow to avenge his nephew's death. A well-honed instinct for self-preservation stirred Ramos to action. He would need more than a little luck to see this through. Baltasar clutched the .45 Colt with all the fervor of a convert, slowly holstered the weapon and stepped away from the confessional.

His forehead was dotted with sweat like droplets of old blood, his crown of righteousness. He shambled down the center aisle, through flickering pools of sacred candlelight. He paused before the penitents; a sideways glance and the Mestizos closest to him gasped and drew back in fear. He had a long ride ahead of him. But he'd make it. This wouldn't be the first time he had lost himself south of the border.

An ill wind forced its way through the front doors and wailing like some wounded seraph, it gusted through the sanctuary, to extinguish the votive candles while it hounded Baltasar Ramos into the profane darkness of the approaching storm.

Made in the USA
Charleston, SC
13 August 2011